Y0-CDB-950

Writings through John Cage's Music, Poetry, and Art

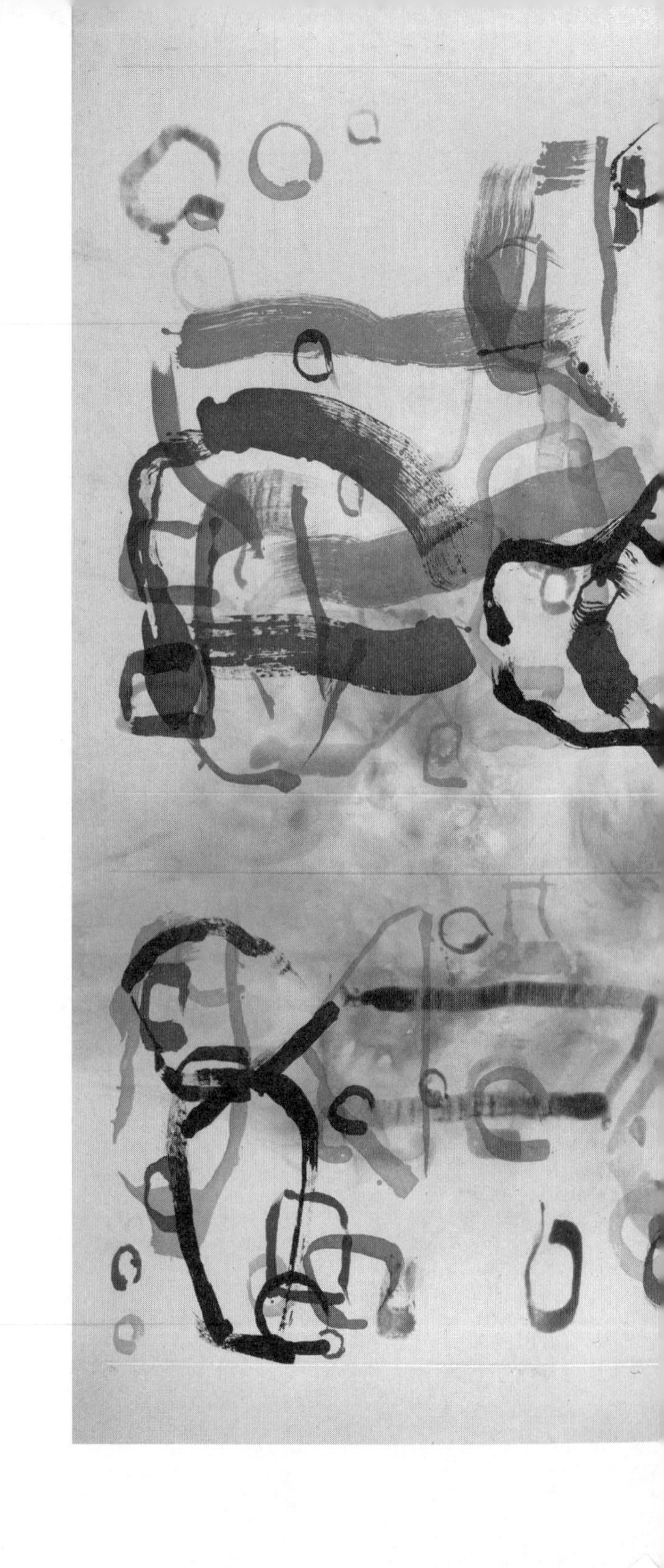

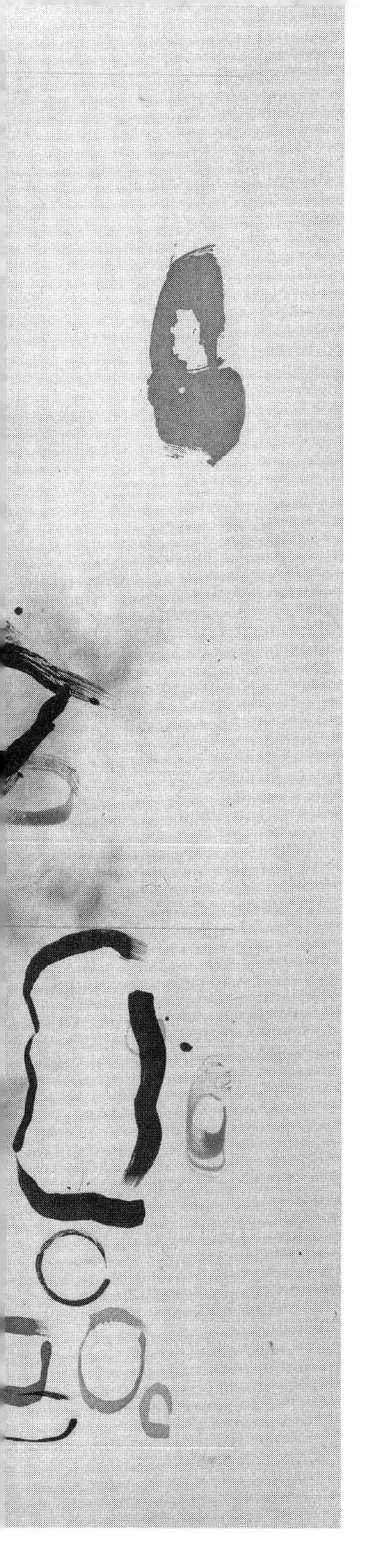

Writings through John Cage's Music, Poetry, and Art

Edited by David W. Bernstein and Christopher Hatch

THE UNIVERSITY OF CHICAGO PRESS CHICAGO AND LONDON

DAVID W. BERNSTEIN is associate professor of music and head of the Music Department at Mills College.
CHRISTOPHER HATCH has retired from the Department of Music at Columbia University.

The University of Chicago Press, Chicago 60637
The University of Chicago Press, Ltd., London
© 2001 by The University of Chicago
All rights reserved. Published 2001
Printed in the United States of America

10 09 08 07 06 05 04 03 02 01 5 4 3 2 1

ISBN (cloth): 0-226-04407-6
ISBN (paper): 0-226-04408-4

Library of Congress Cataloging-in-Publication Data

Writings through John Cage's music, poetry, and art / edited by David W. Bernstein and Christopher Hatch.
p. cm.
Proceedings from the conference entitled "Here Comes Everybody: The Music, Poetry, and Art of John Cage" which took place at Mills College in Oakland, Calif. from November 15 to 19, 1995.
Includes index.
ISBN 0-226-04407-6 — ISBN 0-226-04408-4 (pbk.)
1. Cage, John—Criticism and interpretation—Congresses. I. Bernstein, David W., 1951–. II. Hatch, Christopher.
ML410.C24 W74 2001
780'.92—dc21

00-011440

∞ The paper used in this publication meets the minimum requirements of the American National Standard for Information Sciences—Permanence of Paper for Printed Library Materials, ANSI Z39.48-1992.

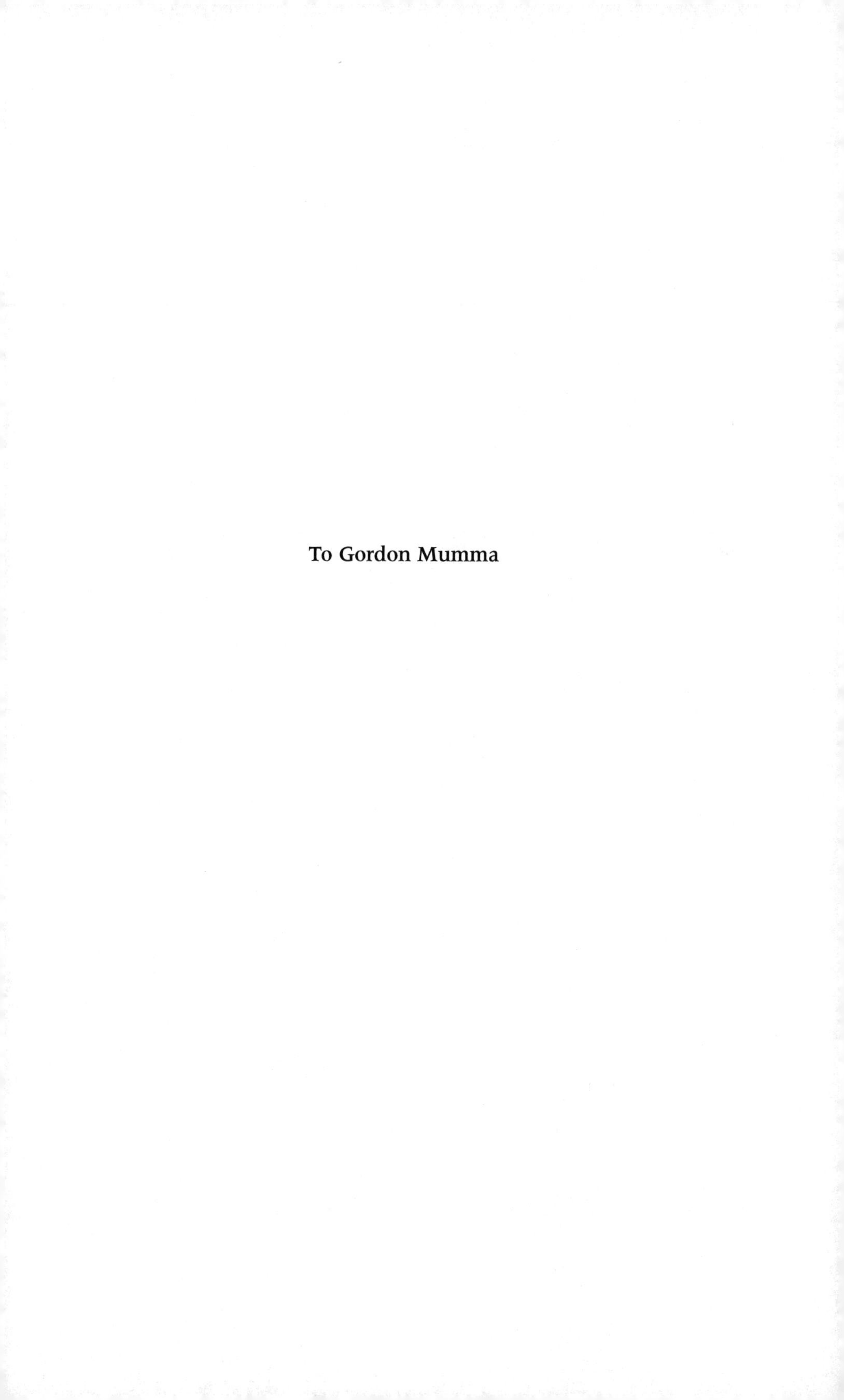

To Gordon Mumma

CONTENTS

ACKNOWLEDGMENTS

This book resulted from a collaborative process that began almost a year after John Cage's death on August 12, 1992. It was during one of many inspiring conversations with Gordon Mumma—a wonderful creative artist, ubiquitous scholar, intellectual, and the person to whom this book is dedicated—that the idea of a conference and festival focusing on Cage's work first emerged. Its location at Mills College, an institution with a rich tradition in experimental music and close ties to Cage, was a splendid choice. The combination of Cage and Mills proved a powerful catalyst, drawing scholars and creative artists to the event from all over the world.

"Here Comes Everybody: The Music, Poetry, and Art of John Cage" took place on November 15–19, 1995. It was supported by funding from the National Endowment for the Humanities, the National Endowment for the Arts, the Mills College Music Department, and the Mills College Art Museum. I would like to thank Laura Kuhn and Joan Retallack for introducing me to the dedicated community of scholars studying Cage's work. I am also grateful to Charles Hamm and Marjorie Perloff for their enthusiastic support of our project. It was especially a pleasure to meet and work with Andrew Culver. I would like to thank my colleagues from the Mills College Music Department and Center for Contemporary Music—David Abel, John Bischoff, Chris Brown, Belle Bulwinkle, Alvin Curran, Elisabeth Eshleman, Michelle Fillion, Fred Frith, Dave Madole, Pauline Oliveros, Maggi Payne, Julie Steinberg, Les Stuck, and William Winant—for their artistic and intellectual inspiration. This debt I also owe to my students at Mills.

From the start, Kathleen Hansell, music editor for the University of Chicago Press, expressed interest in our plan to produce a book from the conference proceedings. Her continued support gave us the opportunity to realize our goal. Moira Roth and George Lewis reminded us that a critical perspective is crucial for Cage research; their ideas influenced this book's final form. It was a pleasure to work with the contributors to this volume; they selflessly committed hours of their time. It is a rare opportunity to work with a group of such talented artists and scholars.

I have had the privilege of collaborating with Christopher Hatch on several projects. As coeditor of this book, he brought his uncanny ability to shape and clarify an author's argument without the intrusion of his own editorial ego. This, as well as his keen intellect, curiosity, and openness, reminds me of John Cage. Finally, I would like to acknowledge the patience and support of my wife, Jamie, and son, Jeremy, who made work on this book possible.

David W. Bernstein

INTRODUCTION

David W. Bernstein

I notice both in writing and in speaking [that] many people are gloomy about the present circumstances and it isn't my nature to be gloomy. . . . I have been so long in reading and thinking of *Finnegans Wake*, "Here comes everybody," and I think our experiences more and more are populated not only with more people, but with more things that strike our perceptions. . . . We live in a time I think, not of mainstream, but of many streams or even, if you insist upon a river of time, that we have come to [a] delta, maybe even beyond [the] delta to an ocean which is going back to the skies.

—John Cage, Radio interview with Charles Amirkhanian, KPFA, Berkeley, January 14, 1992

The epigraph at left expresses the inspiration behind a conference entitled "Here Comes Everybody: The Music, Poetry, and Art of John Cage," which took place at Mills College in Oakland, California from November 15 to 19, 1995. It also conveys in large part the motivation that led to this book. The conference constituted a major landmark in Cage scholarship; it was the first international assemblage of scholars and creative artists to examine Cage's work after his death on August 12, 1992. As such, it marked a new era in Cage research, as scholars began to consider and evaluate his life, influence, and creative output more critically.

Cage, who admired the writings of James Joyce, particularly *Finnegans Wake*, was fond of the phrase "Here comes everybody" because it epitomized his own pluralistic vision of politics, society, and art. For Cage, "Here comes everybody" represented a political and social philosophy celebrating the uniqueness of individuals and the multiplicity of cultural differences around the world. In music, this vision informed Cage's assumption that any combination of sounds, whether they are "musical" sounds or noises, can be aesthetically pleasing; the materials available for a musical work are thus virtually unlimited, and Cage rejoiced in the existence of these infinite possibilities.

Cage extended this idea into an encompassing pluralism that crossed artistic boundaries. His creative energies were not limited to music, for he was at the same time an accomplished writer and an artist. The author of more than seven major volumes of essays and poetry, he was also extremely productive in the visual arts, especially printmaking and watercolors. This richness of artistic output and an almost unprecedented level of productivity continued until his death.

Throughout his career, Cage was known as a tireless provocateur and propagandist for a small community of avant-garde musicians, artists, and writers, but today his work is recognized around the world. We have, in fact, arrived at a pivotal moment in the history of Cage studies. As scholars begin to address his extraordinary legacy, they will need to understand the breadth and importance of his achievements. This process has already begun. The first Cage biography came out in 1992, and others will appear soon.[1] There exist a growing number of excellent dissertations focusing on Cage's work.[2] A major Cage conference that took place at Stanford University in 1992 resulted in an important volume of essays.[3] In 1993, the first book to examine Cage's entire musical output appeared, several new books explore aspects of Cage's work and aesthetics, while others contain substantial sections on Cage.[4] In addition, a collection of interviews published shortly before he died provides fresh insight into the compositional methods and aesthetics of his late

1. David Revill, *The Roaring Silence: John Cage, a Life* (New York: Arcade, 1992). Biographies by Charles Shere, Mark Swed, and Franz van Rossum are currently underway.

2. Deborah Ann Campana, "Form and Structure in the Music of John Cage" (Ph.D. diss., Northwestern University, 1985); James William Pritchett, "The Development of Chance Techniques in the Music of John Cage, 1950–1956" (Ph.D. diss., New York University, 1988); Laura Kuhn, "John Cage's *Europeras 1 & 2:* The Musical Means of Revolution" (Ph.D. diss., University of California, Los Angeles, 1992); Martin Erdmann, "Untersuchungen zum Gesamtwerk von John Cage" (Ph.D. diss., Rheinische Friedrich-Wilhelms-Universität, Bonn, 1993); David W. Patterson, "Appraising the Catchwords, c. 1942–1959: Cage's Asian-Derived Rhetoric and the Historical Reference of Black Mountain College" (Ph.D. diss., Columbia University, 1996); Paul van Emmerik, "Thema's en Variaties: Systematische tendensen in de compositietechnieken van John Cage" (Ph.D. diss., Universiteit van Amsterdam, 1996).

3. Marjorie Perloff and Charles Junkerman, eds., *John Cage: Composed in America* (Chicago: University of Chicago Press, 1994).

4. James Pritchett, *The Music of John Cage* (New York: Cambridge University Press, 1993); Stefan Schädler and Walter Zimmerman, eds., *John Cage: Anarchic Harmony* (Mainz: Schott, 1992); William Fetterman, *John Cage's Theater Pieces: Notations and Performances* (Amsterdam: Harwood Academic Publishers, 1996); Christopher Shultis, *Silencing the Sounded Self: John Cage and the American Experimentalist Tradition* (Boston: Northeastern University Press, 1998); George Leonard, *Into the Light of Things: The Art of the Commonplace from Wordsworth to Cage* (Chicago: University of Chicago Press, 1995); and Daniel Herwitz, *Making Theory, Constructing Art* (Chicago: University of Chicago Press, 1993).

music.[5] An extensive archive containing thousands of Cage's manuscripts and other documents was recently established at the New York Public Library. "Here comes everybody" captures the present situation very well; today's Cage scholars have inherited a wealth of materials that should occupy them for many years to come.

The Mills conference involved participants from a wide variety of disciplines; although the major focus was Cage's music, there were contributions by writers, literary critics, and art historians. This book includes papers presented at the conference, transcriptions of two important panel sessions, as well as several new essays addressing issues that emerged during the conference. The collection begins with my endeavor to place Cage within a broad historical context and examine his relationships to developments in twentieth-century culture and musical style. I explore Cage's ties to twentieth-century modernism, claiming that this retrospective view may facilitate a critical appraisal of his music and thought.

In chapter 2, Jonathan Katz turns to aspects of Cage's life seldom discussed in Cage scholarship. Katz suggests that Cage came to terms with his homosexuality through Zen Buddhism at the same time that he developed an artistic philosophy based upon the negation of self-expression. Cage's "silence" in this sense signifies his reluctance to mention his sexuality. But rather than interpreting this as a strategy for avoiding post–World War II homophobia, Katz maintains that Cage's "silence" was rooted in his ideological convictions. His "silence" was a moral stance. As Katz explains, it was a way to resist the errors of oppositional politics, which according to Cage, only "make matters worse." Cage's "silent piece," *4′33″*, supplies Austin Clarkson with a way to expose the reader to issues associated with listening to and performing Cage's music. Cage believed that the purpose of music was to "sober the mind and make it susceptible to divine influences."[6] As Clarkson points out in chapter 3, *4′33″* "exemplifies quintessentially Cage's tendency to link music and spirituality." Drawing from writings by William James, Carl Jung, Meister Eckhart, and Daisetz Suzuki, Clarkson clarifies our understanding of Cage's views concerning spirituality. He discusses how performing and listening to a composition by Cage has a "transpersonal effect" and, by engaging the creativity of those who experience it, can lead to a heightened state of being. Clarkson shows us that spirituality, for Cage, results from a psychological transformation rather than a reli-

5. *Musicage: Cage Muses on Words, Art, and Music*, ed. Joan Retallack (Hanover, N.H.: Wesleyan University Press, University Press of New England, 1995).

6. "45′ for a Speaker," in *Silence: Lectures and Writings* (Middletown, Conn.: Wesleyan University Press, 1961), 158.

gious one. He identifies a need to develop analytical techniques that address this mode of musical experience and suggests some preliminary methods that can help us perform and listen to Cage's music.

Performance is the focus of the next three essays. In chapter 4, Gordon Mumma, a composer and performer who collaborated with Cage at a time when both worked with the Merce Cunningham Dance Company, documents aspects of Cage's activities as a performer. He covers Cage's work as pianist and percussionist both in concert and as dance accompanist, his performances with David Tudor and others using electronic media, and his virtuosic readings of his own poetry. Mumma dispels the myths (that Cage often helped promulgate) about Cage's musical abilities, demonstrating that he was in fact a skilled and sensitive performer. The two essays that appear here as chapters 5 and 6 also contribute to our knowledge about the performance practices associated with Cage's music. Deborah Campana explores how his concept of musical time evolved from the early compositions for percussion and prepared piano to the "number" pieces written toward the end of his life. She shows that Cage's concern for temporal organization remained constant despite changes in his musical style and notational resources. John Holzaepfel deals more intensively with performance practice in his discussion of piano virtuoso and composer David Tudor's realization of the *Solo for Piano* from Cage's *Concert for Piano and Orchestra* (1957–58). Holzaepfel draws attention to Tudor's disciplined and extremely precise interpretation of Cage's notation, tracing parallels with Cage's own methods and providing valuable insights into the performance practices associated with Cage's indeterminate scores.

In chapter 7, Paul van Emmerik looks toward the future of Cage research. Van Emmerik played an important role in cataloging the collection of more than twenty-five thousand folios of Cage's music manuscripts now located at the New York Public Library. "Here comes everybody" becomes "Here comes everything" for van Emmerik, as the availability of these materials ushers in a new era in Cage research. A careful examination of the Cage *Nachlass* may take many years, but it will certainly lead to significant discoveries. Van Emmerik points out that studying Cage's source materials is crucial when analyzing his music from the 1950s and later, since his compositional decisions took place before a score was realized through chance operations. He demonstrates the usefulness of this methodology through an analysis of *Three,* one of Cage's number pieces, for which thirty-nine folios of source materials exist.

Two symposiums are included as chapters 8 and 9 of this book. The first, entitled "Cage's Influence," provides an opportunity for five of

Cage's former colleagues to discuss his impact on their own work as well as that of others. Allan Kaprow begins with a valuable account of Cage's classes in experimental music at the New School for Social Research in the late 1950s. James Tenney assesses Cage's historical role, claiming that by eliminating personal expression from music Cage brought to an end a period in music history that started with the beginnings of opera in the early seventeenth century. Uncomfortable with the idea of "influence," Christian Wolff stresses that Cage's groundbreaking discoveries helped others pursue their individual and independent creative paths. Comparing the present with the late 1930s, when Cage wrote his famous essay "The Future of Music: Credo," Maryanne Amacher explains that today we face a similar revolutionary moment in music history, propelled by recent innovations in computer science, electronic media, pyschoacoustics, biotechnology, and neuroscience. The technological advances that Cage predicted more than sixty years ago are now a reality. Amacher asks us to remain open to changes of the same magnitude in the not too distant future. The last participant, Alvin Curran, discusses his own work with the improvisatory performing group Musica Elettronica Viva, telling us that although Cage disliked improvisation, he was an important source of inspiration for this group.

In the second symposium, "Cage and the Computer," James Tenney recounts how Cage's aesthetics affected his own pioneering work on computer sound synthesis at Bell Labs during the early 1960s. Tenney credits his interest in noise and algorithmic composition using random number generation to Cage's influence. In describing stochastic processes as *constrained* random processes, he suggests an important point of contact with Cage's working methods, since Cage invariably built constraints into his own compositional systems before using chance operations. Controlled randomness comes up again in Andrew Culver's remarks as he describes the intricacies of the computer programs he created for Cage. Culver, who worked as Cage's assistant from the early 1980s until the composer's death, contributes a fascinating overview of the computer programs that Cage used in composing music and writing poetry. In this way, he provides insight into Cage's working methods, which are also the focus of comments from the third panelist, Frances White.

Cage's involvement in media other than music supplies the inspiration for the last group of essays. In chapter 10, Jackson Mac Low presents a wide-ranging survey of Cage's writings through the 1980s. He discusses Cage's methods and important influences on his writings. Constance Lewallen (chap. 11) is interested in how the asking of questions served Cage as an artist. She concentrates on the structured arena within which Cage applied his chance operations while engaged in printmaking at Crown Point Press and painting at the Mountain Lake Workshop in West Virginia. In chapter 12, Ray Kass, founder of this workshop, gives an account of Cage's activities at Mountain Lake and includes valuable information on Cage's methods as a painter. Henning Lohner, in the final essay of this collection, offers a study of one of Cage's last major works, the film *One*[11]. Lohner describes Cage's working methods during their collaboration over several years. He reveals much about the creative personality of an artist at the end of an incredibly rich and varied career.

This book can by no means claim inclusiveness. The scope and influence of Cage's activities are far too extensive to address in a single volume. It is our hope, however, that it will give readers a sense of the importance of Cage's creative activities in a variety of fields and an understanding of how much research has yet to be done. Finally, our goal here is to contribute to the rapidly expanding knowledge about Cage and his creative output. An end to this task is not in sight and may, in fact, not be desirable. For, as Cage often explained, it is far more interesting to search for new questions than for right answers. This book will inspire many such questions and open up new areas of inquiry. We are confident that this would have pleased John Cage.

ONE

David W. Bernstein

"In Order to Thicken the Plot": Toward a Critical Reception of Cage's Music

I

In an essay entitled "History of Experimental Music in the United States," John Cage paraphrases a question put to Sri Ramakrishna: "Why if everything is possible, do we concern ourselves with history (in other words with a sense of what is necessary to be done at a particular time)?" And Cage answers, "In order to thicken the plot."[1] The essay, written at the request of Wolfgang Steinecke, director of the Internationale Ferienkurse für Neue Musik at Darmstadt, was published in the 1959 issue of the *Darmstädter Beiträge*. Cage's concern was to provide an international audience with a historical context for his work. He traces the radical developments in his style during the 1950s to the first half of the twentieth century and the American Experimentalist tradition. The essay outlines the attributes of experimental music, emphasizing the use of chance, indeterminacy, collage, and noise. It describes a new approach to musical form in which composers no longer felt the need to "stick sounds

1. "History of Experimental Music in the United States," in *Silence: Lectures and Writings* (Middletown, Conn.: Wesleyan University Press, 1961), 68.

together to make a continuity," thus letting "sounds be themselves." Cage also points to the historical inevitability of the changes in his musical style:

> All those interpenetrations which seem at first glance to be hellish—history, for instance, if we are speaking of experimental music—are to be espoused. One does not make just any experiment but does what must be done. By this I mean one does not seek by his actions to arrive at money but does what must be done; by this I mean one does not seek by his actions to arrive at fame (success) but does what must be done; one does not seek by his actions to provide pleasure to the senses (beauty) but does what must be done; one does not seek by his actions to arrive at the establishing of a school (truth) but does what must be done.[2]

The urgency and determinism conveyed by this passage seem out of place; it makes a modernist claim of historical progression—similar pronouncements by Cage's teacher Arnold Schoenberg come immediately to mind—within an essay promoting what today we would define as postmodernist aesthetic elements. Cage's linking of these ideas leads us to questions concerning his position within the history of twentieth-century art and ideas, and particularly his role in the development of modernist and postmodernist aesthetics.

While attempting to disentangle the many meanings of the term "postmodernism" and to clarify its relationship to modernism, critic Charles Jencks has explained that "Post-*Modernism* means the continuation of Modernism *and* its transcendence, a double activity that acknowledges our complex relationship to the preceding paradigm and world view." Jencks objects to the polarizing polemics pitting modernism against postmodernism, often expressed in lists of mutually exclusive elements of each worldview, such as "purpose vs. play," "design vs. chance," or "hierarchy vs. anarchy."[3] Rejecting such reductionism, he argues that the emergence of postmodernism in the second half of the twentieth century does not entail a reversal, an abandonment of modernism. Postmodernism is "a hybridization, a complexification of modern elements with other ones"—which Jencks terms "double-coding."[4]

Jencks's "double-coding" seems especially useful for understanding Cage's position within a broad historical context. There seems to be a

2. Ibid.

3. See "The Post-Modern Agenda," in *The Post-Modern Reader*, ed. Charles Jencks (New York: St. Martin's Press, 1992), 11, 12. The juxtaposition of these terms originally appeared in Ihab Hassan, *Paracriticisms: Seven Speculations of the Times* (Urbana: University of Illinois Press, 1975), 123–24.

4. "The Post-Modern Agenda," 12.

consensus among literary critics that Cage played a vital role in "postmodernizing" music.[5] Similarly, in a recent article, musicologist Charles Hamm maintains that Cage's work from the 1950s on was postmodern.[6] These discussions have contributed to our understanding of Cage's aesthetics and musical style. However, if we draw a dichotomy between modernism and postmodernism with respect to Cage, we may overlook his ties with a modernist project devoted to political and social change through art. Moreover, if we underestimate his dependence on techniques associated with twentieth-century musical modernism, we may miss a valuable opportunity to clarify some of the problematic features of his musical style. The historical, stylistic, and cultural context for Cage's work makes up an extremely "thick" plot consisting of a subtle interplay between modernism and postmodernism. Indeed, as this essay will demonstrate, it is useful to consider aspects of both worldviews in order to find a path through the complex maze of interpenetrations that constitute the historical context for Cage's aesthetics and creative output.

II

Cage's relation to what Jürgen Habermas refers to as the "project of modernity"[7] lies in his connection with the history of the most radical manifestation of modernism, the twentieth-century avant-garde. In placing Cage within this historical context, we must recognize that, while scholars have examined avant-garde aesthetics from a variety of disciplinary perspectives, historians of twentieth-century music have not addressed the topic adequately. Moreover, for the most part, musical historiography lacks a precise definition of the "avant-garde," even though the term is often applied to musical repertories from several different historical periods.

In its well-known military usage, an avant-garde constitutes the leading edge of an invading force. Similarly, in aesthetics and cultural history the avant-garde functions as a vanguard, paving the way for developments in artistic language. But the meaning of the term is far more complex, for it embodies sociopolitical as well as artistic issues. The notion of

5. See, for example, Gregory L. Ulmer, "The Object of Post-Criticism," in *The Anti-Aesthetic: Essays on Postmodern Culture,* ed. Hal Foster (Seattle: Bay Press, 1983), 101ff.; Frederic Jameson, *Postmodernism, or, The Cultural Logic of Late Capitalism* (Durham, N.C.: Duke University Press, 1991), 1; Marjorie Perloff, *The Poetics of Indeterminacy* (Chicago: University of Chicago Press, 1981). Perloff places Cage within a postmodernist literary tradition that included Rimbaud, Stein, Williams, Pound, Beckett, Ashbery, and Antin.

6. "Privileging the Moment: Cage, Jung, Synchronicity, Postmodernism," *Journal of Musicology* 15, no. 2 (1977): 278–89.

7. "Modernity—an Incomplete Project," in Foster, *The Anti-Aesthetic,* 3–15.

an avant-garde was first applied to the arts in the early nineteenth century by the father of utopian socialism, Henri Comte de Saint-Simon. He envisioned a society led by artists and scientists—an avant-garde that would spearhead a radical transformation of society: "What a most beautiful destiny for the arts, that of exercising over a society a positive power, a truly priestly function, and of marching forcefully in the van of all intellectual faculties, in the epoch of their greatest development! This is the duty of the artists, this is their mission."[8]

The association of the avant-garde with sociopolitical radicalism continued in Europe throughout the nineteenth century.[9] However, despite its long-standing historical association with political radicalism, in musical scholarship today, avant-gardism is often equated with artistic activities that have little or nothing in common with social change. Radical innovation and experimentation have in many cases become the sole criteria for the avant-garde. For example, the Ars Nova, the New German school, and the post–World War II generation of composers including Boulez and Stockhausen have all been characterized as avant-garde movements.[10]

The history of the twentieth-century avant-garde began with the iconoclastic radical art movements known as futurism and dadaism.[11] Both futurism and dadaism emerged from the economic, political, moral, and social upheaval surrounding the First World War. But while dadaism was a loose international affiliation of artists, writers, and poets revolted by the butchery of World War I, futurism represented a more insular movement, whose proponents were fervently nationalistic, misogynist, and pro-war. These sentiments were proclaimed by Filippo Tommaso Marinetti, who established futurism with a manifesto published in Italy in 1909: "We will glorify war—the world's only hygiene—militarism, patriotism, the destructive gesture of freedom-bringers, beautiful ideas worth dying for, and scorn for women."[12]

In spite of the political and national differences between the two movements, the aesthetic assumptions underlying dadaism and futur-

8. Quoted in Donald D. Egbert, *Social Radicalism in the Arts* (New York: Knopf, 1970), 121–22.

9. Gabriel Desiré Laverdant, for example, in his book entitled *De la mission de l'art et du rôle des artists* (1845) defined avant-garde art as that which has the potential to initiate social change, and in 1878, Mikhail Bakunin prepared a periodical entitled *L'Avant-garde*, which served as a forum for the anarchist movement. See Renato Poggioli, *The Theory of the Avant-Garde* (Cambridge: Harvard University Press, 1968), 9.

10. See, for example, Glenn Watkins, *Soundings: Music in the Twentieth Century* (New York: Schirmer Books, 1988), 506ff., and the article on the "avant-garde" by Paul Griffiths in *The New Grove Dictionary of Music and Musicians*, 1:742–43.

11. For a history of dadaism, see Hans Richter, *Art and Anti-Art* (New York: Oxford University Press, 1965). RoseLee Goldberg, *Performance Art: From Futurism to the Present* (New York: Abrams, 1988) contains an excellent introductory survey of both movements.

12. Filippo Tommaso Marinetti, *Selected Writings*, trans. R. W. Flint and Arthur Coppotelli (New York: Farrar, Straus and Giroux, 1971), 42.

ism were remarkably similar. Both endorsed a total reformulation of contemporary aesthetic values accompanied by radical political and social change. The futurists adamantly rejected the past, particularly its artistic institutions. In his 1909 manifesto, for example, Marinetti even exhorted his followers to "destroy the museums, libraries, and academies of every kind."[13] Although they were usually not as belligerent, dadaist writings often echo this disdain for the past and for institutionalized art. Thus, Tristan Tzara, a Rumanian artist and writer who played a major role in the Zurich dada movement, wrote: "The beginnings of dada were not the beginnings of an art, but of disgust. Disgust with the magnificence of philosophers who for three thousand years have explained everything to us (what for?), disgust with the pretensions of these artists-God's-representatives on earth, [and] disgust with the lieutenants of a mercantile art made to order according to a few infantile laws."[14] In its most radical form, the early-twentieth-century avant-garde's rejection of institutionalized art was only part of an all-encompassing nihilism that looked forward to the downfall of social as well as artistic institutions. Walter Serner, an Austrian anarchist who was a member of the dadaist circle in Zurich, called for the complete destruction of present-day society. In a work entitled *Letze Lockerung* (1918), he explained that active dissolution of the status quo was itself a form of serious art.[15] Art, or "anti-art" as it is often termed, was a means by which to destroy a corrupt and hopeless society.

The anti-art polemics produced by these movements also arose from a common understanding that art and life praxis are inseparable—a fundamental tenet of avant-garde aesthetics. This view was expressed in a variety of ways. The futurists celebrated the urban environment, with its chaos, noise, machines, and speed. Futurist painters attempted to capture what they termed the dynamism and simultaneity of modern life. Futurist musicians such as Antonio and Luigi Russolo invented noise-making machines (called *intonarumori*) so that they could use citylike sounds in their music. Dadaist artists pioneered collage and photomontage, techniques that sought to represent the real world during a time of chaos and revolution. Their poetry often employed almost random combinations of words and, in some cases, used only abstract sounds devoid of meaning in a new poetic style called "Verse without Words" or "Sound Poetry."[16] This new form of verse was practiced by Hugo Ball,

13. Ibid.

14. "Lecture on Dada, 1922," in *Dada Painters and Poets: An Anthology,* 2d ed., ed. Robert Motherwell (Boston: G. K. Hall, 1981), 250.

15. Richter, *Art and Anti-Art,* 48.

16. For more on this and other genres of early twentieth-century experimental poetry, see László Moholy-Nagy, "Literature," in *The Avant-Grade Tradition in Literature,* ed. Richard Kostelanetz (Buffalo: Prometheus, 1982), 78–141.

who with his wife, Emmy Hennings, opened the Cabaret Voltaire—a nightclub, founded in 1916, that served as a center for dadaist activities in Zurich.

Their fascination with chaos, irrationality, and simultaneity led both futurists and dadaists to the development of multimedia performance art. In a manifesto dated 1913, Marinetti described the "Variety Theater"—an early example of performance art in which jugglers, ballerinas, gymnasts, poets, and musicians all participated simultaneously. The purpose of such a wild spectacle was to engage and even infuriate the audience, as Marinetti's ideas for possible scenarios for his "Variety Theater" make clear:

> One must completely destroy all logic in Variety Theater performances. . . . Systematically prostitute all of classic art on the stage, performing for example all the Greek, French, and Italian tragedies, condensed and comically mixed up, in a single evening—put life into the works of Beethoven, Wagner, Bach, Bellini, Chopin by inserting Neapolitan songs . . . play a Beethoven symphony backward . . . boil all of Shakespeare down to a single act . . . have actors recite *Hernani* tied in sacks up to their necks—soap the floorboards to cause amusing tumbles at the most tragic moments.[17]

Marinetti's collaborative performances, which he called "Futurist Evenings," were staged all around Italy. Similar events were in vogue within dadaist circles.

Chaos and irrationality inspired dadaist experiments with chance. Hans Richter explains that the Alsatian painter and dadaist Jean Arp once, when dissatisfied with one of his paintings, tore it in pieces and threw it on the floor. To his amazement Arp noticed that the new configuration of scraps was more successful than the original. Chance had succeeded where the artist's original intent had not. Tristan Tzara also used chance methods in his poetry. He cut up newspapers into little pieces containing no more than a few words, then either selected pieces randomly from a hat or threw them onto a table. The new combination of words was then pasted together.[18] These experiments anticipate Cage's first compositions using chance methods by more than thirty years. Again, the motivation behind this sort of activity was to bring art closer to the randomness that was seen to characterize real life.

Political and social activism, the rejection of tradition and institutionalized art, chaos, chance and irrationality, simultaneity, and the merg-

17. Marinetti, *Selected Writings*, 120–21.

18. Tristan Tzara, "Seven Dada Manifestoes," in Motherwell, *Dada Painters and Poets*, 92.

ing of art and life were the aesthetic principles endorsed by avant-garde movements in the early twentieth century. Dadaism, futurism, and the artistic movements that grew out of them—collectively known as the "historical avant-garde"[19]—did not survive beyond the fourth decade of the twentieth century. The onslaught of World War I helped bring on the dissolution of futurism, although aspects of its ideology took root in Russia. The futurists' interest in the industrial world, for instance, was echoed by the Russian constructivists, who believed in a utilitarian art committed to the establishment of a classless society. Thus, initially, avant-garde art flourished in postrevolutionary Russia, but the relatively tolerant artistic climate that reached its apogee during the 1920s would decline under an increasingly totalitarian political regime.[20] During the years after World War I, dadaism spread from Zurich to Berlin, Hanover, Cologne, New York, and Paris. It was in Paris that the movement began to break apart as a result of internecine rivalries and, above all, the impossibility of unifying a movement that embraced chaos and disorder. Although many of the artists and writers who helped create dadaism still remained productive, by 1924, after a series of confrontations, polemics, and public disputes, dadaism was finished.[21] Surrealism emerged out of the ashes of dada, but by the beginning of the Second World War, this movement had also run out of steam, owing to its inability to align itself with the Communist party and the fact that few people could concern themselves with "discussions of sex, character, and potential behavior of a scrap of velvet at a time when fascists were burning books and killing people."[22]

The collapse of the historical avant-garde did not prevent the dissemination of its aesthetic principles and artistic techniques. Cage played a crucial role in this development. Although his early percussion works gave noise a musical vitality that went far beyond the dadaist and futurist experiments, this new direction in his musical style was influenced, in part, by the historical avant-garde. Even more important was his in-

19. This term is used by Peter Bürger in his *The Theory of the Avant-Garde* (Minneapolis: University of Minnesota Press, 1984).

20. For a fine survey of the arts in twentieth-century Russia before World War II, see David Elliot, *New Worlds: Russian Art and Society, 1890–1937* (New York: Rizzoli, 1986); *The Great Utopia: The Russian and Soviet Avant-Garde, 1915–1932* (New York: Guggenheim Museum, 1992) is another useful secondary source. For more on the constructivist art movement, see Christina Lodder, *Russian Constructivism* (New Haven: Yale University Press, 1983).

21. For a discussion of the final stages of the dadaist movement, see Richter, *Art and Anti-Art*, 196, and Georges Ribemont-Dessaignes, "History of Dada," in Motherwell, *Dada Painters and Poets*, 116ff.

22. Ilya Ehrenburg, *Post-War Years, 1945–54* (London, MacGibben and Kee, 1966), 287. These words are cited in the following excellent study of surrealism's political context: Helena Lewis, *The Politics of Surrealism* (New York: Paragon, 1988), 122.

terest in breaking down the barriers between art and life, a position with unmistakable parallels to the historical avant-garde.[23] This aesthetic conviction drew Cage to many of the techniques used by the dadaist movement, such as simultaneity and chance methods. It resulted in the now famous "happening" at Black Mountain College in 1952 and the composition of *4′33″* during the same year. The latter work, a piece for piano without sound, challenged the distinction between art and life. In so doing, *4′33″* was perhaps Cage's most important contribution to the midcentury revival of avant-garde aesthetics. Cage's fascination with the sort of layered simultaneities employed in his Black Mountain piece extended throughout his career, from his early experiments with electronic media such as *Williams Mix,* to the enormous superimposition of electronic and other musical media in *HPSCHD,* to later works such as *Roaratorio* and the *Europeras,* which, although not intended in the same antagonistic spirit, resemble Marinetti's plans for his "Variety Theater."

Cage enjoyed a longtime personal association with Marcel Duchamp, and it is not surprising that many of his ideas stem from dadaist aesthetic ideology. From the 1940s on, he increasingly took on the role of an agent provocateur, in much the same spirit as Tristan Tzara and other radicals active in the early part of the century. In 1948, Cage caused quite a stir with his polemics against Beethoven at Black Mountain College. His "Lecture on Nothing," presented at the New York City Artists' Club circa 1949–50, was perhaps an inflammatory jab at the aesthetics of abstract expressionism.[24] The uproar resulting from these activities was surpassed by the first performance of *4′33″* in Woodstock, New York, on August 29, 1952. The audience, although well prepared for an evening of contemporary music, was shocked by what Cage would later call his most important work.

After World War II, there was a resurgence of avant-gardism. Many of the radical groups associated with the postwar resuscitation of the avant-garde—such as the Nouveaux réalistes, the Cobra movement, the International Situationists, and Fluxus—had political and artistic agendas remarkably similar to those of the historical avant-garde and are thus often referred to as the "neo-avant-garde" or "neo-dada." Cage was an important figure in this revival of avant-garde aesthetics. During the late 1950s, he taught a course in experimental music at the New School for Social Research. His students, among whom were George Brecht,

23. Of course, Asian philosophy, Zen Buddhism in particular, was also an important source for this aspect of Cage's aesthetics. Cage attended a lecture entitled "Zen Buddhism and Dada" at the Cornish School in Seattle. He noted that there exist possible connections between dadaism and Zen. See the foreword to *Silence,* xi.

24. Caroline A. Jones, "Finishing School: John Cage and the Abstract Expressionist Ego," *Critical Inquiry* 19 (summer 1993): 628–65.

Dick Higgins, Toshi Ichiyanagi, Allan Kaprow, Jackson Mac Low, and Richard Maxfield, went on to become leaders within such avant-garde artistic circles as the Fluxus movement.[25]

Despite these ties to the historical avant-garde, Cage's work immediately following the war seems apolitical, and thus appears to lack a necessary component of the avant-garde aesthetic program.[26] Much of the high modernist art of the 1950s did not overtly address political concerns. On the surface, Cage's *Music of Changes* (1951) and *Concert for Piano and Orchestra* (1957–58) appear as examples of the apolitical 1950s. These works drew upon the premise that art equals life by "imitating nature in her manner of operation," an approach certainly congruent with the avant-garde's aesthetic claims. But the passivity and apparent absence of political engagement characteristic of Cage's music from this period differ markedly from works by the historical avant-garde.

Toward the end of the 1960s, Cage paid increasing attention to the relation between art and political and social structures.[27] Yet, although he must have supported many of the goals of the 1960s protest movement, he did not endorse its methods. In a conversation with Morton Feldman about the Vietnam War he explained:

> You know, my tendency is to think of these activities—of protest, and of parades, and objections, and all these things—as being like critical actions rather than like composing actions. I know, in my case and certainly in your case, that nothing that the critic said stopped me from composing. Now it seems to me that the war is not going to be stopped by critical action, or, if it is stopped, that it will be succeeded by another war, et cetera. I think something like a composing action needs to be made rather than like a critical action, in order to bring about a world where these things to which we clearly and rightfully object will not take place.[28]

For Cage, a work of art might offer a model of how an ideal world would be constructed. This idea is stated explicitly in Cage's essay "The Future of Music" (1974): "Less anarchic kinds of music give examples of less anarchic states of society. The masterpieces of Western music exemplify

25. These classes are described by Allan Kaprow in the panel discussion entitled "Cage's Influence," chapter 8 below.

26. For a discussion of Cage's activities during this period, see David W. Bernstein, "John Cage and the Aesthetic of Indifference," in *The New York Schools of Music and the Visual Arts*, ed. Steven Johnson (New York: Garland Publishing, forthcoming).

27. Natalie Crohn Schmitt, "John Cage in a New Key," *Perspectives of New Music* 20 (fall/winter 1981): 99–103.

28. John Cage and Morton Feldman, *Radio Happenings I–V, 1966–1967* (Cologne: MusikTexte, 1993), 153.

monarchies and dictatorships. Composer and conductor: king and prime minister. By making musical situations which are analogies to desirable social circumstances which we do no yet have, we make music suggestive and relevant to the serious questions which face Mankind."[29] The political intent of art conceived in this way lies in its offering us alternative epistemologies in the hope that these might lead to a radical reshaping of our political and social structures. This approach exemplifies what Marxist literary critic Raymond Williams has termed alternative culture, as opposed to oppositional culture, which also envisages social change but relies on a much more overt and confrontational political message.[30]

Seen in this light, even Cage's most abstract high-modernist compositions from the early 1950s were steps toward his formulation of musical works as idealized social structures, for by "letting sounds be themselves" in works such as the *Music of Changes,* he created a musical anarchy that would later provide us with models of alternative forms of social and political organization. Cage's early interest in the future of music increasingly became a concern for the state of the world, a preoccupation that was to persist throughout his artistic career.

Cage's renewal of avant-garde aesthetics came at a time when the phrase "the avant-garde is dead" had started to appear in writings by both intellectual historians and literary critics.[31] Noting the failed political, social, and artistic programs endorsed by avant-garde movements in the twentieth century, many scholars had concluded that the avant-garde was no longer viable. But through his own works, and by promoting ideas drawn from Marshall McLuhan, R. Buckminster Fuller, and anarchist politics, Cage transformed the sociopolitical program of the twentieth-century avant-garde, redirecting its concerns to problems facing us at the turn of the twenty-first century. His reformulation of avant-garde aesthetics is a contemporary manifestation of the modernist project initiated by Enlightenment philosophers more than two hundred years ago.

29. "The Future of Music," in Cage, *Empty Words* (Middletown, Conn.: Wesleyan University Press, 1979), 183.

30. See Williams's "Base and Superstructure in Marxist Cultural Theory," *Contemporary Literary Criticism,* ed. Robert Davis and Ronald Schleifer (New York: Longman, 1989), 384. The tactics of alternative culture were taken up by Cage's successors, including Christian Wolff, who experimented with compositional techniques that yield works resembling ideal social communities. Another noteworthy example is Pauline Oliveros's practice of "deep listening."

31. See, for example, Hans Magnus Enzenberger, "Die Aporien der Avant-Garde," *Einzelheiten Poesie und Politik* (Frankfurt am Main, 1962); Leslie Fiedler, *The Collected Essays* (New York: Stein and Day, 1971), 2: 454–61; Bürger, *Theory of the Avant-Garde;* Andreas Huyssen, *After the Great Divide: Modernism, Mass Culture, Postmodernism* (Bloomington: Indiana University Press, 1986), and Marjorie Perloff, *Radical Artifice* (Chicago: University of Chicago Press, 1991).

III

Thus far we have examined Cage's modernist ties in a broad context. Narrowing the focus by considering his relationship to twentieth-century musical modernism sheds light on the development of his musical style. Cage's early musical training included an exposure to several facets of early-twentieth-century modernist music. Upon his return to Los Angeles in 1931, he saw the musical landscape in terms of two camps, populated by followers of Schoenberg on the one hand and followers of Stravinsky on the other: "I came to think that it was fairly clear from a survey of contemporary music that the important figures then were Schoenberg and Stravinsky, and that you could go in one direction or the other. I myself preferred Schoenberg."[32] Cage's early works employ various idiosyncratic interpretations of Schoenberg's twelve-tone system. By the mid-1940s, he had established his career as a composer with connections to the Schoenberg "school."

The historical context for Cage's early music also included work by composers from the American ultra-modernist school, such as Henry Cowell, Ruth Crawford, Charles Seeger, Carl Ruggles, and Johanna Beyer. These composers sought to break their ties to European musical traditions; their dissonant harmonies and experiments with serialism, however, still point to Schoenberg's atonal and twelve-tone music. Henry Cowell, a prominent figure in this group, was an active Schoenberg advocate. In short, the musical milieu that Cage joined after returning from Europe owed much to Schoenberg's influence.

During the 1930s, Cage developed his own idiosyncratic approach to the twelve-tone system. Perhaps the most striking departure from Schoenberg's method was his decision to avoid the thematic articulation of his twelve-tone rows. Cage refrained from any successive presentation of the twelve members of the row. The series was an element of his precompositional process, never appearing in the finished work.[33] He constructed melodic motives based upon the row's intervallic structure. These motives remain constant, not subject to alteration. Cage formed connections between the motives by referring to the final note of each motive and its position within the row. Each subsequent melodic motive

32. *Musicage: Cage Muses on Words, Art, Music,* ed. Joan Retallack (Hanover, N.H.: Wesleyan University Press, University Press of New England, 1995), 88. Cage's interest in Schoenberg's music led him to attend the latter's classes at both USC and UCLA. For a historical account of this period in Cage's career, see Michael Hicks, "John Cage's Studies with Arnold Schoenberg," *American Music* 8 (summer 1990): 125–40. I examine the relationships between the two composers' musical aesthetics in "John Cage, Arnold Schoenberg, and the Musical Idea," in *John Cage: Music, Philosophy, and Intention, 1933–50,* ed. David W. Patterson (New York: Garland Publishing, forthcoming).

33. This is not the case for the second movement of Cage's *Solo for Clarinet* (1933).

begins on the following or preceding note of the row. The first movement of his *Two Pieces for Piano* (1935) illustrates Cage's technique (ex. 1.1).[34] The twelve-tone row for this work reads as follows:[35]

B–B♭–G–D–E♭–D♭–A♭–G♭–C–E–A–F

The melodic motive in the right hand, bar two, consists of interval classes 1 and 5, a succession that appears between the fifth, fourth, and third notes in the row. The last note of the motive, A♭, proceeds to G♭, which begins the next motive (bar three) and also follows A♭ in the row. Similarly, the melodic motive in the left hand (bar one) consists of two intervallic successions stemming from the row: a three-note fragment consisting of interval classes 5 and 4 and a two-note fragment consisting of interval class 5. The final note of the motive, G, proceeds to D, which begins the next motive. D follows G in Cage's row.

Cage's sketches for the 1974 revision of his *Two Pieces* provide further insight into his working methods. The sketches suggest that he began with a series of rhythmic as well as melodic motives (noted in terms of intervals up or down between pairs of pitches). Each melodic motive was assigned its own rhythm, as illustrated in example 1.2, which juxtaposes a page from Cage's sketches and its transcription. The entire first movement consists of repetitions of these motives at different levels of transposition. For instance, the first motive in example 1.2 appears in measures two and twenty-four in the right hand and measures eight, nine, sixteen, and thirty-four in the left hand. Motive six occurs in measures nine and twenty-five in the right hand and measures one, six, twelve, and thirteen in the left hand. It is apparent that the score was assembled in a somewhat mechanical way. Much of the composing of the work took place *before* this process as Cage composed the work's row, derived his melodic and rhythmic materials, and decided upon the procedures governing just how these materials would be put together in the work itself.

The late 1930s marked a breakthrough in the development of Cage's compositional style. It was during this period that he began a lifelong exploration of the musical potential of noise. But at the same time that Cage was mapping out a new, unexplored musical terrain, he was also building upon innovations by his contemporaries and predecessors. His

34. For a discussion of this and other early works by Cage, see David Nicholls, *American Experimental Music, 1890–1940* (New York: Cambridge University Press, 1990), 175ff. Paul van Emmerik also discusses this work in "Thema's en Variaties: Systematische tendensen in de compositietechnieken van John Cage" (Ph.D. diss., Universiteit van Amsterdam, 1996), 34.

35. Nicholls and van Emmerik each present different orderings of the row. The version used here appears in Cage's analytical sketches for his 1974 revision of this work. These sketches are written in a stenographer's pad now part of the John Cage Manuscript Collection at the New York Public Library, JPB 94–24, folder 22. The differences between Cage's, Nicholls's, and van Emmerik's interpretation are not significant, since each preserves the row's intervallic structure.

EXAMPLE 1.1
Two Pieces for Piano, I, Edition Peters. © 1974 by Henmar Press, Inc. Used by permission.

interest in noise was inspired by the work of filmmaker Oskar von Fischinger,[36] the music of Edgard Varèse, and dadaist and futurist experiments with bruitism. Perhaps less obvious was Schoenberg's continuing influence. Cage's first work for percussion, the *Quartet*, was written in 1935, the same year in which he moved back to Los Angeles to study with Schoenberg. In a lecture presented circa 1938–40, Cage explains

36. *For the Birds: John Cage in Conversation with Daniel Charles* (Boston: Marion Boyars, 1981), 73ff.

EXAMPLE 1.2
Sketch for the 1974 revision of *Two Pieces for Piano,* from stenographer's pad, New York Public Library, John Cage Manuscript Collection, JPB 94-24, folder 22. Shown with its transcription.

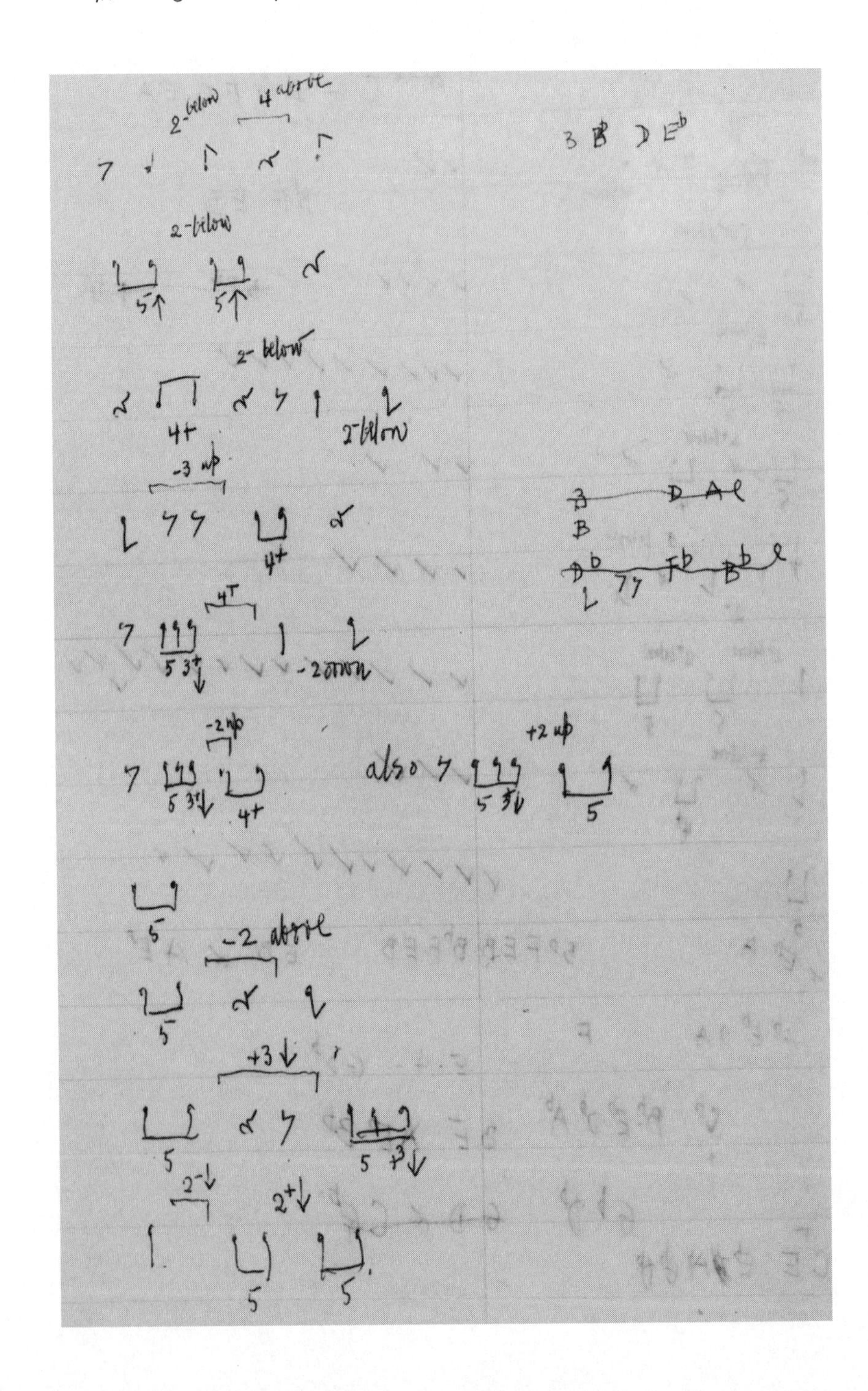

1 -1 +5

2 +7 -1 +7

3 -6 -1 -1

4 +3 6

5 -7-4 6 -1 *
3

6 -7-4+2 +7
or:-7-4+1 6 *
3

7 +7

8 +7 +1

9 +7 -4 -7-4
3

10 -1 5 -2 5

*The triplets transcribed here conform to the way they appear in the final score.

that just as Schoenberg has rejected the distinction between consonance and dissonance, today there exists a needless differentiation between noise and so-called musical sounds:

> Whereas, in the past, the point of disagreement has been between dissonance and consonance, it will be, in the immediate future, between noise and so-called musical sounds. The present methods of writing music, principally those which employ harmony and its reference to particular steps in the field of sound, will be inadequate for the composer, who will be faced with the entire field of sound. New methods will be discovered, bearing a definite relation to Schoenberg's twelve-tone system and present methods of writing percussion music and any other methods which are free from the concept of a fundamental tone.[37]

The parallels with Schoenberg were a matter not only of aesthetics, but also of similar compositional technique. Cage predicted that new methods for writing percussion music would draw upon Schoenberg's twelve-tone system. This seems to have been true of Cage's *First Construction (in Metal)* (1939). In composing the *First Construction,* as in his twelve-tone works written during the period from 1935 to 1938, Cage began with a collection of motivic groups, or cells. He first composed a series of sixteen rhythmic cells, as illustrated by the sketch and its transcription in example 1.3.

In a letter to Pierre Boulez, Cage described the method used in composing this work:

> Now something about the *Construction in Metal.* The rhythmic structure is 4, 3, 2, 3, 4 (16 × 16). You can see that the first number (4) equals the number of figures that follow it. This first number is divided 1, 1, 1, 1 and first I present the ideas that are developed in the 3, then those in the 2, etc. Regarding the method: there are 16 rhythmic motives divided 4, 4, 4, 4 conceived as circular series. When you are on 1, you can go 1 2 3 4 1 or retrograde. You can repeat (e.g., 112233443322 etc.). But you cannot go 2–4 or 1–3. When you are on 2, you cannot only use the same idea but can go back to 1 using the "doorways" 1 or 4. (Very simple games.)[38]

These remarks point to the work's rhythmic structure, which according to Cage's "square root" system consists of sixteen sixteen-bar phrases grouped into larger sections based on the proportion 4:3:2:3:4. Likewise, each sixteen-bar section divides into phrases of 4, 3, 2, 3, and 4 measures long. The work begins with a section made up of four sixteen-bar units (1, 1, 1, 1), which Cages calls an "exposition." This is followed

37. "The Future of Music: Credo," in *Silence,* 4–5.

38. Jean-Jacques Nattiez, *The Boulez-Cage Correspondence,* trans. and ed. Robert Samuels (Cambridge: Cambridge University Press, 1993), 49.

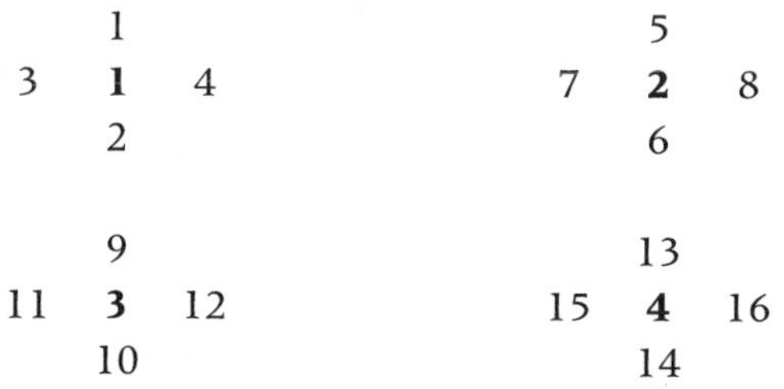

	1				5	
3	**1**	4		7	**2**	8
	2				6	
	9				13	
11	**3**	12		15	**4**	16
	10				14	

FIGURE 1.1
Circular series for *First Construction (in Metal)*, in *The Boulez-Cage Correspondence*, ed. Jean-Jacques Nattiez (Cambridge: Cambridge University Press, 1993), 49.

by a "development" with sections of 16 × 3, 16 × 2, 16 × 3, and 16 × 4 measures, and a "coda."

Cage deployed the rhythmic cells according to the "circular series" described above. As indicated in his sketch, the order of the cells is different. For example, the first group of four cells is numbered 1, 4, 2, 3 rather than 1, 2, 3, 4. This change is taken into account in figure 1.1, which is a revision of the diagram from Cage's letter to Boulez.

Cage's "serial" method is illustrated in example 1.4, which consists of the opening sixteen measures of the second, third, and sixth percussion parts. (The reader should note that in this passage and elsewhere in the work, Cage's rhythmic cells are often accompanied by sustained sounds, such as the thundersheet rumblings in the opening of the movement or the brakedrum half notes in bars eight and nine. These accompaniments do not appear to correspond to Cage's cells. There are some cases, however, in which their total duration matches that of the cells. For example, the brakedrum half notes correspond to the duration of cell 3. That Cage may have been thinking in these terms is suggested by his sketch, in which the durational value of each cell appears in the right-hand column.) In measures ten through sixteen, the sixth percussionist moves around the first circle, playing cells 3, 3, 1, 3, 3, 1, 3, 2, 2, and 4. Precisely as the composer's precompositional rules allow, there are moves in both directions to contiguous cells along the circle and repeated cells, but no moves across the circle. The third percussionist plays cells 4, 1, 4, 2, 3, 3, and 4. This succession adheres to Cage's rules except for the final cell 4, which is preceded by cell 3 from across the first circle. It seems clear that Cage was willing to deviate from his plan for musical reasons;[39] the third and sixth percussionists play cell 4 in unison, thus articulating the end of the first sixteen-bar section.

39. This was also the case in Cage's later work. See, for example, the discussion below of his *Music of Changes*.

EXAMPLE 1.3

Sketch for *First Construction (in Metal),* New York Public Library, John Cage Manuscript Collection, JPB 95-24, folder 37. Shown with its transcription.

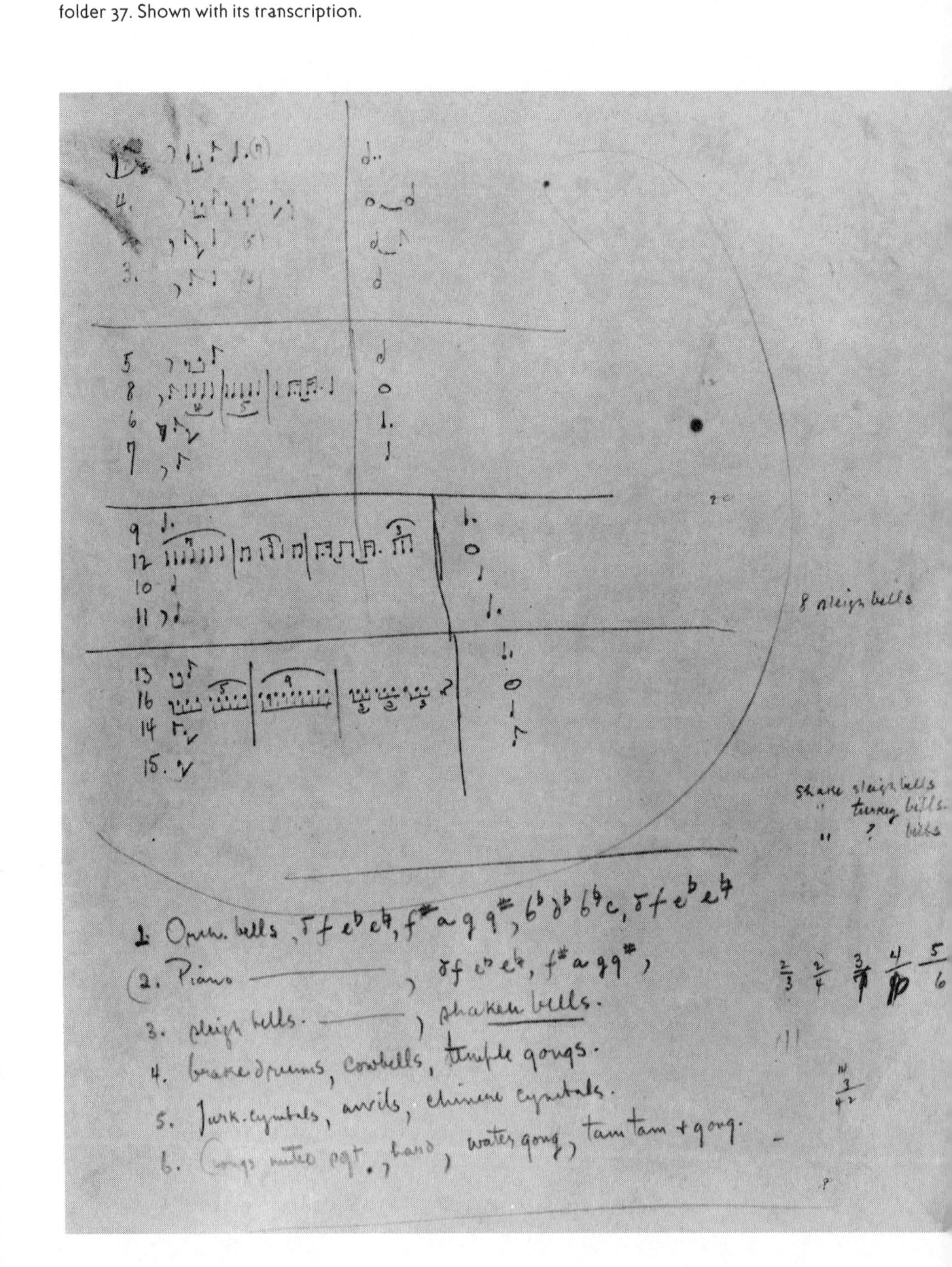

EXAMPLE 1.3 *continued*

1

4

2

3

5

8

4 5

6

7

9

12

3

7 3

10

11

13

5 9

3 3 3

16

14

15

Another noteworthy departure from the rules occurs in the first two measures, where the second percussionist plays cells 1, 7, 9, and 5. If cell 1 is segmented into groups of 4 and 3 eighth notes, the durational values in eighths of these cells are 4, 3, 2, 3, 4 (as indicated by the brackets in example 1.4).[40] Cage's opening "theme" thus foreshadows the rhythmic proportions governing the entire piece. It is almost as if the composer chose to present, in Schoenbergian terms, the composition's "basic shape," or *Grundgestalt,* as the work's initial gesture.[41] This foreshadowing and the quasi-serial structure in the *First Construction* are evidence of Schoenberg's continuing influence. It is important to point out, however, that the cellular permutations in the *First Construction* differ markedly from Schoenbergian motivic techniques, particularly developing variation. The essential difference lies in the fact that Cage's motivic cells are static; they recur unchanged and are never developed. His technique is "constructive," as his title suggests, rather than "developmental," a process involving transformation rather than literal repetition.

During the four sixteen-bar sections in his exposition, which comprises the first large unit of the rhythmic structure, Cage proceeds through each of his four circles. For example, in the second section (which begins at rehearsal letter A), the fourth percussionist alternates cells 5 and 7, the fifth percussionist plays cells 5, 8, 6, 7, 6, 8, and 5 (ex. 1.5). In this passage and elsewhere, a cell is abbreviated (see the first cell 8 in ex. 1.5). In addition, there is an overlap; the passage contains cells 3 and 2 (in the second and sixth percussion parts) from the previous section. But here and throughout the *First Construction,* Cage for the most part adheres to the rigors of his system. In the development, he deploys the cells at a slower rate. Following the remaining units of his rhythmic "macrostructure," he moves through the first circle during three sixteen-bar units (rehearsal letters D, E, and F), the second circle during three sixteen-bar units (rehearsal letters G and F), the third circle during three sixteen-bar units (rehearsal letters I, J, and K), and the fourth circle during four sixteen-bar units (rehearsal letters L, M, N, and O). As in the exposition there are overlaps, and some of the longer cells are condensed. The work ends with a nine-bar coda in which the first percussionist plays cell 16, the last cell from the fourth circle.

The foregoing analyses of two of Cage's early pieces reveal much about the formation of his compositional style. They can, moreover, provide

40. I am grateful to percussion virtuoso and Cage expert William Winant for pointing this out. Note that cell 1 might be construed as cells 5 and 9, thus yielding the same segmentation into groups of 4 and 3 eighth notes.

41. It is very likely that Cage was exposed to this concept during his classes with Schoenberg. See Bernstein, "John Cage, Arnold Schoneberg, and the Musical Idea."

EXAMPLE 1.4
First Construction (in Metal), measures 1–16, second, third, and sixth percussion parts.

EXAMPLE 1.5
First Construction (in Metal), measures 17–23.

us with a valuable perspective for examining his later works. Although Cage began his compositional career exploring aspects of Schoenberg's twelve-tone system, his limited exposure to these methods (Schoenberg preferred not to teach his students serial techniques) and natural inclination to experiment and push boundaries led him to develop his own approach to the twelve-tone system. Perhaps most striking is the extent to which Cage focused on setting up intricate precompositional strategies. A significant portion of the actual "composing" of *Two Pieces* and

First Construction took place before Cage turned to the final score. In the case of *Two Pieces,* Cage first composed his row and then his melodic/ rhythmic motives. He next arranged the motives, according to the rules of his twelve-tone system, into the mosaic that constituted the final score. Similarly, in the *First Construction,* Cage selected the instrumentation, determined the rhythmic structure, composed his motivic materials, and decided upon the method for their systematic deployment before realizing the score. In both cases, a mechanistic process seems to lessen the role that choice plays in the creative process. But Cage's emphasis upon the earliest stages of composition helped him cultivate an acute sense of the potential of his musical materials and methods that would remain a crucial aspect of his compositional technique.

IV

Cage's works from the early 1950s mark critical changes in his musical style and aesthetic philosophy, which seem to indicate a departure from his earlier modernist affiliations. During the previous decade Cage had become interested in South and East Asian philosophy, appropriating elements of Indian, Taoist, and Zen philosophy into his own aesthetics.[42] The focus of his music shifted from the composer to the listener; music now had an ethical and spiritual function—"to sober the mind and make it susceptible to divine influences."[43] After 1950, Cage looked toward a more complete withdrawal of his own subjectivity from the creative process through the use of chance and indeterminacy. The result was a seemingly depersonalized musical style, emphasizing the objectification of musical sound. As Christian Wolff explained in an article on electronic music: "One finds a concern for a kind of objectivity, almost anonymity—sound comes into its own. The 'music' is a result existing simply in the sounds we hear, given no impulse by expressions of self or personality. It is indifferent in motive, originating in no psychology nor in dramatic intentions, nor in literary or pictorial purposes."[44] This development may be seen, as James Tenney argues in chapter 8, as the end of the "operatic era"—a 350-year period in the history of Western music during which the primary function of music was to express human emotion. But to identify Cage's shift as a complete break from the past does not take the full historical situation into account. The radi-

42. For an informative account of Cage's "appropriations" of South and East Asian philosophy, see David W. Patterson, "Appraising the Catchwords, c. 1942–1959: Cage's Asian-Derived Rhetoric and the Historical Reference for Black Mountain College" (Ph.D. diss., Columbia University, 1996). For a discussion of the changes of this period within the context of the development of the New York school, see Bernstein, "Cage and the Aesthetic of Indifference."

43. John Cage, "45' for a Speaker," in *Silence: Lectures and Writings* (Middletown, Conn.: Wesleyan University Press, 1961), 158.

44. Quoted in Cage, "History of Experimental Music," 68.

cal changes in his compositional style notwithstanding, Cage continued to play a role within the evolution of post–World War II modernism. Moreover, the importance of understanding Cage's ties to the past becomes especially apparent when we begin to look toward developing analytical methods for the music he wrote after 1950.

Cage enjoyed a lively correspondence with Pierre Boulez from 1949 to 1954.[45] The two men exchanged detailed notes regarding the compositional techniques they were employing at that time. It is fascinating to observe how much they had in common, despite the fact that Boulez was moving toward integral serialism while Cage was exploring chance and indeterminacy. Each composer promoted the other's work. Cage was an advocate of Boulez's music in the United States. He especially admired the latter's *Second Piano Sonata,* despite the fact that its extroverted, often aggressive style was far from his own. Boulez organized a performance of *Sonatas and Interludes* for a soirée at Suzanne Tézenna's salon in June 1949. He was especially interested in Cage's exploration of complex frequency patterns in his percussion music and compositions for the prepared piano. In Boulez's view, Cage "proved the possibility of creating non-tempered sound spaces, even with existing instruments. Thus his *prepared piano* is not merely an unexpected sidelight on the percussion-piano, whose soundboard is invaded by strange metallic vegetation. It rather calls into question the whole notion of acoustics as it has gradually stabilized in the evolution of western music, becoming an instrument capable, by means of an artisan tablature, of yielding complex frequency patterns." He also praised Cage for "conceiving rhythmic structure as dependent on real time, expressed through numerical relationships in which the personal element plays no part." Boulez noted the similarities between Cage's innovations and his own work. He saw Cage's focus on the "individuality of sound" as an approach that took into account all the attributes of sound: pitch, volume, timbre, and duration. Boulez recognized parallels between his own development of integral serialism and Cage's systematic procedures in such pieces as the *Music of Changes.* Describing how Cage used a system of tables to set up "structural relations between different components of sound," organizing "each component into parallel but autonomous distributions," Boulez remarked, "The tendency of these experiments by John Cage is too close to my own for me to fail to mention them."[46]

45. Nattiez, *The Boulez-Cage Correspondence.* This correspondence is also examined in Deborah Campana, "A Chance Encounter: The Correspondence between John Cage and Pierre Boulez, 1949–1954," in *John Cage at Seventy-Five,* ed. Richard Fleming and William Duckworth (Lewisburg, Pa.: Bucknell University Press, 1989), 209–48.

46. Pierre Boulez, "Possibly. . . ," in *Stocktakings of an Apprenticeship,* trans. Stephen Walsh (Oxford: Oxford University Press, 1991), 134, 135.

In the *Music of Changes,* Cage used eight charts containing sounds (and silences), eight charts with durations, and eight charts with dynamics. In addition, single charts were used to determine tempi and superpositions (the number of contrapuntal layers in each phrase). Several of these charts are reproduced in example 1.6.)[47] Selections from the charts were made through coin tosses according to the procedures in the *I Ching.* In cases where Cage used eight charts, four were mobile and four immobile (or static) at any given point during the compositional process. When elements were selected from mobile charts, they were thereafter replaced. Elements from immobile charts could be used again.

Boulez completed the first *(Ia)* of his *Structures for Two Pianos* in 1951, the same year in which Cage finished his *Music of Changes.*[48] The two composers' letters during this period include an interesting exchange concerning the compositional methods employed in the two works. Boulez's letter to Cage dated August 1951 contains some of the working materials used for *Structures* (ex. 1.7). Boulez's charts are strikingly similar to those used by Cage. The matrices marked A and B can apply to intensity, attack, duration, and pitch. Thus, the permutations of order positions for his pitch series determine the reorderings of his series for intensity, attack, and duration.[49] The first movement, *Structures Ia,* is an extremely deterministic work. Boulez was exploring the limits of total serialism; as he explained, his concern was "to see how far one could pursue the automaticism of musical relationships without allowing individual choice to intervene other than on really basic levels of organization."[50] He was experimenting with an "expressive nadir," a pure and objective musical style devoid of the composer's personality and intent. To this end, *Structures* uses the series composed by Olivier Messiaen for his *Modes de valeurs et d'intensités* (1950). In addition to reconciling the often ambivalent relationship with his former teacher, this strategy diminished the element of choice from the very beginning of Boulez's compositional process.[51]

Thus, in the early 1950s, Cage had strong ties with the ultramodernist Darmstadt school. Like Boulez and Stockhausen, he was intently exploring composition based upon all aspects of musical sound. Ironically, although the ironclad determinism of total serialism seems diametrically

47. The charts and working materials for the *Music of Changes* are located in the David Tudor Archive now housed at the Getty Center for the History of the Arts and Humanities in Los Angeles. Most of the materials are contained in a hardbound notebook. Several of Cage's sound charts appear as separate sheets.

48. Dominique Jameaux, *Pierre Boulez,* trans. Susan Bradshaw (Cambridge: Harvard University Press, 1991), 48.

49. See ibid., 269ff., for a useful discussion of the serial techniques in *Structures Ia.*

50. Ibid., 52.

51. Ibid., 51, 269.

EXAMPLE 1.6
Music of Changes, sound chart 3, amplitude charts 3 and 4, and tempo chart, the David Tudor Papers, 1884–1998 (bulk 1940–1996), Getty Research Institute, Research Library, accession no. 980039.

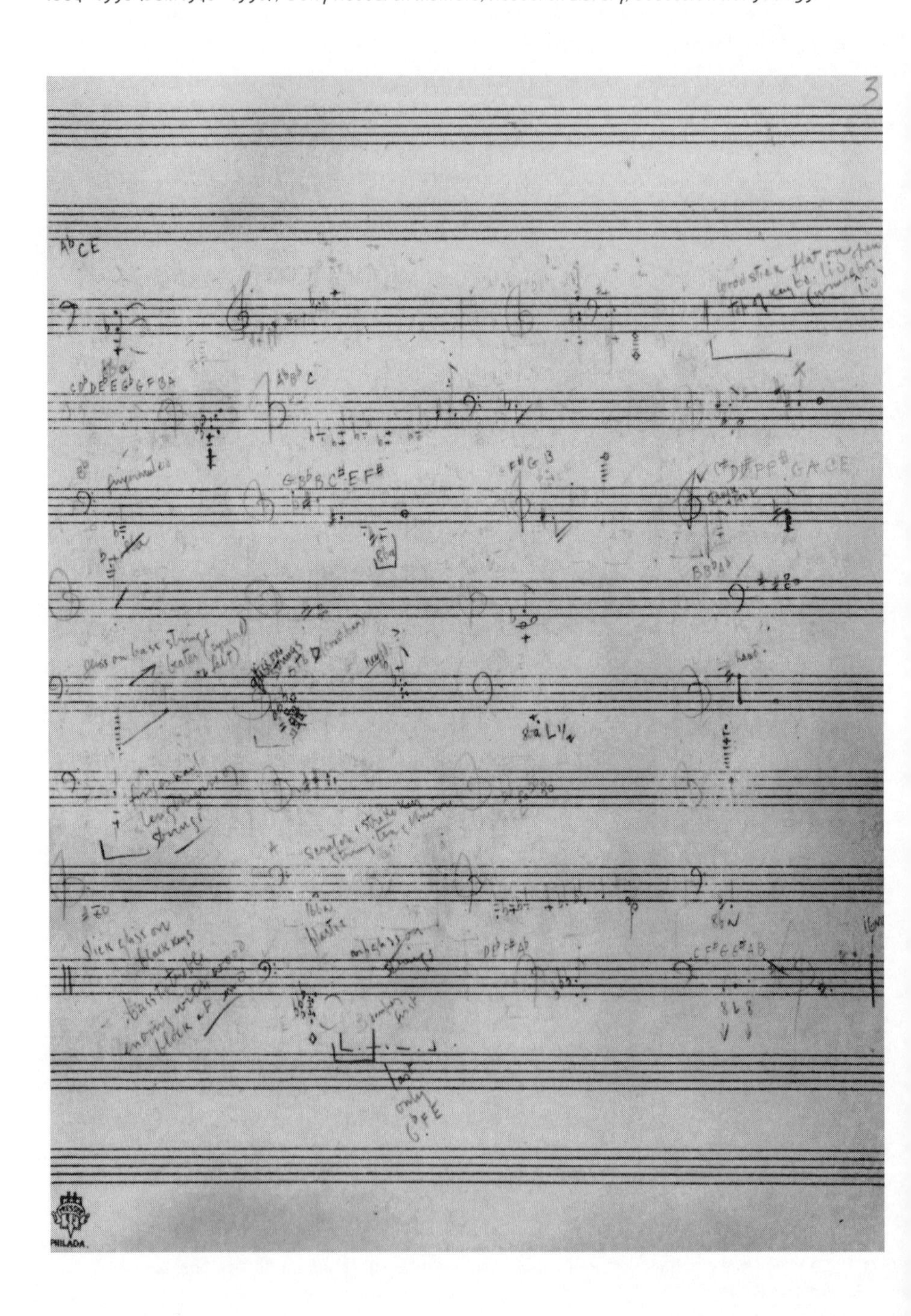

EXAMPLE 1.6 *continued*

opposed to music based on chance, the mechanical "automaticism" of the former procedure appeared to all but eliminate the composer's role just as did the latter. Despite the seemingly paradoxical congruence, Boulez had reservations concerning Cage's use of chance operations, which culminated in 1957 with his well-known article entitled "Alea," in which he denounced the overuse of chance in composition. Boulez attributed the overuse of chance to a weakness in compositional technique. He claimed that a composer working with chance "feels no responsibility for his work, but out of unconfessed weakness and confusion and the

EXAMPLE 1.6 *continued*

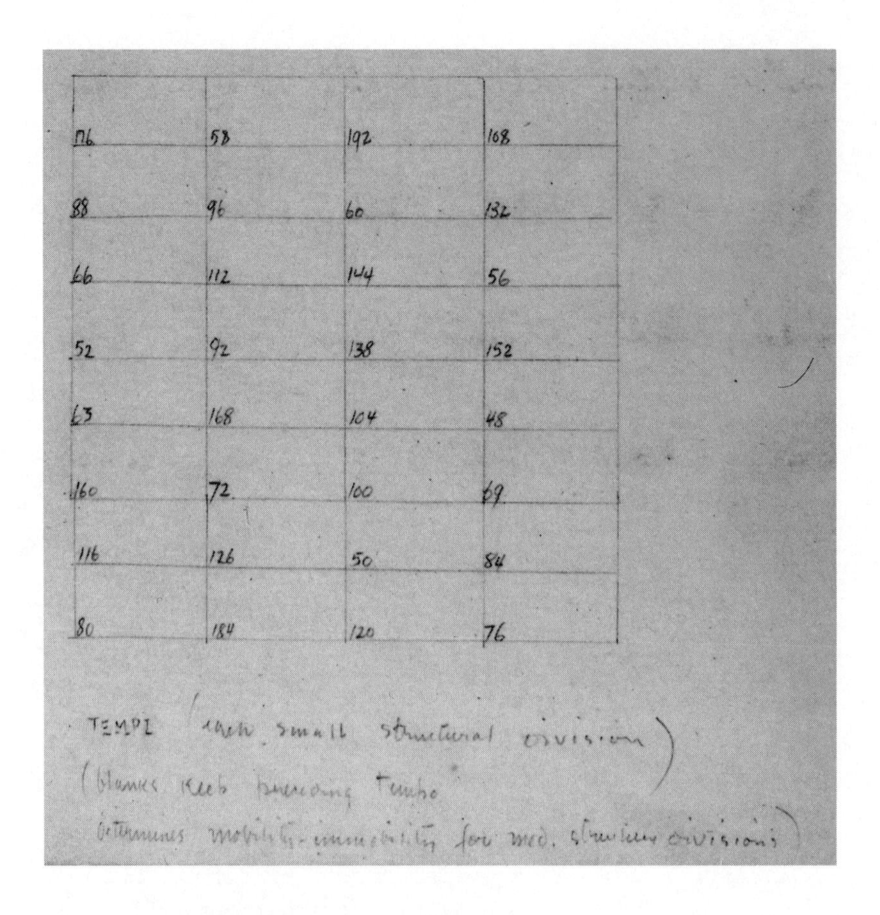

176	58	192	168
88	96	60	132
66	112	144	56
52	92	138	152
63	168	104	48
160	72	100	69
116	126	50	84
80	184	120	76

TEMPI (each small structural division)
(blanks keep preceding tempo
determines mobility-immobility for med. structure divisions)

desire for temporary relief, simply throws himself into puerile mumbo-jumbo. In other words, everything just happens as it will, without control (an intentional but not meritorious omission, since there is no alternative), BUT within a fixed network of probabilities, since even chance must have some sort of outcome."[52] Boulez was unwilling to allow for what he referred to as "accidental chance." He believed that the wholesale adoption of such methods amounted to an abandonment of the creative process. This characterization, however, does not apply to Cage's music. Indeed, it is a persistent misunderstanding that his use of chance operations entails a lack of compositional control.

Cage composed the *Music of Changes* according to the phrase and sec-

52. Boulez, "Alea," in *Stocktakings*, 26. See also his letter to Cage dated December 1951. Nattiez, *The Boulez-Cage Correspondence*, 112–13.

EXAMPLE 1.7
Working materials for Pierre Boulez, *Structures Ia*, Boulez to John Cage, August 1951, in *The Boulez-Cage Correspondence*, ed. Jean-Jacques Nattiez (Cambridge: Cambridge University Press, 1993), 100, 101. Reprinted with the permission of Cambridge University Press.

Which <u>in figures</u> gives the following double serial organisation:

A

1	2	3	4	5	6	7	8	9	10	11	12
2	8	4	5	6	11	1	9	12	3	7	10
3	4	1	2	8	9	10	5	6	7	12	11
4	5	2	8	9	12	3	6	11	1	10	7
5	6	8	9	12	10	4	11	7	2	3	1
6	11	9	12	10	3	5	7	1	8	4	2
7	1	10	3	4	5	11	2	8	12	6	9
8	9	5	6	11	7	2	12	10	4	1	3
9	12	6	11	7	1	8	10	3	5	2	4
10	3	7	1	2	8	12	4	5	11	9	6
11	7	12	10	3	4	6	1	2	9	5	8
12	10	11	7	1	2	9	3	4	6	8	5

B

1	7	3	10	12	9	2	11	6	4	8	5
7	11	10	12	9	8	1	6	5	3	2	4
3	10	1	7	11	6	4	12	9	2	5	8
10	12	7	11	6	5	3	9	8	1	4	2
12	9	11	6	5	4	10	8	2	7	3	1
9	8	6	5	4	3	12	2	1	11	10	7
2	1	4	3	10	12	8	7	11	5	9	6
11	6	12	9	8	2	7	5	4	10	1	3
6	5	9	8	2	1	11	4	3	12	7	10
4	3	2	1	7	11	5	10	12	8	6	9
8	2	5	4	3	10	9	1	7	6	12	11
5	4	8	2	1	7	6	3	10	9	11	12

1	2	3	4	5	6	7	8	9	10	11	12
pppp	*ppp*	*pp*	*p*	·meno *p* quasi *p*	*mp*	*mf*	più *f* quasi *f*	*f*	*ff*	*fff*	*ffff*

for attacks:

>									*sfz*	*sfz*	normal
1	2	3	4	5	6	7	8	9	10	11	12

(See the piece entitled: Modes de valeurs et d'intensités, by Messiaen.) for durations:

1 2 3 4 5 6 7 8 9 10 11 12

tion lengths of a precompositionally determined rhythmic structure.[53] Just as in the *First Construction*, the *Music of Changes* uses Cage's "square root" system; there are 29⅝ sections, each 29⅝ measures long and divided into phrases of 3, 5, 6¾, 6¾, 5, and 3⅛ measures. For each phrase the tempo and the number of layers were determined by a single hexagram.[54] If the phrase appeared at the beginning of a section of 29⅝ measures, the same hexagram would determine whether the odd-numbered or even-numbered duration, pitch, and dynamics charts were mobile or immobile. He selected elements from these charts, composing one layer at a time until the phrase was filled. When the same pitch occurred simultaneously in two different layers, a situation Cage called "interference," one of the pitches was omitted.[55] That he was willing to make adjustments to the musical score after his coin tosses is an important point. There are many examples of his compositional intervention in the *Music of Changes*. Its composition was not an entirely mechanical process; when necessary, Cage shortened, lengthened, and segmented the duration of his sounds according to his own musical judgment. He likewise manipulated the dynamics and used pedaling to alter the results of his chance operations in order to yield what he thought were more musical results.[56]

Cage's control was certainly operative before the score's realization; the final results were a function of the compositional system employed in the *Music of Changes*.[57] This system ensured a varied contrapuntal texture, from single lines to dense polyphonic events. The nature of the materials used in making the *Music of Changes* had an obvious effect upon the end product. The duration charts consisted of rhythms built incrementally from as small as a thirty-second of a beat to a whole note and included sixteenths, eighths, and quarters as well as units based on thirds, fifths, and sevenths (ex. 1.8). These guaranteed a level of rhythmic complexity similar to that found in contemporaneous works by Boulez and others. Cage described the contents of his sound charts in terms of single sounds and silences, intervals, aggregates (simultaneities

53. In his pathbreaking dissertation on the development of Cage's chance techniques in the 1950s, James Pritchett has reconstructed the step-by-step procedure through which Cage composed the *Music of Changes*. See Pritchett, "The Development of Chance Techniques in the Music of John Cage, 1950–1956" (Ph.D. diss., New York University, 1988), 129ff. See also Pritchett, *The Music of John Cage* (New York: Cambridge University Press, 1993), 78–88.

54. Pritchett, "Development of Chance Techniques," 130.

55. Cage, "Composition: To Describe the Process of Composition Used in *Music of Changes* and *Imaginary Landscape No. 4*," in *Silence*, 58.

56. Pritchett, "Development of Chance Techniques," 6ff., 151. See also Prichett, "Understanding John Cage's Chance Music: An Analytical Approach," in Fleming and Duckworth, *John Cage at Seventy-Five*, 249–61.

57. Pritchett, "The Development of Chance Techniques," 6ff.; see also "Understanding John Cage's Chance Music."

EXAMPLE 1.8
Music of Changes, duration chart 6, the David Tudor Papers, 1884–1998 (bulk 1940–1996), Getty Research Institute, Research Library, accession no. 980039.

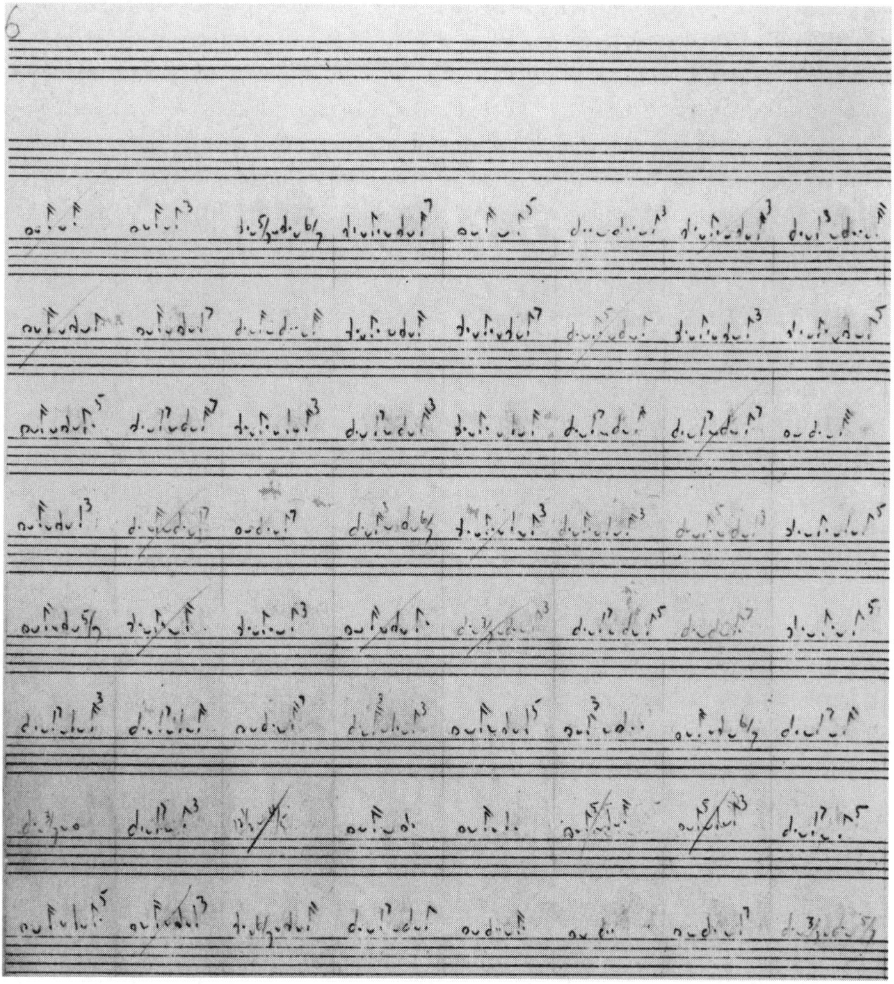

consisting of three or more notes), and constellations (more complex rhythmic combinations).[58] The charts contain a wide variety of innovative piano sounds such as clusters, harmonics, and "string-piano" techniques used by Cage and his mentor Henry Cowell. There are also several instances of sounds produced by slamming the keyboard lid and striking the wood under the keyboard. These sounds as well as the

58. "Composition: To Describe the Process of Composition Used in *Music of Changes* and *Imaginary Landscape No. 4*," in *Silence*, 58.

work's many silences (each sound chart contains as many silences as sounds) yield a distinctly Cagean style. The more traditional "pitched" aggregates and constellations are largely dissonant combinations, which give the work a distinctive chromatic sound markedly different from many of the often diatonic combinations in the gamuts for such works as Cage's *String Quartet in Four Parts* (1949–50). The high degree of chromaticism in the *Music of Changes* was also guaranteed by Cage's precompositional decision that the vertical and horizontal axes of his sound charts must include all twelve tones of the chromatic scale.[59] Note, for instance, in the sound chart given in example 1.6 that the trichord in the upper-left corner (C, A♭, E, or pitch-class set 3–12) is immediately followed by its complement (C♯, F♯, G, A♯, B, D, E♭, F, A, or pitch-class set 9–12). (Pitches could recur on the same axes, once Cage's dodecaphonic requirement was satisfied.)

In composing the *Music of Changes,* Cage sought a sort of perpetual variation resulting from the continued renewal of his materials. This was accomplished through chart "mobility." As noted above, when elements were selected from mobile charts they were replaced. This procedure guaranteed a high degree of entropy; the relative absence of repetition in the *Music of Changes* contrasts with such works as *Sixteen Dances* (1950–51) or the *String Quartet in Four Parts.* When repetitions do occur they are very striking. For example, the repeating occurrences of the constellation (a) that begins the fourth movement and the reoccurring glissandi (b) played with the fingernail inside the piano (ex. 1.9) assume a certain motivic significance, which results from Cage's precompositional plan. The *Music of Changes* was thus as much a product of the composer's intentions and precompositional decisions as of his chance operations.

In short, despite their obvious stylistic differences, Cage's *Two Pieces, First Construction,* and *Music of Changes* show similarities in compositional technique. Each work employs an elaborate precompositional plan laid out in a series of charts or sketches. In addition, the realization of the score was in each case a somewhat mechanical process. Cage's precompositional work is where the actual composing took place. This approach characterizes almost all of Cage's oeuvre, right through his last pieces, as is vividly illustrated in Henning Lohner's essay on Cage's film *One[11]* (chap. 13). Cage learned from Schoenberg that a composer should always have the end in view and understand the developmental possibilities inherent in a work's motives and themes. From early on in his career, he continually refined this ability to understand the potential of his

59. Ibid., 26.

EXAMPLE 1.9
Music of Changes, measures 1, 15, 42, 17, and 97, Edition Peters (Henmar Press, 1961).

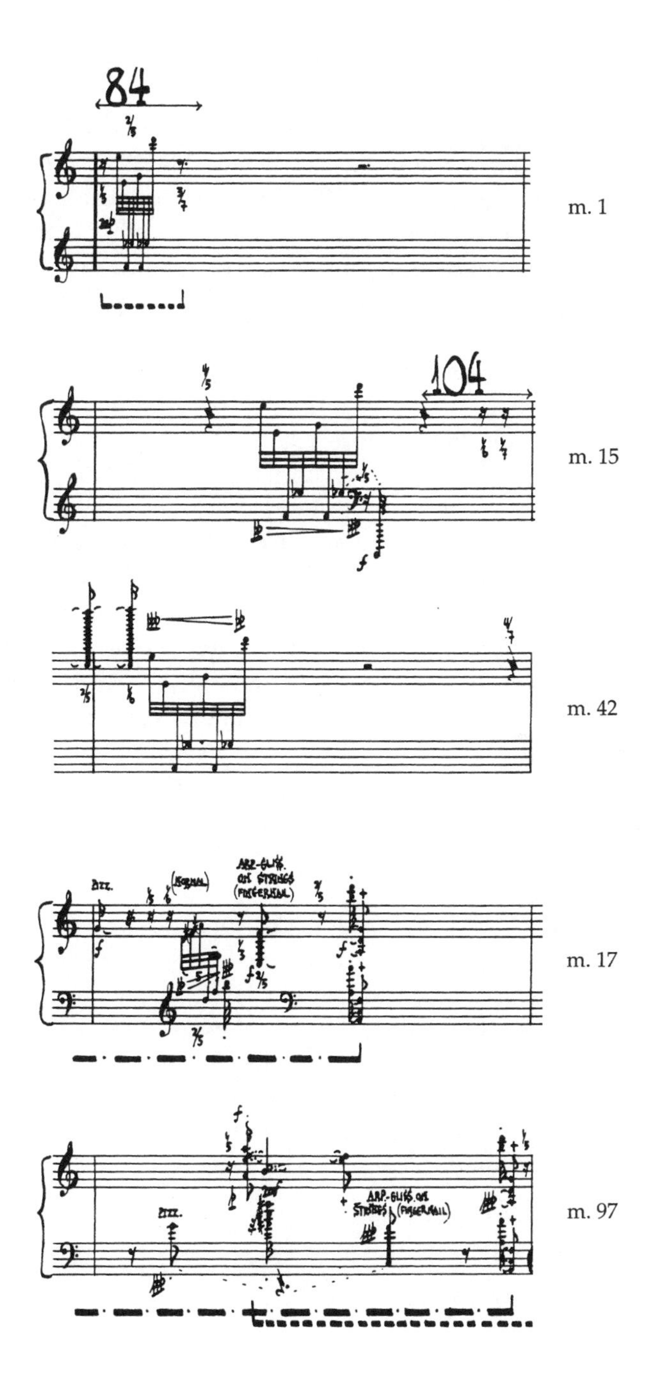

compositional strategies. Cage maintained this tie to the past, concurrent with his use of chance. Thus, the opposition of chance and design invoked during comparisons of postmodernist and modernist aesthetics is a false dichotomy for Cage, since both operate freely within the same musical context.

Such observations should not lead us to ignore the revolutionary aspects of Cage's work. His commitment, for example, to letting "sounds be themselves" resulted in a radically new form of musical continuity devoid of intentional relationships between sounds other than their coexistence in musical space and time. As Cage explained in an essay describing the compositional process in his *Music of Changes* and *Imaginary Landscape No. 4:* "It is thus possible to make a musical composition the continuity of which is free of individual taste and memory (psychology) and also of the literature and 'traditions' of art. The sounds enter the time-space centered within themselves, unimpeded by service to any abstraction, their 360 degrees of circumference free for an infinite play of interpenetration."[60] Cage's redefinition of form entailed a rejection of an organicist assumption that a musical work should be a unified whole, an aesthetic criterion that had been as relevant for composers during the nineteenth century as it was for the high modernist composers who explored the limits of integral serialism during the 1950s. Cage's concept of musical form was revolutionary. But the radical results of his compositional processes were achieved through more conventional means, namely, through modernist precision, with its systematic attention to detail and control of the materials used in composition. When considering Cage's compositional methods, one finds that the postmodern and the modern coexist without contradiction. The same is true of Cage's political and social agenda. Through his redefinition of musical form Cage created works modeling desirable political and social structures. He was able to renew the modernist project dedicated to political and social change through art using postmodernist artistic techniques. As we assess Cage's role within the development of twentieth-century thought and musical style and intensify the critical evaluation of his creative output, it is crucial that we consider both the traditional and the radical aspects of his aesthetics and compositional style. This formidable task may very well occupy scholars for many years to come.

60. Ibid., 59.

TWO

Jonathan D. Katz

John Cage's Queer Silence; or, How to Avoid Making Matters Worse

To know of some is good;
but for the rest, silence
is to be praised.

—Ser Brunetto Latini,
speaking of his fellow
sodomites to Dante
in the *Inferno*

John Cage never did quite come out of the closet. Nonetheless, nearly everybody in the art world who knew him knew of his lifelong relationship with Merce Cunningham, and some even knew about the other men in his life. His sexuality was an open secret within the avant-garde, and as his fame spread, so too did knowledge of his personal life. Still, direct public acknowledgment of Cage's sexuality has been, until quite recently, hard to find; consigned to the realm of gossip, it has been understood as tangential to his historical importance and achievements. Cage himself, while never denying his sexuality, preferred to duck the question. When asked to characterize his relationship with Cunningham, he would say, "I cook, and Merce does the dishes.'"[1] As I hope to

Although originally written for this book, this essay first appeared in the *Gay and Lesbian Quarterly* 5, no. 2 (1999): 231–52. I would like to thank Moira Roth, without whom this essay could not have been written, and Kevin Schaub for his love and patience while it was being finished.

1. Interview with Remy Charlip, San Francisco, April 24, 1996. The most significant historical account of Cage's gay life, based on two remarkably candid interviews with him, is Thomas Hines, "Then Not Yet 'Cage': The Los Angeles Years, 1912–1938," in *John Cage: Composed in Amer-*

show in this essay, such avoidance was not only coy but constituted a form of active resistance within the homophobic culture of postwar America.

I. Gay Life

Cage first met Cunningham at the Cornish School in Seattle in 1938 after taking a job as piano accompanist for the dance classes. In a rare personal revelation, Cage once remarked that he and his wife, Xenia, had an open marriage and that both were attracted to the teenage Cunningham. Cage stated that during their ménage à trois he realized he "was more attracted to Cunningham than to Xenia."[2] The two men moved to New York, without Xenia, in 1942 and there undertook their first collaboration, *Credo in Us.* Its title is the first acknowledgment of the personal and professional partnership that animated so much of their subsequent work. Although they had been involved with one another for nearly four years, *Credo in Us,* born of their new independent life together, marked the public emergence of the relationship as muse.

Tellingly, the music Cage composed prior to his acquaintance with Cunningham was given largely straightforward descriptive titles—*Sonata for Two Voices* (1933), *Solo for Clarinet* (1933), *Five Songs for Contralto* (1938), *Music for Wind Instruments* (1938), for example. That this first joint project should unabashedly express their partnership in such romantic terms seems, in retrospect, remarkable. Yet the titles of many of the compositions Cage wrote between his move with Cunningham to New York and his final separation from Xenia (1942–46) reflect—in a distinctly allegorical, even expressive way—on his involvement with the dancer: *Credo in Us* (1942), *Amores* (1943), *Tossed as It Is Untroubled* (1943), *Root of an Unfocus* (1944), *Perilous Night* (1944), *A Valentine Out of Season* (1944), *Mysterious Adventure* (1945). Of the evocatively titled *Amores,* Cage admitted that its thematic "concerned the quietness between lovers." It was "an attempt to express in combination the erotic and the tranquil, two of the permanent emotions of Indian tradition."[3]

---

ica, ed. Marjorie Perloff and Charles Junkerman (Chicago: University of Chicago Press, 1994), 65–99. By contrast, as late as 1988 an *Architectural Digest* spread on Cage and Cunningham showed them in a photograph together in the apartment they shared but referred to them only as "lifelong friends" (John Gruen, "Architectural Digest Visits John Cage and Merce Cunningham," *Architectural Digest,* November 1988, 198–201). Caroline A. Jones provides an excellent analysis of Cage's silence as a means of opposing the abstract expressionist ego in "Finishing School: John Cage and the Abstract Expressionist Ego," *Critical Inquiry* 19 (summer 1993): 643–47.

2. Hines, "Then Not Yet 'Cage,'" 99 n. 60. Hines kindly let me hear parts of the tape recording of the interview and gave me the entire unpublished transcript. Despite Richard Kostelanetz's rather scurrilous charges as to its genuineness, I can testify to the authenticity of both tape and transcript.

3. "A Composer's Confessions," in *John Cage, Writer: Previously Uncollected Pieces,* ed. Richard Kostelanetz (New York: Limelight, 1993), 40, 9.

That many of these later, "expressively" titled pieces were written, moreover, to correspond with Cunningham's dances only reinforces the point.

But between *Amores* and, a year later, *Perilous Night* there is a change in mood, as if the volubility of the early works produced in association with Cunningham could not be sustained. Cage found it difficult to communicate his feelings in *Perilous Night* and thus began to question the very possibility of a traditionally expressive music: "I had poured a great deal of emotion into the piece, and obviously I wasn't communicating this at all. Or else, I thought, if I were communicating, then all artists must be speaking a different language, and thus speaking only for themselves. The whole musical situation struck me more and more as a Tower of Babel."[4]

What emotions or feelings was Cage struggling to give form to in *Perilous Night?* Uncharacteristically speaking in the impersonal, Cage hinted at their nature: "the loneliness and terror that comes to one when love becomes unhappy." Derived, as he later explained it, from an Irish folktale, "the music tells a story of the dangers of the erotic life and describes the misery of 'something that was together that is split apart.'" The year after *Perilous Night* was finished, Cage officially concluded his separation from Xenia. It was an especially painful and bitter moment; after interviewing Cage, one scholar reports, "Earlier he found it difficult to communicate with Xenia and . . . their later relationship had not been particularly friendly."[5]

Cage had had long-term homosexual relationships prior to his marriage, including one with a man named either Don or Allen Sample, with whom he was involved when he met his future wife. Cage and Sample enjoyed relationships with other men as well. Cage recalled that "contact with the rest of the [gay] society was through [cruising in] the parks. For me it was Santa Monica along the Palisades."[6] No less a figure than Harry Hay, the founding voice of the modern gay and lesbian rights movement, befriended Cage and helped him prepare a course on modern music that he gave to housewives in the mid-thirties.[7] Hay even sang several of Cage's compositions publicly; indeed, he was the first person

4. *For the Birds: John Cage, in Conversation with Daniel Charles* (Boston: Marion Boyars, 1981), 148.

5. "A Composer's Confessions," 40; Richard Francis, introduction to *Dancers on a Plane: Cage, Cunningham, Johns* (London: Anthony d'Offay Gallery, 1989), 26; Hines, "Then Not Yet 'Cage,'" 99.

6. Hines, "Then Not Yet 'Cage,'" 84. In an interview with Joan Retallack in October 1991, Cage refers to his former partner as Allen Sample, but Hines, interviewing Cage in May 1992, calls him Don Sample. See *Musicage: Cage Muses on Words, Art, Music,* ed. Joan Retallack (Hanover, N.H.: Wesleyan University Press, University Press of New England, 1996), 86; and Hines, "Then Not Yet 'Cage,'" 84–85.

7. See Stuart Timmons, *The Trouble with Harry Hay: Founder of the Modern Gay Movement* (Boston: Alyson, 1990), 40, 56–59, 72, 75, 85.

to do so. In 1933–34 Cage lived in New York and, through Virgil Thomson, met and became involved with the architect Philip Johnson; their relationship apparently ended in part because of differences in socioeconomic standing. Johnson recalled, "With his talent and good looks, everyone in Virgil's circle was wild about Cage."[8]

Xenia knew about Cage's past and accepted it. Cage remarked, "I didn't conceal anything so that even though the marriage didn't work any better than it did, there wasn't anyone to blame." Yet the failure of the marriage came to have an unexpected corollary effect, for it troubled his creative life as well. Cage has acknowledged that during this period "I was disturbed both in my private life and in my public life as a composer."[9] In *Perilous Night* he seems, paradoxically, to have discovered the impossibility of communication only while working to express some very specific, highly charged emotions, and his subsequent abandonment of an expressive musicality was thus intimately interwoven with the changes in his private life that followed the start of his relationship with Cunningham. If *Perilous Night* maps the culmination of the dissolution of Cage's marriage, then its theme of unhappy love is of the heterosexual and marital variety, the result of his return to a fully homosexual existence after his failed attempt at normative heterosexuality.

Cage more than once remarked that he turned first to psychoanalysis and then to Zen in response to what he termed these "disturbances" in his personal and creative life. Indeed, his first visit to a therapist and his subsequent involvement in Zen came almost immediately after he had separated from Xenia. As he flippantly put it: "Do you know the story of my relationship to psychoanalysis? It's short. It must have been around 1945. I was disturbed. Some friends advised me to see an analyst." But psychoanalysis did not suit him, and "so through circumstances, I substituted the study of Oriental thought" for it.[10]

Cage clearly associates this newfound curiosity about Zen—and his abandonment of psychoanalysis—with the "personal problems" attendant on his new life with Cunningham: "Well, if you had a disturbance both about your work and about your daily life, what are you going to do? . . . None of the doctors can help you, our society can't help you, and education doesn't help us. It's singularly lacking in any such instruction. Furthermore, our religion doesn't help us. . . . There isn't much help for

8. Quoted in Hines, "Then Not Yet 'Cage,'" 92. On a long car trip across America, Johnson repeatedly called Cage in an effort to keep the relationship alive. See Franz Schulze, *Philip Johnson: Life and Work* (New York: Knopf, 1994), 97, 112.

9. Hines, "Then Not Yet 'Cage,'" 86, and Kostelanetz, *John Cage, Writer,* 239.

10. *For the Birds,* 116; John Cage, interview by Paul Cummings, New York City, May 2, 1974 (transcript housed in the Archives of American Art, National Museum of American Art, Smithsonian Institution, Washington, D.C.), 36.

someone who is in trouble in our society. I had eliminated psychiatry as a possibility. You have Oriental thought, you have mythology."[11] Seeking resolution to "disturbances" in his work and his life in the dominant, authoritative Western traditions—medicine, education, religion—Cage found nothing that was useful. Given the centrality of homophobia to each of these traditions at the time (the American Psychological Association did not remove homosexuality from its list of pathologies until 1973), this is hardly surprising. His turn toward the East, then, was in part a response to a personal need unmet by orthodox Western traditions.

Cage later was to characterize his state of mind at the time as one of desperation. He was separating from his wife; he was embracing his relationship with Cunningham and, concomitantly, his identity as a socially marginal gay man; and during these experiences he was coming to the conclusion that communication in art, the hallmark of an expressive musicality, was not possible. He began to attend the now famous lectures on Zen Buddhism offered by Daisetz T. Suzuki at Columbia University. These lectures seemed to solve both his personal and his artistic problems: "It was after 1945, between 1946 and 1947 I suppose, that I began to become seriously interested in the Orient. After studying Oriental thought as a whole, I took Suzuki's course for three years, up until 1951."[12]

In essence, Zen repositioned the closet, not as a source of repression or anxiety, but as a means to achieve healing; it was in not talking about—and hence not reifying—one's troubles that healing began. Thus, what made Zen so attractive to Cage, perhaps, was its unhinging of the connection between problems and passions. It gave him a way to negotiate trauma by acknowledging the pain and then moving beyond or through it. This is not to say that problems are to be ignored or passions smothered, but neither are they to become obsessively rehearsed. In this Eastern tradition, the expression or articulation of trauma, so central to Western notions of healing (from Christian confession to Freudian talking cures), is devalued. One can hear just this Zen note in Cage's remarks many years later: "You can feel an emotion; just don't think that it's so important. . . . Take it in a way that you can then let it drop! Don't belabor it! . . . And if we keep emotions and reinforce them, they can produce a critical situation in the world. Precisely that situation in which all of society is now entrapped!"[13]

11. Interview by Cummings, 37.

12. *For the Birds,* 94. Cage's chronology of his studies with Suzuki is problematic, since the latter arrived in New York during the summer of 1950. See David W. Patterson, "Appraising the Catchwords, c. 1942–1959: Cage's Asian-Derived Rhetoric and the Historical Reference of Black Mountain College" (Ph.D. diss., Columbia University, 1996), 141ff.

13. *For the Birds,* 56.

Weaving seamlessly from an individual to a communal perspective, Zen Buddhism, as it could be garnered from Suzuki (who, Cage makes clear, did not "teach" in the Western sense), became the means by which Cage aligned the perceived social necessity of the closet with what would become an individual—and ultimately global—liberationist perspective. Paradoxically, at least from a Western perspective, not talking about feelings would eventually yield a society free of the invidious excesses of emotion enacted on the social plane: hatred and oppression. Through Zen, Cage could connect his involuntary, highly individuated experience of the closet with a larger social-ethical politics of monadic noninterference.[14] Through such psychic sleight of hand, social necessity was transformed into moral virtue.

Thus Zen provided a theoretically attractive and emotionally satisfying resolution to the problematics of communication enforced by the closet. The Zen-inspired call to attentiveness to the present, coupled with its transparency to doctrinal or dogmatic claims, led Cage out of the swamp of his problems and toward a new relationship with his "disturbances." He called this new attitude "nobility": "To be 'noble' is to be detached, at every instant, from the fact of loving and hating. Many Zen stories illustrate that nobility."[15] Cage had undergone a remarkable alchemy: his anxiety and pain had metamorphosed into detachment, which was both morally superior and actively therapeutic. Through his early Zen involvement, then, he first theorized a system in which detachment paradoxically yielded engagement, stemming not from an ideological preconception or program, however, but from simple attentiveness to the world. This detached engagement—what Cage often called, simply, "listening"—served as a precursor to his detachment from political doctrines and engendered his explicitly anarchist convictions.

Clearly, Cage had been driven to Zen by a complex set of needs, some born of his new gay life. Widely taken to lie at the core of his aesthetic, Zen detachment is now routinely invoked as an originary moment in the development of postmodernism in the arts: an instantiation of a nonexpressive authorial voice, an early indication of the "death of the author."[16] To pursue the authorial origins of a postmodernist precept that takes meaning making from authors and places it squarely in the hands of the audience may seem a paradoxical, even contradictory, task. Yet meaning as a historical artifact connected to authors (their lives and

14. There remains much work to be done on the relationship between homosexuality and a Westerner's embrace of Zen. A great many influential queer artists, from Lou Harrison to Agnes Martin to Allen Ginsberg, drew from Zen during this pre-Stonewall era.

15. *For the Birds,* 201.

16. See Amelia Jones's excellent book *Post-Modernism and the En-Gendering of Marcel Duchamp* (Cambridge: Cambridge University Press, 1994).

contexts), as opposed to authorial functions or projections of readerly desire, was authorized by Cage himself—tellingly—with regard to another closeted gay composer and critic with whom he was once friendly.

In response to a request by Virgil Thomson, Cage spent ten years attempting a biography of the composer and critic that was acceptable to its subject.[17] Cage found that he simply could not analyze the meaning of Thomson's oeuvre apart from the life of its creator. Unfortunately, Thomson wanted him to do precisely this, and as a result the biography proved to be not only a source of immense difficulty in Cage's life but also the end of his friendship with the composer. Despite his own insistent antiexpressionism and authorial silence, Cage did not believe in Thomson's segregation of life and work: "In the first chapter, I began by dealing with both the life and the work of Virgil Thomson. In fact, I figured that there was no way in this case to separate one from the other. That was what had not pleased him. . . . Once I completed my text, the difficulty arose: he had to find a reader to edit my work—to filter out everything that had to do with his life, and only leave in print whatever dealt with the works themselves and their analyses."[18]

Finding that Cage advocated such a situated, even biographical, approach to music criticism is perhaps a surprising, albeit happy, antecedent for my own analysis of the social dynamics of his silences. But it is not difficult to reconcile Cage's infamous antiexpressionism with his form of situated, social-historical inquiry, for there is a substantial difference between saying that the work is not about the life (antiexpressionism) and saying that the life has nothing to do with the work. There are, after all, modes of revelation of self that have nothing to do with expressionism. One of the points of silence, Cage was fond of reminding his audiences, was to give life itself a more ample hearing: "Sometimes we blur the distinction between art and life; sometimes we try to clarify it. We don't stand on one leg. We stand on both."[19]

Indeed, it is only from such a symmetrical, two-legged stance that we can see how the development of Cage's antiexpressive aesthetic correlates with the wholesale changes in his personal life. Repeatedly, his referencing of "disturbances" slips so easily between the spheres of his creative work and his daily existence as to "blur the distinction between art and life." Cage has remarked: "I saw that all the composers were writing in different ways, that almost no one among them, no one among

17. Thomson even tried Cage out as a music reviewer for the *New York Herald Tribune*, but he found him both too idiosyncratic as a writer and too unreliable about deadlines. See Anthony Tommasini, *Virgil Thomson: Composer on the Aisle* (New York: Norton, 1997), 368.

18. *For the Birds*, 85–86.

19. "Diary: How to Improve the World (You Will Only Make Matters Worse) Continued 1970–71," in *M: Writings, '67–'72* (Middletown, Conn.: Wesleyan University Press, 1973), 106.

the listeners could understand what I was doing in the way that I understood it. So that anything like communication was not possible. I determined to find other reasons [for composing], and I found those reasons because of my personal problems at the time, which brought about the divorce from Xenia."[20] Personal trauma proved artistically fecund.

In understanding himself as homosexual, Cage came to accept as a corollary a new creed as well: an injunction against self-expression in daily life. His newly embraced gay life—in the context of cold war homophobic culture—made it clear in a very personal way that "anything like communication was not possible." This is not to say that the closet alone motivated Cage's deepening involvement with Zen and his concomitant turn toward an antiexpressive art, nor is it to confine his powerfully felt theoretical investments to a species of identity politics. Yet through Zen, Cage found a means to quiet what had once been so disturbing, to transmute trauma into peace. Indeed, in crediting his embrace of Zen to the "personal problems" that had brought about his divorce from Xenia, Cage himself relocated the origins of his Zen sensibility from theoretical to autobiographical grounds.

The developing relationship with Cunningham thus pointed toward a new musical voice not tied to the desire for communication. That voice, Cage shortly concluded, was most at home in the definitionally noble (i.e., detached) aleatoric mode, which achieved its most crystalline form, for four minutes, thirty-three seconds, in the embrace of silence.

II. Silent Lives

A new generation of scholars has tried to break through Cage's silence by describing his reticence with regard to his sexuality as coy and ascribing it to his membership in the pre-Stonewall, preliberationist generation of gay men. As to why a person of Cage's unconventional lifestyle, disdain for public opinion, and anarchist leanings would uphold the highly restrictive social compact of the closet, one longtime acquaintance (who wishes to remain anonymous) has remarked, "Well, he's a fifties queen, you know." Surely according to our contemporary modeling of gay and lesbian identity, which holds being out of the closet as perhaps the central measure of freedom and psychic health, Cage was a fifties queen; his conspicuous silence regarding his sexuality is an index of a time thankfully receding into the past.[21]

20. Interview by Cummings, 36.

21. Philip Brett has argued that music itself constitutes a closet, in which musicians are free to engage in the most public displays of emotion in exchange for not articulating those emotions verbally ("Musicality, Essentialism, and the Closet," in *Queering the Pitch: The New Gay and Lesbian Musicology*, ed. Philip Brett, Elizabeth Wood, and Gary C. Thomas [New York: Routledge, 1994], 9–26).

That Cage's increasingly unexpressive mien was at least partly strategic is clear from the composer Morton Feldman's account of the culture in which Cage traveled throughout the 1940s: the macho, often homophobic community of abstract expressionism.[22] Feldman, a friend of his, underscored the degree to which Cage's unexpressiveness may have done double duty as a shield. As if fearful of violating a confidence, Feldman once told an interviewer, "I don't want to exaggerate this point, because John was very sensitive to it. I remember there was a little gathering in a Chinese restaurant, and Jackson Pollock was taunting John." For his part, Cage has remarked of Pollock: "I . . . tried to avoid him. I did this because he was generally so drunk, and he was actually an unpleasant person for me to encounter. I remember seeing him on the same side of the street I was, and I would always cross over to the other side."[23]

The audience for avant-garde music was notably small, and the abstract expressionist painters, as the chief advocates of an experimental, self-critical art in the postwar American context, became Cage's friends and allies.[24] For a closeted gay man, however, not only was the abstract expressionist premium on self-expression anathema, but so was its too-anxious rehearsal of a performative machismo. The abstract expressionist agreement with dominant cultural attitudes regarding sexuality and gender—including the general assumption of masculine privilege premised in part on the exclusion of women and gay men—made the painters' alliance with Cage tenuous. Feldman, who was not gay, perceived just such a homophobic bias in the abstract expressionist painter Robert Motherwell's relationship to Cage, even though the composer had been his coeditor for *Possibilities:* "I became quite close to Motherwell. I think that they may have had some kind of intellectual or artistic falling out. John never talked about Motherwell. . . . Although everybody cared greatly for him [Cage], and they weren't overly critical, I would say there was a homosexual bias . . . not only against him, but against the younger people who began to associate with him: Rauschenberg, and Jasper [Johns], and Cy Twombly. I would say there was a homosexual bias."[25]

22. Caroline A. Jones correlates Cage's silence to a refusal of the rapacious abstract expressionist ego ("Finishing School," 643–47).

23. R. Wood Massi, "Morton Feldman, John Cage, and Who" (interview, San Francisco, March 3, 1987), 9; Richard Kostelanetz, *Conversing with Cage* (New York: Limelight, 1988), 177.

24. As Feldman recalls: "Cunningham and Cage did not associate with [all] homosexuals. They associated with homosexuals like Obey, landed-gentry types. John Ashbery, the young poets, Frank [O'Hara], they cruised around. If I went to a party at Frank's, I could have straight friends, or tough Jewish intellectuals like me, Norman Bluhm, Michael Goldberg. He would have all these. . . . And then the party will be, for example, Genet . . . Atmosphere" (Massi, "Morton Feldman, John Cage," 9).

25. Massi, "Morton Feldman, John Cage," 4.

To be homosexual in a homophobic culture was to forcefully realize that conversation was not always about expression, that it might be about the opposite: dissimulation, camouflage, hiding. But is there another frame through which to assess Cage's conspicuous silence? For if his silence was an attempt to escape notice—as the silence of the closet presumably is—it was a manifest failure. Cage became notable precisely for his silences—clear proof of the unsuitability of silence as a strategy of evasion. Closeted people seek to ape dominant discursive forms, to participate as seamlessly as possible in hegemonic constructions. They do not, at least in my experience, draw attention to themselves with performative silence, as Cage did when he stood before the fervent abstract expressionist crowd and blasphemed, "I have nothing to say and I'm saying it."[26] If silence was in part an expression of Cage's identity as a closeted homosexual during the cold war, it was also much more. It was not only a symptom of oppression but also a chosen mode of resistance. This silence was not the passive stratagem of someone unwilling and unable to declare his identity in a hostile culture. On the contrary, in contrast to the codes of the closet, if the point of Cage's silence was to escape notice, its effect was surely the opposite.

III. On Nothing

In his infamous "Lecture on Nothing," delivered at the Artists' Club in New York City (c. 1949), Cage denigrated the authorial "I" in favor of the spectatorial "you," emblematizing the too-perfect symmetry between his vaunted musical silences and the less noted silences of his closet. Announcing at the very beginning that "I am here / and there is nothing to say," Cage went on to declare, "Nothing more than / nothing / can be said." Comparing the lecture to an empty glass of milk, he asserted, "Or again / it is like an / empty glass / into which / at any moment / anything may be poured."[27] The "Lecture on Nothing" is a veritable essay in detachment. Whereas five years earlier Cage had "poured a great deal of emotion" into compositions like *Perilous Night,* now he found a Zen peace in limitation, creating works like empty glasses—explicit inducements to the listener to pour into them anything desired. Similarly, by the early fifties, his music had become less an expression of his ideas or tastes and more a product of aleatoric compositional processes in which "meanings," if there were any, were clearly chance products of the listener's cognition. Indeed, the *Concerto for Prepared Piano and Chamber Orchestra,* begun in 1950 and finished in early 1951, thematized Cage's developing distinction between aleatory and expressive modes: "I

26. *Silence: Lectures and Writings* (Middletown, Conn.: Wesleyan University Press, 1961), 109.

27. Ibid., 109, 111, 110.

made it into a drama between the piano, which remains romantic, expressive and the orchestra, which itself follows the principles of Oriental philosophy. And the third movement signifies the coming together of things which were opposed to one another in the first movement."[28]

The agent of that "coming together of things which were opposed" was silence. The musicologist James Pritchett explains: "What makes the third movement sound so different from the others is Cage's arrival at the single most important discovery of the concerto: the interchangeability of sound and silence."[29] With the recognition that silence is coterminous with sound—in that a silence exists as the ground from which sound springs and to which it ultimately returns—Cage finally developed a compositional strategy that favored coexistence ahead of opposition. Silence preceded and exceeded sound and by so doing dissolved the binarism of sound-silence into a form of continuity. Through silence, the domination of one term over another simply dampened into quiescence.

One point of silence, then, is to dissolve the oppositional by freely allowing other voices to be heard. As early as 1928, while still in high school, Cage won the Southern California Oratorical Contest with a speech called "Other People Think," in which he proposed "silence on the part of the United States, in order that we could hear what other people think, and that they don't think the way we do, particularly about us."[30] Many years later, Cage clarified his vision of an ideal society by reference to the notion of conversation: "[The members of this society] would not communicate, but they would talk, they would carry on dialogues. I much prefer this notion of dialogue, of conversation, to the notion of communication. Communication presupposes that one has something, an object, to be communicated. . . . Communicating is always imposing something: a discourse on objects, a truth, a feeling. While in conversation, nothing imposes itself."[31]

Thus communication, which is a form of expression, burdens the listener. It is an attempt to sway, to impose a discourse. In substituting "conversation" for "communication," Cage sought to replace a desire for mastery or control with the open-ended free play of ideas. Indeed, in the "Lecture on Nothing" he described a radical detachment from ideas: "As we go along / (who knows) / an i-dea *[sic]* may occur in this / talk. I have no idea / whether one will / or not. / If one does / let it. Re / gard

28. *For the Birds,* 41. For an excellent discussion of the *Concerto for Prepared Piano and Chamber Orchestra,* see James Pritchett, *The Music of John Cage* (Cambridge: Cambridge University Press, 1993), 62–66.

29. *Music of John Cage,* 71.

30. Hines, "Then Not Yet 'Cage,'" 77–78.

31. *For the Birds,* 148.

it as something / seen / momentarily, / as / though / from a window / while traveling."[32]

Elevating conversation above communication entailed refusing what Gordana P. Crnković has termed the vertical or hierarchical organization of discourse in favor of the horizontal, and Daniel Herwitz has written: "Cage symbolically aims to halt the march of language, meaning, and human control." This analysis of communication as riddled by power dynamics is, of course, the particular insight of the subordinated subject, and as a gay man, Cage was certainly familiar with the often painful impositions of a hostile discourse over his own.[33]

Now replaced by a policy of noninterference, meaning was for Cage freed from any dependence on such a logos, for it was logos, after all, that had marked him as disturbed, marginal, and unworthy in the first place. Discriminations of meaning or value were, Cage argues, inherently discriminatory: "I hold a great deal against this system of organization, that is, [the separation of things which should not be separated]. We categorize everyone. . . . What is a government? That which maintains these divisions. In other words, our body is divided against itself. Just about everywhere anybody has tried to organize, that is *to articulate that body*, it doesn't work; we are not dealing with a healthy organism."[34]

Hence freedom from meaning was also freedom from domination, definition, and control in a very real-world sense. After all, to be a subordinated subject is to be defined by power. To articulate the social body, and one's place or investments in it, was thus to divide that body against itself. In silence, there was instead a wholeness, a process of healing: the interplay between life and art worked both ways. It is just this sense

32. Cage, *Silence*, 110.

33. Gordana P. Crnković, "Utopian America and the Language of *Silence*," in *John Cage*, ed. Perloff and Junkerman, 167–87; Daniel Herwitz, "John Cage's Approach to the Global" in ibid., 190. As a gay white man, Cage felt himself subordinated under one set of discourses (heterosexist) but generally could elect to be interpellated under another as equal or even dominant (white male artist/intellectual)—so long as he remained in the closet. This situation is what Chantal Mouffe terms, in another context, "contradictory interpellation," or an experience of the self in a contradictory manner, as both inside and outside dominant culture ("Hegemony and New Political Subjects: Towards a New Concept of Democracy," in *Marxism and the Interpretation of Culture*, ed. Cary Nelson and Lawrence Grossberg [Urbana: University of Illinois Press, 1988, 89–104]). To be at once inside and outside the structures of domination is a rare and highly revealing subject position, for oppression is most comprehensively understood from the position, or pose, of the dominant. Mouffe argues that this contradictory self-understanding sows the seeds for the deconstruction and challenging of domination, for it reveals the very strategies necessary to the maintenance of the power of the dominant. Since the fact of subordination itself need not produce a challenge or even, for that matter, an antagonism, Mouffe argues that it is this contradictory self-understanding that provides the tools, and the motive, for a destructuring critique. The margins can generate precise anatomies of domination when allowed an insider's point of view. See also Earl Jackson's systematic development of the implications of this idea in *Strategies of Deviance: Studies in Gay Male Representation* (Bloomington: Indiana University Press, 1995), 17–52.

34. *For the Birds*, 111; Cage's interpolation.

of seamless personal and creative existence that is underscored in Cage's assertion that "there's a slight difference between Rauschenberg and me. . . . I have the desire to just erase the difference between art and life, whereas Rauschenberg made that famous statement about working in the gap between the two. Which is a little Roman Catholic from my point of view. . . . Well he makes a mystery out of being an artist."[35] For Cage, there is no mystery in being an artist: art cannot be segregated from the rest of existence—a "noble," hence liberatory art and a "noble," hence liberatory life are one.

The "Lecture on Nothing" exemplified Cage's new approach to the problem of communication or expression, especially in the policed cold war cultural context.[36] The lecture was, in Cage's sense of the term, a conversation, not a communication. He offered the abstract expressionists an empty glass and left them to fill it. He neither endorsed an expressionist practice nor conveyed his opposition to one. Instead, his route lay in the direction of silence.

IV. Silent Music, Silent Politics

> INTERVIEWER: In your Eastern itinerary, first there was India, then the Far East.
>
> CAGE: Yes, you could conclude an evolution of that kind from my works. . . . It sometimes seemed to me that I manage to "say" something in them. When I discovered India, what I was saying started to change. And when I discovered China and Japan, I changed the very fact of saying anything: I said nothing anymore. Silence: since everything already communicates, why wish to communicate?[37]

In the remainder of this essay, I will attempt to recuperate silence as a means of a historically specific queer resistance during the cold war. Silence was much more than conventionally unmusical; it provided a route toward an active challenge of the assumptions and prejudices that gave rise to homophobic oppression in the first place. For Cage, silence was an ideal form of resistance, carefully attuned to the requirements of the cold war consensus, at least in its originary social-historical context.[38] There are both surrender and resistance in these silences, in a re-

35. Quoted in Martin Duberman, *Black Mountain: An Exploration in Community* (New York: Dutton, 1972), 229.

36. As Hines makes clear, however, Cage's interest in the politics of silence can be traced much further back ("Then Not Yet 'Cage,'" 77–78). Compare this with the circa 1949 "Lecture on Nothing" (*Silence*, 109–27).

37. *For the Birds*, 103.

38. For a related account of resistance among the visual artists in Cage's circle, see my "Passive Resistance: On the Critical and Commercial Success of Queer Artists in Cold War American Art," *L'Image*, no. 3 (1996): 119–42. Cage's often-stated defense of what had once been thought

lation not of either/or but of both/and. It is within this complicated nexus of what can be viewed as at once compliance and defiance that the undeniable consistency and congruence in Cage's silence about his sexuality, on the one hand, and all the other manifestations of artistic or creative silence—such as *4′33″*, on the other—need to be understood. That Cage's self-silencing was in keeping with the requirements of the infamously homophobic McCarthy era should not obscure the fact that it was also internally and ideologically consistent with his larger aesthetic politics.

Thus the task at hand is to restore the weight and force of the cold war social context on Cage while granting that his ideological convictions were not simply or purely products of his oppression as a gay man. After all, many similarly oppressed gay artists did not then make silence the touchstone of their aesthetics.[39] Against a web of connections, both personal and political, Cage's many types of silence can be seen as queer—in their common repression of expressivity and identity—while they equally articulate his deeply held aesthetic and political convictions.

Reframing Cage's consistent self-silencing as something other than a timorous refusal to come out of the closet (perhaps even recovering it as a species of politics, however strange, if not self-defeating, it may appear from a contemporary vantage point) may help explain why he was so persistently closeted well after life in the closet had ceased to hold any instrumental benefits. When scholars and activists were rooting for Cage to come out, were they asking him to turn his back on his own convictions about silence and the work it could do and thereby ignoring the distinction between their political claims on him and his own lifelong principles?[40] Yet it is evident that Cage spoke freely about many

---

mere "noise"—he defended it as simply another (unaccustomed and disempowered) form of music—met with much more sympathy than his defense of silence did. The elevation of noise sought only to expand the category of music; the elevation of silence, however, might be—and apparently was—thought of as the negation of it. The premiere of *4′33″* Cage informs us, incited a near riot, a much more forceful protest than any of his earlier compositions had met. Nonetheless, silence was simply the other face of noise, just as noise was the other face of music, and Cage set out quite deliberately to deconstruct these false polarities. Of course, *4′33″* sprang from this intuition, and the incidental noises produced by the audience during its performance only drove home the point. In the "Lecture on Nothing," Cage (underscoring his theme with unpredictable silences and idiosyncratic punctuation) said, "Noises, too, / had been discriminated against; / and being American, . . . I fought / for noises" (*Silence,* 117).

39. Significantly, however, Cage's circle did, most notably Rauschenberg, Johns, and Twombly.

40. A number of scholars have asked Cage if he was gay. Massi, who conducted several interviews while completing his dissertation in musicology at the University of California, San Diego, asked Cage this question at Crown Point Press in 1985 and was told, "Yes, but I don't like to be political about it" (interview by the author, October 25, 1998). Massi then interviewed him formally at a Cage conference in Palo Alto on February 26, 1988, but Cage, accompanied by friends, proved evasive. Hines, in a remarkable five-hour interview in Los Angeles over two days in May 1992, recorded Cage talking explicitly about his gay life.

other aspects of his personal life, from his love of mushrooms to the intimate particulars of his daily routine. Why, then, this silence about his sexuality?

The easy answer—Cage's closeted gay identity compelled his infamous antiexpressionism and self-silencing—is at least partly evident. Indeed, in correlating his embrace of Zen to his personal "disturbances," he says as much himself. And there is a lovely economy to the notion that a closeted gay man made antiexpressionism the hallmark of his career, culminating in a work of absolute authorial silence. But this notion may also put the cart before the horse.

Instead, could it be that Cage's antiexpressionist convictions compelled his closetedness, that his belief in the utility of silence caused him to stifle or at least mute his public acknowledgment of his sexuality? Perhaps both factors, his fear of exposure and his belief in the efficacy of silence, simply coexisted, so that his closetedness and his antiexpressive ideology reinforced one another. I think that we can best make sense of Cage's closetedness by analyzing it as both an individual tendency and an ideological conviction, as a social-historical phenomenon common among gay men of his generation and as a coherent aesthetic and political philosophy.

How can silence be understood politically, as a remedy for oppression? I propose that its particular utility as a means of resistance for Cage and his circle was its evasion of a politics of opposition. Not only could closeted homosexuals ill afford to call attention to themselves with an articulated, entrenched oppositional stance, but actively opposing power would only "make matters worse," as Cage claims in the eponymous series of diary entries from which the title of this essay comes.[41] Indeed, he argues that any attempt to improve the condition of the world will only worsen it. But Cage was hardly one to believe that the world was fine as it was. He objected not so much to a desire to improve the world (a desire that I dare say animated his prodigious output in many different media) as to what he thought were bad strategies by which to put this improvement into practice.

Repeatedly, Cage powerfully objects to modes of redress of which active opposition to entrenched authority is a hallmark. What silence offered was the prospect of resisting the status quo without opposing it. Cage's divorce and continuing involvement with Cunningham coincided with a dangerous time for gay men in America, a time of long prison sentences, McCarthyite witch-hunts, and cold war hate monger-

41. The full title of the series is "John Cage Diary: How to Improve the World (You Will Only Make Matters Worse)." The first three parts appear in *A Year from Monday: New Lectures and Writings* (Middletown, Conn.: Wesleyan University Press,1967), the last two in *M.*

ing. Cage knew these dangers well: years before, his friend and teacher Henry Cowell had been imprisoned at San Quentin on a trumped-up "morals" charge.[42] That silence-as-resistance allowed its author to escape both complicity in the dominant culture and detection as a homosexual was not the least of its charms.

Cage comes closest to describing his politics of silence in a 1962 article about Rauschenberg, whose *White Paintings* Cage himself publicly acknowledged as a precedent for *4′33″*. Rauschenberg, Cage wrote, "is like that butcher whose knife never becomes dull simply because he cut with it in such a way that it never encountered an obstacle."[43] Cage might just as well have been—and, I speculate, was—referring to himself. To cut yet not encounter an obstacle is paradoxical, for cutting implies the existence of what is cut into. But one mode of cutting avoids such direct incision: irony.

Few have noted how profoundly ironic it is for a composer to make silence the hallmark of his work.[44] That Cage's initial encounter with Zen may have been motivated in part by an emotional search for a resolution to his postmarital "disturbances" should not obscure the fact that he continued for his entire life to explore its ramifications, including the use of irony. The distinction irony draws between what is said and what is meant opened up for him a space of otherness that was not understood as specifically oppositional. As a "readerly" relation, irony is recognized, not written; understood, not declared. It would prove a means through which resistance could figure in a culture of coercion. By ironizing expression in all of its forms, Cage created room in which to maneuver against modernist hierarchies; hence his canonization as a postmodern today. But his efforts were not originally oppositional so much as they were "other": seductions away from dominant expressive discourse and toward other meanings for other purposes.[45]

What were these purposes? Silent music inaugurated a process of reading that moved the listener, potentially, from unselfconscious complicity with dominant forms of expression (in which the expressive was passively registered as inherent in the music) toward a degree of self-

42. See John D'Emilio, "The Homosexual Menace: The Politics of Sexuality in Cold War America," in *Passion and Power: Sexuality in History,* ed. Kathy Peiss and Christina Simmons, with Robert A. Padgug (Philadelphia: Temple University Press, 1989), 226–40; and Michael Hicks, "The Imprisonment of Henry Cowell," *Journal of the American Musicological Society* 44 (1991): 92–119.

43. "On Robert Rauschenberg, Artist, and His Work," *Metro,* May 1961; reprinted in *Silence,* 101.

44. Cage has remarked that *4′33″* was his most important work.

45. For a groundbreaking analysis of modes of opposition, to which this entire section is indebted, see Ross Chambers, *Room for Maneuver: Reading (the) Oppositional (in) Narrative* (Chicago: University of Chicago Press, 1991).

consciousness about one's role as a listener or a maker of meaning. In this way silence paradoxically contributed to the destructuring of music's discursive norms. Cage denaturalized heretofore "naturally" expressive musical forms through silence, fostering an awareness that music was the result of a reading, an exegetical process that had been naturalized. (In this context, silence destructures because an audience has gathered to hear something; in other contexts, that would not necessarily be so.) Music's seemingly automatic or transparent claim to meaning is thus replaced by an awareness of the conditions in which or through which the subset of sound known as music comes into being.

Importantly, this embrace of silence cannot itself be conceived of as a politics, a position, or a statement; rather, it exists in perpetual alterity, always appended to its host—music—in a parasitic relationship. Like any parasite, it eventually weakens its host. But it also works invisibly, never declaring its aims, its purpose, or its project. Having inaugurated a problematizing of dominant expressive forms, it acts like a shock wave, destabilizing the foundations of what was once understood, more simply and solidly, as music. Since silence constitutes an oppositional mode that refuses articulated oppositionality, it offered precisely the cover required to seed destabilization in the policed consensus of the fifties, especially for closeted homosexuals.

Silence achieved these effects without uttering a sound. Cage's many silences did succeed as a form of resistance. That his work was not discussed at the time as specifically oppositional is in this sense evidence of its discursive success in the consensus-based culture of the fifties. Silence made a statement through the absence of statement. It constituted an appeal to the listener for a new relationship to authority and authoritative forms in music—and potentially in other arenas as well.

Silence, in short, is not another kind of music but a challenge to the construction of music itself. Neither musical nor unmusical, Cage's silence was quite precisely other, escaping the binaries that circumscribed the status quo as the sole arena for contestation. As a result, it managed to be an antiauthoritative mode that was nonetheless not oppositional. Revealing the power of the individual to construct meanings unauthorized by, and under the very nose of, the dominant culture, silence was, in a sense, seditious.[46]

Cage's silences can in this way give rise to potent "misreadings," profoundly unauthorized interpretations that allow, for example, a silence to be read as a silencing. However, since dominant interests lie above all

46. In my forthcoming book, *Opposition, Inc.*, I address more fully the notion that it was left to a man marked as other within the binary authoritative discourse of heterosexuality to develop the potential for resistance inherent in a nonbinary term like silence.

in preserving authoritative discursive control (as a means of social control), such silences are permitted to flourish because they are not presented as a direct challenge or opposition to authority. Misreadings remain the responsibility of the listener, while Cage, ever the cold war warrior, stays under cover.[47]

Significantly, Cage's silence can recast the audience from passive to active, from consumer to producer, from co-opted to resistant. Authority shifts from outside the individual to inside, and the new relationship to authority within the concert hall potentially suggests new ways of being outside it as well. Queer culture has long recognized that this silence-as-resistance not only makes it possible to escape proscription (since the discursive norm is upheld) but, paradoxically, may assist the establishment of resistance, even nurture it, providing it with precisely the cover it needs to prosper. In the long history of queer culture, the closet has emblematized just such a potential. As a requisite effect of domination, the silence of the closet in this way opens a space for oppositional existence.

No wonder McCarthyism understood every homosexual as a potential Communist, the figure of seditious resistance.[48] The most dangerous enemy is the one that cannot be seen, the most dangerous threat the one that is not heard. And silence—of many different kinds—was what enabled these threats to thrive. Hence the powerful cultural anxiety over the "invisibility" of homosexuals and Communists in cold war culture—testimony to the oppositional potential of silence, real or imagined, in authoritative discourse.

Yet there is also a second, related political effect of silence. It avoids the recolonizing force of the oppositional: what permits the dominant culture to consolidate its authority by reference to the excluded other. Some recent poststructuralist analyses of both textual and cultural oppositionality stress the utility of opposition as a means of control.[49] In these accounts, opposition may simply reproduce the binary logic through which domination writes itself, and so the oppositional becomes the outside that allows the inside to cohere in a series of exclusions. Given its instrumentality to oppression, then, opposition continually risks co-optation as a mere tool of hegemony; indeed, as we have seen, the outsider (e.g., the Communist or, for that matter, the homosexual) has long supported, if not actually authorized, the production of

47. I take up the question of the peculiar fit between these closeted modes of queer resistance and the cold war cultural climate in my "Passive Resistance."

48. See, e.g., Arthur Guy Mathews, "Homosexuals Are Stalin's Atom Bomb against America," *Bernarr MacFadden's Vitalized Physical Culture*, May 1953, 12–13.

49. See, e.g., Chambers, *Room for Maneuver;* and Hugh Silverman, "Writing (on Deconstruction) at the Edge of Metaphysics," *Research in Phenomenology* 13 (1984): 107–9.

the power that controls him or her. Once marked as oppositional, any disturbance can be incorporated into a discourse of oppositionality that only catalyzes oppressive constructions, just as homosexuality supported heterosexuality and Communism stabilized the cold war consensus.

Cage had a clear understanding of how to avoid the recolonizing force of the oppositional, and it was, again, by recourse to silence. He indirectly attributed this insight to his studies in Zen: "Daisetz Suzuki often pointed out that Zen's non-dualism arose in China as a result of problems encountered in translating India's Buddhist texts. . . . Indian words for concepts in opposition to one another did not exist in Chinese." Since, as Cage once wrote, "classification . . . ceases when it is no longer possible to establish oppositions," he concluded that "protest actions fan the flames of a dying fire. Protest helps to keep the government going." [50] Cage never protested in the usual sense; yet, through a performative silence that refused any direct opposition to dominant culture, his work constituted a seduction away from authority.

Of course, there is a powerful alternative tradition to the Cagean paean to silence-as-resistance; it is perhaps best represented by Foucault and his careful analysis of relations of power.[51] Surely, the weight of contemporary resistant practice falls in line with this Foucauldian tradition. But, as they say, the times have changed. Silence-as-resistance was keyed to a context of constraint that I have thankfully never experienced. Even Foucault wrote, in an often quoted passage,

> that silence itself—the things one declines to say, or is forbidden to name, the discretion that is required between different speakers—is less the absolute limit of discourse, the other side from which it is separated by a strict boundary, than an element that functions alongside the things said, with them and in relation to them within over-all strategies. There is no binary division to be made between what one says and what one does not say; we must try to determine the different ways of not saying things, how those who can and those who cannot speak of them are distributed, which type of discourse is authorized, or which form of discretion is required in either case. There is not one but many silences, and they are an integral part of the strategies that underlie and permeate discourses.[52]

Cage would certainly have agreed in principle, and the coexistence of sound and silence in the *Concerto for Prepared Piano and Chamber Orchestra* makes much the same point. But he would also have demurred from

50. *M*, xiii, 10, 12.

51. See David M. Halperin, *Saint Foucault: Towards a Gay Hagiography* (New York: Oxford University Press, 1995), 15–37.

52. Michel Foucault, introduction to vol. 1 of *The History of Sexuality*, trans. Robert Hurley (New York: Pantheon,1978), 27.

Foucault's insistence on determining the import and meanings of what has been left unsaid. For Cage, the unsaid could never have a meaning; it would differ for every (non)speaker. In fact, Cage stated quite specifically that simple opposition to the dominant culture would never produce real social change:

> It is unimaginable that one particular attitude alone would be able to unleash what you envision under the name revolution. I believe instead that the revolution is in the process of unrolling right before our eyes on all levels—and that we aren't aware of it. . . .
>
> Protest movements could quite easily, and despite themselves, lead in the opposite direction, to a reinforcement of law and order. There is in acceptance and non-violence an underestimated revolutionary force. But instead, protest is all too often absorbed into the flow of power, because it limits itself to reaching for the same old mechanisms of power, which is the worst way to challenge authority! We'll never get away from it that way![53]

In short, there is an "underestimated revolutionary force" in modes of resistance that are not oppositional, and there is equally the prospect of being co-opted ("absorbed into the flow of power") through an opposition that is "itself . . . reaching for the same old mechanisms of power."

That Cage understood his particular form of acceptance—silence—as an expressly political force is evident in the connections he draws in *For the Birds* between his composing and the larger social situation in 1976:

> When I really began making music, I mean composing "seriously," it was to involve myself in noise, because noises escape power, that is, the laws of counterpoint and harmony. When I spoke about [Pierre] Schaeffer [founder of "musique concrete," which used recorded natural sound as the basis of music], I said that noises had not been liberated but had been reintegrated into a new kind of harmony and counterpoint. If that were the case, that would mean that we had only changed prisons! My idea is that there should be no more prisons. Take another example: Black Power. If blacks free themselves from the laws whites invented to protect themselves from the blacks, that's well and good. But if they in turn want to invent laws, that is, to wield power in exactly the same way as whites, what will the difference be? There are only a few blacks who understand that with laws that will protect them from the whites, they will just be new whites. They will have come to power over the whites, but nothing will change. . . . Today, we must identify ourselves with noises instead,

53. *For the Birds*, 236.

> and not seek laws for the noises, as if we were blacks seeking power! Music demonstrates what an ecologically balanced situation could be—one in which whites would not have more power than blacks, and blacks no more than whites. A situation in which each thing and each sound is in its place, because each one is what it is. Moreover, I'm not the one who's inventing that situation. Music was already carrying it within itself despite everything people forced it to endure.[54]

The goal is thus not to challenge power but to escape it. Active opposition would mean that "we had only changed prisons." By "identify[ing] ourselves with noises instead"—and noises are, of course, audible only when the music quiets down—we will free ourselves from our prisons. And what makes a noise a noise is precisely its freedom from any preordained conceptual or ideological system. Thus music permeates the culture, and the culture permeates music: change one and you change the other. As Cage demonstrates time and again, there is life (even his life), and there is music (even his music), and it is all the same thing.

54. Ibid., 230–31.

THREE

Austin Clarkson

The Intent of the Musical Moment: Cage and the Transpersonal

I. The Pragmatic Background

The conversations Joan Retallack recorded with John Cage during the last two years of his life roam through highways and byways that provide fresh perspectives on the major themes of his career. While Cage repeats stories and opinions from previous writings and conversations, in these interviews he often sharpens the focus with fresh formulations. One theme that recurs like a deeply pulsing wave is a spiritual attitude, which throughout his career aroused criticism and even derision, but which he continued to affirm to the end (see appendix [21a–c]). The question that arises, therefore, is whether his interest in spirituality was relatively superficial and in service only to his aesthetic program or was, on the contrary, a core condition that informed both his life and his art. In her introduction, Retallack responds to

The author dedicates this chapter to the esteemed memory of David Tudor. I am most grateful to several colleagues who responded to a draft of this essay, and in particular to John Holzaepfel, Jackson Mac Low, David W. Patterson, and Joan Retallack, whose comments resulted in changes. I am especially grateful to Professor Patterson, who not only made helpful queries and comments, but also generously sent me a copy of his dissertation.

this theme, observing that Cage's spirituality was "not at all 'transcendent' in the sense of removal from daily life but in fact a constant return to pragmatic concerns with a resonant sense of the interconnectedness of things—that we are all, persons and environment, 'in it' together." She conjures up a kaleidoscope of other perspectives—from Epicurus, Kierkegaard, Dewey, Jung, Duchamp, and Wittgenstein to utopianism, dada, Japanese humor, and fractals—but it is the connection with pragmatism that strikes home. In the end, Retallack finds that Cage eludes the categories of current critical theory with a "post-skeptical poetics of public language, a post-ironic socioaesthetic modeling without denial or naiveté—a *complex*, not naive, realism." Although this series of "posts" might suggest that what is "pre" is past, Retallack dubs Cage a "utopian avant-pragmatist" and links him to Dewey's "spiritually rich, aesthetic pragmatics of everyday life." And yet, despite the strong link she makes with the tradition of pragmatism, she writes: "Very little in twentieth-century Western culture prepares us for Cage's work."[1] On the premise that Cage's project is indeed planted deep in the seedbed of a spiritually informed American pragmatism, I would like to explore that background in order to better understand his art in general, and in particular the problems raised in the performance of his indeterminate music.

The pragmatic background in philosophy, psychology, aesthetics, and religion antedates John Dewey (1859–1952). It includes C. S. Peirce (1839–1914), William James (1842–1910), G. H. Mead (1863–1931), Daisetz T. Suzuki (1870–1966), and C. G. Jung (1875–1961). A spiritually rich pragmatism was an everyday reality of abiding interest to these pioneers, and the empirical attitude to spiritual experience that marked their work proved fundamental to many twentieth-century developments in the arts, humanities, and social sciences. As we shall see, William James, the crucial figure in this background, was a seminal thinker for both Suzuki and Jung, two of the leading players in Cage's story. In *The Varieties of Religious Experience*, James credits Peirce with providing his approach to the study of religious experience. Since pragmatism is at issue, here is James's synopsis of the method as he took it from Peirce:

> Thought in movement has for its only conceivable motive the attainment of belief, or thought at rest. Only when our thought about a subject has

1. *Musicage: Cage Muses on Words, Art, Music*, ed. Joan Retallack (Hanover, N.H.: Wesleyan University Press, University Press of New England, 1996), xxxix, xx, xli. The conversations were recorded from 1990 until shortly before Cage's death in August of 1992. David W. Patterson's thorough-going analysis of the ideas, turns of phrase, and formulations from South and East Asian texts in Cage's writing leads him to conclude that Cage's interest in Eastern philosophies stemmed more from his aesthetic interests than from spiritual concerns. See "Appraising the Catchwords, c. 1942–1959: Cage's Asian-Derived Rhetoric and the Historical Reference of Black Mountain College" (Ph.D. diss., Columbia University, 1996), 241.

> found its rest in belief can our action on the subject firmly and safely begin. Beliefs, in short, are rules for action; and the whole function of thinking is but one step in the production of active habits. . . . To attain perfect clearness in our thoughts of an object, we need then only consider what sensations, immediate or remote, we are conceivably to expect from it, and what conduct we must prepare in case the object should be true.2

In his own lectures on the subject of pragmatism, James caused a furor with his attack on idealism and his assertion that "[t]ruth *happens* to be an idea. It *becomes* true, is *made* true by events." In setting out his own version of the pragmatic method, he said:

> You must bring out of each word its practical cash-value, set it at work within the stream of your experience. It appears less as a solution, then, than as a program for more work, and more particularly as an indication of the ways in which existing realities may be *changed.*
>
> *Theories thus become instruments, not answers to enigmas, in which we can rest.* We don't lie back upon them, we move forward, and, on occasion, make nature over again by their aid.[3]

For James theories are not articles of faith, but instruments for discovery and change. Thus his conception of the "field of consciousness" asserts its vague, shifting, and indefinite "margins" from reports of his own and others' ordinary experiences of their mental states:

> The important fact which this "field" formula commemorates is the indetermination of the margin. Inattentively realized as is the matter which the margin contains, it is nevertheless there, and helps both to guide our behavior and to determine the next movement of our attention. It lies around us like a "magnetic field," inside of which our centre of energy turns like a compass-needle, as the present phase of consciousness alters into its successor. Our whole past store of memories floats beyond this margin, ready at a touch to come in; and the entire mass of residual powers, impulses, and knowledges that constitute our empirical self stretches continuously beyond it. So vaguely drawn are the outlines between what is actual and what is only potential at any moment of our conscious life, that it is always hard to say of certain mental elements whether we are conscious of them or not.[4]

Incorporating research on parapsychology, automatisms, and mediumistic and religious experience, James observed that outside the field of

2. William James, *The Varieties of Religious Experience: A Study in Human Nature* (1902; London: Fontana, 1960), 426.

3. *Pragmatism: A New Name for Some Old Ways of Thinking* (1907; New York: Dover, 1995), 77–78, 21. The emphases are James's.

4. *Varieties of Religious Experience,* 233.

consciousness lies the subliminal consciousness, which contains everything from the instinctual to the spiritual that is not in consciousness. Harry T. Hunt finds that James's contributions to the science of the mind are still of fundamental value:

> William James, in his chapter in *The Principles of Psychology* (1890) entitled "The Stream of Thought," was probably the first western thinker and scientist to address ordinary lived consciousness as an empirical phenomenon in its own right. How curious that it is this recent. In so doing, he also addressed the relationship between consciousness and physical reality in ways which have not yet been fully assimilated. James's work informed subsequent schools of thought that are generally held to be antithetical—in psychology, functionalism and behaviorism as well as the Gestalt tradition; in philosophy, Wittgenstein as well as Husserl, Heidegger, and Merleau-Ponty. Since subsequent approaches to consciousness within psychology can in no sense be said to have "gotten past" James, we will need to engage his phenomenology of awareness as "streaming," to consider it as metaphor and as physical and neural reality.
>
> In many ways, William James is one of our first modern thinkers. Within what he would help to establish as an emergent "science" of psychology, and writing in the wake of Nietzsche, he offers his own North American version of pluralism and the relativity of truth to human purposes. Neils Bohr mentioned his reading of James on consciousness as foreshadowing the principles of complementarity and indeterminism in quantum mechanics. Just as light becomes both wave and particles, consciousness is both substantive and transitive, both a pulsing and a continuous wave: "Nature is simple and invariable; makes no leaps or makes nothing but leaps; . . . what do all such principles express save our sense of how pleasantly our intellect would feel if it had a Nature of that sort to deal with?"[5]

As the founder of modern empirical studies of consciousness, James sets the frame for this essay, in which I hope to sketch the context for Cage's contribution to the science of the musical mind. Studies of the field of consciousness and what lay beyond it in the subliminal realms fascinated many painters, poets, and musicians, Cage among them, and led them to regard dreams, fantasies, chance occurrences, archetypes of the collective unconscious, and numinous experience in general as the matter of art. What marked their pragmatism as non-ironic, non-naive, and complex is the premise that the unconscious has a noetic function

5. *On the Nature of Consciousness: Cognitive, Phenomenological, and Transpersonal Perspectives* (New Haven: Yale University Press, 1995), 115–16.

in supplying the conscious mind with creative portents.[6] I shall attempt to show that Cage's achievement was to realize the implications of that premise in experimental music.

II. Experimental Music and the Silent Prayer

In a pioneering study of experimental music from the 1950s and 1960s, Michael Nyman singles out Cage as the creator of a music that departs in fundamental ways from the European concert tradition.[7] From Cage's manifesto of 1955, Nyman calls it "experimental music" and distinguishes it from fully structured and notated contemporaneous compositions, which he names "avant-garde." For Nyman the paradigmatic piece of experimental music is *4′33″*, "tacet for any instrument or instruments." As the extreme instance of pieces that are not prescriptively notated, *4′33″* is impervious to theories of analysis and criteria of criticism generally applied to avant-garde music. It forces us to contend with Cage's statement that he was writing music on the water and was more interested in the moment of listening than in pieces as such [17a]. The term "experimental" was rejected by composers who took their works to be fully realized creations and not experiments in the sense of trials or tests. But the idea appealed to Cage: "[Experimental music] is understood not as descriptive of an act to be later judged in terms of success and failure, but simply as of an act the outcome of which is unknown. What has been determined?"[8] For Cage the outcome of a fully structured piece is predictable and therefore occludes the act of performing with memories of historical styles and expectations of definitive readings [8]. And so he conceived of a music of actions that do not have predictable outcomes. If the musical content were reduced to a minimum and the outcome stripped of expectations, the performer would be open to the spontaneous flow of the musical imagination, and performing music would be a creative rather than a re-creative act. When each sound is the Buddha [13], then the performer becomes likewise.

Cage's experimental music is not an art of representation, where meaning is derived from the relation between a signifier and a referent. It is presentational. Of presentational states, Hunt writes,

> meaning emerges as a result of an experiential immersion in the expressive patterns of the symbolic medium. It appears as spontaneous, preemptory imagery and is fully developed in the expressive media of the

6. "William James insisted that the state of mind in mystical states was not just affective or emotional but specifically 'noetic'" (ibid., 111–12).

7. *Experimental Music: Cage and Beyond* (New York: Schirmer Books, 1974), 2.

8. "Experimental Music: Doctrine" (1955), in *Silence: Lectures and Writings* (Middletown, Conn.: Wesleyan University Press, 1961), 13.

> arts. Here, felt meaning emerges from the medium in the form of potential semblances that are "sensed," polysemic and open-ended, and so unpredictable and novel. It is the receptive, observing attitude common to aesthetics, meditation, and classical introspection that allows such meaning to emerge.

By limiting representation as much as possible, Cage intensified the presentational function of music. However, Hunt argues that the two states are complementary: "Referential language use is filled with intonation, gesture, and emphasis as its presentational aspect, while presentational states, although ineffable in ordinary discursive terms, nonetheless have their definite *sense* of intentional meaning in the form of an incipient portent."[9] To extend the argument from language to music, we can suppose that music translates the presentational aspects of language—intonation, gesture, and emphasis—into properties that have been sedimented historically as melody, harmony, rhythm, and so forth. By rejecting these parameters as representational, Cage set out to explore presentational aspects of music that are even more elusive—incipient portents that might be harbingers of the ineffable.[10]

"Experiment" and "experience" both come from Latin *experiri* (to try, prove, put to the test). Experimental music thus shifts attention from the piece of music as a representable, transcendent object to the felt meanings and potential semblances. Just as Dewey affirmed that aesthetic experience "occurs continuously, because the interaction of live creative and environing conditions is involved in the very process of living," so for Cage experimental music dissolves the boundary between art and

9. *On the Nature of Consciousness*, 42.

10. The distinction in aesthetics between representation and presentation has had a long and varied history. For Edmund Gurney, for instance, it is the means for differentiating poetry, sculpture, and painting, which "represent in various aspects things cognisable in the world outside them," from architecture and music, whose function it is "to present, not to represent, and their message has no direct reference to the world outside them" (*The Power of Sound* [1880; New York: Basic Books, 1966], 60). Suzanne Langer makes a more general distinction between two kinds of symbolization: the discursive (i.e., representational) symbolism of language and the presentational symbolism of an art object, which is understood from its direct presentation through the interrelations of the symbolic elements within the total structure (*Philosophy in a New Key* [1942; Mentor, 1948], 78–79). Peter Kivy now advances the important notion that representational symbolization is at work even within pure music: "Since all music, even the most frankly representational, has pure musical parameters as well—harmonic, rhythmic, contrapuntal, melodic—it follows that all music, of the kind we are talking about, has a deep layer of representationality" (*Music Alone: Philosophical Reflections on the Purely Musical Experience* [Ithaca: Cornell University Press, 1990], 44). Kivy's "music alone" is "a quasi-syntactical structure of sound understandable solely in musical terms and having no semantic or representational content, no meaning, making reference to nothing beyond itself" (202). But Kivy does not investigate "presentationality." By emphasizing presentationality, Cage seeks to evade both the "deep layer of representationality" and the "quasi-syntactical structure" of Kivy's "music alone." Hunt's presentation-representation model is founded on Langer, the psychoanalyst Marshall Edelson, and the cognitive psychologist Robert Haskell (41). (I am grateful to an anonymous reader for the suggestion to amplify the notions of presentation and representation.)

life. Dewey based his philosophy of art on the integrity and abundance of experience, which he described as follows:

> We have *an* experience when the material experienced runs its course to fulfillment. Then and then only is it integrated within and demarcated in the general stream of experience from other experiences. A piece of work is finished in a way that is satisfactory; a problem receives its solution; a game is played through; a situation, whether that of eating a meal, playing a game of chess, carrying on a conversation, writing a book, or taking part in a political campaign, is so rounded out that its close is a consummation and not a cessation. Such an experience is a whole and carries with it its own individualizing quality and self-sufficiency. It is *an* experience.[11]

Cage's notion that experimental music should dissolve the distinction between art and life, between subject and object, follows from the all-encompassing plenitude and uniqueness of Dewey's "experience." Aesthetic experience, according to Dewey, merges the listener and the music in a greater whole: "For the unique distinguishing feature of esthetic experience is exactly the fact that no such distinction of self and object exists in it, since it is esthetic in the degree in which organism and environment cooperate to institute an experience in which the two are so fully integrated that each disappears." For Dewey the outcome of an aesthetic experience is a blissful, procreative union, as "when varied materials of sense quality, emotion, and meaning come together in a union that marks a new birth in the world."[12] Aesthetic experience is not merely receptive, but creative, for something new is born from the union, the "incipient portent." Dewey did not speculate on what that new thing might be, but Cage was interested in defining "what is to be determined." In the essay "Experimental Music," he said that magnetic tape was a means of getting rid of old patterns of thought, as it "introduces the unknown with such sharp clarity that anyone has the opportunity of having his habits blown away like dust."[13] Later, in conversation with Daniel Charles, Cage said that the goal was "those experiences that contribute to changing us and, particularly, to changing our preconceptions" [17e]. Thus the incipient portent for Cage was the potential for bringing into conscious awareness some unknown factor that would effect a spiritual and life-changing experience, some hitherto unconscious content that would promote personal growth and renewal.

11. *Art as Experience* (1934; New York: Capricorn Books, 1958), 35.
12. Ibid., 249, 267.
13. "Experimental Music," in *Silence*, 16.

Presentational listening was a creative agent for change because it admitted the unknown into the experience of music [5].

Nyman selected *4′33″* as the paradigmatic piece of experimental music because it is the most empty of its kind and so the most full of possibilities. The emptiness of *4′33″* is filled by the listener, whose focus must be open, free-flowing, and capable of supplying his or her own meanings:

> *4′33″* is a demonstration of the non-existence of silence, of the permanent presence of sounds around us, of the fact that they are worthy of attention, and that for Cage "environmental sounds and noises are more useful aesthetically than the sounds produced by the world's musical culture." *4′33″* is not a negation of music but an affirmation of its omnipresence. Henceforward sounds ("for music, like silence, does not exist") would get closer to introducing us to Life, rather than Art, which is something separate from Life.[14]

For Nyman *4′33″* demonstrates a number of theorems: There is no such thing as silence, music is everywhere, and life and art are indivisible. Let us survey the literature for other views of the silent piece, on which any theory of experimental music must turn. Just as Charles Ives asked what has sound got to do with music, so *4′33″* questions the idea that it is sufficient to define music as a structure of sounds. Jean-Jacques Nattiez describes *4′33″* as a metamusical critique of conventional music: It is a "'speaking' in music about music, in the second degree as it were, to expose or denounce the institutional aspects of music's functioning." And so, he concludes, "(without too much soul-searching) that sound is a minimal condition of the musical fact." But by bracketing *4′33″* as a metamusical thought experiment, Nattiez misunderstands Cage's explicit demand that it be regarded as his most important piece of music. For one does hear sounds at each performance of *4′33″*, even though they are not prescribed. And the experience of listening evokes an engagement of the whole being that may well involve soul-searching. Richard Kostelanetz accepts *4′33″* as a piece of music, but brackets it as the null instance. For him *4′33″* states that "anything is possible in art including . . . *nothing at all.*" Thus Kostelanetz thinks that Cage was speaking ironically when he said that the music he prefers is "what we hear if we are just quiet," and so regards *4′33″* as primarily philosophical speculation. David Cope also favors the conceptualist stance when he says that the composer's contribution to *4′33″* is the idea alone: "The act of the creator is minimal *and* conceptual." Or, as Eric Salzman wrote,

14. Nyman, *Experimental Music,* 2, 22.

once you have done *4′33″*, you cannot really do it again: "One man's silence is, after Cage, much like another's." In general, the conceptualists interpret *4′33″* as the collection of sounds, whether from the audience or outside the auditorium, that are noticed during the given time. But by concretizing the silent piece as a particular collection of physical sounds or as the null and void, they miss Cage's requirement that the act of listening is paramount, and that the minimal condition of the musical fact is the reflexive relationship between sound and the listener.[15] Cage was not a conceptualist [17e].

By contrast to the conceptualists, the pragmatists accept at face value Cage's statement that *4′33″* is his most important piece and fundamental to his entire oeuvre. They also take note of David Tudor's assertion that *4′33″* is one of the most intense listening experiences you can have.[16] Heinz-Klaus Metzger views Cage's oeuvre in light of the Hegelian dialectic between pure being and pure nothingness and sees that Cage pushed this flux to the extreme, where "the material is expanded to embrace everything, and contracted to the point of nothingness." Metzger evidently regards *4′33″* as an instance of the intersection of pure being and pure nothingness. For Schwartz and Godfrey, while *4′33″* is purposeless in the sense that the composer and performer renounce individual creative input, it nevertheless has a serious purpose, because a period of silence or nonexpression allows ultimate truths to be realized. Jonathan Kramer goes a step further. He states that the listener becomes a creative participant in the performance and thus is "*more* important to the music than the composer." The distinction between the self and the other, the listener and the music is minimized. Kramer emphasizes the role of the listener, who, while listening to what he calls "vertical" or "nonteleological" music, is in a blissful state of "fusion of the self with the environment." Kramer's idea of fusion is reminiscent of Dewey's notion of aesthetic experience, but he does not speculate on what is "to be determined." That Cage does not call for the listener to lose contact with consciousness is affirmed by Eric de Visscher, who understands that a dynamic process is involved. For de Visscher the act of listening to *4′33″* is a process in which the listener takes an active part in negotiating his or her relationship to the outer world. De Visscher also notes that there is a paradox between Cage's clear statement of his intentions and his

15. Jean-Jacques Nattiez, *Music and Discourse: Toward a Semiology of Music* (Princeton: Princeton University Press, 1990), 43; Richard Kostelanetz, *John Cage (Ex)plain(ed)* (New York: Schirmer Books, 1996), 11–12; David Cope, *New Directions in Music*, 6th ed. (Madison, Wis.: Brown and Benchmark, 1993), 172–73; Eric Salzman, "Imaginary Landscaper" (1982), in *Writings about John Cage*, ed. Richard Kostelanetz (Ann Arbor: University of Michigan Press, 1993), 6.

16. Harold C. Schonberg, "The Far-Out Pianist," *Harper's Magazine*, June 1960, 49. Thanks to John Holzaepfel for the source of this reference.

desire for nonintention. He reasons that an art without intention and preconceptions is probably unfeasible. But de Visscher concludes that for Cage it was likely an unattainable ideal.[17]

Here de Visscher raises the issue of whether it is possible to understand *4′33″* without admitting contradiction. Those who tackle Cage's favorite paradoxes and oxymorons—"interpenetration and nonobstruction," "chance operations," "purposeful purposelessness"—often rest content with demonstrating that they are logically fallible. Like de Visscher, they usually conclude that these formulations may be hoped-for ideals but are unattainable in practice.[18] Which is another way of saying that Cage approached but never achieved his goal. But Cage knew already in 1948 that his goal was paradoxical [4]. Paradox is designed to subvert rational cognition, and oxymoron, a form of condensed paradox, is the poet's stock in trade for extolling the ecstasies of love and spirituality. Paradoxical though it seems, *4′33″* offers listeners the opportunity of performing in the purely presentational mode. If they choose to perform the piece, they find, as Dewey would say, that it calls not for understanding but for "undergoing."

That *4′33″* is a spiritual exercise is affirmed both by David Revill, who writes that *4′33″* exemplifies quintessentially Cage's tendency to link music and spirituality, and by James Pritchett, who recalls that the title Cage originally had in mind when he announced that he was going to compose a silent piece was "Silent Prayer." Pritchett writes that the silent piece serves a "personal, spiritual purpose," and he makes an analogy between experiencing structure that is without content and Cage's intent to follow Eckhart's injunction to empty oneself in order to hear "the hidden word." For Pritchett *4′33″* is "a mental, spiritual, and compositional exercise," and "its literal silence reflects the silence of the will necessary to open up a realm of infinite possibilities." In their recent monographs on Cage, these authors at last acknowledge the spiritual intent of the silent piece and so endorse a theory of Cage's experimental music that assumes a transpersonal context.[19] But *4′33″* is paradoxical

17. Heinz-Klaus Metzger, "Europe's Opera: Notes on John Cage's *Europeras 1 and 2*," in Kostelanetz, *Writings about John Cage*, 240; Elliott Schwartz and Daniel Godfrey, *Music since 1945: Issues, Materials, Literature* (New York: Schirmer Books, 1993), 214; Jonathan D. Kramer, *The Time of Music* (New York: Schirmer Books, 1988), 384, 382; Eric de Visscher, "'There's No Such Thing as Silence . . .': John Cage's Poetics of Silence" (1991), in Kostelanetz, *Writings about Cage*, 127, 130.

18. Cf. Charles Junkerman, "'nEw / foRms of living together': The Model of the Musicircus," in *John Cage: Composed in America*, ed. Marjorie Perloff and Charles Junkerman (Chicago: University of Chicago Press, 1994), 58–60; and N. Katherine Hayles, "Chance Operations: Cagean Paradox and Contemporary Science," in ibid., 226.

19. David Revill, *The Roaring Silence: John Cage, a Life* (New York: Arcade, 1992); 167; James Pritchett, *The Music of John Cage* (Cambridge: Cambridge University Press, 1993), 59, 60.

in another way. Cage arrived at the durations of the three "movements" by means of *I Ching* operations, yet when one adds up 4 minutes and 33 seconds, the sum is 273 seconds. Translated into negative degrees of temperature, this happens to be absolute zero on the Kelvin scale (actually −273.2°C). As substances approach that temperature, molecular motion ceases and they begin to exhibit peculiar properties. Although Cage heard sounds in an anechoic chamber and concluded that silence does not exist, his silent prayer of 273 seconds is a metaphor for a physical state in which matter is maximally ordered, vibratory activity is stilled, and silence is, in principle, absolute. When Tudor said that *4′33″* is the most intense listening experience you can have, he was describing a state in which mind, body, and spirit are at the highest possible level of concentration, analogous to the condition of minimum entropy. But just as materials at very low temperatures have anomalous properties of superfluidity and superconductivity, so a listening experience of utmost intensity gives rise to surprising epiphanies occasioned by a superflowing and superconducting imagination.

III. Performance and "The Social Problem"

Cage discovered early that music has a magical effect. While in his mid-twenties he gave a talk in which he said that listening to music attentively creates a state in which one experiences an exalted sense of unity with the order of things, a mysterious participation in the flow of nature [1]. He found that through music one can enter another world in which the natural flow of sounds brings a sense of excitement and mystery. The pleasure, peace, and spiritual abundance that he found affirmed for him that this transformed state of being was most desirable. For Cage the musical piece was merely the agent or conduit for evoking an act of listening that advances the individual's spiritual development. When his compositions of the thirties and forties did not produce the effects he hoped for, he was ready to make the radical move (at least for a composer) from a representational to a presentational aesthetic.

As Cage progressed from pieces that were indeterminate as to composition but determinate as to performance (that is, still fully notated) to compositions that were indeterminate in both respects, he ran into resistance from performers and listeners who did not understand the demands of a purely presentational aesthetic. Though the tactics of his experimental pieces vary greatly, the overall strategy remains consistent, namely, to set in motion processes that engage the musical imagination of the performer. The success of a performance depends on finding musicians who are willing to put not only their abilities as performers on the line, but their imaginative and spiritual capacities as well. Even musicians with whom Cage worked individually were unable to meet the challenge. At the New York and Cologne premieres of the *Concert for Piano and Orchestra* in 1958, Cage was very disappointed when some of the musicians made inappropriate sounds, including snippets from Stravinsky. He wanted musicians to be free so that they would become noble rather than foolish. He concluded that his problem was not simply musical, it was also social.[20]

Giving performers too much freedom had let in regressive and disruptive behaviors. After the radical openness of pieces like the *Concert for Piano and Orchestra,* Cage developed ways of limiting choice but still allowing considerable freedom. And yet he continued to run into the so-called social problem throughout his career. In the case of a performance of *Cheap Imitation* in Holland in 1972, he put its failure down to a lack of devotion in the musicians, and he ascribed that to the faulty organization of society. After a production of *Europeras 1 & 2* in 1991, his anger boiled over. In an open letter to the orchestra of the Zurich Opera, he accused the musicians of departing from the instrumental parts and playing operatic melodies that had been reserved for the singers, and, what was worse, playing them in harmony. He berated them for faulty tone production, which he believed showed their disgust for his work, and generally for misrepresenting his music and causing *Europeras* to fail.[21] He stated his credo: society will change only when the individual changes, and the individual musician changes only by playing music that is unfamiliar and does not mean anything in particular, namely, when it is "vibratory activity needing no support to give us pleasure." By failing to understand his music, the musicians showed, according to Cage, that they did not know what was best for the future of the world. Although Cage titled his diary "How to Improve the World (You Will Only Make Matters Worse)," he clearly intended that his music would change the world for the better. But at the height of his career, laden with fame and honors, he was unable to persuade a professional orchestra to take the right attitude and practice the needed discipline. Experimental music was evidently not in their repertoire. If Cage had grasped the magnitude of the problem he posed musicians, he would have taken

20. John Cage, *A Year from Monday* (Middletown, Conn.: Wesleyan University Press, 1967), 136. The retrospective *Concert* has been reissued (Wergo WER 6247–2). Sporadic bursts of laughter and applause from the audience begin at about the eight-minute mark of that twenty-six-minute version of the *Concert for Piano and Orchestra.*

21. *For the Birds: John Cage in Conversation with Daniel Charles* (Boston: Marion Boyars, 1981), 184; "Letter to Zurich" (1991), in *John Cage: Writer,* ed. Richard Kostelanetz (New York: Limelight, 1993), 255–56. We need to acknowledge the difficulty Cage had in meeting such resistance to his music and not pass over it by saying that Cage was never impatient. Cf. Junkerman, "nEw / foRms," 60. In the filmed interview *19 Questions* (1987), Cage said on the subject of *Europeras,* "Many people have no regrets. But I must say I regret that I ever said yes."

further steps to solve the "social problem" and might not have regretted composing *Europeras.* Perhaps a series of exercises in presentational music-making, including several "run-throughs" of *4′33″*, should have been scheduled before the actual rehearsals began.

Of course *Europeras* would have succeeded if the orchestra had consisted entirely of David Tudors. As Cage said, "Everything I have composed since 1952 was written for David Tudor."[22] Tudor's phenomenal powers as an executant and his devotion in realizing and performing indeterminate scores are legendary. What marked Tudor's approach, aside from his musical gifts, was his openness to the transpersonal. As Cage recognized, Tudor understood that the unconscious was involved in bringing about change in the conscious attitude [17d]. Tudor's participation became a benchmark in performances of experimental music. At a thirty-fifth anniversary presentation of the *Concert for Piano and Orchestra* that I attended in New York City, Tudor demonstrated his exemplary way of making sounds that, in Cage's words, "arise from actions, which . . . arise from their own centers" [12d]. Had all the musicians present noticed and emulated Tudor's poised presence as he made sounds from in and around the electrified piano, the performance would have been truly successful. Sounds that seemed connected to the unfolding sound organism happened when the musicians' postures and gestures indicated that the sounds they were making were valued gifts to the whole ensemble. But too many of the musicians appeared to sit inertly and play perfunctorily, without a sense of attentively listening to everything that was happening and taking full responsibility for their part in the piece. The proceedings were not marred by ugly sounds from the orchestra and raucous laughter and applause from the audience as in 1958, but too many sounds were tossed out casually, even carelessly, unconnected to the fabric of the evolving process. A few weeks after the concert, I had the opportunity to ask David Tudor how he thought the performance could have been improved. He replied, "It would have been better if they were more fully aware that they are all individuals."

By "individual," Tudor did not mean someone who is egoistic, willful, and ethically uncommitted to the enterprise. The individual for Cage and Tudor is someone whose actions arise not only from the ego-system, but also from the guiding center of the personality, the source of ethical impulses that link the individual to society. By contrast to the ego-system, that center can be referred to as the self-system [17f]. New music frequently challenges performers to reinvent themselves, but Cage's con-

22. *For the Birds,* 120. See also John Holzaepfel, "David Tudor and the Performance of American Experimental Music, 1950–1959" (Ph.D. diss., City University of New York, 1994).

ditions are even more stringent. He requires that musicians not only reinvent themselves, but do so by means of a "vibratory activity" that they themselves must invent. The challenge for orchestral musicians, whose powers of invention must usually submit to other demands, is to be like composers, taking responsibility for their individual creativity and engaging the self-system as they play. This cannot be accomplished with a few hours of rehearsal. Even performers long committed to Cage's music have struggled to meet these demands, as Margaret Leng Tan reveals in the story of her last meeting with Cage.

Tan visited Cage in early August of 1992 to work on some pieces she was preparing for festivals in Europe that fall. Two years earlier, after her performance of *One²*, a piece Cage had written for her, the composer had made a comment that still bothered her: "I would really prefer it, Margaret, if you didn't take it so seriously, but rather, play whatever comes to hand when you get to each piano without knowing what you are going to do until you get there." Tan had worked out in detail her earlier versions and felt secure with them, but Cage had said that she should forget her planned realization and play what came to her in the moment. This required a change of attitude—a leap of faith—for which she did not yet feel ready. The problem baffled her, and so she returned to work on *One²* for the third time with great trepidation. Cage had written extensively on what he meant by indeterminate performance [12–16], but it was another thing to achieve it in practice. Tan is celebrated for her renditions of Cage's music. Her admission that she was stumped reveals the humility and dedication that is needed for this work. Then the breakthrough happened:

> It was very simple: I didn't have to do anything. Having prepared the material thoroughly, I had only to draw spontaneously on the reservoir of possibilities at the moment of performance to make a truly indeterminate performance, the outcome of which would be different each time and unpredictable even to me. As I arrived at each piano, I would find not that I was going to play but, rather, that I (or "It") was playing. At the instant of sound, I would be simultaneously performer and audience; evaluating the results would be irrelevant. "Simply let sounds be sounds," in John's words.

The solution had eluded her because she was relying on old habits for preparing pieces. The moment of illumination came when she discovered that if the conscious mind gives up some measure of control, the ego will trust that a transpersonal "It" will play [15]. From this transpersonal position where the ego-system shares control with the self-system, the ego becomes deintegrated and permeable. The conscious attitude of the performer becomes more flexible and can expand to incorporate the roles of the composer and the listener. Tan found that when the ego-system comes in touch with the self-system, the ego becomes less critical and judgmental, facilitating rather than inhibiting the creative process. She continues:

> As I shared these discoveries with John, he made me feel that I was on the right track. He confirmed that *One*^{2} is about "space-time" (embodied in the Japanese concept of *ma*, where space and time are perceived as coincidental and indivisible). He suggested that I use an *I-Ching* chart of possibilities in my various approaches to the three pianos so I would not be "wandering around aimlessly." When I observed that I would be like the bell ringer who goes about sounding the bells yet letting them speak for themselves, John beamed and said, "You've got it."

Cage was still not satisfied with how Tan moved from piano to piano and suggested that she consult the *I Ching* to guide her movements. She must have been surprised at this. First Cage said to prepare less, and now he was telling her to prepare more. But consulting the *I Ching* is not the same as preparing out of the ego-system, for it models how to operate out of the self-system. And perhaps Cage knew that in the *I Ching* Tan might find the teacher who would replace him when he was gone. As Tan left, Cage was preparing to bake cookies, and twenty-four hours later he suffered the fatal stroke. At the time he died, Tan relates, she was practicing and trying to apply what she had learned the previous day. New questions came up, but she did not call right away thinking that the issues might resolve themselves. When she heard the news of Cage's death, she was filled with terror that he would no longer be there to answer her questions. But then she realized that like him she should hold onto the questions rather than seek the answers. Tan had found her new teacher.[23]

Tan's story can be taken as a paradigm of how the self-system has a noetic function in respect to the ego-system. Cage had to show Tan that the task of preparing the materials is a prelude to playing spontaneously and creatively in the presentational state. When Cage suggested that she be less serious, he was implying that she play more playfully, but he meant the serious play that for D. W. Winnicott is the basis of the healthy development of the child. It is the kind of play that operates out of the self-system, where "the individual child or adult is able to be creative and to use the whole personality, and it is only in being creative that the individual discovers the self."[24] Tan discovered that by playing

23. Margaret Leng Tan, "John Cage Poses a Few Last Questions," *Musicworks* 59 (summer 1994): 47–48.

24. *Playing and Reality* (London: Tavistock Publications, 1971), 54.

this way she could achieve the presentational state of awareness Cage desired [17a]. At each moment the ego-system must leave open the question as to what is to be next so that the self-system may participate [13]. The ego must let go the fear of failure, have faith that the question will be answered and that the self will respond. The sounds that suddenly happen will not be predictable according to canons of style, but the ego trusts that they will realize the intent of the moment. The questioning, playful, and devoted attitude of the performer invites the listeners to be present openly in the abundance of their own imaginations. The performance is a discovery of the potential of the moment to be infused with meaningful sounds, where meaning does not arise from a rhetoric of expressive devices, a grammar of signs, or implications that depend on being realized. There is no need for interpretation, as there is no space between the listener and the sounds for translating symbols into discursive meanings. Hermeneutic windows cannot be opened, as they have no handles. Sending and receiving are simultaneous in a continuous creation of felt meanings. To the critic who says that "musical understanding cashes out in the ability to describe music,"[25] Cage would reply that "nothing one does gives rise to anything that is preconceived," and "the complex of existence exceeds mentation's compass" [13, 14]. The listener does not stand outside the experience in order to describe, analyze, and understand it, but co-creates and undergoes it. Undergoing cashes out in the capacity to reside in the liminal zone between consciousness and unconsciousness. Objectivity and subjectivity begin to float freely on the sea of selfhood. It is the point in the "Lecture on Nothing," before a full-page pause, when the listener is carried into the borderland between the ego-system and the self-system: "Originally we were nowhere; and now, again we are having the pleasure of being slowly nowhere. If anybody is sleepy, let him go to sleep" [6]. If listeners stay awake, they are in the hypnagogic realm, where opposites interflow—the listener is yin and the sound is yang—or the sound is yin and the listener is yang. As the music ends and consciousness floats back to firm shores, there is a feeling of awe and fulfillment. "That is finished now," Cage continues after the pause. "It was a pleasure." The "Lecture on Nothing" shows the phases of undergoing the act of listening in the presentational mode.

Professional musicians experienced in performing experimental music confirm Tan's account of letting a transpersonal agency take over. A pianist remarks on performing experimental music: "You are in a sense outside yourself. You are anonymous, and the interpreter's and author's role[s] are secondary to the moment of now. That now takes precedence.

25. Kivy, *Music Alone,* 101.

That now is almost playing you." And a percussionist says: "It's not the instrument alone, it's not the player alone, there is an anonymity to that sound. It is precisely this unanalysable quality, this anonymity, which defies categorization, that allows the sound to communicate to others."[26] These musicians describe how they enter a transpersonal state where there is just "a sound happening." The diminished functioning of the ego-system is felt as a loss of identity, a state of anonymity, and a loss of rational discrimination among the components of the event. But there is a gain in the state of heightened awareness that incorporates the roles of performer, composer, and listener. And a spiritual quality pervades when the musician senses a merging with the instrument and the music in a holistic "sound" that is happening, as though the musician is being played by the music. Moreover, this presentational state enfolds the musician and the attentive members of the audience in a communal flow of felt meanings.

IV. The Synthesis: Mace, Eckhart, Jung, Suzuki, and the *I Ching*

When Oskar Fischinger told the young Cage that "everything in the world has a spirit which is released by its sound," he gave Cage permission to regard the career of a composer as a spiritual vocation.[27] By his mid-thirties, Cage was sorting out his stance as a composer in regard to the religious question. In a talk on the impact of Eastern music on the West, he listed composers according to whether they were openly affiliated to an organized religion (Hovhaness and Messiaen), wrote sacred music that was not sectarian in nature (Lou Harrison), or did not write sacred music as such but had a strong element of the spiritual in their music (Varèse, Ruggles, and Thomson) [2]. It is clear that Cage sided with the last group, that is, with those who, as he said, "imbue their music with the ineffable" by incorporating Oriental or other non-Western elements. In an aside he declared his opposition to those who, like Schoenberg, intellectualize music, and who, like the Freudians, dwell on neurosis. Here Cage stood opposed to what he took to be an analytical and reductionist attitude to both music and the mind. He implied that his calling was to heal the mind with music grounded in Eastern principles of spirituality.

From about 1948 on, when Cage spoke about the purpose of music he would generally offer two types of statements, one spiritual and

26. The musicians were interviewed as part of a research project in presentational states. The interview with the percussionist was recorded in Toronto, April 26, 1996, and with the pianist on January 19, 1997. The percussionist had known Cage since the 1970s and had worked with him on many performances.

27. Thomas Hines, "Then Not Yet 'Cage': The Los Angeles Years, 1912–1938," in Perloff and Junkerman, *John Cage*, 90–91.

the other psychological. For the spiritual statement he quoted Thomas Mace, the seventeenth-century English composer, lutenist, and author [3a]. Mace's book, *Musick's Monument* (1676), does not contain the sentence Cage refers to as such, but the component phrases can be found in separate passages: "[T]o *Season, and Sober his Mind, or Elevate his Affection to Goodness*" comes from one passage, and "*[M]aking us capable of Heavenly, and Divine Influences*" comes from another.[28] Thomas Mace (ca. 1612–1706) began as a chorister and then became a clerk of Trinity College, Cambridge, where he was closely associated with the school of philosophers and theologians known as the Cambridge Platonists. Leading members of the school, Ralph Cudworth and Henry More, appear in the list of subscribers to his book. Cudworth (1617–88) was the principal systematic philosopher of the group, while More (1614–87) was the chief exponent of its mystical side. These philosophers and theologians gathered their ideas from Pythagoras and the supposedly pre-Platonic Hermes Trismegistus and the Chaldaean Oracles. Some of them believed that the Platonic tradition, which led back from Ficino, Plotinus, and Proclus to Pythagoras and Plato, could be traced to the biblical wisdom of Moses and the Jewish Kabbalah. The Cambridge Platonists were united in their opposition to Calvinist predestination, sectarianism, atheism, and to certain doctrines of the new generation of experimental scientists and philosophers, in particular, the materialism of Hobbes and the mechanistic theories of Descartes. In fact, More is credited with coining "materialist" and "Cartesian" as derogatory epithets for those modes of thought.[29]

Since the sentence from Mace is evidently Neoplatonic in origin, it is tempting to describe Cage as a Pythagorean, but when Joan Retallack suggested to him that he stood closer to Pythagoras than to the *I Ching*, he disagreed.[30] For the Pythagorean numbers have divine powers, and Mace explains how the Great Chain of Being is organized by musical octaves to draw all existence harmoniously to the Godhead. One of his doggerels states the doctrine: "Mysterious Center of All Mysterie; / All

28. "[W]hich [modern music of which Mace does not approve] is rather fit to make a Mans *Ears Glow*, and fill his *Brains full of Frisks*, &c. than to *Season, and Sober his Mind, or Elevate his Affection* to *Goodness*" (Thomas Mace, *Musick's Monument* [London, 1676; Paris: Centre National de la Recherche Scientifique, 1958], 236). "*That They* [the "Grave Musick" of the past] *have been to my self, (and many others) as Divine Raptures, Powerfully Captivating all our unruly Faculties, and Affections, (for the Time) and disposing us to Solidity, Gravity, and a Good Temper; making us capable of Heavenly, and Divine Influences*" (ibid, 234). The typography is original.

29. "Cambridge Platonists" and "Henry More," in *The Cambridge Dictionary of Philosophy*, ed. Robert Audi (Cambridge: Cambridge University Press, 1995). For a survey of the Cambridge Platonists, see Basil Wiley, *The Seventeenth-Century Background* (1934; New York: Anchor, n.d.), chap. 8.

30. *Musicage*, 236.

Things Originate Themselves in Thee; / And in Their Revolution, wholly tend / To Thee, Their Octave, Their Most Happy End."[31] On one level the end of music for Cage was not to resound in the perfect consonances of the cosmos, but to activate the creative process in the individual musician. "Square root" temporal schemes, magic squares, and throwing the *I Ching* were not designed to achieve harmony with a transcendent Godhead, but rather to liberate sounds from the constraints of tradition. And yet Cage's ethical intent, while not Neoplatonic as such, was to strive for a spiritual transcendence. And he did share other traits with Mace. Both enjoyed telling amusing anecdotes that were in fact teaching stories, and both were opposed to current trends in contemporary music. Mace's comment on the role of music is drawn from passages in which he praises the ability of the older styles to achieve the proper effects of music. He utterly disapproves of the music of his own day, which makes the "Ears Glow" and "fills his Brains full of Frisks." Cage, too, did not much like modernist music, and his enthusiasm for the music of Satie is somewhat similar to Mace's defense of the reserved music of the past. In later years, Cage forgot the original source of this view and attributed it to the musician Gita Sarabhai, who had introduced him in the late forties to Indian music and the writings of Sri Ramakrishna. Thus, for Cage, Mace's comment came to stand on a deeper level for a perennial philosophy of music that links spiritual traditions in both the West and the East.[32]

The psychological rationale for music also appears in Cage's lectures from 1948 and 1949. It is that music brings together the conscious (or rational) and the unconscious (or irrational) by integrating split-off parts of the psyche and so leading to psychological wholeness [3b–c, 4, 5]. He mentions specifically a book of essays by Jung with the title *The Integration of the Personality.*[33] These essays were selected and translated by Stanley Dell so as to cover the principal concepts of Jung's psychology—the unconscious, the complex, archetypes, the dream, the problem of the opposites, the transcendent function, the technique of active imagination, the individuation process, the mandala as symbol of the self, and so forth. In this book and perhaps other books by Jung, Cage found a

31. *Musick's Monument,* 269.

32. Aldous Huxley and Ananda Coomaraswamy both provided Cage with ideas about a perennial philosophy. Cf. Pritchett, *The Music of John Cage,* 36; Patterson, "Appraising the Catchwords," 73.

33. This was formerly not recognized to be the title of a book. *The Integration of the Personality,* ed. Stanley Dell (New York: Farrar and Rinehart, 1939), contains the following essays: (1) "The Meaning of Individuation," (2) "A Study in the Process of Individuation," (3) "Archetypes of the Collective Unconscious," (4) "Dream Symbols of the Process of Individuation," (5) "The Idea of Redemption in Alchemy," and (6) "The Development of the Personality." The essays, somewhat revised and expanded, appear in Jung's *Collected Works* as follows: (1) *CW* 9/1:275; (2) *CW* 9/1:290; (3) *CW* 9/1:3; (4) *CW* 12; (5) *CW* 12; (6) *CW* 17:167.

pragmatic approach to the psyche that valued religious experience in general and Eastern spiritual traditions in particular. That Jung linked his psychology to Zen, Taoism, and medieval mysticism must have strengthened its appeal for Cage.

Jung was deeply influenced by the pragmatism of William James, whose research into the nature of consciousness went beyond the borders of academic psychology into typology, parapsychology, and religious experience. Eugene Taylor shows that for Jung, who also was greatly interested in these areas, James was a pioneer of fundamental importance to his development. Already in his doctoral thesis on occult phenomena (1902), Jung had cited cases from James's *Principles of Psychology* (1890). During the Clark University conference of 1909 at which Freud and Jung were both given honorary degrees, Jung met with James and discussed James's work with a medium. James's writings were fundamental to many of Jung's basic formulations. In the introduction to his Fordham University lectures of 1912, Jung quoted from James's *Pragmatism* the passage given above, which begins, "You must bring out of each word its practical cash-value." He cited James at that juncture to indicate that after parting ways with Freud he was returning to his roots in a pragmatic approach to the mind in which empirical method takes precedence over dogmatic theories. James also provided a foundation for Jung's concepts of psychological types and the unconscious.[34] In the essay "On the Nature of the Psyche," Jung quotes the passage by James (also given above) that begins "The important fact which this 'field formula' commemorates," which describes the liminal realm beyond consciousness as containing the past memories, residual powers, impulses, and knowledge that constitute the empirical self.

Oriental religions and Jung's depth psychology aroused much interest among artists and humanists in the United States during the 1930s and thereafter, and Cage's study of these subjects intensified when he came to New York in the early 1940s. He was then friends with Joseph Campbell, who published his key to *Finnegans Wake* in 1944 and his first treatise on mythology, *The Hero with a Thousand Faces*, in 1949. Campbell acknowledged his debt to Jung for pioneering studies in comparative mythology and for the concept of the archetypes.[35] Artists with whom

34. Eugene Taylor, "William James and C. G. Jung," *Spring* (Dallas), 1980, 157, 163, 166; Henri F. Ellenberger, *The Discovery of the Unconscious* (New York: Basic Books, 1970), 706–7.

35. Cage stayed with Joseph Campbell in the summer of 1942 (Revill, *Roaring Silence*, 80). *The Integration of the Personality* is among the books by Jung that Campbell quotes in *The Hero with a Thousand Faces*, which was published the year after Cage gave the lecture at Vassar College. That lecture concluded with Cage saying that he planned to collaborate in writing operas with Campbell, who presumably was sitting in the audience (in Kostelanetz, *John Cage: Writer*, 44). For Campbell's view of Jung, see "Mythological Themes in Creative Literature and Art," in *Myths, Dreams, and Religion*, ed. Joseph Campbell (New York: Dutton, 1970), 138.

Cage associated in the forties were interested in Jung for similar reasons, namely, for his view of the unconscious as more than a repository of repressed contents and for his concept of the libido as manifesting itself in drives other than sexuality. He was also noted for treating the image not only as a symptom to be rationally explained, but as the bearer of the unknown factor that points the way to individuation. Thus Jung warned against reductive analyses of images through a fixed system of interpretation. Furthermore, he was known as a commentator on texts that were of interest to those who looked to the Orient for alternatives to Christianity.[36] Jung was for Cage and many artists an authority on depth psychology as well as on the psychological implications of Eastern religions. Cage believed that the goal of the creative process was the transformation of the individual, a concept for which he found much support in Jung, who regarded the purpose of psychological work as discovering from images thrown up from the unconscious the meanings that guide the individual on the path to wholeness. Jung called it "the process of individuation" and looked to the East for an analogy, which he found in Zen and the *I Ching*. In particular, the Taoist idea of the Way accorded with his notion of the individuation process: "The undiscovered vein within us is a living part of the psyche; classical Chinese philosophy names this interior way 'Tao,' and likens it to a flow of water that moves irresistibly towards its goal. To rest in Tao means fulfillment, wholeness, one's destination reached, one's mission done; the beginning, end, and perfect realization of the meaning of existence innate in all things. Personality is Tao."[37]

Cage's search for a new spiritual and psychological basis for his compositional practice ended in 1949 when he created a synthesis between Meister Eckhart and Jung in the lecture "Forerunners of Modern Music." Since Jung himself often quoted Eckhart, the synthesis was readily accomplished. Cage begins by citing Eckhart to the effect that the purpose of music is to set "the soul in operation," defining the soul as "the

36. Cf. Terree Grabenhorst-Randall, "Jung and Abstract Expressionism," and "Artists' Roundtable: Jung's Influence," in *C. G. Jung and the Humanities*, ed. K. Barnaby and P. d'Acierno (Princeton, N.J.: Princeton University Press, 1990), 185–216. Artists of New York who acknowledged the impact of Jungian ideas on their work include John Ferren, Adolph Gottlieb, Ibram Lassaw, Jackson Pollock, Robert Rauchenberg, and Mark Rothko.

Jung wrote commentaries on *The Secret of the Golden Flower* (London: K. Paul, Trench, Trubner, and Co., 1931), *The Tibetan Book of the Dead* (Oxford: Oxford University Press, 1953), *The Tibetan Book of the Great Liberation* (Oxford: Oxford University Press, 1954), Suzuki, *Introduction to Zen Buddhism* (London: Rider, 1949), and *The I Ching* (written in 1945; published in 1950). Also the essays "Yoga and the West," *Prabuddha Bharata* (Calcutta), 1936, and "The Psychology of Eastern Meditation" (1943), in *Art and Thought, in Honor of Ananda Coomaraswamy*, ed. K. Bharatha Iyer (London: Luzac, 1947).

37. Jung, "A Study in the Process of Individuation," in *The Integration of the Personality, CW* 9/1 : 340; Jung, "The Development of Personality," *CW* 17 : 186.

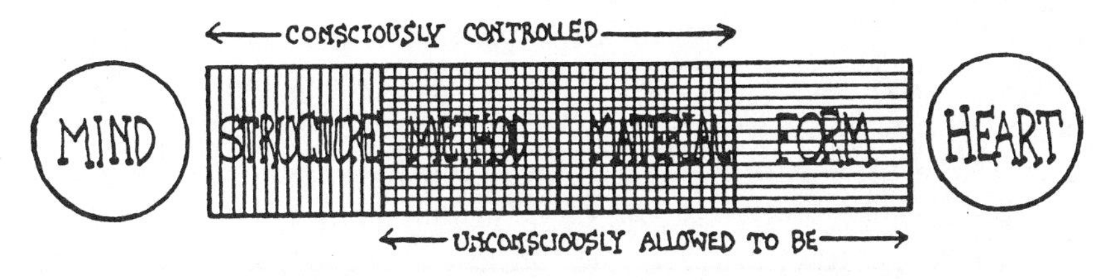

FIGURE 3.1
Diagram from Cage's "Forerunners of Modern Music," in *The Boulez-Cage Correspondence,* ed. Jean-Jacques Nattiez (Cambridge: Cambridge University Press, 1993), 39.

gatherer-together of the disparate elements . . . , its work fills one with peace and love."[38] The soul here is not the totality of the psyche, but rather the several elements that together form the personality, as in Jung's terminology. Cage then quotes a paragraph verbatim from a sermon of Eckhart that speaks of how "unselfconsciousness" is achieved by means of "transformed knowledge." This passage, which has puzzled Cage's commentators, becomes clear in the light of the structure of the psyche as outlined by Jung.

The original version of Cage's lecture differs in important respects from the version reprinted in *Silence.* The principal change is the omission of a diagram that Cage drew to illustrate the section titled "Strategy" (see fig. 3.1). The diagram has two phrases that do not appear in the main text and thus are altogether missing from the later version. The two phrases read: "consciously controlled" and "unconsciously allowed to be." The former is written in the upper margin and positioned toward the left-hand side, where the word "mind" is inscribed in a circle. The latter phrase is in the lower margin and positioned toward the right-hand side, where the word "heart" is inscribed in another circle. The meaning of the opposition between the "conscious mind" and "unconscious heart" is made clear in the footnote, in which Cage asserts emphatically that to exclude the irrational from composing is irrational in the extreme. Thus the diagram is even more explicit than the text in presenting Cage's new paradigm, namely, that musical form is to structure as the freedom-to-be of the heart is to the mind, and as the (irrational) unconscious is to the (rational) conscious. The phrases "consciously controlled" and "unconsciously allowed to be" clearly refer both to Jung's concept of unconscious contents that are allowed to flow

38. "Forerunners of Modern Music," in *The Boulez-Cage Correspondence,* ed. Jean-Jacques Nattiez (Cambridge: Cambridge University Press, 1993), 38. This passage is cited more completely in the appendix to this chapter [5].

into consciousness through the activated imagination and to Eckhart's notion of "our ignorance" (that is, Jung's ego) being "informed by the divine unconsciousness" (that is, Jung's unconscious). The paragraph from Eckhart then affirms the concept of the dynamic process by which the ego becomes more conscious of the infinite field of the unconscious. The words of Meister Eckhart, that "our ignorance will be ennobled and adorned with supernatural knowledge," could as cogently have been Jung's: "The whole must necessarily include not only consciousness but the illimitable field of unconscious occurrences as well, and that the ego can be no more than the centre of the field of consciousness."[39] The synthesis of Eckhart and Jung that Cage achieved in 1949 formed the basis for the praxis that became the music of indeterminacy. His later writings, as in the 1958 lecture titled "Indeterminacy," continue to elaborate this paradigm [12a–d].

Cage's next step was to introduce chance as the means of breaking down the "ignorance" of the ego in order to let in the "divine unconsciousness." In January of 1950, that is, before Cage saw the Bollingen edition of the *I Ching,* he wrote to Pierre Boulez about composing music for a film on Alexander Calder. He recounted how he started the piece in a dream and wanted to use unrelated sounds by recording material four times, changing the preparation of the piano each time. He then found he had to write the music anyway and concluded, "Chance comes in here to give us the unknown" [7a]. In other words, chance served to break down the ego's resistance to the unconscious. Chance is here for Cage the agent for releasing musical "form" from the unconscious "heart" into the conscious "mind." It was this concept of chance that caused the split with Boulez, who answered Cage many months later (December 1951) that "chance must be extremely controlled . . . as there is already quite enough of the unknown." There is an uncanny resonance here with the split that occurred some forty years before between Jung and Freud, when they broke off their association over a similar difference of belief.

When Christian Wolff presented Cage with the Bollingen edition of the *I Ching* sometime later in 1950, Cage discovered the means for putting the new synthesis into operation. The *I Ching,* with the foreword by Jung, brought Eckhart, Jung, Zen, Taoism, and chance into a fortunate synchrony. From then on the *I Ching* was Cage's sage, whether he consulted it about life issues or used it as a source of numbers for his music of indeterminacy [18].

The Bollingen edition of the *I Ching* had been conceived twenty years

39. Jung, "A Study in the Process of Individuation," 276.

before. Jung had begun to experiment with the Legge translation of the *I Ching* in about 1920 and became fascinated with its ability to provide meaningful answers to his questions. He was soon using the *I Ching* in psychotherapeutic sessions with his patients as a means of bringing unconscious factors into clearer focus. When Richard Wilhelm's German translation of the *I Ching* came out in 1923, Jung invited Wilhelm to demonstrate the method of consulting the *I Ching* to his colleagues and students at the Psychology Club in Zurich. Wilhelm died in 1930, and Jung was invited to give the eulogy. He paid tribute to Wilhelm's enormous achievement in translating and commenting on the *I Ching,* for as Jung saw it, the *I Ching* provided "an Archimedean point from which our Western attitude of mind could be lifted off its foundations." Jung then took the opportunity to articulate for the first time his theory of acausal order, which he believed underlay the operation of the *I Ching:* "The science of the *I Ching* is based not on the causality principle but on one which—hitherto unnamed because not familiar to us—I have tentatively called the synchronistic principle." Although Jung had reservations about the applicability of some aspects of Eastern thought and practice to Western life, he held no doubts about the cardinal importance of the *I Ching:* "We must continue Wilhelm's work of translation in a wider sense if we wish to show ourselves worthy pupils of the master. The central concept of Chinese philosophy is tao, which Wilhelm translated as 'meaning.' Just as Wilhelm gave the spiritual treasure of the East a European meaning, so we should translate this meaning into life."[40]

Jung encouraged Cary Baynes, who had already rendered several of Jung's works into English, to translate the German edition under Wilhelm's supervision, and she began work on it in 1929. The translation was accepted for publication in the Bollingen Series, and the first Bollingen catalog, issued in the fall of 1943, listed the *I Ching,* with "Dr. C. G. Jung's valuable commentary." Baynes received Jung's foreword in late 1945, but she put off translating it because she was worried lest Jung be branded even more an occultist than he already had been. In the commentary, Jung describes how he consulted the *I Ching* in order to receive advice from the oracle on the right attitude to take in presenting the book to Western readers. Baynes was finally persuaded to translate the fore-

40. Jung, "Richard Wilhelm: In Memoriam," *CW* 15:55, 56, 59. In a later reminiscence of Wilhelm included with his memoirs, Jung described in more detail his early experiments with the *I Ching* and its application to his work with patients, which led him to the idea of "acausal parallelism," later termed "synchronicity" (*Memories, Dreams, Reflections* [New York: Vintage, 1965], 373–77). Thus, Jung first articulated the notion of synchronicity in 1930, not in the foreword to the Bollingen edition of the *I Ching.* Cf. Charles Hamm, "Privileging the Moment: Cage, Jung, Synchronicity, Postmodernism," *Journal of Musicology* 15, no. 2 (1997): 285.

word as Jung wrote it, and the manuscript went to the printer in 1948. When the proofs came back, Baynes contacted Wilhelm's son Hellmut, also a scholar of Chinese literature, for assistance in checking them with the original sources. This took another year, and the English edition was published at last in April of 1950.[41] The copy of the *I Ching* that Christian Wolff presented to Cage in 1950 was thus the product of a lengthy collaboration between scholars from the East and the West.

In the foreword, Jung sets out the crisis of chance and necessity in Western thought in terms that Cage must have found of absorbing interest: "The axioms of causality are being shaken to their foundations. . . . If we leave things to nature . . . every process is partially or totally interfered with by chance, so much so that under natural circumstances a course of events absolutely conforming to specific laws is almost an exception." In respect to the concept of chance, Jung continued:

> I have termed synchronicity a concept that formulates a point of view diametrically opposed to that of causality. Since [causality] is a mere statistical truth and not absolute, it is a sort of working hypothesis of how events evolve one out of another, whereas synchronicity takes the coincidence of events in space and time as meaning something more than mere chance, namely a peculiar interdependence of objective events among themselves as well as with the subjective (psychic) state of the observer or observers.[42]

Cage had already been experimenting with chance, but throwing coins while consulting the ancient Chinese book of wisdom for the numbers of its hexagrams gave chance the spiritual context for which Cage was searching. Jung's enthusiastic advocacy of the *I Ching* and the cardinal importance he gave to chance as a corrective to Western materialism could only have strengthened Cage's intent. By basing his compositional practice on the *I Ching*, Cage too would assist in applying the oracle to contemporary life. Cage also fell in with Jung's bias against causality. Like Jung, Cage sought to compensate for the Western emphasis on logic and causality with an equal and opposite emphasis on chance. However, it has been demonstrated that the *I Ching* is as open

41. This account of the publishing history of the *I Ching* is drawn from William McGuire, *Bollingen: An Adventure in Collecting the Past* (Princeton, N.J.: Princeton University Press, 1982), 19, 73, 101, 179–81. The date of publication of the Bollingen edition has been placed somewhat later. Cf. Revill, *Roaring Silence*, 131.

42. C. G. Jung, foreword to *The I Ching; or, Book of Changes*, translated into English by Cary F. Baynes from the German of Richard Wilhelm (Princeton, N.J.: Princeton University Press, 1950), xxii–xxiii. It was the foreword to the *I Ching* that Cage recalled as the source for Jung's concept of synchronicity [11]. Cage recommended to Joan Retallack that she read the *I Ching* in the Bollingen edition with the essay on synchronicity by Jung (see *Musicage:* xviii). Jung wrote separate essays on synchronicity in 1951 and 1952, see "Synchronicity: An Acausal Connecting Principle," in *CW* 8:419–519; and "On Synchronicity," in ibid., 520–31.

to causality as it is to chance. Lama Govinda shows that the *I Ching* does not reject the principle of causality, but rather includes it as the basis for the temporal ordering of things.[43] Nevertheless, Cage thereafter used the formulation "*I Ching* chance operations" to describe his method of putting into operation the Eckhart-Jung paradigm, as though the *I Ching* were the source of chance alone [18]. The *I Ching* was for Cage far more than a quaint and antique source of random numbers, as it is so often characterized. It was the way of seasoning and sobering the mind, bringing Eckhart's ignorance in touch with *Grund*, Jung's conscious in touch with the unconscious, and finally Suzuki's small-*m* mind in touch with Mind [17c, 17f].

Cage was working out the compositional applications of the new synthesis while he attended the lectures of Daisetz T. Suzuki. He was already experimenting with the *I Ching* when he said to Suzuki that he was making a connection between his work and Zen and asked what the master had to say about art.[44] Cage's studies in Oriental thought during the forties had led him to the Indian theory of *rasa* as a source for a representational aesthetic, but when this did not achieve what he desired, he gravitated toward Zen Buddhism. Suzuki, who was the leading interpreter of Zen for the Western reader, came to the United States in 1897 to work for Paul Carus, publisher of the Open Court Press in La Salle, Illinois, and a philosopher in his own right. Suzuki's writings and translations first began to appear in English in the following year. Through Carus, who was the principal publisher of the writings of Peirce and who corresponded with William James, Suzuki came to know James's writings and was greatly influenced by them.[45] Suzuki repeatedly casts his argument in the form of a comparison and contrast between Zen and Christian mysticism as treated by James in *The Varieties of Religious Experience*, which he often cites. For instance, he quotes James on the noetic quality of mystic experience and finds that this applies to Zen *satori*. In characterizing Zen, Suzuki sometimes links it to James's pragmatism, as when he describes "its simplicity, its directness, its pragmatic tendency, and its close connection with everyday life." In this fashion Suzuki built a bridge between Zen and the pragmatism of James, which accounts in part for the wide acceptance his writings found among Western read-

43. "The *I Ching* is based on the principles of synchronicity and causality, which proves that they need not be mutually exclusive, but that the one can contain the other, while going beyond it. We therefore need not choose between the systems of Fu Hi and King Wen, but can accept both, depending on whether we want to see the world in its universal or its temporal aspect" (Lama Anagarika Govinda, *The Inner Structure of the I Ching* [Weatherhill: Wheelwright Press, 1981], 157).

44. See Revill, *Roaring Silence*, 124.

45. Harold Henderson, *Catalyst for Controversy: Paul Carus of Open Court* (Carbondale: Southern Illinois University Press, 1993), 102–7.

ers.[46] After returning to Japan in 1909, Suzuki remained there as professor of English at Tokyo Imperial University. He continued to make translations of Buddhist texts and publish his essays on Zen Buddhism, while keeping in touch with developments in the West, particularly with the writings of C. G. Jung. In 1933, as a mark of his regard, Suzuki sent Jung a copy of the *Second Series of Essays in Zen Buddhism,* to which Jung responded with a letter in which he wrote that he was already an admirer of Suzuki's work and describing Zen as "a true goldmine for the needs of the Western 'psychologist.'" Jung's interest in Suzuki's writings continued, and six years later he wrote a foreword to the German edition of Suzuki's *An Introduction to Zen Buddhism.* Jung's foreword was then translated into English for the republication of that book in 1949. In that year, at the age of seventy-nine, Suzuki again left Japan. He spent a year in Hawaii and another year at Claremont College in California before going on a tour of American universities. He finally arrived in New York in 1951, where he taught at Columbia University as professor of religion until 1957.[47]

Suzuki continued to engage with developments in depth psychology, and in his book *The Zen Doctrine of No-Mind,* which first appeared in 1949, he investigates the similarities and differences between the Zen and Western ideas of the unconscious. Suzuki criticizes Jung's concept of "the Unconscious" as a concrete entity and writes that the psychoanalytical unconscious cannot go deep enough to include Zen No-Mind-ness. Suzuki develops a structure of the psyche that is based on the James-Jung model but goes beyond it in elaborating the interactions between the conscious and unconscious levels. Thus, when Cage attended the lectures of Suzuki and consulted his writings, he encountered an interpretation of Zen that was richly charged with the pragmatism of James and the depth psychology of Jung. And so it is important to keep in mind the link between James, Suzuki, and Jung when considering the impact of Zen on Western culture in general and on Cage in particular.[48]

46. Daisetz T. Suzuki, *The Essentials of Zen Buddhism,* ed. Bernard Phillips (London: Rider, 1963), 8, 164. Suzuki's most widely circulated writings: three series of *Essays in Zen Buddhism* (London: Luzac, 1927, 1933, 1934); and *An Introduction to Zen Buddhism* (Kyoto: The Eastern Buddhist Society, 1934), translated into German by Heinrich Zimmer and published in 1939 with a foreword by C. G. Jung. The English edition of the book was reprinted in London and New York in 1949 with Jung's foreword translated by Constance Rolfe; *Zen Buddhism and Its Influence on Japanese Culture* (Kyoto: The Eastern Buddhist Society, 1938) was revised and republished as *Zen and Japanese Culture* in the Bollingen Series (New York: Pantheon Books, 1959).

47. See *C. G. Jung Letters,* ed. Gerhard Adler and Aniela Jaffé (Princeton, N.J.: Princeton University Press, 1973), 1:128; and Bernard Phillips, introduction to Suzuki, *The Essentials of Zen Buddhism,* xxxvii–xil.

48. Suzuki, *The Zen Doctrine of No-Mind* (1949; York Beach, Me.: Samuel Weiser, 1972), 144. Cage was eagerly awaiting the publication of Suzuki's writings at this time, as he indicates in a letter to Boulez (January 1950); see *The Boulez-Cage Correspondence,* 50. Cf. J. J. Clarke, *Jung and Eastern Thought* (London: Routledge, 1994), 131.

The central fact of Zen is *satori,* a mental state to which meditating on a *koan* is a guide. Suzuki explains that the *koan* was devised in order to counteract two tendencies in Zen Buddhism, one being quietism and the other, intellectual analysis:

> The worst enemy of Zen experience, at least in the beginning, is the intellect, which consists and insists in discriminating subject from object. The discriminating intellect, therefore, must be cut short if Zen consciousness is to unfold itself, and the *koan* is constructed eminently to serve this end. On examination we at once notice that there is no room in the *koan* to insert an intellectual interpretation. The knife is not sharp enough to cut the *koan* open and see what are its contents. For a *koan* is not a logical proposition but the expression of a certain mental state resulting from the Zen discipline.[49]

That mental state is *satori:*

> *Satori* may be defined as an intuitive looking into the nature of things in contradistinction to the analytical or logical understanding of it. Practically, it means the unfolding of a new world hitherto unperceived in the confusion of a dualistically-trained mind. Or we may say that with *satori* our entire surroundings are viewed from quite an unexpected angle of perception. Whatever this is, the world for those who have gained a *satori* is no more the old world as it used to be; even with all its flowing streams and burning fires, it is never the same one again. Logically stated, all its opposites and contradictions are united and harmonized into a consistent organic whole. This is a mystery and a miracle, but according to the Zen masters such is being performed every day. *Satori* can thus be had only through our once personally experiencing it.[50]

It was the concepts of the *koan* and *satori* that led Jung to find in Zen a validation of some of his more radical conceptions. In looking back on his work in later years, Jung often cites Zen as a close parallel to his own thinking. For Jung the Buddha provides a more complete expression of the self than does the Christ, and Zen, like his own psychology, is based on cognition of the self. *Satori* was for Jung an unmatched expression of the numinous, meaningful, and unrepeatable moment when the self-system breaks through into the ego-system:

> When the old Chinese master asked the pupil with whom he was walking at the time of the blossoming laurel: Do you smell it? and the pupil

49. Suzuki, *Essentials of Zen Buddhism,* 293. This passage is from the second series of essays (1933).

50. Ibid., 154. Originally from the first series of essays (1927).

> experienced *satori,* we can still guess and understand the beauty and fullness of the moment of illumination. It is overwhelmingly clear that such a *kairos* [the right or proper time, the favorable moment] can never be brought back by a willful effort, however painstaking and methodical.[51]

In the foreword to Suzuki's *Introduction to Zen Buddhism,* Jung tries to find analogies between Zen and Western thought, as the conception of *satori,* which he takes to be the raison d'être of Zen, is of such "unsurpassed singularity." Jung was fascinated by the concept of *satori* because, no matter how strange it may seem to the Western mind, it is a very simple, natural occurrence akin to Eckhart's *Durchbruch,* and not a system of abstract thought. Jung connected this breakthrough with his own conception of the relation of the self to the ego: "However one may define the self, it is always something other than the ego, and inasmuch as a higher insight of the ego leads over to self, the self is a more comprehensive thing which includes the experience of the ego and therefore transcends it. Just as the ego is a certain experience I have of myself, so is the self an experience of my ego. It is, however, no longer experienced in the form of a broader or higher ego, but in the form of a non-ego."[52] The only parallel to Zen *satori* that Jung finds in the West is in Meister Eckhart, whose "paradoxical statements," he says, "skirt the edge of heterodoxy or actually overstep it," and he quotes a passage from Eckhart on the "breakthrough." Jung is also attracted by the iconoclasm of the Zen masters and the extreme individualism of their methods. And in the technique of the *koan* he sees a radical attack on the integrity of the ego that he could find nowhere else in Western thought:

> Since no logical sequence can be demonstrated, it remains to be supposed that the *koan* method puts not the smallest restraint upon the freedom of the psychic process and that the end-result therefore springs from nothing but the individual disposition of the pupil. The complete destruction of the rational intellect aimed at in the training creates an almost perfect lack of conscious assumptions. These are excluded as far as possible, but not unconscious assumptions—that is, the existing but unrecognized psychological disposition, which is anything but empty or unassuming. It is a nature-given factor, and when it answers—this being obviously the *satori* experience—it is an answer of Nature, who has succeeded in conveying her reaction direct to the conscious mind. What

51. *Jung Letters,* 2:453 (1958), 601 (1960), respectively.

52. Jung, foreword to Suzuki's *Introduction to Zen Buddhism,* in *CW* 11:548, 542.

> the unconscious nature of the pupil opposes to the teacher or to the *koan* by way of an answer is, manifestly, *satori*.[53]

Jung explained the ability of the *koan* to produce *satori* as a breakdown of the rational defenses of the ego-system so that contents from the unconscious can flow in and activate the self, which for Jung was the key to spiritual and mental health and to the successful outcome of the individuation process. Jung's comments on the *koan* and *satori* illuminate Cage's description of the music of indeterminacy, his call for dangerous, sudden listening, and his belief that a piece of music should be like a work of Nature [12a–c, 16]. Cage's compositions provide musicians a *koan*-like guide to a breakthrough that brings musical enlightenment.

V. The Tertiary Process

Working with chance and the Eckhart-Jung-Zen paradigm, Cage devised an extraordinarily rich and varied repertoire of schemas for activating the musical imagination. Representation continued to play a part in his later compositions, as in *Lecture on the Weather,* but the time-bracket pieces emphasize the presentational state. The time-bracket method fulfills Cage's desire for actions without symbols or intellectual references [8], actions that provide little knowledge about what is going to happen next [17e], actions that are about attention to the sounds suddenly appearing [20], actions that have an element of risk [21c–d], and actions that result in the continuous creation of meaning [17b]. The act of letting sounds happen evokes presentational states of musical cognition. But, as Suzuki said about the *koan,* there is no room in the presentational state to insert an intellectual operation. The analytic knife is not sharp enough to cut the music open and examine its contents, because the meaning is not in the sounds alone. We can record performances of time-bracket pieces and transcribe them, but the sounds carry limited meaning in themselves when detached from the act of producing them and from the felt meanings of the performers and the listeners—which is why Cage said that a recording is as much like the thing itself as a postcard is of a landscape [12c]. A recording provides audial documentation of the musical event, but does not convey the transpersonal outcome. Experimental music requires us to orient our discovery procedures away from structures of sounds as such to encompass the presentational aspects of performing and listening.

Harry T. Hunt sets out a framework of concepts for researching the presentational states that Cage regarded as central to his music. After a

53. Ibid., 549.

survey of the field, Hunt points to the "peak experience" of Abraham Maslow and the "flow experience" of Mihalyi Csikszentmihalyi as concepts of the core condition:

> All these terms describe a special sense of felt reality and clarity, with a concomitant sense of exhilaration, freedom, and release. Such experience is also involved in many accounts of lucid dreaming, where the sudden realization that one is dreaming entails a special attention to one's immediate here-and-now experience for its own sake and in a way that is rare, not only within ordinary dreaming but in everyday life as well. This sense of vital presence is sought more formally as the "subtle" or "imaginal" body experience of the meditative traditions.[54]

Performing and listening in the presentational state allow felt meanings, a sense of vital presence, and subtle or imaginal body phenomena to come into consciousness, and so we need to develop a methodology for working with such outcomes of aesthetic experience. These features of the peak or flow experience are vital elements of Cage's musical actions, but he would prefer that, like *satori,* they be natural, everyday occurrences rather than occasional flights into "higher consciousness."

Experimental music as Cage conceives it greatly emphasizes presentation over representation and, by so doing, points up the fundamental importance of presentation to all aesthetic experience. As we have already found, representation and presentation are complementary. In fact, it can be shown that activating the presentational state enhances greatly reception of the representational aspects of an artwork.[55] If presentational states in music are valued, then felt meanings, subtle body experiences, and creative outcomes will be accepted as an essential part of musical experience. This calls for understanding how the liminal zone between the conscious and the unconscious is mediated by the imaginal intelligence. The dadaists and surrealists were familiar with these principles from their experiments with automatic writing, dream imagery, collage, frottage, and the stream of consciousness. In this respect, Cage's experimental music belongs to the history of artistic and psychological investigations of the active imagination.[56] We must beware

54. *On the Nature of Consciousness,* 200.

55. An installation at the Art Gallery of Ontario (Toronto) was designed to evoke the presentational state in the visitor while in the presence of an artwork. Visitors listen to a thirteen-minute audio program that guides them through an active imagination exercise while viewing the painting *The Beaver Dam* by J. E. H. MacDonald. The installation has been in operation since January 1993. See my "The Sounds of Dry Paint: Animating the Imagination in a Gallery of Art," *Musicworks* 63 (fall 1995): 20–27.

56. Among many sources for this literature, see Lucy R. Lippard, ed., *Surrealists on Art* (Englewood Cliffs, N.J.: Prentice Hall, 1970), and *Dadas on Art* (Englewood Cliffs, N.J.: Prentice Hall, 1971).

the rationalistic prejudice that the data of mental experience cannot be independently tested and verified. But support is now on its way even from the tough-minded (as James liked to call rationalists). Some leading neurobiologists now affirm that the era of stimulus-response behaviorism is well and truly dead, that all mentation is mediated by imagery, and that concepts of value and the self may have a neural basis.[57] Nevertheless, it will take still more evidence to persuade the tough-minded that the unconscious is a domain of the mind and has a noetic function for consciousness.

Those who are interested in the background to James's pragmatism will find it fascinating to explore the extensive literature of research in psychic phenomena from the late nineteenth century.[58] In the present era, psychologists and psychiatrists have come to posit a border zone between consciousness and the unconscious in which mental experiences occur that confound logical reasoning and literal thinking. James defended his interest in this area from those who want to reduce every mental phenomenon to biology, for whom "ideals appear as inert by-products of physiology," and who explain what is higher by what is lower and treat it forever as a case of "nothing but something else of a quite inferior sort." In his book on religious experience, James referred to the liminal zone as the region where we come in touch with what he referred to as the mind's "germinal higher part": an individual "becomes conscious that this higher part is conterminous and continuous with a MORE of the same quality, which is operative in the universe outside of him, and which he can keep in working touch with, and in a fashion get on board of and save himself when all his lower being has gone to pieces in the wreck."[59] "Primary consciousness" for James is what we now refer to as ordinary ego consciousness, whereas the "primary process" for Freud is the unconscious, and the "secondary process" refers to ordinary ego consciousness. That the notion of what is primary shifted from consciousness with James to the unconscious with Freud conveys the fundamental change of emphasis that ushered in the era of depth psychology. The intermediate or liminal zone between the unconscious and the conscious is called by Jung the "transcendent function" because it transcends the standpoints of both the ego and the unconscious. In language reminiscent of Dewey's description of aesthetic experience, Jung

57. See, for instance, Antonio Damasio, *Descartes' Error: Emotion, Reason, and the Human Brain* (New York: Putnam, 1994), 280. Damasio gives a nod to William James, who, he says, "might be pleased to discover that today there are plausible if not yet proven hypotheses for the neural basis of the self" (244).

58. Cf. Ellenberger, "On the Threshold of a New Dynamic Psychiatry," chapter 5 in *Discovery of the Unconscious.*

59. James, *Pragmatism*, 6; *Varieties of Religious Experience*, 484.

defines the transcendent function as the union of the opposites, the conscious and the unconscious, but goes further in defining the outcome of this union. For Jung the transcendent function generates an irrational life-process that expresses itself in images out of which arise new conscious attitudes. This "rounding out of the personality into a whole may well be the goal of any psychotherapy that claims to be more than a mere cure of symptoms." [60] The idea of a transcendent function that has a noetic value for the ego also underlies Cage's descriptions of the effects of the music of indeterminacy [12b].

The study of the liminal zone between the conscious and the unconscious was advanced by D. W. Winnicott, who referred to a "transitional space," which he defined as a potential, or intermediate, or third area in which the cultural experience that is a derivative of play arises. Silvano Arieti was the first to name the area of intersection between the primary and secondary processes the tertiary process and to identify it as the source of creativity: "The tertiary process ultimately comes into being as a 'click,' or match, between the primary and secondary processes, which brings about an accepted emerging representation. Eureka! The new unity is created!" The psychoanalyst Nathan Schwartz-Salant describes the phenomenon of the "tertiary process" as follows: "This space is a transitional area between the space-time world (where processes are characterized as an interaction of objects) and the collective unconscious—the *pleroma*. This area has a fundamentally different quality from the space-time world. In its pathological form, the pleroma invades the conscious personality as primary-process thinking. But in its creative form, it is the source of healing through one's experience of the *numinosum*." [61] The experience described here, one that occurs between two individuals, is similar in many respects to presentational states arising from aesthetic encounters with an artwork. Both have outcomes that are felt to be illuminating, healing, and numinous.

Cage regarded experimental music as a means of investigating hidden regions of the mind and spirit, and the excitement he conveyed to Boulez in their correspondence is that of someone setting off to explore an unknown continent. Cage believed that he was conducting leading-edge research in an area of immense potentiality, which was correct so far as music was concerned. Although composers such as Richard Wagner have reported that they create music by activating the imagination in the tertiary process, Cage intended that musicians perform from that mode also.

As one enters the tertiary process, the categories that appear distinct

60. Jung, "A Study in the Process of Individuation," 289.

61. *The Borderline Personality: Vision and Healing* (Wilmette, Ill.: Chiron Publications, 1989), 107.

in the secondary process of the rational space-time world begin to blur and the imagination takes over as the principal faculty. Synaesthesia is the norm, with sense modalities (vision, hearing, touch, bodily sensations, and spatial perceptions, etc.) blending in surprising combinations.[62] Past and future interflow with the here-and-now. Logical and causal orderings give way to acausal synchronicities. And last but not least, the borders between body, mind, and spirit begin to dissolve, which accounts for subtle body phenomena and the numinosity of experiences in the tertiary process. Cage indicated his familiarity with the tertiary process in a rich trove of language: lost awareness of time and space [3b], deeply pleasurable moments of completeness [3c], the air so alive that one is simply part of it [7d], sounds centered within themselves in an infinite play of interpenetration [9, 10a], the union of spirit and matter that partakes of the miraculous [10b], moving out in all directions from the center when time is luminous [11], not interrupting the fluency of nature [12a], and the participation of life in sounds [17b]. These evocations of the presentational state convey the effects of the mind, body, and spirit as they merge with sound, and in particular the perception that the individual's physical body takes on an imaginal or virtual form, which is sometimes referred to as the subtle body. That the subtle body experience is a normal outcome of activating the tertiary process is affirmed by Schwartz-Salant: "The subtle body can be experienced imaginally as a kind of energy field that extends from our physical being. While invisible to ordinary perceptions, it can be seen imaginally. . . . The question is not whether or not the subtle body exists, but whether or not its existence can be perceived. For when we deal with the subtle body, we are concerned not with ordinary perceptions but with imaginal ones."[63] Since the presentational state immerses one in "imaginal" perceptions, it is not surprising that many musicians have found it difficult to adapt to indeterminate music. Some of the resistance that Cage encountered, and which he interpreted as opposition to change and labeled the "social problem," can be understood as a justifiable apprehension about activating the tertiary process among those who are unfamiliar with its effects.

In 1912 and 1913, when Jung undertook explorations of his own psyche during the crisis that followed the break with Freud, he discovered that the tertiary process can be employed in a therapeutic fashion. Later he used the technique with his patients and soon recognized that

62. Hunt makes an important case for synaesthesia, or cross-modal translation, as the basis of cognition in presentational states. See *On the Nature of Consciousness*, chap. 7. My own research in musical imagery from the tertiary process documents many narratives that embody cross-modal and numinous experiences, and archetypal images for music. See "Uncursing the Silence: An Exploration of Sonic Imagination," *Musicworks* 57 (winter 1994): 38–46.

63. *The Borderline Personality*, 132–33.

he needed to make a distinction between the passive fantasy, which is dystonic and harmful to the ego standpoint, and the active fantasy which is syntonic and highly creative:

> Whereas passive fantasy not infrequently bears a morbid stamp or at least shows some traces of abnormality, active fantasy is one of the highest forms of psychic activity. For here the conscious and the unconscious personality of the subject flow together into a common product in which both are unified. Such a fantasy can be the highest expression of a person's individuality, and it may even create that individuality by giving perfect expression to its unity.[64]

During the 1920s, Jung developed what he called the active imagination method in order to stimulate the active fantasy through drawing, body movement, and automatic writing. When Richard Wilhelm in 1928 sent Jung his German translation of the Taoist manual on meditation and alchemy, *The Secret of the Golden Flower,* Jung was delighted to find confirmation of his work on active imagination from a hitherto unknown source. His commentary on that text describes active imagination as a technique that needs to be continued until the rational mind relaxes its hold, that is, "until one can let things happen, which is the next goal of the exercise. In this way a new attitude is created, an attitude that accepts the irrational and the incomprehensible simply because it is happening."[65]

At the same time as Jung was experimenting with active imagination as a therapeutic method, and in the same city of Zurich, Jean Arp, Sophie Tauber, and others were investigating the tertiary process in the interests of revolutionizing art. Arp describes how he and Tauber began in 1915 to paint, embroider, and do collages drawn from the simplest forms, which were the first examples of what he came to call "concrete art." For Arp, concrete art rather than abstract art gives direct and palpable shape to inner reality, "for nothing is more concrete than the psychic reality that it expresses." And so he focused on presentational states: "We rejected all mimesis and description, giving free rein to the elementary and the spontaneous."[66] Max Ernst admitted images from dreams and active fantasy, but did not paint his dreams as such. In 1934 he wrote that surrealists do not paint their dreams, which would be descriptive and naive naturalism, but rather, "they freely, bravely, and self-confidently move about in the borderland between the internal and

64. "Psychological Types" (1921), in *CW* 6:428.

65. Jung, foreword to the second German edition of *The Secret of the Golden Flower,* in *CW* 13:16–17. Wilhelm's German translation of the Chinese text together with Jung's commentary was published in 1929. It appeared in English, translated by Cary F. Baynes, in 1931.

66. *Arp on Arp: Poems, Essays, Memories,* ed. Marcel Jean, trans. Joachim Neugroschel (New York: Viking, 1966), 222, 232. The items were written in 1948.

external worlds which are still unfamiliar though physically and psychologically quite real ('sur-real'), registering what they see and experience there, and intervening where their revolutionary instincts advise them to do so."[67] Ernst is describing here the artist's experience of James's subliminal consciousness and Jung's transcendent function. For these pioneers of the tertiary process, chance was an essential means for exploring the liminal zone between the conscious and the unconscious. Arp wrote, "Since the arrangements of planes and their proportions and colors seemed to hinge solely on chance, I declared that these works were arranged 'according to the law of chance,' as in the order of nature, chance being for me simply a part of an inexplicable reason, of an inaccessible order."[68] Arp's friend and colleague Hans Richter also recalled discovering the importance of chance: "Chance appeared to us as a magical procedure by which one could transcend the barriers of causality and of conscious volition, and by which the inner eye and ear became more acute, so that new sequences of thoughts and experiences made their appearance. For us, chance was the 'unconscious mind' that Freud had discovered in 1900."[69]

Chance was the path of liberation out of the categorical constraints that separated art from life. But chance also had another purpose, which was to restore to the work of art its immediacy and primeval power: "By appealing directly to the unconscious, which is part and parcel of chance, we sought to restore to the work of art something of its numinous quality of which art has been the vehicle since time immemorial, the incantatory power that we seek, in this age of general unbelief, more than ever before." Richter linked Arp's belief that the law of chance could only be comprehended by complete surrender to the unconscious to Jung's notion of synchronicity.[70] Richter and Arp found that engagement in the tertiary process had a numinous effect, and they looked to Kandinsky as the artist who reclaimed for art the spiritual dimension. In an appreciation of Kandinsky, Arp wrote, "He discovered 'the spiritual in art.' An explorer like Kandinsky particularly stresses the invisible, impalpable life that our defective eyes cannot distinguish and that sometimes leads the explorer along the angel's road."[71]

Thus more than three decades before Cage created his experimental music with chance operations in a search for "the spiritual in music,"

67. "What Is Surrealism," in Lippard, *Surrealists on Art,* 136.

68. "Dadaland," in *Arp on Arp,* 232.

69. *Dada: Art and Anti-Art* (New York: Abrams, 1965), 55. The The term "unconscious mind" is from the book Jung wrote in collaboration with the physicist Wolfgang Pauli, *The Interpretation of Nature and the Psyche* (New York: Pantheon Books, 1955).

70. Ibid., 59, 57.

71. "Kandinsky" (1948), in *Arp on Arp,* 228.

the dadaists and surrealists found that chance engaged the tertiary process and released numinous felt meanings from the liminal zone of imaginal cognition. Arp describing what happened in 1917 prefigures Cage in 1950: "I became more and more removed from aesthetics. I wanted to find another order, another value for man in nature. . . . Dada wanted to replace the logical non-sense of the men of today by the illogically senseless. . . . Dada is for nature and against art."[72] Both Arp and Cage regarded chance as the means by which they could remove taste, memory, and tradition from art and infuse it with the numinous.

In this perspective, Cage's experimental music is the long-delayed application to music of a development that had begun thirty-five years earlier in the other arts. This confirms the notion that in some respects music is an extremely conservative art form. That the experimental revolution in music was delayed does not diminish the achievement of Cage and others who sought to revolutionize the traditional concept of the musical composition as the *opus perfectum et absolutum.* Cage's accomplishment as a composer can be seen in the imaginative and resourceful playfulness with which he adjusted the framing of the presentational state that will activate the musician's tertiary process. If the schema is too loose, the musician has too much freedom and the imagination is not sufficiently engaged. If the schema is too tightly controlled, the response is not spontaneous enough, and the musical imagination has too little scope. Finally, in the time-bracket pieces, Cage achieved a sensitive balance between too tight and too loose a frame. And yet in the 1990s, in the city that had seen the inception of depth psychological approaches in the arts and psychotherapy, the musicians of the opera orchestra were not able to perform Cage's *Europeras* satisfactorily. Conservatories and music schools evidently still do not equip musicians to make music out of the presentational state. Cage's contribution as a composer will be fully realized only when musicians can make music in the tertiary process by engaging in spontaneous music making that activates the creative imagination. The fear that experimental music seeks the destruction of composed music will abate if we can establish that presentational and representational states are complementary. But this calls for a program that will help traditionally trained musicians make what Margaret Leng Tan described as her leap of faith.

VI. Preparing to Perform Experimental Music

Research into musical experience in the presentational state is needed so that we can guide students to perform and listen to experimental mu-

72. "I became more and more removed from aesthetics" (1948), in *Arp on Arp,* 237–38. The analogies between Cage's music post-1950 to the aesthetic of Satie and to the experiments of

sic. It is only by undergoing such activities and discovering the results for ourselves that we overcome our mistrust. We need to take a leaf out of James and look *"away from first things, principles, 'categories,' supposed necessities"* and turn *"towards last things, fruits, consequences, facts."*[73] A pragmatic attitude to transpersonal experience accepts the outcomes in spite of inhibitions and preconceptions. A pilot project in the application of the presentational state was designed with that objective in mind. In the fall of 1996, over the course of seven weeks, a small group of graduate student volunteers from York University in Toronto undertook a program of musical exercises that activated the tertiary process. Meeting once a week for about three hours, the students engaged in a variety of activities. There is space here to mention only one component of the program, a two-phase exercise for imagining music in silence: Working in pairs, participants sit in chairs facing each other.[74] First they are asked to imagine a musical solo. After six minutes, they are asked to write about or draw what they have imagined. Then they share their experiences and the discussion is taped. For the second phase, they again sit in pairs and this time imagine performing a musical duet with the partner. After six minutes, they again write or draw the results and then share with the group.

In general, participants respond to the duet exercise by imagining that they are engaged in a musical exchange as separate individuals. Then, after a while, they experience an entity to which both partners seem to contribute actively. In the pilot project, Participant A (female, candidate for the master's degree in education) and Participant B (female, vocalist, candidate for the master's degree in women's studies and music) were partners at the beginning of the exercise. Participant A reported the imagined entity as light energy that formed a strong, harmonious bond with her partner, while Participant B reported that it was a column made of sounds and colored lights that took shape between them and became an egglike form: "I felt that right between us there was this round thing made out of lights and blues and purples. It was music also. It was both of our musics together, so it wasn't one answering the other—it was both of them occurring at the same time as one. I

Arp, Richter, and others in the visual arts after World War I put in question the view that Cage's experimental music is a precursor of postmodernism (cf. Hamm, "Privileging the Moment," 278–79), or "ultra-modernism" (cf. Patterson, "Appraising the Catchwords," 241). If Cage's position can be demonstrated to be postmodern, we may have to posit that the seeds of the reaction to modernism were sown simultaneously with those of modernism itself, and that the two position have coexisted as shadow aspects of each other throughout the twentieth century.

73. *Pragmatism,* 22; James's italics.

74. The exercise was modeled after one used by Henry Reed. See "Close Encounters in the Liminal Zone: Experiments in Imaginal Communication," *Journal of Analytical Psychology* 41, no. 1 (1996): 81–116 (part 1); 41, no. 2 (1996): 203–26 (part 2).

knew that both of our sounds were together." With no other stimulus or guidance than the instruction to imagine a musical solo and then a duet, the transitional space between the participants became a highly charged transpersonal field of synaesthetic images. Each participant perceived that her separate identities had merged in a mutually generated "third thing" that was different from what either contributed alone.

At the next session, the same exercise was repeated with different partners. The following is a synopsis of the exchange between Participant A and Participant C (female, zheng player, Ph.D. candidate in musicology):

> PARTICIPANT A: We started with spirals and it kept turning into figure eights. And it was all over the place. It wasn't just going up, it was all over, and it was all movement. Waltzes kept coming in. There was this spiral that's pulling down and collecting up. Plunging and diving. That is bizarre! It was so physical! We were just dancing and colliding together and moving in and moving out. Very amazing! My jaw was just dropping when you were speaking. Wow! Those figure eights, and moving!
>
> PARTICIPANT C: It was really, really amazing—swirling upwards. It is also a geometric figure that gets into my mind, and I also started off with woodwinds. A very sinuous figure goes in the shape of an eight, but in three dimensions, definitely. Full of motion and energy at a very, very fast pace. At first this shape goes at a plane level between my head and yours, and we are exchanging. This really comes back and forth between us and includes our bodies, so it goes around us. And then it runs into a vertical shape where we dance around, kind of up and down. The whole shape is moving all the time, never ending. And we bump against each other; we are dancing. And a whole orchestra was there—I can't even differentiate the sound. It was such a lively, vibrant situation! We were just having fun frolicking.

This exercise again produced an intense engagement between the participants, who imagined a highly active and playful exchange of audial, spatial, and kinesthetic elements. The mutual energy field was manifested in a geometrical form, which for C was a figure eight that was at first horizontal and then became vertical, and for A was a spiral that turned into a figure eight, which also had a vertical orientation. The similarities between their images astonished the two participants greatly.

The results of this exercise have a precedent in the findings of psychologist Henry Reed, who conducted experiments in transpersonal communication with large numbers of participants. His informants reported similar spiraling energy forms, heightened states of awareness, synchronous images, synaesthesias, and intense felt meanings.[75] It can be affirmed that sitting and intending mutual musical communication results in the activation of a transpersonal field of collaborative images that are valued as enriching, pleasurable, and creative. We can suppose that musicians who have developed this ability will bring an awareness of the tertiary process to any music they play, whether a Haydn trio or a time-bracket piece by Cage.

Although he was active as a writer and a visual artist, Cage found music appealing as a medium because the performance situation offers a model for the relationship between the individual and society. Cage often defined his goal as the spiritual transformation of the individual on the assumption that social change begins with individual change. The data from the pilot program in presentational states lend support to Cage's premise that focusing on transpersonal communication has an effect on social interactions. Four to six weeks after the last session, the participants were interviewed and asked to comment on the effects of the program. Participant A remarked in particular on how impressed she was by the silent solos and duets. She spoke of the exchanges with her partners as definitely changing her idea of how to relate to another person. She had realized that communication is more than just separate individuals sending and receiving information—"something else" is also present: "It became a living breathing entity, we created another life, or another experience, or another energy. . . . Just the awareness of doing a duet with somebody changed the whole communication process in terms of relating with other people and realizing that it's not just an exchange of my words and their words, and my hearing and their hearing, but this flow starts to happen." She found that becoming aware of the "flow" experience revealed that communication takes place against a transpersonal background. She said, "It creates a kind of sacredness about life or about the connection between people. It gives a whole different idea of what community really is. And it is totally the unseen world."

Cage evidently trusted that musicians who bring a similar attitude to performing his pieces will create music together in a spiritually enriching social context. His experimental music assumes that with sufficient discipline and devotion the flow experience will happen, and the music will become manifest as "the third thing." But, as Margaret Leng Tan shows us, it takes practice to ensure that that "it" will play. At the core of the musician's problem is what Cage identified as the alienation of Art from Nature, which on a personal level becomes a split between music and the musician. A fourth participant in the pilot program, a Ph.D. can-

75. Ibid., part 2, 220.

didate in musicology and professional pianist spoke to this issue when she reflected on the effect the program had on her:

> PARTICIPANT D: I did feel a kind of reconnection with the musical part of myself. I didn't feel as much as if it was me here and music over there. . . . I was the music in a sense. . . . The music was already there, and it was a question of just letting go, and relaxing, and letting it happen. In summary, I felt music was within me, and music was a part of who I was, who I am. . . . It was a blending of the exercises in which we discovered things about ourselves, like the drawings, or when we threw the *I Ching* and interpreted it, that blended with the idea of the music, of listening to music, and talking about music, made me feel more like the music was my own too. I didn't feel that it was an object of study. It was just very natural.

For this participant, the program had allowed the music, which had been identified with the ego-system, to find a place in the self-system. Her words resonate with Cage's desire that music provide a moment when the multiplicity of elements that make up an individual become integrated and she is one [3b].

VII. Conclusion

In the tertiary process, opposites conjoin and paradox is at home. It is where we experience nonobstruction and interpenetration, and purposeful purposelessness. We should expect that here, too, the competing claims between the individual and the social will be reconciled. Harry Hunt points out that the fathers of the pragmatic approach to the transpersonal addressed this problem, which they saw as the need for spirituality: "James, Jung, and contemporary transpersonal psychology understand our crisis as a loss of 'soul,' 'inwardness,' or 'sense of meaning'—the loss of a sense of being and felt reality of equal concern to Heidegger's analysis of culture and to the psychoanalysis of Winnicott." As I noted at the beginning of this essay, when Cage expressed the same need, many interpreted it as a retreat into solipsism. But, Hunt argues, the move to inwardness and transpersonal experience is not a denial of the social:

> Indeed their psychological conception of religious experience makes James, Jung and contemporary transpersonal psychology both the beginnings of a "science" of what is traditionally termed "soul" and the outward expressions of this sociocultural shift toward inner-worldly mysticism. The search for a holistic cognitive psychology and neurophysiology of the transpersonal can be seen both as a genuine extension of the science of mind and as an expression of incipient social collectivity.[76]

76. *On the Nature of Consciousness*, 279–80, 281.

In this perspective, Cage belongs among those who suppose a radical reflexivity between the individual and the social. Hunt suggests that Durkheim's conception of an emergent collective consciousness is most directly expressed in the shared unity of presentational states. He finds that while Durkheim's collective consciousness has been studied in respect to public opinion in complex societies, what has been bypassed is Durkheim's assertion "that the fullest access to a collective consciousness will be through the maximum development of the very presentational states that modern society has come to regard as the most inward and subjective."[77] While the surrealists had explored this premise in the years between the world wars, Cage was in the forefront of its application to music in the second half of the century. Cage focused on a music of *satori*-like presentational states because he found they generate experiences in which individual and social meanings interpenetrate. His pieces offer occasions for realizing the intent of each moment in invented musical images that are both personally and collectively meaningful even though the meanings cannot be otherwise represented than in their effects. The tough-minded continue to look askance at Cage's belief in the immanence of spirit in music and nature. They will need to reckon with the facts of experience evoked readily and reliably from activating the tertiary process through experimental compositions or other exercises for the musical imagination. Hunt proposes that such facts be referred to a holistic cognitive psychology or a neurophysiology of the transpersonal. On the basis of such an approach, music theorists and historians would be able to treat the effects of performing music, including *4′33″*, as constitutive of the music itself.

For James, the universe of the rationalist has many editions, "one real one, the infinite folio, or *édition de luxe,* eternally complete; and then the various finite editions, full of false readings, distorted and mutilated each in its own way." Indeed Joan Retallack finds that the irony and skepticism of critical theory is inimical to Cage, who like James recommends to us the universe as it actually is. Cage thus stands in the tradition of James, who finds "only one edition of the universe, unfinished, growing in all sort of places, especially in the places where thinking beings are at work." By insisting on the transpersonal effects of musical experience, Cage asks that we regard the acts of performing and listening as means of continuing the process of creating that pragmatic universe. And so he would surely have agreed with James:

> Our acts, our turning-places, where we seem to ourselves to make ourselves and grow, are the parts of the world to which we are closest, the parts of which our knowledge is the most intimate and complete. Why

77. Ibid., 286.

> should we not take them at their face-value? Why may they not be the actual turning-places and growing-places which they seem to be, of the world—why not the workshop of being, where we catch fact in the making, so that nowhere may the world grow in any other kind of way than this?[78]

Cage hoped that his music of indeterminacy would provide a means of contributing to that pragmatic universe the "facts in the making" from the individual and shared invention of such music.

APPENDIX

Quotes

1. What can we expect to be the result of attentive listening to music? I believe that listening to music makes for our lives another world, living in which, somehow, our hearts beat faster and a mysterious excitement fills us. And the natural flow of sounds which music is reassures us of order just as the sequence of the seasons and the regular alternation of night and day do.

"Listening to Music" [c. 1937], in *John Cage: Writer,* 19

2. Schoenberg analyzes and fragmentizes his music, so that he seems with Freud to be a founding father of today's cult of the neurosis. The composers who today wish to imbue their music with the ineffable, seem to find it necessary to make use of musical characteristics not purely Western; they go for inspiration to those places, or return to those times, where or when harmony is not of the essence.

"The East in the West" [1946], in *John Cage: Writer,* 25

3a. Lou Harrison found a passage by Thomas Mace written in England in 1676 to the effect that the purpose of music was to season and sober the mind, thus making it susceptible of divine influences, and elevating one's affections to goodness.

"A Composer's Confessions" [1948], in *John Cage: Writer,* 41

b. After eighteen months of studying oriental and medieval Christian philosophy and mysticism, I began to read Jung on the integration of the personality. There are two principal parts of each personality: the conscious mind and the unconscious, and these are split and dispersed, in most of us, in countless ways and directions. The function of music, like that of any other healthy occupation, is to help to bring those separate parts back together again. Music does this by providing a moment when, awareness of time and space being lost, the multiplicity of elements which make up an individual become integrated and he is one. This only happens if, in the presence of

78. *Pragmatism,* 100, 111.

music, one does not allow himself to fall into laziness or distraction. . . . Neuroses act to stop and block. To be able to compose signifies the overcoming of these obstacles.

Ibid., 41–42

c. If one makes music, as the Orient would say, *disinterestedly,* that is, without concern for money or fame but simply for the love of making it, it is an integrating activity and one will find moments in life that are complete and fulfilled. Sometimes composing does it, sometimes playing an instrument, and sometimes just listening. . . .

We were simply transported. I think the answer to this riddle is simply that when the music was composed the composers were at one with themselves. The performers became disinterested to the point that they became unselfconscious, and a few listeners in those brief moments of listening forgot themselves, enraptured, and so gained themselves. It is these moments of completeness that music can give, providing one can concentrate one's mind on it, that is, give one's self in return to the music, that are such deep pleasure, and that is why we love the art.

Ibid., 42

4. The function of a piece of music and, in fact, the final meaning of music may be suggested: it is to bring into co-being elements paradoxical by nature, to bring into one situation elements that can be and ought to be agreed upon—that is, Law elements—together with elements that cannot and ought not to be agreed upon—that is, Freedom elements—these two ornamented by other elements, which may lend support to one or the other of the two fundamental and opposed elements, the whole forming thereby an organic entity.

Music then is a problem parallel to that of the integration of the personality: which in terms of modern psychology is the co-being of the conscious and the unconscious mind, Law and Freedom, in a random world situation. Good music can act as a guide to good living.

"Defense of Satie" [1948], in *John Cage: An Anthology,* 84

5. *The purpose of music.* Music is edifying, for from time to time it sets the soul in operation. The soul is the gatherer-together of the disparate elements (Meister Eckhart), and its work fills one with peace and love. . . . *Strategy.* As is repeated . . . schematically [see fig. 3.1 above], structure is properly mind-controlled. Both delight in precision, clarity, and the observance of rules. Whereas form wants only freedom to be. It belongs to the heart; and the law it observes, if indeed it submits to any, has never been and never will be written. [*footnote:* Any attempt to exclude the "irrational" is irrational. Any composing strategy which is wholly "rational" is irrational in the extreme.]

"Forerunners of Modern Music" [1949], in
The Boulez-Cage Correspondence, 38

6. Slowly, as the talk goes on, slowly, we have the feeling we are getting nowhere. That is a pleasure which will continue. If we are irritated, it is not a pleasure. Nothing is not a pleasure if one is irritated, but suddenly, it is a pleasure, and then more and more it is not irritating (and the more and more and slowly). Originally we were nowhere; and now, again, we are having the pleasure of being slowly nowhere. If anybody is sleepy, let him go to sleep. * * * That is finished now. It was a pleasure.

"Lecture on Nothing" [1950], in *Silence,* 123–24

7a. I have just finished recording my cinema music. I started that piece of work in a dream: I wanted to write without musical ideas (unrelated sounds) and record the results 4 times, changing the position of the nails each time. . . . I abandoned the dream and I wrote some music. . . . Chance comes in here to give us the unknown.

Letter to Pierre Boulez, January 1950, in
The Boulez-Cage Correspondence, 48

b. All this brings me closer to a "chance" or if you like to an un-aesthetic choice. I keep, of course, the means of rhythmic structure feeling that that is the "espace sonore" in which [each] of these sounds may exist and change. Composition becomes "throwing sound into silence" and rhythm which in my Sonatas had been one of breathing becomes one of a flow of sound and silence.

Letter to Pierre Boulez, December 1950, in ibid., 78

c. [Re the Calder music] No synchronizing was attempted and what the final result is is *[sic]* rather due to a chance that was admired. . . .

. . . At this point my primary concern became: how to become mobile in my thought rather than immobile always. And then I saw one day that there was no incompatibility between mobility & immobility and life contains both. This is at the basis of the manner of using the *I-Ching* for the obtaining of oracles. . . .

[After explaining the use of the *I Ching.*] I have the feeling of just beginning to compose for the first time. I will soon send you a copy of the first part of the piano piece *[Music of Changes].* The essential underlying idea is that each thing is itself, that its relations with other things spring up naturally rather than being imposed by any abstraction on an "artist's" part.

Letter to Pierre Boulez, May 1951, in ibid., 93, 94, 96

d. The experience of the 8 loudspeakers is extraordinary. There is no room for anything but immediate listening. The air was so alive one was simply part of it.

Letter to Pierre Boulez, May 1953, in ibid., 143

8. [T]he accepting of what comes without preconceived ideas of what will happen and regardless of the consequences. This is, by the way, why it is so difficult to listen to music we are familiar with; memory has acted to keep us aware of what will happen next, and so it is almost impossible to remain alive in the presence of a well-known masterpiece. Now and then it happens, and when it does, it partakes of the miraculous. Going on about what someone said: at the root of the desire to appreciate a piece of music, to call it this rather than that, to hear it without the unavoidable extraneous sounds—at the root of all this is the idea that this work is a thing separate from the rest of life, which is not the case with Feldman's music. We are in the presence not of a work of art which is a thing but of an action which is implicitly nothing. Nothing has been said. Nothing is communicated. And there is no use of symbols or intellectual references. No thing in life requires a symbol since it is clearly what it is: a visible manifestation of an invisible nothing.

"Lecture on Something" [1951], in *Silence*, 136

9. It is thus possible to make a musical composition the continuity of which is free of individual taste and memory (psychology) and also of the literature and "traditions" of the art. The sounds enter the time-space centered within themselves, unimpeded by service to any abstraction, their 360 degrees of circumference free for an infinite play of interpenetration.

Value judgments are not in the nature of this work as regards either composition, performance, or listening. The idea of relation (the idea: 2) being absent, anything (the idea: 1) may happen. A "mistake" is beside the point, for once anything happens it authentically is.

"Composition: To Describe the Process of Composition Used in *Music of Changes* and *Imaginary Landscape No. 4*" [1952], in *Silence*, 59

10a. And I imagine that as contemporary music goes on changing in the way that I am changing it what will be done is to more and more completely liberate sounds from abstract ideas about them and more and more exactly to let them be physically, uniquely, themselves. This means for me: knowing more and more not what I think a sound is, but what it actually is in all of its acoustical details and then letting this sound exist, itself, changing in a changing sonorous environment.

They are with respect to counterpoint, melody, harmony, rhythm, and any other musical methods, pointless. They are indeed without purpose but in their purposelessness expressing life itself which centers out from them in every direction. Silence surrounds many of the sounds so that they exist in space unimpeded by one another and yet interpenetrating one another for the reason that Feldman has done nothing to keep them from being themselves.

"Juilliard Lecture" [1952], in *A Year from Monday*, 100

b. To accept whatever comes, regardless of the consequences, is to be unafraid or to be full of that love which comes from a sense of at-oneness with whatever. . . .

. . . In other words there is no split between spirit and matter. And to realize this, we have only suddenly to awake to the fact. I have noticed it happens and when it does it partakes of the miraculous.

Ibid., 105, 111

11. That two or more / things happen at the same time is / It is entirely possible for something to // their relationship: Synchronicity. That / Break for instance / means at the center moving out in all // directions and then time is clearly / Should one stop and mend it? / luminous. It could not be easily otherwise.

"45′ for a Speaker" [1954], in *Silence,* 184

12a. [The performer] may perform his function of colorist in a way which is not consciously organized (and therefore not subject to analysis)—either arbitrarily, feeling his way, following the dictates of his ego; or more or less unknowingly, by going inwards with reference to the structure of his mind to a point in dreams, following, as in automatic writing, the dictates of his subconscious mind; or to a point in the collective unconsciousness of Jungian psychoanalysis, following the inclinations of the species and doing something of more or less universal interest to human beings; or to the "deep sleep" of Indian mental practice—the Ground of Meister Eckhart—identifying there with no matter what eventuality. Or he may perform his function of colorist arbitrarily, by going outwards with reference to the structure of his mind to the point of sense perception, following his taste; or more or less unknowingly by employing some operation exterior to his mind: tables of random numbers, following the scientific interest in probability; or chance operations, identifying there with no matter what eventuality.

"Indeterminacy" [1958], in *Silence,* 35

b. How is each performer to fulfill this function of being alert in an indeterminate situation? Does he need to proceed cautiously in dualistic terms? On the contrary, he needs his mind in one piece. His mind is too busy to spend time splitting itself into conscious and not-conscious parts. These parts, however, are still present. What has happened is simply a complete change of direction. Rather than making the not-conscious parts face the conscious part of the mind, the conscious part, by reason of the urgency and indeterminacy of the situation, turns towards the not-conscious parts. He is therefore able, as before, to add two to two to get four, or to act in organized ways which on being subjected to analysis successfully are found to be more complex. But rather than concentrating his attention here, in the realm of relationships, variations, approximations, repetitions, logarithms, his attention is given inwardly and outwardly with reference to the structure of his mind to no matter what eventuality. Turning away from himself and his ego-sense of separation from other beings and things, he faces the Ground of Meister Eckhart, from which all impermanencies flow and to which they return. "Thoughts arise not to be collected and cherished but to be dropped as though they were void." . . . Similarly in the performance of *Duo II for Pianists*, each performer, when he performs in a way consistent with the composition as written, will let go of his feelings, his taste, his automatism, his sense of the universal, not attaching himself to this or to that, leaving by his performance no traces, providing by his actions no interruption to the fluency of nature. The performer therefore simply does what is to be done, not splitting his mind in two, not separating it from his body, which is kept ready for direct and instantaneous contact with his instrument.

Ibid., 39

c. A performance of a composition which is indeterminate of its performance is necessarily unique. It cannot be repeated. When performed for a second time, the outcome is other than it was. Nothing therefore is accomplished by such a performance, since that performance cannot be grasped as an object in time. A recording of such a work has no more value than a postcard; it provides a knowledge of something that happened, whereas the action was a non-knowledge of something that had not yet happened.

Ibid.

d. There is the possibility when people are crowded together that they will act like sheep rather than nobly. That is why separation in space is spoken of as facilitating independent action on the part of each performer. Sounds will then arise from actions, which will then arise from their own centers rather than as motor or psychological effects of other actions and sounds in the environment.

Ibid.

13. What is the nature of an experimental action? It is simply an action the outcome of which is not foreseen. . . . However, more essential than composing by means of chance operations, it seems to me now, is composing in such a way that what one does is indeterminate of its performance. In such a case one can just work directly, for nothing one does gives rise to anything that is preconceived. . . .

Why is this so necessary that sounds should be just sounds? There are many ways of saying why. One is this: In order that each sound may become the Buddha. If that is too Oriental an expression, take the Christian Gnostic statement: "Split the stick and there is Jesus."

"History of Experimental Music in the United States" [1958],
in *Silence*, 69–70

14. One cannot determine exactly what effect the notation causes—thus indeterminacy. The observer-listener is able to stop saying I do not understand, since no point-to-point linear communication has been attempted. He is at his own center (impermanent) of total space-time. How are his ears and eyes? Serious questions. The complex of existence exceeds mentation's compass. Emptiness of purpose does not imply contempt for society, rather assumes that each person whether he knows it or not is noble, is able to experience gifts with generosity, that society is best anarchic.

"Form Is a Language" [1960], in *John Cage: An Anthology*, 135

15. We see that to look at an object, a work of art, say, we have to see it as something happening, not as it did to him who made it, but as it does while we see it. We don't have to go anywhere: it comes to us.

"Where Are We Going? and What Are We Doing?" [1961], in *Silence*, 223

16. We learned from Oriental thought that those divine influences are, in fact, the environment in which we are. A sober and quiet mind is one in which the ego does not obstruct the fluency of the things that come in through our senses and up through our dreams. Our business in living is to become fluent with the life we are living, and art can help in this.

"Memoir" [1966], in *John Cage: An Anthology*, 77

17a. I have decided that my task is to open up the personality; I also want to open up the work so that it may be interpreted in various ways.

For the Birds, [1970–71], 59

b. Sounds have no goal! They are, and that's all. They live. Music is this life of sounds, this participation of sounds in life, which may become—but not voluntarily—a participation of life in sounds. . . .

. . . I believe that information never stops appearing.

Ibid., 87, 89

c. That is precisely the first thing the *I Ching* teaches us: acceptance. It essentially advances this lesson: if we want to use chance operations, then we must accept the results. . . . If I am unhappy after a chance operation, if the result does not satisfy me, by accepting it I at least have the chance to modify myself, to change myself. But if I insist on changing the *I Ching*, then it changes rather than I, and I have gained nothing, accomplished nothing!

Ibid., 94–95

d. When David Tudor began work on *Variations II*, he decided to begin with what was unknown—to start with the unknown rather than to force the unknown to become the known. His point of view was that we must use the unknown to make the known unknown. And not the other way around.

Ibid., 128

e. [On performing *Vexations*, by Satie] In the middle of those eighteen hours of performance, our lives changed. We were dumbfounded, because something was happening which we had not considered and which we were a thousand miles away from being able to foresee. So, if I apply this observation to conceptual art, it seems to me that the difficulty with this type of art, if I understand it correctly, is that it obliges us to imagine that we know something *before* that something has happened. That is difficult, since the experience itself is always different from what you thought about it. And it seems to me that the experiences each person can have, that everyone is capable of appreciating, are precisely those experiences that contribute to changing us and, particularly, to changing our preconceptions. . . . I, on the contrary, attempt to deconcentrate attention, to distract it.

Ibid., 153–54

f. The Self is not an ego; it is rather the fact that each of us is at the center, is the center of the world, without being an ego. The Self is what I do not impose on others. It is not a kind of "subjectivity," but a reference to something which comes much before that and which—beyond that—allows that "subjectivity" to be produced. It is a reference to the Nothingness that is in all things, and thus also in me. It would be more appropriate here to invoke, as I did concerning Suzuki, the soul's Base, Meister Eckhart's *Grund*. Or society!

Ibid., 234

18. Following my studies with Suzuki Daisetz in the philosophy of Zen Buddhism, I have used in all my work, whether literary, graphic, or musical, *I Ching* chance operations in order to free my mind (ego) from its likes and dislikes, trusting that this use was comparable to sitting crosslegged, and in agreement with my teacher that what Zen wants is that mind not cut itself off from Mind but let Mind flow through it.

"Notes on Compositions III" [1967–78], in *John Cage: Writer,* 107–8

19. I began using chess and the hunting of wild mushrooms as a balance to my involvement with chance. They are both situations in which chance cannot be used. They are both life and death matters of winning and losing. One prefers to live.

"42 Seconds on Chess," from *19 Questions,* a film by Frank Scheffer [1987]

20. We are living in a period in which many people have changed their minds about what the use of music is or could be for them. Something that doesn't speak or talk like a human being, that doesn't know its definition in the dictionary or its theory in the schools, that expresses itself simply by the fact of its vibrations. People paying attention to vibratory activity, not in relation to a fixed ideal performance, but each time attentively to how it happens to be this time, not necessarily two times the same. A music that transports the listener to the moment where he is.

"An Autobiographical Statement" [1989], in *John Cage: Writer,* 246–47

21a. We have the feeling that many people pay no attention to culture. And that they also don't pay any attention to anything else that is connected with spirituality or with things other than physical necessity. . . . I do miss what one might lump together under the word "spirituality." . . .

I think that the hope, any hope, any future in fact, has to be viewed from the viewpoint, not of the masses, but from the viewpoint of the individuals. . . . If the masses are going to get any culture that is really useful to them, they will get it individually rather than as a group. . . .

Because no individual knows how his life is going to change, hmm? Even the cultured ones *(laughter)*, let alone the uncultivated ones. But even the uncultivated ones, the hopeless ones, the homeless ones—all of those—can in the next ten minutes change their lives. And we don't know why, or what will have stimulated them to do that. But they do it. And that is how life is . . . don't you think?

Musicage [1992], 46–47

b. *But,* what is marvelous is that the opposites are not opposite. And that's part of what we might call the spirituality—art in life.

Ibid., 110

c. But in the sudden school [of Buddhism]—which I prefer—there are three principal truths. They're called the whispered truths. Which means you oughtn't to talk about them. People shouldn't know about them. And the reason people shouldn't know about them is because they won't understand them, hmm? So they have to be spoken of so that they won't know that they're being talked about. *(laughs)* And the first is that creation is endless, hmm? That it's vast! *Incomprehensibly* . . . great. And the next is that your action in that situation—of vast creation—your action should be as though you were writing on water. Isn't that beautiful? Or, pulling yourself up into the tree in winter. In other words, not to make an impression. And the final thing is to realize that the opposites are not opposite. *(pause)* And that's what's so dangerous. And what's why it's whispered. Because if you learn that the important thing is to meditate when you're not meditating, hmm? then how will we persuade people to meditate? *(laughter)*

Ibid., 163–64

d. It challenges, well, how you behave in the face of uncertainty, hmm? And that's one of the exciting things about music—that it's instantaneous behavior, hmm? . . .

. . . It's dangerous to make an action, hmm?

Ibid., 252

FOUR

Gordon Mumma

Cage as Performer

In the last part of his life, John Cage's performance virtuosity was mostly vocal: reading (or singing or chanting) from his writings, and responding to questions in lively public encounters. Most currently available recordings of his performances were made during this time. And since his work seems to have had greater impact on people younger than himself, most of those who heard him are probably less familiar with his earlier instrumental and live-electronic performances.

Cage's performances in the earlier part of his career were unique and as memorable as his later vocal performances. Typical of musicians who have considerable playing experience, he had developed a reliable technique while accompanying modern dance classes and during many years of concerts. Though at no time in his career was he primarily a performer (as, say, the composer Rachmaninov was), his performances were always remarkable.

Cage made use of four performance resources in the course of his career: piano, percussion, electronic-music equipment, and voice. His performing life, which began in 1933, divides roughly into three periods, each about two decades long. In the first period, 1933–53, Cage was primarily a performer with piano and percussion; during the 1940s, he also conducted percussion ensembles. In the second period, after 1953, Cage continued as a pianist (and sometimes as conductor) and developed performance with electronic equipment and with his voice. In the third period of his creative life, after 1973, he performed mostly with his voice.

Cage's early formal musical training was as a pianist. After the five-finger exercises of his elementary school years, he studied nineteenth-century piano music with his aunt, Phoebe James, and during the mid-1920s with pianist-composer Fannie Charles Dillon in Los Angeles. His formal study of piano concluded in the 1930s, with Richard Buhlig in Los Angeles. As a performer of percussion and electronic resources, and with his voice, Cage was essentially self-taught. He did not develop his performing skills as a percussionist by learning the classical rudiments of the orchestral or band percussionist. Rather, he learned what was necessary for each situation. Cage developed as a percussionist as one does in gamelan traditions, by progressing through levels of skill from relative beginner to mature virtuoso. The development of his creative skills with electronic equipment resulted from a disciplined exploration of possibilities (rather than a formal background in science and engineering), nourished by his productively unorthodox imagination. His vocal skills developed from his love of writing and speaking and grew out of his major innovations as a poet with the written word. (It was also in this third period that he extended his creativity as a graphic artist.)

Throughout his first period, Cage performed as a pianist in concert and as an accompanist for dance. His repertory included his own compositions. He had good sight-reading proficiency and considerable technical skill, sufficient for notably challenging pieces such as *The Perilous Night* (1944) and the *Sonatas and Interludes* (1946–48). He also performed with piano virtuosos, such as Maro Ajemian, Grete Sultan, William Masselos, Marcelle Mercenier, and David Tudor. With these colleagues he performed his *Experiences No. 1* (1949), *Music for Piano 4–84* (1953–56), and *34'46.776"* (1954).

In the late 1940s, Cage was introduced to Tudor by composer Stefan Wolpe. Merce Cunningham was at work on choreography (*Pool of Darkness,* premiered in January 1950) for a technically difficult piano piece by the American composer Ben Weber; Cage engaged Tudor to perform the Weber piece. The profoundly nourishing creative relationship between Tudor, Cage, and Cunningham did not end with Cage's death in 1992. As a pianist Tudor established benchmarks for performance of the challenging, innovative piano music by Cage, Pierre Boulez, Karlheinz Stockhausen, Christian Wolff, Wolpe, and many others. Tudor's association with Cage and with the Cunningham Dance Company relieved Cage from a sense of obligation about performing as a pianist.

Cage continued to perform as piano soloist with the Cunningham Dance Company into the late 1960s, notably in the work *Nocturnes* (1956; the music was Erik Satie's *Three Nocturnes*). Cage's approach to the Satie was lyrical, gently liquid rather than markedly articulated, and with a subtle lilt like a barely perceptible perfume. In this second period, several Cunningham repertory works involved Cage and Tudor as duo pianists; these included *Minutiae* (1954) and *Suite for Five* (1956), both of which used Cage's *Music for Piano 4–84*. The piano duo of Cage and Tudor also performed Morton Feldman's *Ixion* (1958) for Cunningham's choreography entitled *Summerspace* (1958). After the early 1970s, Cage performed as a pianist mostly in one work, *Cheap Imitation* (1969). The context of this work offers insight into an aspect of his creative life.

In the late 1960s, Cage and Cunningham returned to work on a project begun many years earlier: a choreography for Satie's *Socrate.* The situation was extraordinary for the Cunningham ensemble: the choreography was coordinated with the music, and the dancers rehearsed with the music. (In most of the Cunningham repertory, the dance and music are independent of each other, created, rehearsed, and performed independently, though in performance their independence occurs simultaneously.)

Cage had made a two-piano transcription of *Socrate,* intending that he and Tudor would perform it. In the many years since the project's inception, Cage had become busy with commissions and other creative activity (and was increasingly troubled with arthritis). Cunningham was completing the *Socrate* choreography while Cage was at work on the extravagant, multimedia *HPSCHD* (1969; a compositional collaboration with Lejaren Hiller). Unforeseen legal issues interfered: the Satie estate denied permission for the use of Cage's transcription. He resolved the problem by composing *Cheap Imitation* for solo piano, in which he maintained the architecture of *Socrate* but, by using chance operations, replaced Satie's music with his own. In response to the situation and to Cage's title for the music, Cunningham gave the title *Second Hand* to this long-gestated choreography.

Cage's *Cheap Imitation* is now well known. It is a half-hour single melodic line in three movements for solo piano, and Cage performed it widely on the Cunningham tours into the early 1970s. He also made other versions of it, including one for solo violin, and an orchestration. Playing *Cheap Imitation* was the last substantial performing that Cage did as a pianist.

As a percussionist during the first period of his creative life, Cage was encouraged particularly by Henry Cowell and inspired by compositions of Amadeo Roldán and Edgard Varèse. His collaboration with Lou Harrison is celebrated, both for their percussion ensemble and for the collaboratively composed *Double Music* (1941). The members of this percussion ensemble included Doris Dennison, Margaret Jansen, and Xenia Kashevaroff (to whom Cage was then married). His work with percussion media continued after the 1950s primarily as a resource for live-electronic music.

In the late 1930s, and continuing through the second period of his creative life in collaboration with David Tudor, Cage developed performance skills with live-electronic resources. His *Imaginary Landscapes* (1939) and the classic *Cartridge Music* (1960), as well as the works using amplified plant materials—*Child of Tree* and *Branches* (1975)—are important examples. He also performed with live-electronic resources in Cunningham repertory with music by other composers, such as David Behrman's *For Nearly an Hour* for the choreography *Walkaround Time* (1968) and Alvin Lucier's *Vespers* for the choreography *Objects* (1969).

The reasons for Cage's progression from piano to percussion to electronic instruments to voice, were both practical and artistic. Though the practical circumstances may seem mundane, they were important. His contributions to the percussion genre declined as he grew weary of travel with a cumbersome menagerie of heavy instruments. One reason for his development of the prepared piano was to have a multi-timbral resource of sonorities without the heavy labor of moving percussion instruments.

Cage's gradual retirement as pianist was due to arthritis. By 1960 his hands were already troubled with this affliction. He had increasing difficulty performing the music for *Suite for Five,* an exquisite choreography that had an unusually long life in the repertory. In 1960, following the first performance I saw of this work with Cage and Tudor as duo pianists, I expressed my appreciation to Cage at intermission and shook hands with him. He said, "Please be careful," and continued: "The sponsor worries that we are hurting the pianos by playing inside them, and some of the audience think the sound hurts their ears." Then, with his unique grin: "But this piece hurts me more than it hurts them."

By the late 1970s, Cage had changed his diet to minimize fatty foods and alcohol, and had given up smoking. Though his arthritis improved for a time, it gradually became a burden again, along with sciatica, in the 1980s. But by this time he had developed his activities as a vocal performer into a major effort and had also extended his prolific creative life as a writer and graphic artist, activities that were less physically stressful. I last saw Cage in May 1992, between a rehearsal and performance of *Music for* (1984) by the San Francisco Contemporary Music Players. Cage, Betty Freeman, and I walked five blocks to a vegetarian restaurant for dinner. His arthritis made the journey for him slow and uncomfortable.

Cage's performing voice and the writing that he performed with it in his third creative period are well known.[1] An early example is his reading of the one-minute stories from *Indeterminacy* (1958). He also read these stories to accompany Merce Cunningham's celebrated choreography *How to Pass, Kick, Fall, and Run* (from the 1960s repertory). Some of his vocal skills were developed with the Cunningham Dance Company's many *Events,* which date from 1964. *Events* were not repertory works, but were collaboratively conceived for single performance occasions, often in non-proscenium spaces, using materials from the choreographic repertory. By 1995 the Cunningham Dance Company had made several hundred unique *Events.* The music for *Events* was often a collaboration between several musician-composers. Cage sometimes performed with electronic equipment and sometimes used his voice.

This vocal aspect of Cage's contribution to *Events* was concurrent with the development of his mesostics (1971) and similar asyntactical writing. Cage commonly performed mesostics as a solo vocalist. But on occasion he presented them in other contexts, such as in simultaneous performance with David Tudor's live-electronic composition *Untitled* (1972). In a performance at Pro Musica Nova in Bremen, Cage stood before four microphones, each of which was amplified to a loudspeaker in a different corner of the performance space. He spoke close to each microphone and moved from one to another, sometimes rapidly. The sound of his voice moved weightlessly around the space.

Cage was usually comfortable as a performer. In show-business vernacular, he was a "trouper." But some circumstances made him anxious. One of these was his performance in Lukas Foss's clever production of Stravinsky's *L'Histoire du soldat* in New York in the late 1960s. The three speaking parts were to be performed by the "three C's of American music"—Aaron Copland as narrator, Elliott Carter as the soldier, and John Cage as the devil. Cage accepted the invitation with misgivings. He told me that he did not think he would be able to do the rhythmic coordinations between his part and the instruments. He said "it should be devilish, not foolish." Cage overcame his apprehension, partly because he wanted to meet Stravinsky to ask for a manuscript for his in-progress book *Notations* (1969). Perhaps Cage thought that his *L'Histoire*

1. And notorious for those familiar with his Charles Elliot Norton Lectures at Harvard University in 1988–89, published as *I–VI* (Cambridge, Mass.: Harvard University Press, 1990).

participation would give him some cachet. And they did meet, in Stravinsky's New York City hotel suite—it was the first meeting between two twentieth-century giants in the development of rhythm in Western art music. The *L'Histoire* performance was a glamorous success, and Cage had no trouble with the rhythmic coordinations. He was a brilliant devil, equaled only in devilish virtuosity by Vanessa Redgrave's recorded performance.[2]

With the Cunningham Dance Company, Cage often played the music of other composers; examples besides the Behrman and Lucier works already cited include the work of Toshi Ichiyanagi for *Scramble* (1967) and Pauline Oliveros for *Canfield* (1969). Separate music concerts were sometimes presented as part of the dance tours. On one of these, at Cornell University in New York State, Cage and I played one of my works, entitled *Swarm.* This music was for two vernacular, or "folkloric," instruments, concertina and bowed saw. Cage played the concertina.

The Cornell concert was a last-minute arrangement. We had time for only one rehearsal, *Swarm* was a new piece, and Cage said he had never played the concertina. He learned what was necessary during a morning rehearsal that preceded our afternoon concert. *Swarm* required close and responsive connections between the two players. We did not play from a notated score; similar to many folkloric musics, *Swarm* was a music of "oral tradition." I explained the piece to Cage at the beginning of the rehearsal. The rules of *Swarm* specified a limited number of choices. Each player could choose a single pitch, or at the most two pitches played simultaneously. When two pitches sounded together, a limited number of pitch intervals could be used.[3] After each choice was made, it could not be used again. Thus each player had to remember what had been previously played in the performance. This is similar to chess and some card games, and Cage was an avid player of both.

During that one rehearsal Cage chose only single pitches. He said, "I'll make the easy choices first." Because he was unfamiliar at first with the concertina, he made a few incorrect choices. But he was from the very start skilled in matters of continuity, grasping immediately when sounds occurred in time, and how they overlapped. Owing to limited time, Cage did not use the two-pitch sonorities in rehearsal. Just before the performance was to begin, I assured him that it was legitimate to play only the single-pitch choices. He smiled (again with his unique grin) and said, "I think it will be fine."

2. With the London Sinfonietta, Kent Nagano, conductor, on Pangea CD-6233.

3. The specific interval vocabulary was limited to m3, P4, m6, M7, M9, and P12. Among the syntactical restrictions each of the two simultaneous pitches had to be different from the pitch(es) sounded just previously by the other player. Further, a player could not use any pitch from the immediately previous choice, and not more than one pitch from the two previous choices.

We began the performance. Cage's first choice was a two-pitch sonority. After my responding sound from the musical saw, he continued with the next choice—a single pitch. As the performance continued, Cage used, variously, single pitches and two-pitch sonorities. He followed securely the logic I had explained during the rehearsal. By the end of the performance he had included many of the possible two-pitch sonorities, including some that were quite difficult. I never heard him repeat a choice that he had already used. The continuity of his concertina part with my musical saw was excellent. He was bold with choices and subtle with musical nuances. It was as though he had learned the concertina and we had rehearsed the piece many times.

This performance of *Swarm* contradicts the legend that Cage had "no ear for pitch or melody." Cage encouraged this legend. He enjoyed saying that he could not do solfège, and that Schoenberg had told him that he had "no sense for harmony." I do not think this is the truth—certainly not the whole truth. Cage told those stories about his being "unmusical" because they were good stories. He was a virtuoso storyteller, a happy raconteur. But Cage was also quick with complex ideas and structures, and a fast learner. As a performer he was disciplined, reliable, and imaginative with creative decisions.

Cage loved performing. He was nourished by the performing experience, even under difficult circumstances. He usually found an appropriate match of his technical proficiency with a given situation. Indeed, quite often his unique performance virtuosity—with music, with words and verbal repartee, and with graphic materials—was astonishing, even to practitioners of those arts not easily astonished.

FIVE

Deborah Campana

As Time Passes

The work of John Cage is difficult to describe and nearly impossible to codify. The variety of musical forces and their uses, the compositional techniques he developed over almost six decades, serve to delight and, at times, confound audiences. The air of mystery his work evokes may be attributed, in part, to his use of chance operations, yet there is one constant that can be examined to elucidate his compositional process: from his earliest compositions for chamber ensembles to his last works for large-scale forces, the parameter of time appears to be Cage's initial and often dominant concern when planning a work. This essay focuses on temporal design, on how Cage fashioned ideas and channeled them through a variety of temporal structures. By analyzing several pieces representing different aspects of his output, I attempt to demonstrate how this temporal element helps define his distinctive compositional style.

The shaping of musical time, so prominent in Cage's work, can be viewed from two angles: formal concerns, or the shape of something, the essential nature as distinguished from its matter (or, in Cage's compositions, the musical materials), and structure, something that is constructed or arranged in a definite pattern often evolved from, or resulted from, temporal organization. Seven compositions can act as examples: *Imaginary Landscape No. 1, Sonatas and Interludes,* the time-length pieces, *Concert for Piano and Orchestra, Score and 23 Parts: Twelve Haiku, Roaratorio,* and *108.* It is impossible to discuss time and its evolution in Cage's music without considering three specific aspects of a composition: the sounds, or musical materials, as Cage has referred to them; the score's notation, or the manner of designing ideas on paper to instruct performers how to play; and finally, the organization of the work, how its formal or structural design reflects an integral whole.

To those whose musical training derives from a Western art music tradition, the idea of musical time passing evokes many images. Visually, one recognizes the symbolic representation of sound and timbre expressed by notes and rests assigned to particular instruments or voices. One reads a page of music from left to right, proceeding from top to bottom. With training, one can read a score and mentally hear a specific sound upon seeing a note; for example, a loud clarinet pitch in its high register is associated with a notated symbol for a high D above the treble staff marked fortissimo.

Traditionally, time in music has been described in terms of measurement represented on the page as measures, phrases, and movements. Implied in the designation of measures, for example, is meter, or recurring pulses grouped in a variety of patterns related by strong and weak stresses and by their proximity to one another. Groups of measures or phrases and, on the larger scale, movements suggest the recurrence of events or a periodicity, planned contrast, and return. In essence, such patterns implicitly acknowledge the role memory plays in the musical experience. Cage was fond of referring to the fact that "composing's one thing, performing's another, listening's a third. What can they have to do with one another?"[1] I posit that the awareness of time passing could be a primary level for observing how this interaction brings the three together.

Composed in 1939, while Cage was working at the Cornish School in Seattle, *Imaginary Landscape No. 1* is scored for what he called muted piano, sizzle cymbal, and sound-effects recordings (ex. 5.1).[2] He committed the work to paper by employing rather traditional notation: pitch was indicated insofar as possible, and measures marked the passage of time. By looking deeper, one can distinguish phrases: motives are linked to specific instruments and reappear intact throughout the course of the

1. "Experimental Music: Doctrine," in *Silence: Lectures and Writings* (Middletown, Conn.: Wesleyan University Press, 1961), 15.

2. *Imaginary Landscape No. 1* (New York: C. F. Peters, 1960).

EXAMPLE 5.1
Imaginary Landscape No. 1, measures 1–40, Edition Peters. © 1960 by Henmar Press, Inc. Used by permission.

short work. A rather roughly defined rondo form evolves from the juxtaposition of a general feeling of stasis or undulation provided by the piano in contrast with the sensation of moving forward exhibited in the sound-effects recording. In the Peters catalog of 1962, compiled by Robert Dunn, Cage described this contrast in formal terms:

EXAMPLE 5.1 *continued*

Each interlude is one measure longer than the preceding one. The first, one measure long, introduces three rhythmic elements which one by one are subtracted from the interludes to be added one by one to the middle parts of the second and third and to the final part of the fourth 15-measure section. The completion of this process reestablishes the original form of the interlude, which, by means of repetition (first of the whole and then of the second half only) is extended, concluding the piece.[3]

3. Notes to *Imaginary Landscape No. 1,* in Robert Dunn, *John Cage* (New York: C. F. Peters, 1962), 35–36.

During the mid-1940s, having moved to New York a few years earlier, Cage composed music for dancers and made the acquaintance of others in the arts community. Although this was a time of tremendous creativity for Cage, he was unhappy with the general reception of his work. Too often his heartfelt expressions cast in percussive sound or presented on his newly inspired prepared piano were misinterpreted by audiences. His serious moments were considered flights of fancy and, therefore, at times rewarded with laughter.

One of Cage's most popular works, the *Sonatas and Interludes,* composed in 1946–48 for prepared piano, reflects a pre-chance mindset, not unlike *Imaginary Landscape No. 1.*[4] Cage employed the prepared piano to compose the *Sonatas and Interludes* "by playing the piano, listening to differences, making a choice." In fact, he described his compositional method as "considered improvisation (mainly at the piano), though ideas came to me at some moments away from the instrument."[5]

Because Cage improvised or composed the *Sonatas and Interludes* primarily at the piano, the construction of motives or thematic material grew out of a tactile awareness of the piano keyboard and a familiarity with those fingering patterns associated with traditional music. The manner in which a musical idea is played or "felt under one's fingers" influenced him. Scalar passages, arpeggios, and triadic-chordal constructions found throughout the score reflect a feeling for the fingering patterns or hand positions more closely associated with traditional keyboard music than with the more exotic timbres of the prepared piano.[6] Cage found a certain tonality in the work, as he noted in a letter dating from 1968, in which he discussed the preparation of the piano for *Sonatas and Interludes:* "At the time that I wrote the music, the sounds were in my memory, so to speak, and I was able, going to another piano to capture them. There is a certain gravity or 'tonality' about the piece, and this can generally be known from the cadences. If at those points, the music seems to come 'to earth,' then it is right preparation. . . . The pitches resulting from preparation were intentional, picked up as one does shells on a beach."[7]

In considering the organization of the *Sonatas and Interludes,* beyond merely that of the overall collection (four sonatas followed by an interlude, four sonatas and an interlude, followed by the mirror image

4. *Sonatas and Interludes* (New York: C. F. Peters, 1960).

5. "Composition as Process," in *Silence,* 34, 19.

6. See Deborah Campana, "Form and Structure in the Music of John Cage" (Ph.D. diss., Northwestern University, 1985).

7. Cage to Gregory Clough, Champaign, Illinois, typed and signed letter, January 18, 1968, John Cage Archive, Northwestern University Music Library, Evanston, Illinois.

of this pattern), one must acknowledge what Cage has described as an example of his macro-microcosmic structure. Sonata 4, for example, is one hundred measures long, divided into ten-measure units that are grouped according to a proportion 3, 3, 2, 2; the same proportion is used internally within the ten-measure units (ex. 5.2).[8]

Cage claimed that the musical materials employed in the *Sonatas and Interludes* were not related to the actual temporal structure, yet there is no denying that the musical elements fit within the prescribed overall or macro-, if not the microstructure of each movement. In the earlier work, *Imaginary Landscape No. 1,* Cage consciously defined the temporal evolution as indicated in both the changing length of the work's interludes and the shifting of the motivic characters to suit this process. In *Sonatas and Interludes,* this idea appears to have crystallized. In spite of the formal traits associated with the term "sonata," and the resurfacing of the interlude as a means of contrast, each movement is organized around a proportional scheme that is confirmed aurally only by cadences, or in Cage's words, by coming "to earth." Cage noted the dominance of what he termed "rhythmic structure" in a 1944 article in the *Dance Observer:* "It may seem at first thought that rhythmic structure is not of primary importance. However, a dance, a poem, a piece of music (any of the time arts) occupies a length of time, and the manner in which this length of time is divided first into large parts and then into phrases (or built up from phrases to form eventual larger parts) is the work's very life structure."[9]

From 1952 through 1956, Cage wrote a series of compositions all titled by lengths of time. Although these works capture the flavor of the temporal structures in the *Sonatas and Interludes,* they are actually quite different. The first and perhaps his most notorious work, *4'33",* is in three movements, the lengths of which were determined by chance. The work may be performed by any instrument or combination of instruments. The other five time-length works—two for string players (*59½"* [1953] and *26'1.1499"* [1955]), two for pianists (*31'57.9864"* and *34'46.776"* [1954]), and one for percussionist (*27'10.554"* [1956])[10]—are presented in graphic notation with space on the page measured horizontally to represent time (ex. 5.3 on p. 128). Cage specified that the rhythmic structure's divisions indicate points at which other instruments or works may join in the performance. According to the notes to *27'10.554" for a Percussionist* in the 1962 catalog published by C. F. Peters, "This

8. Cage, "Composition as Process," 19.

9. "Grace and Clarity," from "Four Statements on the Dance," in *Silence,* 89–93; originally published in *Dance Observer,* November 1944, 108–9.

10. All were published by C. F. Peters in 1960.

EXAMPLE 5.2

Sonata 4 from *Sonatas and Interludes*, Edition Peters, 13. © 1960 by Henmar Press, Inc. Used by permission.

piece may be segmented at structural points indicated by dotted lines and the segments superimposed in any way to provide duets, trios, etc."[11]

Cage might have described these works as indeterminate with respect to performance. In committing such musical ideas to paper, he gave the performer great responsibility for interpreting the notation of the individual parts as well as in determining how each musician will play with others. There are prescribed sections, but whether or not they will become aurally distinctive to a listener is up to the performers who choose to enter or exit on these cues. With the performance of *4′33″*, the audience can perceive the opening and closing of the keyboard cover, for example, when a pianist performs the work and thereby defines the sections of the composition.[12]

The Concert for Piano and Orchestra was completed in 1958, one decade after the *Sonatas and Interludes* and a few years after the series of time-length compositions.[13] The work has no master score, but comprises individual parts for piano, three violins, two violas, and one cello, double bass, flute, clarinet, bassoon, trumpet, trombone, and tuba. The *Concert* may be performed by one part or any combination of parts, or in conjunction with other works, such as *Aria* and *Fontana Mix*, two works written soon after.

Cage composed the *Solo for Piano* for the *Concert* by selecting events from either *Winter Music* or *Music for Piano* and using them exactly as they appear, or by varying them, or, a fourth possibility, by composing a completely new event.[14] Although the work is not Cage's first graphically notated score, the piano part in particular is one of the most elaborate examples of this technique. The notation resembles traditional music notation that has been calligraphically altered. In the piano part, individual letters or combinations of two letters precede all events. These letters refer to eighty-four different descriptions or, according to Cage, "kinds of composition" included in the preface to indicate how particular notational elements in a given event should be interpreted.[15]

Time is represented by the horizontal dimension of the score, read from left to right. Cage did not define a scale or standard for measurement, but left this determination to the performer.[16] In lieu of metric specifications, duration is measured chronometrically: a conductor's

11. Cage, Notes to *27′10.554″* for a Percussionist, in Dunn, *John Cage*, 26.

12. Instructions to *4′33″* read: "If performed by a pianist, the 3 sections are indicated by opening and closing the keyboard lid" (New York: C. F. Peters, 1960).

13. *The Concert for Piano and Orchestra* (New York: C. F. Peters, 1960).

14. Cage to author, June 25, 1985, typed and signed letter.

15. Notes to *Concert for Piano and Orchestra* in Dunn, *John Cage*, 31.

16. Preface to *Concert for Piano and Orchestra*.

EXAMPLE 5.3

Excerpt from *34′46.776″ for a Pianist*, Edition Peters, 14. © 1960 by Henmar Press, Inc. Used by permission.

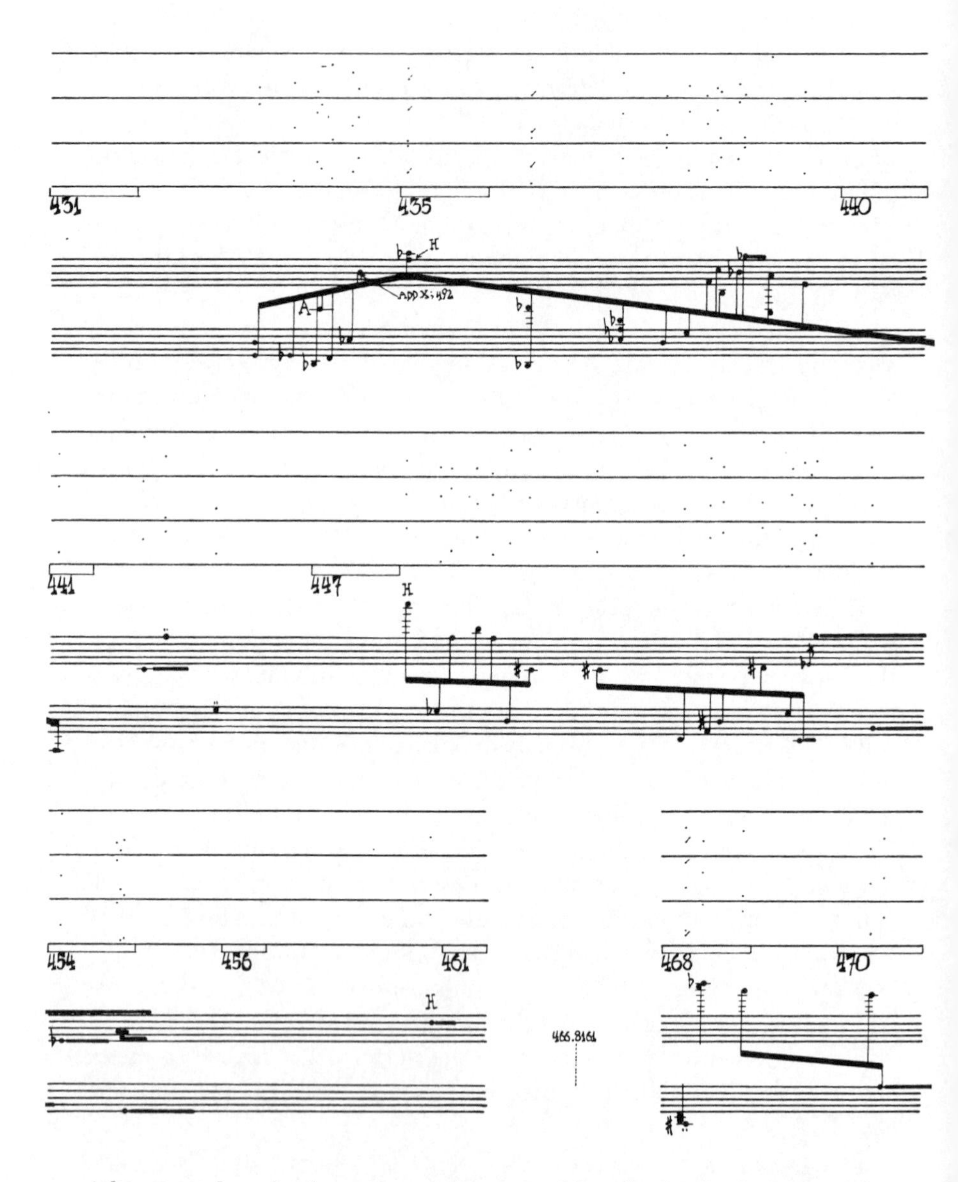

right arm takes the function of the second hand of a clock, incorporating varied motions, while the left hand indicates the proportion of the entire work that has passed. In this way, the performer can judge at any given point his or her temporal standing on each page and within the work based upon the position of the conductor's arms. The page becomes the basis for temporal organization, because the proportion of notated elements to blank space, or the spatial arrangement of the page, conveys to the performer the number of events, density of texture, and sound volume that should occur within the period of time expressed by the page (see ex. 5.4).

The spatial arrangement on the page also plays a significant role in defining a composition that dates from a decade and a half later, commissioned by Dennis Russell Davies and the St. Paul Chamber Orchestra: *Score (40 Drawings by Thoreau) and 23 Parts (for Any Instruments and/or Voices): Twelve Haiku, Followed by a Recording of the Dawn at Stony Point, New York, August 6, 1974.* The score itself consists of illustrations that Henry David Thoreau drew in the margins of his *Journals* (ex. 5.5a, below on p. 134). Having selected certain images by chance operations, Cage reproduced them on a grid, which is marked for the passage of time, that is, divided into seventeen sections grouped five plus seven plus five, in keeping with a haiku-like structure. Since the musicians' improvisations are to be based on segments of images that appear on the pages of their parts (ex. 5.5b), the conductor alone can see the complete images or the entire work.

To perform *Score,* Cage indicates that horizontal measure refers to time and that the performance of an individual haiku should be followed by silence approximately equal to the length of its performance. All twelve haiku are to be followed by a recording by David Behrman that is equal in length of performance to the entire set of haiku.[17]

In one sense, Cage used the haiku proportions, seventeen units in a 5–7–5 grouping, as a template, or a means for organizing time on a micro-level. It is apparent that he did not intend these measures to frame recurring pulse patterns. Instead, they aid the conductor and performer by serving as indication of icti-occurrences, marking the passage of time. Each haiku serves as a section, defined by the silence that surrounds it. The musicians' performance is but half the work's duration, however, since Cage indicated that the tape of environmental sounds should be heard after the musicians complete their performance, specifically, as long as the sum of the twelve haikus' durations.

Periods of silence also frame the sections of one of Cage's more popular late works, *Roaratorio.* Composed in 1979 as a radio play, or *Hörspiel, Roaratorio* is a compilation of four basic layers of sound activity all taken from or directly related to James Joyce's *Finnegans Wake.* In "writing through" the entire book, Cage derived mesostics based on the words or identity of James Joyce; this process resulted in a forty-one-page text that serves as the basis for the most significant layer of *Roaratorio,* the

17. Preface to *Score (40 Drawings by Thoreau) and 23 Parts (for Any Instruments and/or Voices): Twelve Haiku, Followed by a Recording of the Dawn at Stony Point, New York, August 6, 1974* (New York: Henmar, 1974).

EXAMPLE 5.4

Solo for Piano, from *Concert for Piano and Orchestra*, Edition Peters, 56 and 63. © 1960 by Henmar Press, Inc. Used by permission.

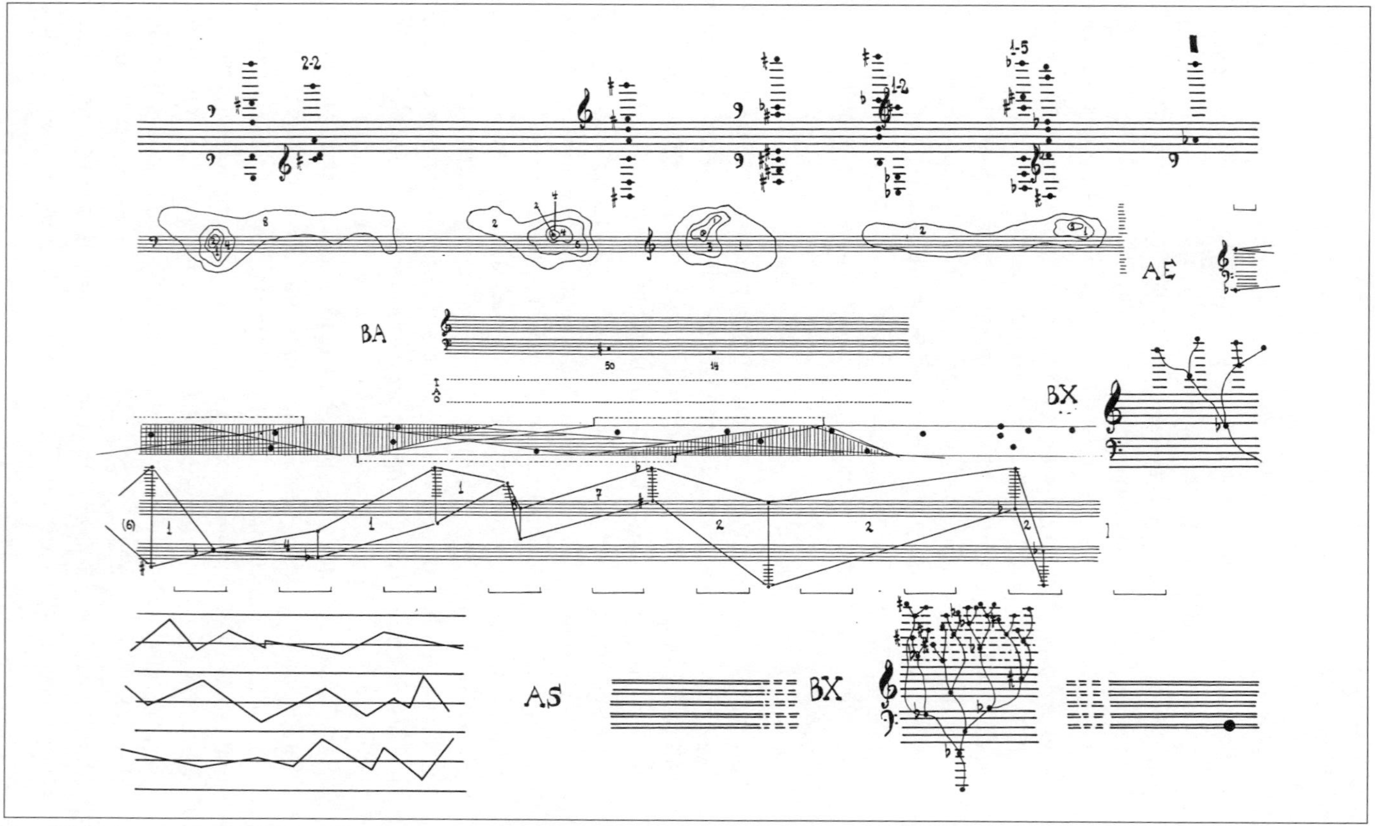

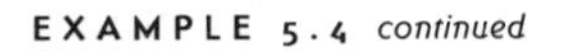
EXAMPLE 5.4 *continued*

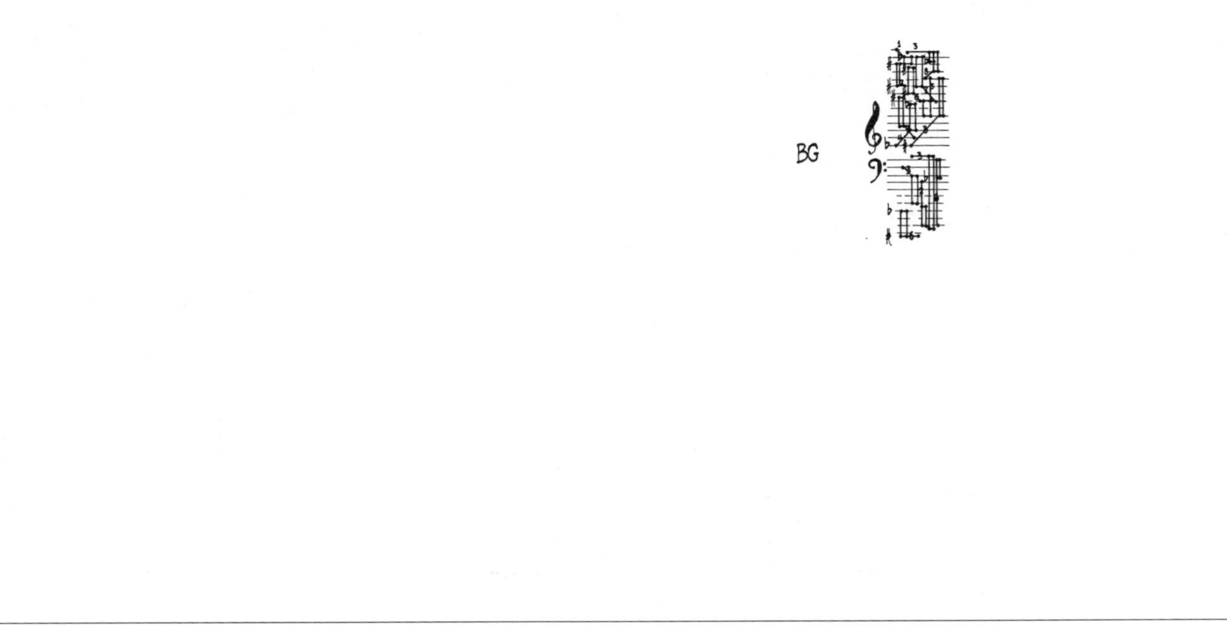

time template. Cage's intention in composing mesostics using *Finnegans Wake* as the source of material was to magnify the many different meanings associated with single words in Joyce's text and to point up the poetry inherent in his language. When asked to write music to this text, Cage created an Irish circus—music for which "there is not one center but . . . a plurality of centers." As Cage put it, "I wanted to make a music that was free of melody and free of harmony and free of counterpoint: free of musical theory. I wanted it not to be music in the sense of music, but I wanted it to be music in the sense of *Finnegans Wake*."[18]

Cage taped his own reading of the text, preserving the line and page numbering of Joyce's work as well as the author's designation of seventeen chapters assembled in four books. Determining that the tape of *Roaratorio* would be one hour long, he took the difference in time that remained after his reading of the mesostics and inserted periods of silence or unrecorded tape between each of the seventeen chapters. The divisions between the four books are emphasized by longer periods of silence. In effect, the divisions of line, page, chapter, and book act as mensural increments that define his temporal framework and become a ruler or standard by which the remaining three layers are added. These layers include (1) tapes of ambient sounds recorded at chance-selected locations mentioned in *Finnegans Wake* as derived from Louis Mink's *A Finnegans Wake Gazetteer;* (2) recordings of sounds mentioned in Joyce's text ("baywinds" or "lute," for example); and (3) traditional Irish music performed by Irish musicians. The sounds in the first two layers were added to Cage's taped reading of the mesostics at precisely the points corresponding to those at which they were encountered in Joyce's text.

One of Cage's last large-scale works, *108,* is scored for orchestra and constructed as a series of time brackets or durational ranges. Within a given range, for example, a performer may choose to begin and end the sound of traditionally notated pitches at any point during the temporal window. Such actions need not be coordinated specifically with another individual's performance; in fact, it is better for the performers to focus only on their own parts, rather than think in accord with what and when other members of the ensemble are playing. Cage specified that in a given time bracket, pitches should not be repeated. The 108-member ensemble is divided into five groups: the first group includes four percussionists; the second, violins; third, violins, violas, and cellos; fourth, cellos, basses, upper woodwinds; and fifth, clarinets, bassoons, brass,

18. *Roaratorio, ein irischer Circus über Finnegans Wake/An Irish Circus on Finnegans Wake,* edited by Klaus Schöning (Königstein: Athenaum, 1982), 85, 107, 89.

and one percussionist.[19] The large ensemble is seated onstage according to these groups. In performance, its playing is coordinated by a videoclock, a videorecording that marks the passage of minutes and seconds and provides the metric standard for the sound material performers place in their temporal windows.

To say that time is the element common to all the works described herein would be a truism. Yet, among Cage's many compositions, commonalties do exist with regard to temporal organization that can serve to illuminate his compositional process. On a basic level, the variety of notational practices notwithstanding and in spite of his understanding of Zen Buddhism and other Eastern philosophies, the temporal elements found in the scores examined here hold to the convention of time moving on a horizontal plane and the performer reading from left to right. This is not to say that the performer's work is accomplished easily, however, for even when employing conventional symbolic music notation, a half note does not necessarily maintain a relation to two quarters, nor do bar lines designate a metric flow. In fact, the performer must negotiate considerable differences in notational practice in order to interpret the composer's wishes.

Today we recognize that Cage's own description of "object" and "process" surfaced in the early to mid-fifties, after he adopted chance procedures and began exploring aspects of indeterminacy.[20] Thus, the term "object" referred to his earlier works, which were notated fully and left little room for interpretation if one were a musician trained in the Western art music tradition. On the other hand, the works considered to fit the category "process" were usually indeterminate and gave great interpretative license to the performer. For this reason, it is interesting to note that even as early as 1939, Cage described what is in essence an early manifestation of rhythmic structure in *Imaginary Landscape No. 1* as an evolving process. Evidently, in striving to work with a plan for designing this rhythmic evolution, he talked about the composition in terms he was more apt to use in describing indeterminacy, a concept that he didn't fully articulate until nearly two decades later.

While it is possible to trace seeds of Cage's interest in process back to his earliest work, we can also reflect on a convention he employed then that changed little over the passing of time. In *Imaginary Landscape* and the *Sonatas and Interludes,* for example, we observe temporal patterns—metric patterns, phrase patterns, and even sectional patterns—all of

19. Michael Bach to author, facsimile transmission, October 22, 1991. Bach, the solo violoncellist for whom *One⁸*, a solo work written to be performed with *108*, was written, provided a copy of the orchestration and how the orchestra members should be grouped.

20. Cage, "Indeterminacy," part 2 of "Composition as Process," 35–40.

EXAMPLE 5.5

Score and 23 Parts: Twelve Haiku, Edition Peters, 1 and 3. © 1974 by Henmar Press, Inc. Used by permission.

a.

b.

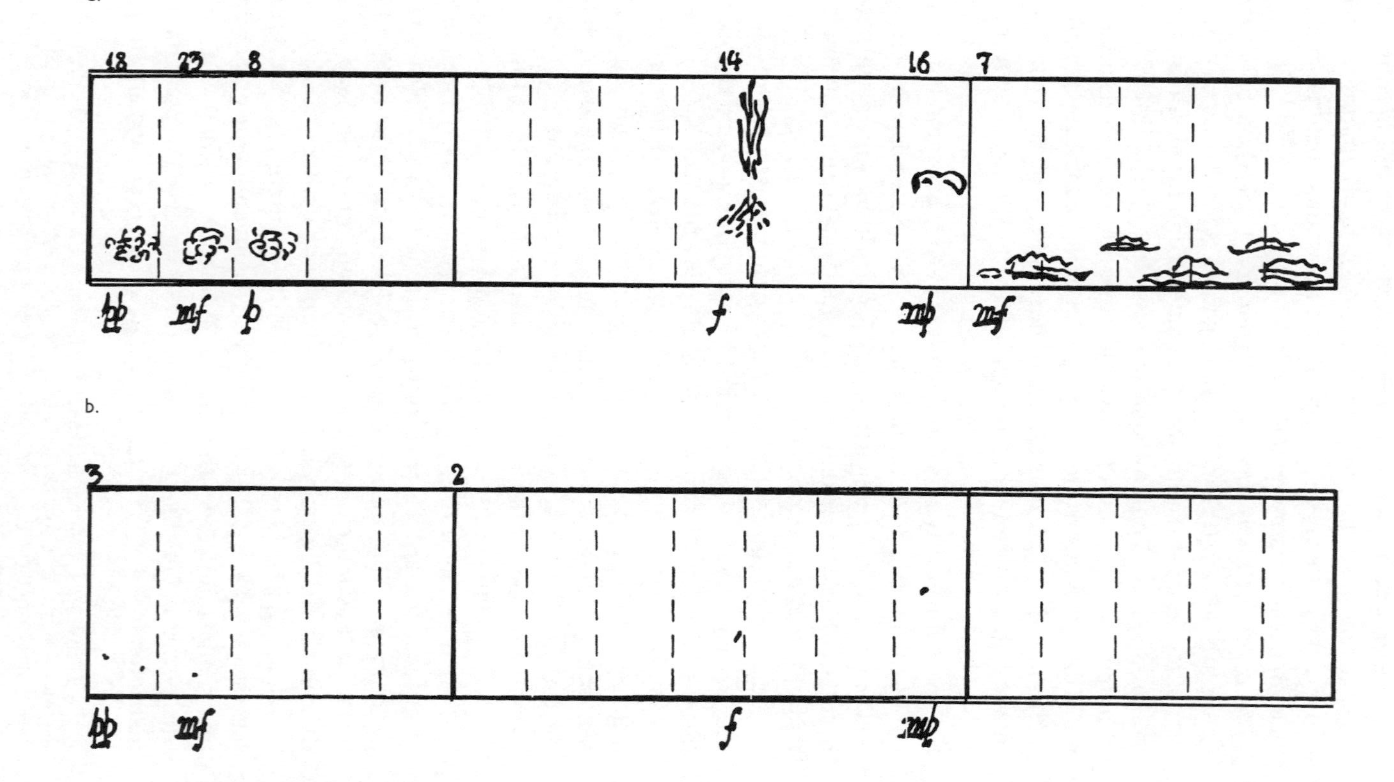

which can be perceived by a listener. But even within his chance-inspired works dating from several years later and those works that are indeterminate with respect to performance, Cage composed sections within the score that could serve as indication of a number of changes, including (1) the point at which an ensemble might be altered, as in the time-length pieces and *108,* (2) a change in physical action as in *4′33″,* and even (3) contrasts in texture, as in *Score and 23 Parts* and *Roaratorio.* In all these examples, the divisions into sections are not merely cosmetic, but instead act in a functional capacity. Indication of metric pattern does not necessarily represent the means by which an ensemble stays together, as in traditional music notation. Instead, meter serves to indicate when ensemble members might choose to enter or exit the work and thereby effect a change in texture. Moreover, they can be perceived by listeners, who are thus enabled to organize their sense of the time flow.

In *Score,* the recurrence of musical haiku interspersed with silence and ultimately followed by the tapes of environmental sound sets the audience's mood: expectation of the alternating texture, then at last resolution in the dawn, or the environmental sound captured on tape. Such sections defined by silence in *Roaratorio* may appear less evident to the audience, yet their design and meaning as based upon an extramusical device, the chapters and books of *Finnegans Wake,* act as a means of organizing the flow of time.

Even in the absence of meter and phrases, or of preexistent or literary forms, Cage sought creative solutions to the organization of time. In the *Concert,* the page itself stood as a temporal unit that was conducted based on real time, rather than symbolic or meter-derived time. Similarly for *108,* the durational windows may be the means of temporal organization, though rather than expressing this visually to the audience by a conductor, a videoclock seen only by the musicians serves this function just as well.

To move from the perception of time and meter to its interpretation by performers, the score and its parts pose an intriguing conundrum. Of particular interest are the later examples or those works for larger forces. In the *Concert,* for example, there is no score, but a conductor is needed in performance. His only job, however, is marking the passage of time, both at the micro-level (as a second hand of the clock) and the macro-level (as signaling the portion of the work that has passed in the performance). In *Score,* the conductor does have a score, at least for that part of the piece that is performed by musicians. However, aside from the haiku-grid it has in common with the parts, the score bears little resemblance to what the players themselves see. In essence, the conductor again marks time; he oversees the work's unfolding so that musicians can enter at their respective cues, which are indicated by the icti-points on the haiku-grid. In *108*, again there is no score and, moreover, no conductor. The videoclock takes the place of such a leader, and template markings in each performer's part provide guidance toward interpreting her performance.

As demonstrated in these examples, Cage was fascinated with the social relationships that arise between a score and the performers' parts or, more precisely, the conductor and the members of an ensemble that must interpret them. How do instrumentalists play for a given period of time without playing together? Can a group of musicians become an ensemble without each person losing his own identity or individuality? Can musicians come together without becoming an ensemble or group? Can a group come together without a leader? Can a leader lead without becoming more important than any one member of the group she leads? Can a conductor lead without imposing personal influence (especially with regard to expressivity)?

Although we cannot be certain that Cage ultimately was able to answer these questions, the continuum of his thoughts is apparent in these examples. Moreover, one must wonder if he did not feel that he had achieved a point of satisfaction in the latter works that employed templates similar to that of *108*, considering the number of works he composed that exhibit its traits. We can speculate that perhaps he had finally devised a notational method that pleased him—one that would successfully communicate his thoughts about sound through a two-dimensional medium of writing on a page. Whatever the truth, an audience may hear Cage's music as free flowing and ever changing, and the basis for such change rests on a temporal plan that he established early in his compositional process. While the template takes on a variety of guises, it always functions as the "work's very life structure."[21]

21. Cage, "Grace and Clarity," 90.

SIX

John Holzaepfel

David Tudor and the *Solo for Piano*

Although David Tudor spent the last three decades of his life creating his own music, his name continues to be inseparably linked with the music of John Cage. For fifteen years, from his performance of *Music of Changes* in 1952 to his recording of *Variations II* in 1967, Tudor gave the first performances of all of Cage's post-1950 piano music. By 1962, when Cage's publisher, C. F. Peters, issued its descriptive catalog of the composer's works, Tudor's name appeared in the indices of performances at least as often as did that of Cage himself. From this profusion of musical activity one work stands out in affording a comprehensive view of Tudor's methods in preparing his performances of Cage's scores. It can, in other words, illuminate Cage's reflection that, during the 1950s and 1960s, "David Tudor was present in everything I was doing." [1]

The scope of the *Concert for Piano and Orchestra* of 1957–58 was the largest of Cage's works since the *Music of Changes* of 1951. The *Concert* was an encyclopedic summary of his compositional development as well as a fore-

1. *For the Birds: John Cage in Conversation with Daniel Charles* (Boston: Marion Boyars, 1981), 178.

runner of its immediate future. Moreover, the pianist's part of the *Concert,* called *Solo for Piano,* is a compendium of notational techniques in experimental music (and not only Cage's). As a result, it offers an opportunity to consider Tudor's solutions to a large number of notational problems, which are in many cases identical to those found in other works by Cage that he performed in the 1950s.

The *Solo for Piano* is a collection of eighty-four different notational techniques distributed across sixty-three pages 11 by 17 inches in size (ex. 6.1). Each of the notational techniques produced a discrete graphic object whose coordinates, or visual and spatial dimensions, may be plotted in order to obtain information for preparing a performance. It is for this reason that Tudor referred to the eighty-four techniques as "graphs," a term I shall employ here.

Tudor began by tabulating all the occurrences of the eighty-four graphs according to the page number or numbers (several graphs overlap two pages) on which they appear in Cage's score. He then had to decide whether to use all eighty-four graphs or to make a selection from them. Probably because of the predetermined length of the performance, Tudor chose the latter course. The basis for his selection was the inclusion of at least one of each graph type; that is, his realization would represent each of the eighty-four notational techniques found in Cage's score. By surveying his list of graphs, Tudor could quickly note not only Cage's multiple uses of the same graph type but also those graphs which were, in Cage's words, "varieties of others." In eliminating these varieties, Tudor found a total of sixty-three distinct graph types; he used each of these once. (That the number of graph types is identical to the number of pages in the score of the *Solo for Piano* is, so far as I know, coincidental.)

After making his selection of graphs, Tudor referred to Cage's instructions, which are frequently little more than clues, for reading each graph type. Where necessary, he made content sketches, translating Cage's more abstract graphs into conventional notation. These sketches show that Tudor's readings of the graphs are complete and cumulative; each sketch represents the entire content of each graph used. He then transcribed the contents, in timings based on the dimensions of Cage's graphs, to separate sheets of staff paper, which he gathered in a small ring-binder notebook. The result was Tudor's first realization of the *Solo for Piano;* it was from this realization that Tudor played when he gave the premiere of the *Concert for Piano and Orchestra* on May 15, 1958, as part of the Twenty-five Year Retrospective Concert of the Music of John Cage, given in Town Hall in New York.[2]

2. The concert was recorded by George Avakian and has been reissued on compact discs (Wergo 6247–2).

Solo for Piano, from *Concert for Piano and Orchestra*, Edition Peters, 1. © 1960 by Henmar Press, Inc. Used by permission.

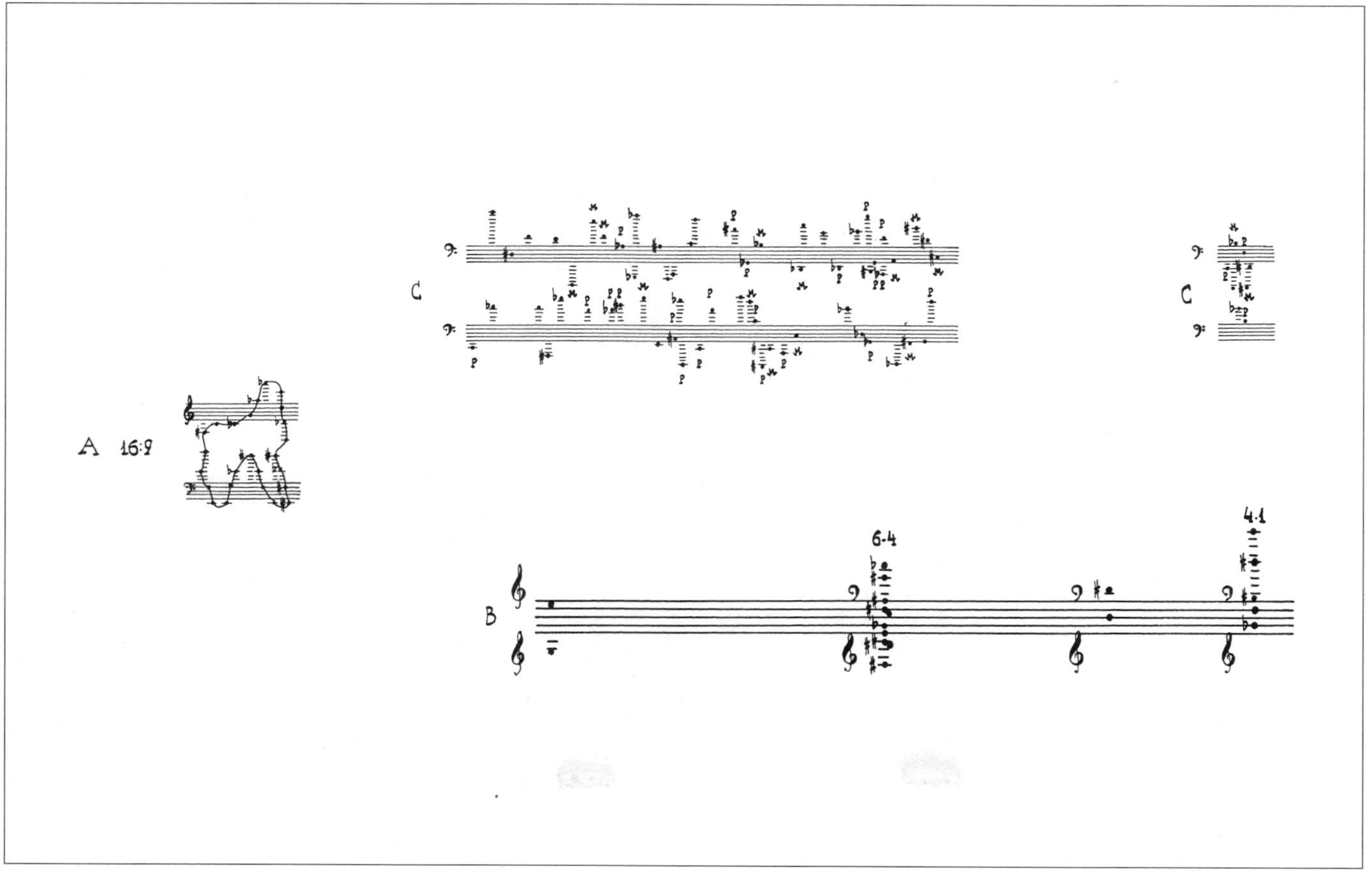

C

C

A 16:9

B

6·4

4·1

I shall devote the remainder of this essay to Tudor's second realization of the *Solo for Piano*. In doing so, I follow Tudor's own emphasis. Taken as a whole, the two realizations of the *Solo for Piano* constitute Tudor's most extensive preparation of any composer's work. But Tudor used the first realization for a rather brief period, perhaps for no more than two years. In contrast, he continued to use his second realization, in various and evolving forms, from the time of its inception in 1959 until as late as 1993, on one of the rare occasions when he still performed at the piano. Furthermore, Tudor made two recordings of the later realization, and a third recording, of a live performance in 1992, has also appeared.[3] Another reason for addressing Tudor's second realization of the *Solo for Piano* is more personal: it has been my long-standing belief that the original recording of the work documents the first great culmination of the Tudor-Cage collaboration.

In the spring of 1959, Cage was invited to give a lecture at Teachers College of Columbia University in New York. Fearing that he would not have enough time in which to write a new text, Cage expanded a lecture he had read the previous fall at the Brussels World's Fair, a lecture that had consisted of thirty stories, each read over the course of one minute. For the Columbia lecture, Cage added sixty more stories and asked Tudor to provide music of his choice to complement the lecture, now ninety minutes long. Tudor used the *Solo for Piano* again. But this time he took a new approach to Cage's score by including only the graphs that, as he put it, "had the possibility of being read as single icti," that is, those graphs whose notations could be played as discrete and separate attacks. There were, Tudor found, fifty-three graphs in the *Solo for Piano* conforming to this criterion.

Tudor next prepared any content sketches needed for the graphs he had not used in his first realization. He determined the contents much the same way as he had done previously, transcribing Cage's graphs to more standard notation and drawing up lists of calculations of the more morphological graphs, some of which I shall discuss below. As before, Tudor sketched the contents of each graph in its entirety. An exception are those graphs, such as graph BY on pages 54–55 of Cage's score, whose contents are to consist of otherwise unspecified noises. In

3. The first recording comprised two simultaneous performances: Tudor playing the *Solo for Piano* and Cage reading his lecture "Indeterminacy: New Aspect of Form in Instrumental and Electronic Music." Made in July 1959 and released on Folkways Records during the same year, the recording has been reissued on compact discs (Smithsonian/Folkways SF40804/5). In 1982, Tudor recorded the *Solo for Piano* alone (Atonal 3037). The third recording (Mode 57), the only current documentation of Tudor performing this realization with orchestra, is of a performance in Frankfurt on September 4, 1992. The occasion was the Festival of Anarchic Harmonies, originally planned as a celebration of Cage's eightieth birthday on September 5; owing to the composer's death the previous month, the concert became a memorial tribute.

these cases, Tudor used tape tracks from Cage's sound collage *Fontana Mix* (1958).

At this point, Tudor had determined the overall content of the new realization. He compiled the results in a master table written on five pages of typescript (fig. 6.1). The underlined numbers represent the ninety-minute duration of the realization. Under the number 0, the first column of figures shows the attack point, in seconds, of each of Tudor's readings; column 2 identifies the graph on which the reading is based, followed by the ordinal number of the specific graph notation being used; and column 3 refers to the page on which the graph begins in Cage's score. For example, the second entry under minute 0, "24.3 T-1 41," means that Tudor's first reading of graph T, as that graph appears on page 41 of Cage's score, is to begin at attack point 24.3 seconds (the first, parenthetical entry ".0 BV-1 53," was not used in the realization). The next entry, "27.65 I-1 46," means that the attack point of Tudor's first reading of graph I on page 46 is to be 27.65 seconds, and so forth.

But the master table gives no indication of why these readings occur at these attack points, or, for that matter, how Tudor generated the attack points themselves. Nor does it explain why Tudor's first two readings from graph BB 45, both of them occurring at attack point 90, are, according to the master table, the eighth and eleventh readings of the graph, rather than the first and second. And neither Cage's notations nor his instructions for reading them have anything to say about these questions. The answer lies in the internal temporal structure Tudor conceived for the new realization.

To determine the attack points of his readings of Cage's graphs within the ninety-minute time frame of the realization, Tudor measured either the area or the length of each graph according to its particular morphology and with whatever means of measurement he found appropriate to a graph's individual form and shape. Each measurement gave him an area or length A for each graph. Next, he measured the position of each ictus, or notational point, within the graph, usually in terms of its distance from the beginning of the graph. Then he multiplied each position measurement by the total duration of the realization, 5,400 seconds (90 minutes) and divided the result by the number representing the relevant area or length A. The quotient was the attack point, in Tudor's realization, of the ictus from Cage's score. In this way, Tudor designed a temporal structure that reflected both the specific attack points of the source material in Cage's score and the order of their occurrence.

This structure placed a new restriction on Tudor's knowledge of his own actions. With his content sketches and calculations he had determined the actions he would perform but not the times at which he

0		
(.0	BV-1	53)
24.3	T-1	41
27.65	I-1	46
40.5	B-1	9
42.65	B-1	34
47.66	AC,AE-1	21
1		
64.55	B-1	1
71.12	B-2	34
72	BZ-1	55
81.15	BS-1	52
83.85	BY-1	54
90	BB-8	45
	BB-11	45
97.65	BC-1	47
108	BZ-2	55
112.5	AT-1	39
2		
121	I-2	46
128.3	BB-1	53
139.66	B-1	23
144	BZ-3	55
145.5	T-1	16
(160.15	BV-2	53)
162	BI-1	50
165	BC-2	47
167	BB-2	53
175.5	B-2	9
176.08	BY-2	54
3		
187.25	T-2	41
189	BT-2	54
197.3	BV-3	53
206.6	BV-4	53
214.7	T-2	16
216	BR-1	51
	BT-1	54
217.2	AB-1	20
222.53	AI-1	36
223.45	CE-1	59
237.83	BY-3	54
4		
255.5	B-3	34
260.69	CE-2	59
263.1	BV-5	53
270	AC-1	31
	BB-7	45
288.8	AE-1	56
5		
307.1	B-4	34
309.2	AG-1	20
311.4	T-3	16
312	I-3	46
319	B-1	55
322	BK-1	52
327.8	BS-2	52
330.75	CA-1	55
337.5	B-3	9
354.86	BR-2	51
6		
381.2	BS-3	52
381.6	I-4	46
384	B-5	34
389.8	BC-3	47
405.12	AC,AE-2	21
419	BK-2	52
7		
425.25	CA-2	55
440	I-5	46
441	BV-6	53
442.2	T-3	41
447.34	U-3	16
450.1	BC-4	47
462.86	BR-3	51
468	BZ-4	55
474	BS-4	52
8		
494	BS-5	52
504	BZ-5	55
505.4	B-2	55
511.24	U-1	16
516	BK-3	52
521.38	CE-3	59
526.5	I-6	46
540	B-4	9
	BI-2	50
	B-6	34
9		
562.3	T-4	41
592	AB-2	20
595	BI-3	50
596.4	T-1	12
10		
(600.4	BV-7	53)
612.5	BK-4	52
617.14	BR-4	51
621	P-1	9
	BT-4	54
643.42	AC,AE-3	21
644.1	T-4	16
645.5	I-7	46
11		
(665.2	BV-8	53)
665.9	AB-3	20
675	CD-12	57
680.5	N-1	9
697.5	B-3	55
702.96	U-2	16
703.5	BI-4	50
703.6	T-5	41
710	BK-5	52
711.2	B-7	34
(712.6	BV-9	53)
713	I-8	46
715.5	P-2	9
12		
744.83	CE-4	59
748.8	N-2	9
751.5	BC-5	47
755.8	T-5	16
756	BZ-6	55
756.5	BI-5	50
	BS-6	52
756.59	AI-2	36
764	BS-7	52
13		
786.86	BR-5	51
797.5	Hb-1	50
797.6	T-6	16
810	BT-3	54
	B-5	9
	CD-1	57
812.2	T-2	12
822	T-6	41
835	I-9	46
837.5	BK-6	52
14		
840.2	BS-8	52
868	N-3	9
877.5	B-6	9
882	B-8	34
892.2	BS-9	52
894.5	N-4	9
15		
911.5	Ca-2	1
913	I-10	46
925.71	BR-6	51
928.5	T-7	16
929	BV-10	53
932.7	BB-3	53
935	BK-7	52
936	BZ-7	55
945.8	AB-4	20
16		
971.5	BS-10	52
990	BB-4	45
1005	BV-11	53
1008	BZ-8	55
1012.5	P-3	9
1016	BV-12	53
17		
1026	BT-5	54
1030.9	AV-1	37
1039.75	BY-4	54
1040	I-11	46
1043	K-1	43
1062.5	B-9	34
1066	T-8	16
1066.5	CA-3	55
1072.37	AC,AE-4	21
1080	B-7	9
	BR-7	51
	BZ-9	55
(	BV-13	53)
18		
(1088	BV-14	53)
1094	BK-8	52
1097	T-7	41
1097.55	CA-4	55
1119	T-8	41
19		
1143	BB-4	53
1164.56	AI-3	36
20		

FIGURE 6.1
David Tudor, second realization of *Solo for Piano*, first page of master table, the David Tudor Papers, 1884–1998 (bulk 1940–1996), Getty Research Institute, Research Library, accession no. 980039.

would perform them. And to keep this aspect beyond his control, he formulated a temporal structure that was at once unpredictable and determinate.[4] A secondary consequence of the new temporal structure was the coincidence of as many as five graph readings, whose individual contents may be mutually exclusive, at a single attack point (as happens at attack point 2025, for example). There is nothing new, of course, about requiring a pianist to do a number of things at once. But as a rule these simultaneous acts of performance are, like the musical results to which they are directed, interrelated. In Tudor's second realization of the *Solo for Piano,* the performer's actions are intentionally disconnected, then reassembled in new and unforeseeable ways.

To prepare the performance score itself, Tudor typed his list of attack points and their sources into his master table, then transcribed the appropriate reading to its place in his score. But this transcription took two forms.

Tudor may have originally intended to use the entire contents of his master table, although its total 789 attack points implies a resulting texture of extreme density. Moreover, if Cage had insufficient time in which to write his Columbia lecture, then Tudor had probably less time to prepare his realization. In any event, he divided the readings in his master table into two parts, copying 472 entries into a small packet of paper and the remaining entries into a second packet. The packets are complementary; together, they contain all the information in the master table.

Referring to the first packet of paper, Tudor transcribed the contents from Cage's score on ninety miniature sheets of staff paper. This was the first version of his second realization of the *Solo for Piano,* which he performed in conjunction with Cage's lecture at Teachers College in April 1959. Later, Tudor began a second version, if for no other reason than to use up the "leftovers," so to speak, which he had copied from the master table into the second packet of paper. This version, too, was written on small sheets of staff paper, but after thirty-two pages the manuscript breaks off. Tudor then began again, writing out the entire second version on ninety pages (forty-five sheets) of blank, rather than staff paper. The result was the second version of his second realization of the *Solo for Piano.*

The reason for the incomplete manuscript seems clear: blank paper offered a notational advantage. Because the new realization consisted entirely of discrete events, Tudor did not need a continuous staff, only a means of denoting the ninety-minute time scale. In both versions, each page equals one minute; at two systems per page, each system, denoted by vertical lines on the left and right, represents thirty seconds. To enter

4. We can show Tudor's method formulaically, where attack point ap = position measurement p times total duration D divided by area or length A, or $(p \times D) \div A = ap$.

each of his readings of Cage's graphs, Tudor simply placed the entry, whatever its notational form, at its proper location on the timeline. In the second version, if a reading called for more or less conventional notation, Tudor used a rastrum. If the notation was in graphic or verbal form, Tudor dispensed with lines and spaces. Staff notation became simply one notational tool among many.

In reconstructing Tudor's process of preparing both versions of his second realization of the *Solo for Piano,* I traced the derivations of his 472 readings of Cage's graphs used in the first version as well as his first reading of each graph used in the second. Using his master table and the two packets derived from it, plus his work sheets, sketches, and two performance scores, I have been able to identify and describe Tudor's methods of determining both the content and the attack point of each sonority in the realization. I shall discuss here a few of the problems posed by Cage's notations in the *Solo for Piano* and Tudor's solutions to them, beginning with the more straightforward notations in Cage's score.

Some graphs present no particular problems in reading or interpretation. In the family of graphs labeled "B," for example, the notation is fairly standard, consisting of noteheads on a staff, and the pitch content is partly determinate. The only ambiguity lies in individual pitch identity, owing to the "floating" clef signs: if both clef signs are present at a given sonority, they are accompanied by numbers signifying how many of the noteheads in that sonority are to be read in each clef, although the assignment of the specific clef is indeterminate. All the B graphs in Cage's score are notated in this manner (that is why they are labeled "B").

The first sonority of graph B 9 consists of six noteheads (ex. 6.2). According to Cage's instructions, four of these are to be read with the treble clef, the remaining two with the bass. Tudor's content sketch for the graph sorts out the pitch identity of all twenty-seven of its sonorities (ex. 6.3). The sketch dispenses with Cage's numerical dispositions, but Tudor's determination of pitch content of sonority 1 is clear. Reading from bottom to top, the four noteheads Tudor read with the treble clef are noteheads 1, 3, 4, and 5, or $G\sharp_2$, $B\sharp_4$, $E\flat_5$, and G_5. The remaining two noteheads, therefore, he read with the bass clef, so that these became $C\flat_2$ and E_5. In his content sketch, Tudor renotated the sonority enharmonically. He then entered the notation on the first page of his score at its proper attack point of 40.5 seconds (ex. 6.4). The first entry in the lower system shows Tudor's first reading of graph B 9 in Cage's score. In his subsequent readings of graph B 9, Tudor replaced Cage's numerous ledger lines with octave signs to facilitate reading; this alteration is unnecessary in the case of sonority 1.

EXAMPLE 6.2
Solo for Piano, from *Concert for Piano and Orchestra*, graph B 9, Edition Peters, 9. © 1960 by Henmar Press, Inc. Used by permission.

Some graphs appear to be more abstract than they actually are. An example of this is the group of K graphs, beginning with graph K 8 (ex. 6.5), one of the most famous of Cage's notations (it adorns the cover of the 1962 Peters catalog of Cage's works). Graph K 8 consists of eight geometric shapes in which pitch names are entered in each angle, so that the number of pitches corresponds to the number of angles in each shape. Some of the shapes overlap, and overlaying all of them is a large grand staff. The instructions for the K graphs read: "Disregard time. Play only odd or even number of tones in a performance, using others of a given 3, 4, 5, or 6 sided figure as graces or punctuations."

Tudor saw that Cage had notated not simply pitch classes but specific pitch content inside each geometric shape, since the pitch names are also aligned with the corresponding lines and spaces on the grand staff. He numbered the eight shapes and wrote down the pitch names found in each, transcribing the resulting sonorities to standard notation in his content sketch. The sketch appears at the bottom of the page containing

EXAMPLE 6.3
David Tudor, second realization of *Solo for Piano,* content sketch for graphs B 9 and K 8, the David Tudor Papers, 1884–1998 (bulk 1940–1996), Getty Research Institute, Research Library, accession no. 980039.

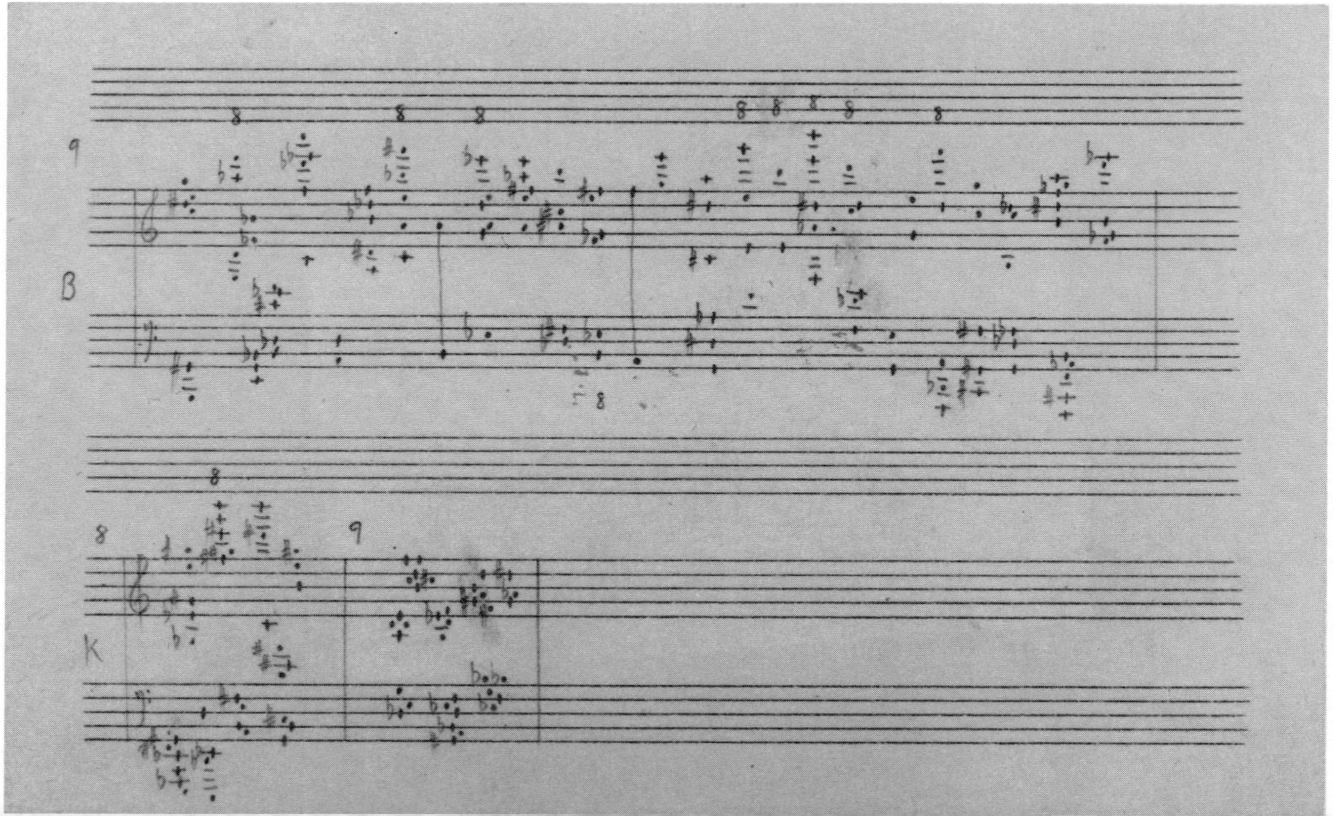

EXAMPLE 6.4

David Tudor, second realization of *Solo for Piano*, the David Tudor Papers, 1884–1998 (bulk 1940–1996), Getty Research Institute, Research Library, accession no. 980039. The first notation, the hexachord B_1–$G\sharp_2$–C_5–$D\sharp_5$–E_5–G_5, reflects Tudor's first reading of graph B 9.

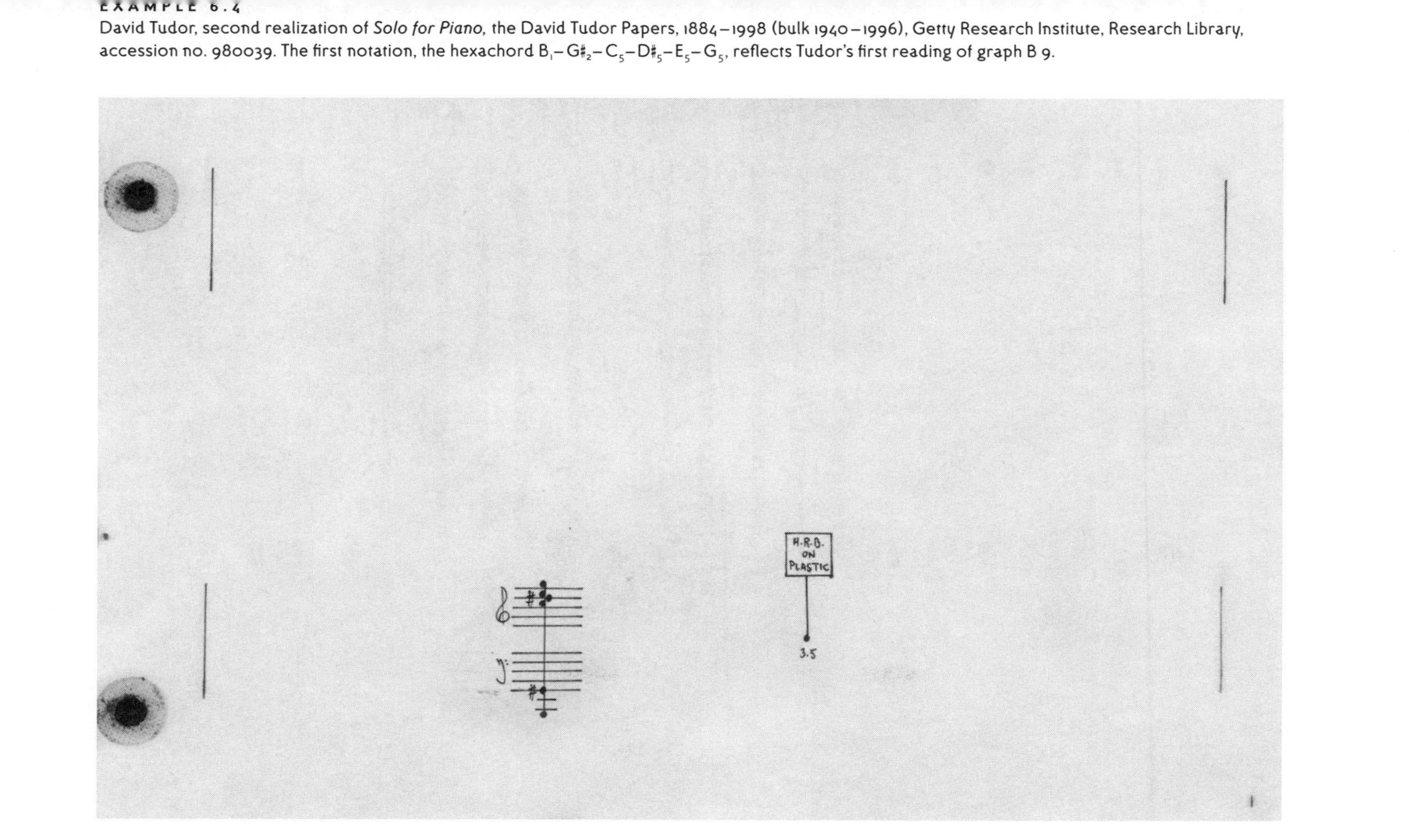

EXAMPLE 6.5

Solo for Piano, from *Concert for Piano and Orchestra*, graph K 8, Edition Peters, 8. © 1960 by Henmar Press, Inc. Used by permission.

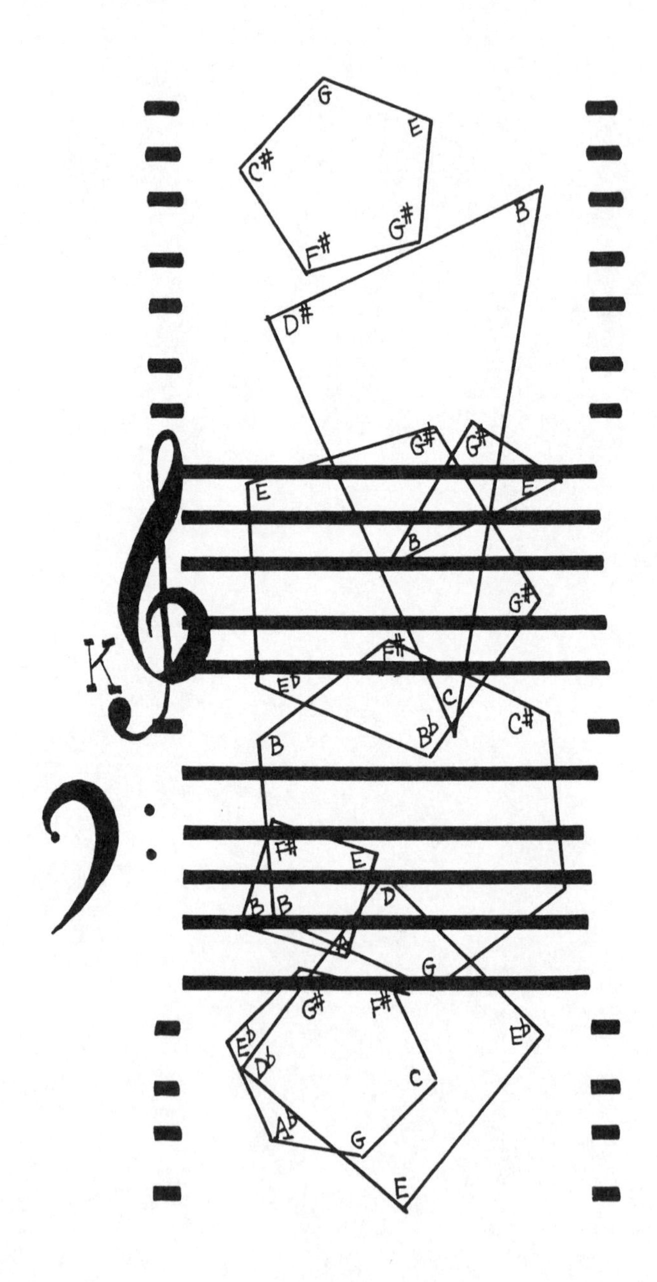

Tudor's content sketch for graph B 9 (ex. 6.3). The first sonority in the sketch, for example, the hexachord G1–A♭1–C2–E♭$_2$–F♯$_2$–G♯$_2$ in the bass staff, shows the pitch content of the hexagon near the bottom of Cage's graph.[5] When the graph is read from the left, however, the first shape is the square inside the bass clef and containing the letter-names for pitches A_2–B_2–E_3–F♯$_3$. Consequently, the first reading of graph K 8 in Tudor's realization corresponds to the fourth notation in the content sketch (the third group of noteheads in the bass staff); both show the tetrachord A_2–B_2–E_3–F♯$_3$. In accordance with Cage's instructions to play either an odd or an even number of notes within each group within a shape, Tudor extended three of the noteheads with a brace to signify an odd number, leaving the F♯$_3$ to serve as "punctuation" (ex. 6.6).

The most abstract notation in the *Concert for Piano and Orchestra* is the series of graphs made with line-and-point drawings, beginning with graph BB 45 (ex. 6.7). The line-and-point drawing was the most efficient of Cage's early techniques of indeterminate notation. While many of the graphs in the *Solo for Piano* primarily confound the order of occurrence of an otherwise specific content, the line-and-point drawings place the musical material itself beyond the composer's control. This in turn requires the performer to determine a content that embodies the character of each sound. And to do this, the performer must first obtain a sufficient description of the sound's characteristics by measuring the graph according to Cage's instructions. The instructions for reading graph BB 45 are as follows: "Notes are single sounds. Lines are duration (D), frequency (F), overtone structure (S), amplitude (A), and occurrence (succession) (O). Proximity to these, measured by dropping perpendiculars for notes to lines[,] gives, respectively, longest, lowest, simplest, loudest, and earliest."

There are twelve notes or noteheads in graph BB 45. Tudor measured the distance in centimeters of each notehead from each of the five lines D, S, F, O, and A and from their hypothetical extensions beyond the graph when this was necessary. He compiled the results in a list of specifications (fig. 6.2).[6] Under the column showing order of occurrence O, the measurements of entries 8 and 11 are both 0.1 cm. This does not reflect a literal reading of Cage's score, where the corresponding noteheads 8 and 11 in fact touch line O and where their distance from the

5. The sketch actually shows seven noteheads in this sonority. Tudor may have initially read the extra A_2, which belongs to the group written within the square above the hexagon in Cage's graph, as part of the first sonority. If this was the case, he saw his error, for he omitted the note from his realization.

6. Graph BB 45 has been reduced in the reproduction shown in example 6.7. All of Tudor's measurements refer to the original 11-by-17-inch dimensions of Cage's score.

EXAMPLE 6.6

David Tudor, second realization of *Solo for Piano*, first reading of graph K 8, the David Tudor Papers, 1884–1998 (bulk 1940–1996), Getty Research Institute, Research Library, accession no. 980039.

EXAMPLE 6.7

Solo for Piano, from *Concert for Piano and Orchestra,* graph BB 45, Edition Peters, 45. © 1960 by Henmar Press, Inc. Used by permission.

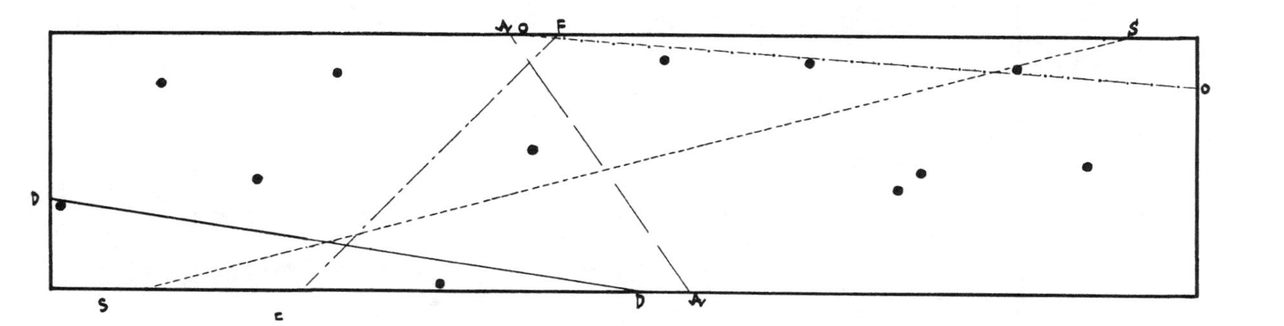

BB

45-46
BB

35.

1 H
2 C
3 N
4 A

-4 x6

9.2=10.5

D .1	S 2.1	F 4.6	O 4.2	A 9.2
D 2.7	S 3.9	F 4.9	O 1.6	A 6.2
D 1.1	S 1.6	F 2.2	O 3.3	A 5.7
D 3.4	S 3.3	F 2.6	O 1.1	A 3.3
D .5	S 1.4	F 1.9	O 5.1	A 4.
D 2.5	S .8	F 1.3	O 2.3	A 1.
D 4.6	S 1.9	F 1.9	O .3	A 2.2
D 5.1	S 1.1	F 4.	O .1	A 4.5
D 2.8	S 1.9	F 6.9	O 2.5	A 4.5
D 3.2	S 1.6	F 7.	O 2.2	A 5.
D 5.5	S .1	F 6.9	O .1	A 7.8
D 3.8	S 2.3	F 9.2	O 1.8	A 7.8

FIGURE 6.2
David Tudor, second realization of *Solo for Piano*, list of specifications for graph BB 45, the David Tudor Papers, 1884–1998 (bulk 1940–1996), Getty Research Institute, Research Library, accession no. 980039.

line is therefore zero. But Tudor needed a positive number in order to calculate the attack points of these noteheads; therefore, he used the nearest available integer, which in centimeters is 0.1.

The figure "× 6" above column O is Tudor's measurement of the area *A* of graph BB 45. I confess I do not know how he arrived at this figure, for the area of the graph in Cage's score is eighteen square inches (two inches high by nine inches long). But whatever Tudor's scale of measurement may have been, the factor $A = 6$ works in determining the order of occurrence of each of the twelve noteheads in the graph. For example, multiplying position measurement 0.1 of noteheads 8 and 11 by the duration 5,400 and dividing the result by 6 yields the common attack point of ninety seconds.

Tudor later revised his list of specifications for graph BB 45, grouping the measurements pertaining to overtone structure S into four categories (these categories also appear at the top of Tudor's first list). Noteheads measuring less than one centimeter from line S (numbers 11 and 8), went into category H. Those more than one but less than two centimeters from the line were labeled C.[7] He also converted the frequency measurements F to piano-key numbers, multiplying each measurement by 10. But the largest product of this operation was 92 (i.e., the 9.2 cm shown in the F column for notehead 12), and the piano has of course only 88 keys. Consequently, Tudor reduced the product of each multiplication by 4; this is the meaning of the figure "− 4" above the F column in the first list of specifications. At some point (this is not reflected in the surviving work notes), Tudor replaced all but the first two piano-key numbers with nonpitched sounds, probably because the inverted scale of Cage's instructions for reading line S, representing the "simplest" overtone structure, required sounds more complex in overtones—noises, in other words—than could be obtained by pitches played on the piano. Finally, Tudor converted the amplitude measurements to a dynamic scale of 0 to 10.5 and equated the largest measurement, 9.2, to the highest degree on this scale, adjusting the other measurements accordingly and incrementally: 0, 0.5, 1, 1.5, 2, 2.5, etc. Only the duration measurements remained unchanged in the new list (fig. 6.3).

7. The meaning of these initials, though not entirely clear, can be inferred from the results in Tudor's realization. H refers to the two notes ($C\sharp_6$ and F_1) played as harmonics; N probably stands for "noise," since the corresponding notations are cues for the use of a Klaxon; and the two appearances of A—"Tap Klaxon" and "Ruler End on Tenor C[enter] B[ar]"—seem to mean the use of auxiliary sound sources. Finally, the realization of all six of the noteheads grouped under category C is the same cue FB, meaning a sound to produced with the fall-board of the piano; on Tudor's first two recordings of the *Solo for Piano* one hears at these six attack points a sound suggesting that Tudor knocked or clapped the fall-board against the case of the instrument.

53 BV

	O	10 S	5 S	F	D	A
1.3	197.3	7	3	45	VL	10
9	712.6	5	3	19	VL	4
2.4	206.6	4	2	72	MS	7
23	1847.4	8	4	59	VL	6.5
51	4403	1	1	30	ML	3.5
3.5	263.1	5	2	64	M	7.5
20	1527	7	4	48	VL	5.5
46	3905	1	1	25	ML	5
4.6	441	7	4	60	ML	10.5
7	600.4	7	3	42	VL	3
5.10	929	2	1	79	S	5
34	2896	9	4	69	VL	9
6.11	1005	9	4	65	M	10.5
2	160.15	7	4	51	VL	2
7.12	1016	4	2	45	VL	7.5
21	1633.3	5	2	15	VL	6
8.18	1370	5	2	30	VL	8
16	1344	3	2	8	L	6
9.22	1691	1	1	58	ML	5
35	2928	7	3	34	L	10.5
10.25	2114	1	1	39	VL	5.5
33	2768	4	2	7	ML	10.5
29	2368	4	2	45	VL	10.5
11.27	2292	1	1	14	ML	8.5
14	1088	2	1	33	ML	10.5
12.30	2498	1	1	51	L	4
44	3613	6	3	22	ML	10
36	3114	5	2	59	VL	8
17	1350	7	3	11	M	6
13.32	2526	2	1	21	L	6
31	2512	2	1	21	ML	9
15	1278	5	2	41	VL	8
14.37	3174	2	1	36	0	3.5
45	3791	4	2	0	M	8.5
26	2202	6	3	61	VL	10.5(0)
1	.0	7	4	17	ML	4.5
15.38	3194	1	1	5	MS	6
28	2307	2	1	62	M	9
16.39	3332	1	1	8	ML	5.5
17.40	3334	1	1	23	VL	4
42	3507	3	1	18	M	10.5
19	1412.5	6	3	56	VL	8.5
18.41	3481	1	1	1	M	5.5
19.47	3966	2	1	6	M	4
43	3517	1	1	47	MS	9
8	665.2	7	4	57	VL	5
20.48	4035	3	1	18	ML	3
49	4165	2	1	32	MS	7.5
13	1080	7	4	67	L	7
24	1957.5	8	4	26	VL	3
21.50	4224	4	2	25	L	2
22.52	4423	3	2	4	M	3
23.54	4990	6	3	12	ML	1.5
53	4968	1	1	41	S	5

12 T
0,R,LR,R,L,0,L,R,LR,LR

53 BB

-	Q	F	D	10 S	5 S	A
1.	128.3	47	M	1	1	7
2.	167	34	M	1	1	8.5
3.	932.7	42	ML	4	2	5.5
4.	1143	28	S	2	1	8.5
5.	1464	16	ML	3	1	9
6.	1772	37	L	5	3	4.5
7.	1911	24	M	6	3	6
8.	2725	2	L	4	2	8.5
9.	3022	21	L	3	2	8.5
10.	3471	10	VL	5	3	10.5
11.	4027	54	VL	3	2	7.5
12.	4776	2	VL	9	4	5

45-46 BB

	O	S	F	(35) D	A
1.	3780	N	42	.1	10.5
2.	1440	A	45	2.7	7
3.	2970	C	18	1.1	6.5
4.	990	A	22	3.4	4
5.	4590	C	15	.5	4.5
6.	2070	H	9	2.5	1
7.	270	C	15	4.6	2.5
8.	90	C	36	5.1	5
9.	2250	C	65	2.8	5
10.	1980	C	66	3.2	5.5
11.	90	H	65	5.5	9
12.	1620	N	88	3.8	9

50 BJ
O2025 SC F61 D3.75 A6

50-51 BI
13457959103711641448539331218235532

364101324159610362835124

50 Ha
1. 1437.5 C^{1} P
2. 4385 F^{1} M
3. 4880 G^{2} M

56-57 AS
3118 G^{1}

15,32,41,61:silence

54 BT (30')

				30':	
1.035	C	24.175	C	1-4	59
1.12	P	27.45	C	8-11	61
3.27	P	29.16	C	14	73-76
4.30	P			17-18	83-84
5.42	P			21	
10.57	P			25	
11.425	P			31-35	
16.39	P			37-38	
17.15	C			42	
21	P			52	

FIGURE 6.3
David Tudor, second realization of *Solo for Piano*, second list of specifications for graph BB 45, the David Tudor Papers, 1884–1998 (bulk 1940–1996), Getty Research Institute, Research Library, accession no. 980039.

EXAMPLE 6.8

David Tudor, second realization of *Solo for Piano*, concurrent readings 8 and 11 of graph BB 45, the David Tudor Papers, 1884–1998 (bulk 1940–1996), Getty Research Institute, Research Library, accession no. 980039.

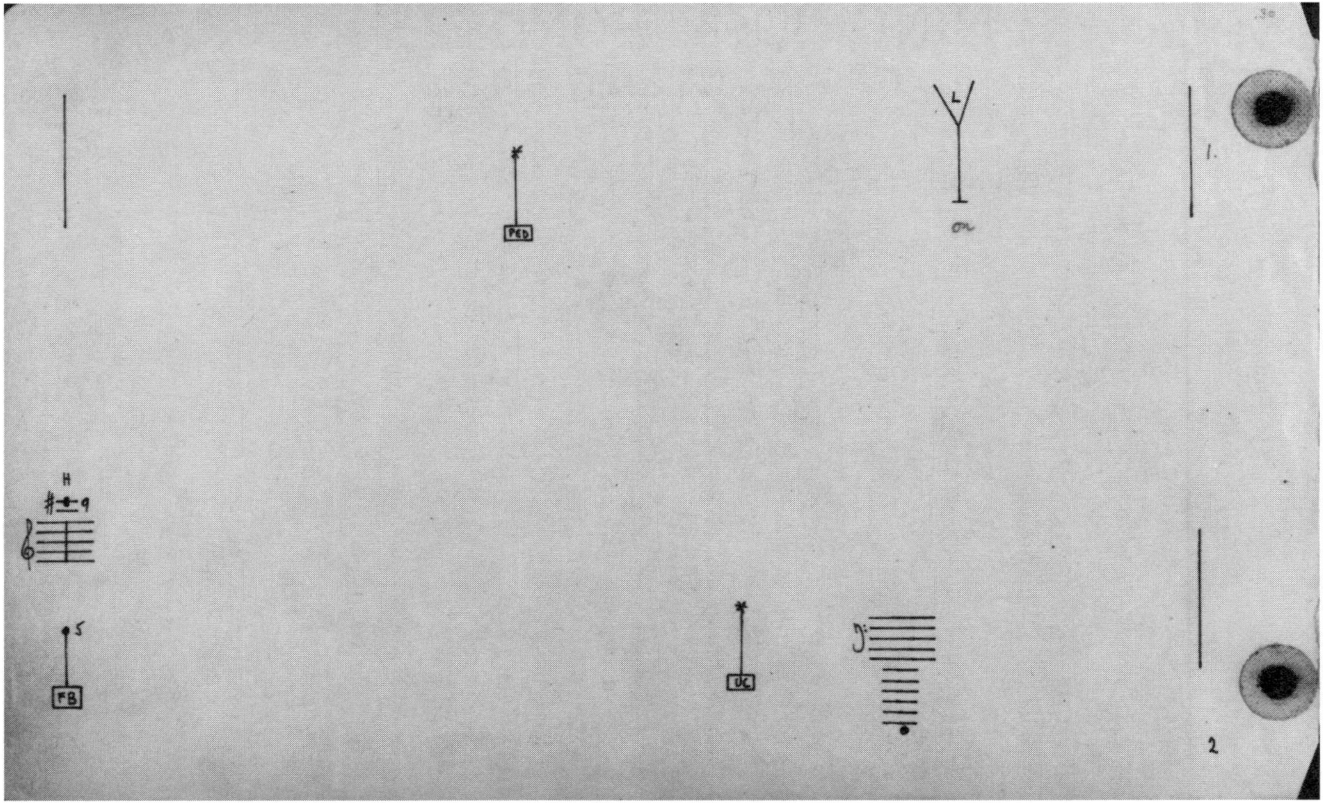

The revised list enables us to distinguish the two readings at attack point 90 in Tudor's realization by noticing that the dynamic level 9 in the upper portion of the notation corresponds to that found at reading number 11 on the list of specifications, and that dynamic level 5 in the lower part of the notation corresponds to reading number 8 (ex. 6.8). In place of frequency (or piano-key number) 36 shown in the entry for reading 8 on Tudor's list, the realization shows the cue FB for a sound to be produced with fall-board at dynamic level 5. Above this notation is an entry whose amplitude level 9 shows that the notehead represents reading 11 on Tudor's list. In Cage's score, notehead 11 lies one centimeter from the line S. Since proximity to the line represents "simplest" overtone structure, Tudor represented this quality through the frequency itself, that is, piano key 65, or C$\sharp_6$, played as a harmonic H.[8]

◻ ◻ ◻

With his second realization of Cage's *Solo for Piano,* Tudor began to move beyond piano playing as he had redefined it in the 1950s. His first realization of the *Solo,* which merits an extended discussion it has not received here, offered Tudor the opportunity to summarize both his virtuosity as a pianist and his innovations in the techniques of piano playing. In his second realization, Tudor entered a new phase. While showing connections with his earlier work, Tudor's second realization of the *Solo for Piano* marks the beginning of a transition from pianist to what Larry Austin has called sonic artist. It was a journey that would lead him away from the piano and into the world of live electronic music. Characteristically, Tudor would create much of this new world himself.

8. Tudor treated the other notehead closest to line S in like manner: page 35 of his realization shows his reading of notehead 6 to be an F_1 (frequency/piano key 9) to be played as a harmonic.

SEVEN

Paul van Emmerik

Here Comes Everything

I

John Cage's death in 1992 is not only a loss, but also a challenge for a new appreciation of his work. This is not to suggest that Cage was somehow "in the way" to anyone interested in his work, since everybody who knew him knows that he considered being accessible "a part of twentieth-century ethics."[1] However, with the death of this charismatic composer, events that seem so recent have unexpectedly become history. Consequently, especially for those who knew him personally, experiences and recollections are being overgrown by the problems of historical method, of interpreting what remains in order to testify about Cage and his work, as happens with all interesting relics from the past.

My own involvement with these "relics" began during Cage's lifetime, in the early 1980s, during the compilation of a bibliography of writings by and about him. Since ample attention, including bibliographical attention, had been given to American mu-

This chapter is dedicated to Charles Hamm.

1. "Conversation with John Cage," in *John Cage,* ed. Richard Kostelanetz (New York: Praeger, 1970), 6.

sic in the now defunct German annual *Neuland,* I approached its editor, the German pianist Herbert Henck, about publishing this bibliography. It turned out that Henck had also been working on a Cage bibliography. Nevertheless, he generously accepted me as coauthor, since our independent efforts had produced quite different lists. Our joint effort resulted in the *Cage-Bibliographie 1939–1985,* published in the fifth and final volume of *Neuland.*[2] Comprising about two thousand entries, it is the most comprehensive bibliography of Cage to date.

After the publication of this bibliography, Henck and I agreed that it should be published as a book and that a catalog of works should be added. It was Cage himself who told us about the catalog of his works already compiled by the Hungarian musicologist András Wilheim, which had resulted from Wilheim's research in Cage's apartment in New York in late 1984. When approached, Wilheim agreed to join the project, and his compilation became the basis for the *catalogue raisonné* included in *A Cage Compendium,* a book currently in preparation. In addition to the catalog and the bibliography, the *Compendium* will include an extensive biographical chronology and, of course, an index. The original bibliography has been expanded and updated steadily in the past few years, and it now comprises approximately ten thousand entries, documenting the reception of Cage's work as extensively as possible. In the *catalogue raisonné,* separate sections are given to Cage's music, writings, and works of art—even though in several cases there is no clear line of demarcation between the three categories—and the arrangement of items within each section is chronological. The following entry exemplifies the format of the music section in the catalog, this particular composition having been chosen for a reason that will become clear below.

Three

For three recorder players using sopranino, soprano, alto, tenor (player 1); sopranino, soprano, alto, basset, tenor, bass (player 2); and soprano, alto, basset, tenor, double bass (player 3)

Extent: 6 sentences (instructions for performance); (1) 2 systems; A through I, each part 3 systems; (2) 2 systems; duration indeterminate

Completed in July 1989 in New York; first performed 27 July 1990, Speyer, Dom, Internationale Ferienkurse für Neue Musik Darmstadt; Trio Dolce: Christine Brelowski, Geesche Geddert, Dorothea Winter (Clemens 1990, Lenz, S. 1990)

Dedicated to Trio Dolce

Manuscripts: New York Public Library at Lincoln Center, JPB 94–24 folder 786 (worksheets, 2 leaves, 28 cm, white paper, ink), folders 787–788 (sketches and draft, 8 leaves, 32 cm, vellum music paper, ink),

2. "Cage-Bibliographie 1939–1985," *Neuland* 5 (1984–85): 394–431.

folder 789 (galley proof and draft of instructions for performance, 29 leaves, 28 cm, white paper, ink, pencil, colored pencil)
Publication: New York: Henmar Press (C. F. Peters 67303), 1989
Literature: Cage/McLellan 1989; Geddert 1994–95; Gronemeyer 1993, 21–22)

This example can be used to clarify the basic set-up of the catalog. Where known or applicable, details about a composition in the catalog are presented under several headings: the title of the work, appearing in standardized form; the performing forces; models, musical or otherwise, used by Cage; for vocal works, the author of the text or libretto; for works originally conceived as music for dance, film, or theater, the name of the choreographer, director, or playwright; the extent, that is, the number of measures, systems, or sentences (in the case of performance notes or verbal notation) and the duration; dates and places of beginning and of completion of the work, information about the first performance and about commissions and dedications; basic information about the manuscripts, described on the basis of direct examination or taken from library or exhibition catalogs (unless otherwise noted, all items listed are Cage's autograph); publication data; publicly distributed recordings on record, tape, and compact disc; and finally, references to literature discussing the work in some detail. Such references usually range from Cage's own statements in published writings, interviews and conversations, accounts by performers of his music, reviews of published scores, first performances and recordings, to analytical or critical essays or studies. The entries for literature on *Three* are given below.

Cage, John / McLellan, Joseph. 1989. "John Cage's Realm: the Din of Manhattan," *International Herald Tribune* (9 May), 18.
Clemens, E. 1990. "Länge statt Meditation," *Speyer Tagespost* (30 July), 10.
Geddert, Geesche. 1994–95. "*Three*—das Blockflötentrio von John Cage," *Tibia* 19–20, 40–43.
Gronemeyer, Gisela. 1993. "'I'm finally writing beautiful music': Das numerierte Spätwerk von John Cage," *Musiktexte*, no. 48 (February), 19–24.
Lenz, Sonja. 1990. "Sternenmusik," *Darmstädter Echo* (30 July), 21.

I continued in early 1992 to expand upon Wilheim's 1984 research and also began an inventory of Cage's music manuscripts in his New York apartment. With more than twenty-five thousand leaves, this assemblage constitutes the largest and most important collection of Cage manuscripts. Shortly after the composer's death, the estate of John Cage requested a team of musicologists to continue this work. In 1993, Wilheim, Martin Erdmann, Laura Kuhn, James Pritchett, and I completed our assessment of the music manuscripts in Cage's possession at the time of his death. After considering the sale of the music manuscripts to a European archive, the estate of John Cage made the wise decision to keep them in the United States. They are now housed in the Music Division of the New York Public Library at Lincoln Center.

II

The six parts of the *Cage-Bibliographie* were arranged chronologically in an attempt to document the reception, scholarly and otherwise, of Cage's work from year to year as closely as possible. Unfortunately, at the time the bibliography was published critics were only just beginning to write about Cage's music on the basis of analysis of the sketches. Consequently, many items testifying to this approach are missing from the list, especially the dissertations of Deborah Campana, James Pritchett, Martin Erdmann, in addition to my own.[3] In the preface to his dissertation, Pritchett defended his use of sources for a study of Cage's chance music of the 1950s as follows: "Some may find the notion of applying such traditional methods to chance music a peculiar one. In my work, I have found otherwise: the methods of source study are not only appropriate, but are, in fact, uniquely suited for this task."[4] Taking *Three*—the composition referred to above—as an example, one may demonstrate how productive this approach can be for an understanding of Cage's music, by pointing out several facets that could not have come to light without a study of the sources for this work.

The essay by Geesche Geddert on *Three* consists of a descriptive analysis with several suggestions for performance of the work, based on a rehearsal of the Trio Dolce with the composer on the day of the first performance in Speyer. As appears from her description, Cage composed seventeen groups of three tones for each of the outer movements of the work, numbered 1 and 2. Using chance, he selected the individual pitches for these thirty-four groups from the total range of the recorders used, F to c''''', or sixty-eight chromatic pitches. The constituent tones of each three-tone group were then distributed among the three players, who change recorders constantly, mostly as a melody and occasionally as a chord.

Between the outer movements of *Three* are interpolated nine short

3. Deborah Ann Campana, "Form and Structure in the Music of John Cage" (Ph.D. diss., Northwestern University, 1985); James William Pritchett, "The Development of Chance Techniques in the Music of John Cage, 1950–1956" (Ph.D. diss., New York University, 1988); Martin Erdmann, "Untersuchungen zum Gesamtwerk von John Cage," (Ph.D. diss., Rheinische Friedrich-Wilhelms-Universität, Bonn, 1993); Paul van Emmerik, "Thema's en Variaties: Systematische tendensen in de compositietechnieken van John Cage" (Ph.D. diss., Universiteit van Amsterdam, 1996).

4. Pritchett, "Development of Chance Techniques," iv.

movements lettered from A to I, any number of which may be performed. On one of the unfoliated worksheets for these lettered movements (folder 786 in the entry for *Three* given above), the numbers 91, 728, and 3003 appear, followed by twenty-seven 3s, 4s, and 5s, arranged in nine groups of three. The former numbers stand for the number of entries in three tables listing collections of all conceivable harmonies consisting of three, four, or five tones, respectively, having a range not exceeding a major ninth. These tables resulted from Cage's wish to use chance in order to compose harmonies that can be played by one hand on a piano, beginning with *Etudes Australes,* composed in 1974 and 1975. "Thus," he stated, "by means of chance operations I am able to introduce harmonies into a music which is not based on harmony but rather on the uniqueness of each sound, of each combination of sounds."[5] In slightly revised form, Cage used these tables in almost all his subsequent music involving keyboard instruments. So the last twenty-seven numbers on the worksheet stand for three-, four-, or five-tone harmonies to be selected from these tables, three for each of the nine lettered movements of *Three.*

Before delving into the question of what numbers referring to keyboard music may possibly have to do in a work for recorders, it will be necessary to detail the selection process insofar as it can be deduced from the sketches (folder 787 in the list of manuscripts). The twenty-seven harmonies to be selected from the precompositionally defined collections or "gamuts" of harmonies were but abstract constellations of interval relationships, which had to be "concretized" by assigning pitches to each. The starting point for this assignment was a given tone, henceforth to be called the "basic tone." (Using the term "root"—Rameau's *son fondamental*—would result in a misleading and contradictory terminology, misleading since the tone in question exclusively acted as such during the compositional process and contradictory since the context of these harmonies is atonal.) The basic tones themselves were selected from the twelve-tone range from g′ to f♯″. In the tables they are represented by the number 0, and the distance to them, counted in minor seconds, by numbers from 1 through 14, positive numbers for pitches higher than the basic tone, negative ones for pitches lower than it. The basic tone never is the lowest or highest tone of the chord. Taking the three harmonies Cage composed for movement A as an example (ex. 7.1), the five-tone harmony b♯, c♯′, d′, a′, c♯″ (henceforth to be called harmony 1) must have arisen from the interval constellation −9, −8, −7, 0, 4, its basic tone being a′; the three-tone harmony 2, f′, b♭′, e♭″,

5. *"Etudes Australes I, II,* and *VIII," Stagebill* 2, no. 5 (January 1975): 23.

EXAMPLE 7.1
Three, harmonies for movement A.

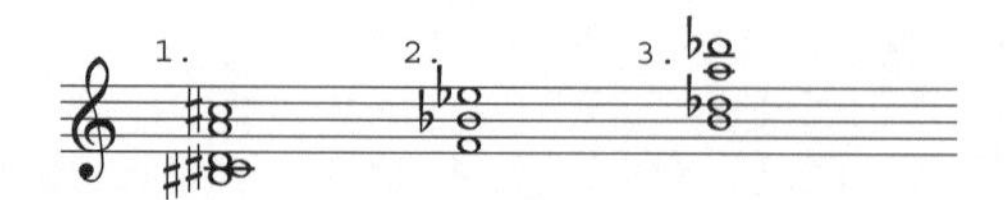

must have arisen from the constellation −5, 0, 5, its basic tone being b♭′; and the four-tone harmony 3, b′, d♭″, a″, d♭‴ from the constellation −2, 0, 8, 12, d♭″ being its basic tone. (The basic tones are not given in the sketches, but they can be deduced, since potential basic tones falling outside the given range from g′ to f♯″ are to be excluded.)

Using chance, Cage then distributed the constituent tones of these three harmonies among the three parts by assigning random numbers 1, 2, or 3 (denoting player I, II, or III) to each pitch. As a rule (a rule that has exceptions), Cage copied the individual tones from the original harmonies as a sequence of pitches in descending order. This procedure resulted in the following sequences within each part: d′ (from harmony 1), a″, c♯″, b′ (all from harmony 3) for player I; c♯″, a′, d♭′, c′ (all from harmony 1) for player II; e♭″, b♭′, f′ (from harmony 2), and b♭″ (misread by Cage while copying d♭‴ from harmony 3) for player III (ex. 7.2). (Enharmonically equivalent tones are considered identical in this work.) Finally, the sequences were notated within what Cage called "time brackets." These brackets, three in each of the nine movements in this case, are periods of time indicated in terms of elapsed time. During these periods of time, performers may begin and end the tones at their discretion, the actual durations being indeterminate for each player. Consequently, it is unpredictable which tones will sound together within each bracket, if at all. (All the tones within each "measure" in music example 7.2 have the potential to sound together, except for the individual tones from the two-tone groups within each part, which are actual sequences of pitches.)

Armed with this knowledge, one can attempt to answer the question why Cage used a collection of harmonies originally intended for keyboard instruments in a piece for recorders. It will be recalled that for each of the outer movements of the work, Cage composed seventeen three-tone groups, for which he selected the individual pitches from the total range of the recorders used, F to c′′′′′, or sixty-eight chromatic pitches. Given these extreme ranges, it is no surprise to find the composer, who obviously wanted to contrast the nine inner movements with the two outer ones, looking for a solution in the realm of ranges.

EXAMPLE 7.2
Three, outline of movement A.

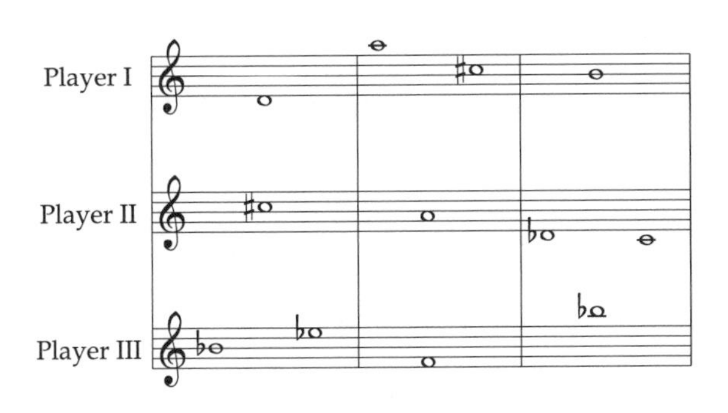

By using keyboard harmonies that have a maximum range of a major ninth and by restricting himself to the twelve-tone range from g′ to f♯″ for the basic tones, he assured himself of a restricted range for the inner movements, which indeed turns out not to exceed the range from g♯ to c‴, or twenty-nine chromatic pitches. Conversely, Cage expanded the three-tone groups of the outer movements into a gamut of three-, four-, or five-tone groups for the inner movements, in order to vary the number of tones within each of the three time brackets of each movement.

The transformation, then, of the original harmonies for the nine inner movements of *Three* into sequences of pitches in parts that have no fixed rhythmic relationship results in a partially unpredictable order and sounding-together of these pitches, related to the original harmonies only by virtue of the mechanism used. Not only is this highly abstract compositional technique strongly reminiscent of Schoenberg's partitioning of twelve-tone rows into hexachords conceived as harmonic units, with little concern for the ordering of the tones; it also points to Stravinsky's method of deriving "verticals" (i.e., harmonies) from a given twelve-tone row by means of transposition-rotation. As Paul Schuyler Phillips has defined it, this transposition-rotation is "produced by following the presentation of a source set with five successive rotations of the set, each rotation beginning one note further into the set and aligned directly below the previous set or rotation, with transposition levels determined by the first note of each rotation being the same pitch as the first of the original set."[6] By reading the six resulting sequences of pitches vertically, Stravinsky obtained a series of harmonies resulting

6. "The Enigma of *Variations:* A Study of Stravinsky's Final Work for Orchestra," *Music Analysis* 3 (1984): 70.

from a mechanism partly beyond his immediate control. In this context, it is a matter of secondary significance that a serial mechanism logically speaking is the exact opposite of a chance mechanism. In the final analysis, this does not change the fact that the resulting music comes about through mechanisms a substantial part of whose workings are unpredictable and therefore escape the composer's control.

III

Referring to the music of Schoenberg as well as to his own, Stravinsky once drew attention to the importance of numbers in musical composition. His remark that "numbers are things"[7] illustrates an aesthetic attitude that has been summarized more than once by the phrase "work in progress" and that has characterized a large part of twentieth-century art music, especially since World War II: the tendency among composers to shift their attention from products to procedures, procedures in which numbers play an important part. In the case of *Three,* however, the principle of numbers generating musical structures is ambiguous. On the one hand, numbers act as a means to control a variety of musical characteristics in a systematic fashion. "With endless inventiveness, Cage assigned compositional parameters to numbers," Mark Swed has observed.[8] On the other hand, the music thus composed could have been different from what it is, since it came into being by means of chance mechanisms. Moreover, it was composed in such a way that the audible structure varies from performance to performance. Yet it is another illustration of the tendency mentioned at the beginning of this paragraph. "The urge not to bind oneself, but to keep possibilities open, compositionally means that instead of the product which one creates, the materials and methods that one uses come to the fore and attract attention."[9] Richard Taruskin is right in arguing that Cage "embodied what may be called the 'research model' (as opposed to the 'communication model') of composerly behavior, so characteristic of midcentury modernism."[10]

Indeed, generalizing about *Three,* one may argue that these observations testify to a facet of Cage's compositional technique that has largely been ignored: its modernist nature. "Most people who believe that I'm

7. Igor Stravinsky and Robert Craft, *Dialogues and a Diary* (Garden City, N.Y.: Doubleday, 1963), 58.

8. "Cage and Counting: The Number Pieces," brochure in *Rolyholyover: A Circus,* ed. Russell Ferguson and Sherri Schottlaender (Los Angeles: Museum of Contemporary Art and Rizzoli, 1993).

9. Carl Dahlhaus, "Die Krise des Experiments," in *Komponieren heute: Ästhetische, soziologische, und pädagogische Fragen,* ed. Ekkehard Jost (Mainz: Schott, 1983), 90.

10. "No Ear for Music," *New Republic,* March 15, 1993, 29.

interested in chance," Cage once said in an interview, "don't realize that I use chance as a discipline—they think I use it—I don't know—as a way of giving up making choices. But my choices consist in choosing what questions to ask."[11] This statement alone suffices to demonstrate that the common belief that Cage's music since 1951 is based exclusively on chance is untenable. Incredulity about the fact that in his music rational and irrational factors go together has often led to an overemphasis on the latter. These irrational factors have then been ascribed to the role Eastern thought played in his aesthetics. Chou Wen-chung's contention, in his study on the influence of Asian concepts on Western composers, that Cage's aesthetic thought since the late 1940s "is actually a modern American product for which certain external aspects of the Eastern originals served as the stimulant," should warn against seeking an explanation for his use of chance exclusively in the Far East.[12] Cage's eclecticism can be illustrated by the fact that in chance composition, he used only the mechanism and ignored the oracular utterances of the ancient Chinese book of wisdom, the *I Ching*. It can also be seen in the way he justified the use of a book of wisdom presumably dating from the twelfth century before Christ by calling upon Zen Buddhism, a form of Buddhism that developed in Japan in the twelfth century after Christ.

However, calling attention to Cage's eclecticism is less important than pointing out that the advent of chance and unpredictability at the expense of musical cohesion can be traced back to a musical problem that fascinated Cage from the very beginning of his career, namely, the search for systems of composition enabling him to disavow inherent relationships between sounds and to emphasize the identity of each individual sound. "Each sound must be considered as essentially different from and independent of every other sound," the composer had already written in the early 1940s.[13] Because of his disavowal of the inherent relationships, the characteristics of the sounds themselves no longer offered him criteria for their continuity or simultaneity. In using systematic techniques having unpredictable results, Cage's conception of music as a universe of sounds that can be freely related to each other but whose relations are arrived at by means of systematic compositional techniques was put into practice long before he adopted the twin concepts "unimpededness" and "interpenetration" from Zen Buddhism to formulate his notion of relations between sounds, human beings, and objects.

11. Interview by Robin White at Crown Point Press, Oakland, California, 1978, *View* 1, no. 1 (April 1978): 5.

12. "Asian Concepts and Twentieth-Century Western Composers," *Musical Quarterly* 57 (1971): 225.

13. "For More New Sounds," *Modern Music* 19 (1941–42): 245.

> Now this unimpededness is seeing that in all of space each thing and each human being is at the center and furthermore that each one being at the center is the most honored one of all. Interpenetration means that each one of these most honored ones of all is moving out in all directions penetrating and being penetrated by every other one no matter what the time or what the space. . . . In fact each and every thing in all of time and space is related to each and every other thing in all of time and space.[14]

In addition, Cage's conception is remarkably similar to Schoenberg's notion of twelve-tone music as a phenomenon manifesting itself in a "unity of musical space" in which

> there is no absolute down, no right or left, forward or backward. Every musical configuration, every movement of tones has to be comprehended primarily as a mutual relation of sounds, of oscillatory vibrations, appearing at different places and times.[15]

Whether the similarities between these quotations were intended by Cage or not, it is beyond doubt that his conception of a universe of sounds that can be freely related to each other but whose relations are arrived at by means of systematic compositional techniques would have been inconceivable without Schoenberg's "method of composing with twelve tones which are related only with one another."

Living at the end of the twentieth century, an era in which notions such as poststructuralism, deconstruction, and ideology critique have challenged the traditional historical method based on source studies and philology, one cannot avoid being aware of the possibility of different interpretations of Cage's work. Nevertheless, in light of the far-reaching implications contained in just thirty-nine leaves—the manuscripts for *Three*—out of more than twenty-five thousand, it is hard to agree with, for example, Rose Rosengard Subotnik's contention that "Cage has exerted influence on Western music through a career that produced relatively little of musical interest—at least in the sense of interesting music."[16] Referring back, then, to the opening statement of this essay, one cannot escape the conviction that the study of "interesting relics from the past" will profoundly change the image of Cage's work as we know it now. As far as the *Nachlass* is concerned, scholars are sitting on top of a gold mine or, to put it differently, "here comes everything."

14. "Communication," in *Silence: Lectures and Writings* (Middletown, Conn.: Wesleyan University Press, 1961), 46–47.

15. Arnold Schoenberg, *Style and Idea,* ed. Dika Newlin (New York: Philosophical Library, 1950), 113.

16. *Deconstructive Variations: Music and Reason in Western Society* (Minneapolis: University of Minnesota Press, 1996), xx.

EIGHT

Gordon Mumma (chair), Allan Kaprow, James Tenney, Christian Wolff, Alvin Curran, and Maryanne Amacher

Cage's Influence
A Panel Discussion

GORDON MUMMA: The topic is Cage's influence, and the extraordinary group of people we have here are probably not enough, in the sense that we have four composers and Allan Kaprow. It seems to me that Allan comes close to filling in some of the gaps, but we really need poets and printmakers and biologists and God knows what to be appropriately extravagant with the topic.

Let me introduce the other speakers: James Tenney, Christian Wolff, Maryanne Amacher, and Alvin Curran.[1] This group has one thing in common, and that is they are all individuals in the great American tradition. And when I say "American," I mean the Americas. The whole Western Hemisphere is filled with people like this who don't fit. They have made their own worlds, without being in some sense "bent," without being influenced in pushy ways by what other people do. These are really unique creative artists, as John Cage was a totally unique figure.

One of the panelists said to me yesterday, "Why this business about influence?" Well, I

1. Maryanne Amacher's comments now appear as a postscript to the panel discussion, having been revised and expanded for this volume.

don't think of us analyzing or constructing and deconstructing the syntax of influences between this, that, and the other. But maybe influence is not such a confining word as long as we don't expect to find connections that are absolutely clear: this happened and then that followed. No, how Cage might have influenced people is not a cause-and-effect kind of activity.

ALLAN KAPROW: Just to fill in a bit of background. I first became aware of John Cage's music in 1952. I remember the year exactly. The occasion was the new Living Theater's concert series down in Greenwich Village. I remember sitting with an art critic I knew and looking at the crowd, most of them from the visual arts and very few musicians, at least very few that I could recognize as such. I asked this critic whether that didn't seem peculiar to him because the reputation of John Cage as a kind of enfant terrible was widespread at the time and should have attracted a lot of musicians, but didn't. He said something to the effect that Cage was appreciated more by artists than musicians because he really wasn't a musician. For a moment I bristled at that, thinking it was unkind. But then a moment later I thought, well, maybe there's something interesting here.

I suppose I met Cage on the level of a handshake here and there for the next few years, and indeed throughout his life I remained a rather distant friend. That is, I was not a part of his social circle, while at the same time benefiting very much from many acts of kindness on his part toward me—getting grants, for example, and getting teaching jobs. He was always there for me, and I never doubted his friendship.

As some of you may know, in the mid-fifties I started to break away from being an action collagist, that is to say, someone who makes what are basically paintings with lots of torn-up material stuck to a surface, and began to expand into environmental proportions so that now you don't just look at what is shown but actually move in and amongst its parts the way you would in a thicket, a thorn thicket. And I began at that time (very quickly in fact, in '56) to incorporate lots of other sensory elements, like sounds. Among the sounds were those produced by those wonderful Japanese toys you could buy in those days; some of these you could wind up and some had batteries, and they would growl. There was a gorilla that I loved very much; it had flashing lights and raised its arms up and would go "uhrrr!" So I bought these at some wholesale house in Manhattan by the cartload (as many different ones, of course, as possible) and fixed them into hidden recesses around the ceiling and underneath the lights of the old gallery-like spaces that most of us used in those days (loft space essentially, not the fancy galleries we have today). And I remember the artist Bob Watts made for me a big wheel that had little bumps on it with micro-switches that rode on the bumps so that the sounds could be randomized (or to the point where they would seem random), so that they would come on at various time lengths and places, here at this side of the room, there at that, and so on. For a while I was pleased with the result, but very quickly I began to figure out the sequences so that as they recurred, though nobody else might hear them in any order, I began to hear the order and grew tired of the repetition. So I called up John Cage and I said: "You may not have any experience with this"—although I expected he did—"but what would you do?" And I explained what the problem was. He said, "Why don't you come to my class at the New School and we can chat. Come a little early."

The very next week, when the class was given, he drove up in a Model A Ford, and I drove up in my Model A Ford, which immediately struck a bond between us. (I asked him where he got his extra parts.) He would drive all the way from a small co-op dwelling up on the Hudson River (where he lived at that time) in that flivver, and I drove from Rutgers University (where I was teaching at the time) in my flivver. And I can tell you it was a foolhardy venture trying to get on the freeway in that machine and wondering if it would break down. In a sense, a "baling wire" attitude of you-can-fix-anything-with-chewing-gum prevailed even in driving that car, as it did with those Japanese toys. Everything had a sleaze element to it. If you remember, that was a part of the taste of the time; it was a period of artists and musicians finding junk in the environment and just incorporating it or in some way pointing to it as Duchamp might and saying, "That's interesting, that's it." We were paying attention to a world that had been disfavored up until that moment. So the fact there was a meeting in heaven, Model A Ford heaven, did something to both of us that we never actually mentioned again, but it was always there.

I came to that class—this is the more meaty part of these memories—with George Brecht at that time, who also lived in New Brunswick, New Jersey, as a research scientist for Johnson and Johnson. (He once told me with great pleasure that he held a patent on Kotex production for a certain number of years.) We drove in and had lots of time in the thirty-odd miles between the two cities to discuss things. George had actually decided to join the class a few weeks before I did, and he told me a little about it: how open-ended it is and how Cage in a way encourages you to experiment, experiment, experiment.

The class was called "Experimental Music" or something like that. I sat in, waved to Cage and he waved back, and the class began. Student works were immediately performed by everyone, including Cage, and

I joined in with great pleasure. I mean, here were the kinds of experimental works which required no unusual skills. So, although I do not play a musical instrument, I was able to simply jump in and bang on the side of the desk or scrape my fingernail on the blackboard and it fit in perfectly, because that's what everyone was doing. Afterward I went up to speak to Cage, and as the class finished I explained what my problem was with those toys which made those repetitive patterns and how I couldn't stand it any more. I said, "Nobody else notices this, since they come in and poke around for a while, but I see that every day and hear that awful sequence. Tell me what to do!" He smiled in a pixyish way and said, "You're a collagist, aren't you?" and I said, "Yes . . . so?" and he said, "Well, why don't you go into tape?" (I knew what he meant because I had heard concerts by him and others using tape sounds, which was the newest rage in music-making possibilities.) Then he said, "All you have to do is record a whole lot of sounds and stick them into envelopes marked accordingly, such as high sounds, low sounds, middle sounds, scratchy sounds, smooth sounds, glissandi, whatever you want, and just put them together the way you do a collage." Except, he said, "I have my way and you'll probably have yours," and he went "Hmmmm . . ." We all remember that kind of pregnant silence. And he actually wrote down an address where I could get wholesale tape decks very cheap, unboxed, with just the motors on them, and he said that those would be called slaves. You paste all the pieces together in some way, run them on the slaves in the right speed combinations, and record on the recording machine, which has to be technically better than the slaves. I said, "That's pretty easy."

I applied at Rutgers University for a research grant, which I got. They knew very little about me in those days, and they lived to regret that. I immediately found an office space at the university and set up my studio, which miraculously started to produce sounds that I could not follow the pattern of. And I remember having the joy of running tape loops from one end of the room to the other on spools, big bumps of tape going by and breaking off in the middle and causing all kinds of static on the recording machine. My musician friends will know what I'm talking about. Remember when we had those little grooved cutting tools with the single-edge razor with which we would cut out long angles and put them together, would cut out short ones and absolutely perpendicular ones, so that you get a real shut-off sound and a harsh attack after that. I got to know a good bit about what musicians were doing in those days because among them was Richard Maxfield, who was advanced beyond anyone I knew in electronics and just collage and tape. This opened up a whole new area which I tried to learn from, but I found myself outclassed and out-knowledged by almost all my musician friends, so I didn't pursue the electronic side at all beyond a few experiments done with Richard Maxfield's expert help.

What I am driving at here is that Cage at the end of our first meeting asked me one more question. He said, "I would like to invite you to join this class, but if you do join the class, why would you want to be here? You seem to know what you want to do." I said, "Well, the reason is because I want to make noise. And I don't want to make music." And he said, "Ah, that's nice." He said, "Please come and you don't have to pay anything." I discovered subsequently that just about everyone in the class had the same privilege. And that's where I met most of our friends—Jackson Mac Low and so on—in that class.

On the pedagogical level Cage was very helpful, because I was a young teacher at the time, as I've said. He introduced me to a kind of permissive teaching that I had not expected from a specialist in some kind of art. That is, usually as you become a teacher you become an authority and have all sorts of assumptions about how learning takes place, what you should do to get that, and so on, including homework assignments. To the best of my memory, Cage never assigned anything; he'd say, "I hope you will consider this class a place where we can experiment and, if you wish, you can bring in pieces and we will, as well as we can, perform them here all together." But he also suggested possible homework projects, such as "prepare a two-minute piece for barely audible sounds." It was like a playground. It was really marvelous; someone came up with some kind of plan and we all carried it out. I remember that my interests at the time were mainly interests in sound rather than in what I somewhat challengingly call noise (everybody enjoys that). This kind of thing, to exploit attention, was something that was not allowed or was frowned on and considered out of the range of proper behavior in traditional musical circles. But we discovered that hearing a pin, for example—an ordinary straight pin—being dropped on the floor required an enormous amount of attention. One of the pieces that became intriguing to me after finding Cage's interest in apparent silence was if you prepare to be as quiet as you can, the world is very noisy. You can even hear a pin drop! So I prepared a number of pieces of torn paper following Hans Arp's early experiments and suggested that everybody have a handful of these according to some plan of how many pieces were in each fist and when they would be dropped. They were usually short "compositions" lasting two or three minutes, and you would see, using your eyes along with your ears, everybody's hand like this, then a thumb would pull apart from the forefinger and one piece of paper would flutter down and everyone would watch it—there would be one on this side and one over there (or two over there and five over here). There were some people, like myself, who desperately wanted to hear what they couldn't. Afterwards, in the discussion period, they would say, "I heard that piece of paper drop. I did, I did; it was like a butterfly." Well, that was fabulous—what we would later call sensitizing. It was an amazing kind of teaching, Cage's encouraging in a playful way what would ordinarily sound very academic, and perhaps intolerable to practice if one were a traditional teacher.

Finally, I would say that Cage's teaching not only affected me, but it also affected all the others in the class, which included Dick Higgins and Al Hansen, one coming from literature and the other from visual arts. A much deeper influence, I think, probably grew—I was going to say "like mushrooms," but really much more slowly—over the years, that has to do with my Zen interest, which was something I was always drawn to but had not practiced. As you know, Cage studied under one of America's most distinguished importers of Zen Buddhism to Western thinking, Daisetz Suzuki, and benefited greatly. Cage talked a lot about that—about the implications of Zen practice. I think that this philosophical side of Cage, which was by no means playful but actually quite dedicated, affected me (and many others in the class), so much so that I began to practice Zen and found an excellent teacher—and to this day I study with her. So that was a very big influence, having more to do with attitude than specific kinds of behavior or belief systems, none of which really matter that much. Attitudes about such things as being the boss, being in control, having others follow my will, making art as a contest between my creative powers and the imperfection in the world—all of these unquestioned assumptions and attitudes that we ordinarily put up with in the West were questioned very openly by Cage's study of Zen and in what he taught in the class and what he seemed to exemplify as an artist. I didn't say as a musician but simply in the broadest sense of the word: an art-making person.

A very important point to consider: I think the profoundest influence on me and, I suspect, on many, many others who have been touched by John Cage is that it doesn't matter if you make music, or art, of any kind. Ultimately music is what he quoted from one of his colleagues, an Indian student: "The purpose of music"—I paraphrase here—"is to calm the mind to make it receptive to divine influence." Well, that sounds terribly mystical and very pious, and it's not the kind of language I would use, being, as Gordon said, an American (we have little patience with this kind of stuff). Nevertheless, and, I think, cutting through the linguistic problem, there is the sense of being quiet (first intending to be and then finding that it is possible, as one's own behavior makes it possible) in everything. Whether you call the result divine influence or simply being attentive, which I would prefer, it is very, very important to me and, I expect, to many others. One sees this openness translated not into going to a concert or making music or whatever, but taking place in the meeting of friends, in conversations, without thinking. It's like what the Buddhists call "right living." This begins to replace ambition. I think that's the most profound influence of all: that John Cage the artist made it possible to give up art.

JAMES TENNEY: I want to tell you what I think is Cage's historical role. In a sense this is a conclusion that I've come to after many years of his influence. (Later, I can talk about that influence on me.) Somewhere—I think it's in a postface to *A Year from Monday: New Lectures and Writings*—he wrote, "Sounds we hear are music." If we take that as a definition and take it seriously, it implies a very radical redefinition of music, which is very interesting. There is no composer implicit in that definition. That is, the sounds in the forest—or on the street corner—may be music. And it's my sense that in that definition, if we take it seriously, Cage caused us to shift the attention, the focus, of the music-making enterprise from the mind and thoughts and emotions of the composer to the experience of the listener. I think this is a very profound shift.

It begins in 1951 with the *Music of Changes* and marks a change in aesthetic viewpoint such that 1951 can be said to be the beginning of the end of a period of about 350 years, a period that began with the beginnings of opera, with Monteverdi and the Camerata. I think a case could be made—I'm not a historian so I can't make it, but I believe the case could be made—that this whole 350-year period, from 1600 to 1950 roughly, is really the operatic era, that the conception of the function of music (and here was a wonderful new discovery on the part of the composers of opera in the early seventeenth century) was a new conception of what music could do: it can express human emotion. Wow! And it can generate similar, perhaps parallel emotions on the part of the listeners. That was a new idea in 1600. It wasn't long before it came to be taken for granted that this was what music was about and that it was all that music should be—that this was somehow natural. Well, that's OK, but it's not the only thing that it can be. Cage shifted our attention from the composer to the listening experience by repeatedly talking about sound, the nature of sound, and a music based on the nature of sound and by not focusing on the ideas or the emotions of the composer. I think it's going to turn out that although the history books now tend to assume that a new era somehow began around the early part of this century, we'll see the work of Schoenberg and the second Viennese school, Stravinsky, and so forth, as really an end: the end of the long period, closing with what Charles Hamm called "terminal modernism." (I liked that term.) Although I don't care for the term "postmodernism," I think that Cage's importance is to be understood as implying the end of a 350-year period.

Nineteen fifty-one was just the beginning—*Music of Changes* and when he wrote about *Music of Changes*. Read again what he said. I can't quote it, but if you again take it seriously and literally, it's astonishing. And it was scary to a lot of people. I believe the negative reaction to Cage—which continues, as you all know—was more to what he said than to the music, because the music can be heard as part of something that was happening in 1950. But what he said about it was that this is music free of the history and traditions of the art, free of psychology and the like. Amazing. And that was the beginning, I think. The *Europeras* were the coup de grâce, the end of the operatic era. (I hope somebody argues with me on that!)

To talk about John Cage's influence really is to talk about the future, isn't it? The future is in all of our hands; it will be what we make of it. The dilemma that we all face is how to go on doing something which is not simply continuing to do what John Cage did. We can't. We can't do that in good conscience. But how to go on doing something else which is not a reaction against what Cage taught us? (There's a lot of that around—not here, but in the world out there.) As Gordon suggested, I think the future will be as diverse and individual as there are individual artists working.

In my own case, twenty some years ago I began to get interested in the question of harmony. Again, after what seemed to me to have been a good half-century in which it was considered more or less irrelevant to new music, I began working on this both in my composing and in theoretical ways, thinking about problems in the theory of harmony. But very soon I realized that it was not going to be a good thing just to try to replace all the rules, all the old ideas about harmony, without deeply renovating what the idea of theory might be. My thoughts on what we had to do about theory were very deeply influenced by Cage's aesthetic. What's needed in this area is not another prescriptive body of rules but a descriptive theory where we try to understand what happens when we hear sounds. Is there an aspect of this that we can distinguish and refer to as a harmonic aspect? I ended up, as some of you know, writing an article that seemed very strange to some people because it is called "John Cage and the Theory of Harmony." It's in two parts. The first part is about John Cage, and the second is about the theory of harmony. In fact, at one point a certain editor of books, many about Cage, asked me if he could include that essay, but only the first part. I said, "No, it has to be both parts or none." Well, with some kicking and screaming, it finally got published, both parts together. Cage read the article, and I think it influenced his thoughts about harmony, which is enough to say here. We are all going to be doing individual things. Many of them will be very strange—or seem so—because they'll be things you might not predict. Who would ever have thought that Cage could be connected to harmony in spite of all his protestations about it! But it can happen and it will.

CHRISTIAN WOLFF: I think I'm the one that Gordon referred to who's uneasy about the subject of this panel—Cage's influence—partly because on the one hand it's extraordinarily diffuse and in some ways it seems very obvious.[2] It seems to me that no one (except a complete idiot) who had met Cage or encountered his work could fail to be affected by him in some way. It's just unthinkable. So his influence is there and it will be, no matter what. Also, I haven't looked into this carefully, but my impression is that Cage has never written a mesostic on the word influence. It is not a subject that he seemed to be very interested in, and that also tells me a little bit. In fact, once I was supposed to write about influence, and I told him about it and he just made a face.

But, anyway, I did find one reference to the word influence in the writing *Themes & Variations*, where he so conveniently lists one hundred and ten ideas that he gleaned from the reading of his work up to that time (I think, around 1980). This is what he said: "Influence derives from one's own work, not from outside it," which is quite a mysterious thing to say, I think. I guess my first take on this was that which affects your work is doing it, is the very process of doing it—having done it, doing it, and what you are going to do with it. Then, perhaps a more ordinary meaning would be what influences you is work—not the person attached to the work nor the ideas surrounding the work, but the actual, practical work, the piece of music, the process of preparing it, presenting it, and so forth. But in any case, it's quite distant from the very notion of what we think of as influence. The other idea I found in that collection that might be connected to influence—at least I thought I might connect to it—is the following: "Impossibility of repeated action, loss of memory—to reach these two is the goal." And, in parentheses, "Duchamp." I don't know enough about Duchamp to know where that comes from, and again it's a little mysterious. But let me read it again: "Impossibility of repeated action, loss of memory—to reach these two is the goal." What this seems to be saying is that you're trying to repeat the

2. The reader may wish to refer to Christian Wolff's essay on this subject, "Under the Influence," in *A John Cage Reader*, ed. Peter Gena and Jonathan Brent (New York: C. F. Peters, 1982), 74–76.

influence—go back to something that's already there, but you should try to do it in such a way that when you achieve it, you have forgotten what it was you were repeating, which may be another way of thinking about the whole issue of influence.

The other thing I like to remember is Cage's citing of Willem de Kooning's remark when de Kooning was asked, "What painters of the past have influenced your work?" De Kooning responded, "The past doesn't influence my work, my work influences the past." In this connection one could mention Cage's influence on figures like Satie and Thoreau. I think that his engagement with them has meant a drastic change for us.

While dealing more generally with influence, I'm happy to talk about particulars too. It seems to me that one could think about Cage's influence in two terms: one is what I call negative influence and the other, which is perhaps very similar, is the notion of facilitating. Let me start with the last one, because there is a very famous remark by Morton Feldman, who when asked what was the influence of Cage or how Cage had affected his work, simply answered, "It gave me permission to do my work." (Rather similar to what Allan was talking about.) I've also thought of the notion of negative influence in this sense, actually in several senses. The simplest one is, if Cage did something, I felt I didn't have to do it. So, for example, I didn't have to use the *I Ching;* I didn't have to use chance operations to make my compositions. Perhaps I should say parenthetically that when I met him, I was sixteen years old and so inevitably very impressionable, and he was in his late thirties then and a figure of potentially great authority. He fascinated me in many ways, and his work I found extraordinarily interesting. So you might expect that I would fall under that spell very powerfully, and in some ways I obviously did. Yet at the same time, I was given the feeling (how, I don't quite know) of this negative influence about not having to do it because he had done it. I've already mentioned the *I Ching;* also I didn't feel I had to do theater pieces, I didn't feel I had to do sound text pieces, and so forth.

To put this in a rather different way, which struck me at the concert last night, concerning several of the pieces—not all of them, certainly not the first one, *Imaginary Landscape,* and perhaps not the *Cartridge Music,* but certainly the *Variations* and the last piece, the *Sculptures Musicales.* I enjoyed the performances immensely (they were very beautiful), yet I also thought that what I was hearing was not the music of John Cage, but the music of those particular performers. A friend of mine who was there, Chris Bobrowski, said she knew a number of the performers and could identify their sounds. It was their presence that was there, and in some way that seems to me the most striking example of Cage's influence. It was Cage's piece that allowed these people to make those sounds and have those sounds be their own sounds. It was an opening of the space for other people to do their own work in and to do it in the best possible way.

ALVIN CURRAN: I might begin by saying that I was inoculated against the Cage virus in 1961; the inoculation, however, didn't take. I was a student of Elliott Carter's at Yale, and at the same time John Cage was in residence at Wesleyan University—a very fruitful residency that has had lasting repercussions. Getting to Middletown from New Haven was an easy trip, but for the quarantine placed on the Yale students, confining them to New Haven only during that period—such was the administration's reaction to that fearful virus imagined to be centered in Middletown, Connecticut. Nonetheless, the students, even though largely steeped in twelve-tone theology, had a natural curiosity to know who the devil this devil was—and thanks to Richard Teitelbaum and the music theory lecture series he curated, we were able at last to bring the musical antichrist to New Haven.

Cage at last appeared, talked and performed, unleashing an uproar of raucous contestation—the expected *scandale*. Yet at this memorable event I saw a man, unflappable and simple as he was brilliant and magnetic (and as it turned out for me highly contagious), though what my poor Ivy League ears were hearing in 1961 was definitely not music, that I was sure of. Extramusically speaking, I was deeply impressed by the full-length leather coat that Cage wore—conferring on him instant elegance and distinction. Today we'd call it "cool." But then it simply conveyed an air of European chic, and struck me in some way as a magical garment. We—the pro-Cage group among whom were Joel Chadabe, Tom Johnson, David Barron, and Richard Teitelbaum—hung out with Cage after his lecture in a nearby tavern, delighting in Cage's aura and his ability to field anything thrown at him, good or bad. Relaxed and funny, he spoke about things no twelve-tone composers would dare consider: sound and silence. Some years later I got one of these coats myself—bought it in the flea market in Rome—such was Cage's influence. In all seriousness, this was the beginning of a wonderful friendship; his influence seeped in bit by bit without my even knowing it.

In the mid-sixties I moved to Rome, and as most of you know, I was joined by a group of people there: Frederic Rzewski, Richard Teitelbaum, Carol Plantamura, Ivan Vandor, Alan Bryant, John Phetteplace, and Steve Lacy. A group was formed known as Musica Elettronica Viva. Largely unaware of and unconcerned by the direct Cage/Tudor influence on the origins of MEV (primarily through Rzewski's enthusiastic stay in Buffalo with them, prior to his own return to Rome), we found ourselves busily soldering cables, contact mikes, and talking about "circuitry" as if it were a new religion. By amplifying the sounds of glass, wood, metal, water, air, and fire, we were convinced that we had tapped into the sources of the natural musics of "everything." We were in fact making a spontaneous music which could be said to be coming from "nowhere" and made out of "nothing"—all somewhat a wonder and a collective epiphany. And learning that Cage had done these things even ten years earlier was no shock, but a confirmation of a "mutual" discovery. What really mattered to us then was not who got there first, but that we were in fact *there*—a radical group of young people making music from zero. And in the spirit of Cage, that was the issue.

Like many Americans of my generation, I had an abysmal ignorance of history and social and political ideas. At the time, I am sure I never heard the word "anarchy," and I'd just begun to discover the significance of Marxism. Nonetheless I was there in the midst of a tumultuous student revolution, barricades, occupations, riots, tear gas, dogs and dope—this was 1968. Consonant with all of this—considering our basic pacifist position—was our aim to make a spontaneous music which we began to call "collective," a timely buzzword that resounded then in almost all activity. MEV, its music and behavior, was highly charged with all of the complex psychosocial dynamics of group behavior, save our willingness to relinquish our individual egos completely. We were not a cult. What was happening here was that we were improvising in ways to question and to test the limits of all known and even unknown musical codes and behaviors; more often than not, musics—forms of pure transcendent energies—emerged, though no one could rightly say who made them or how. You all know that Cage abhorred improvisation—he shunned the word, concept, and practice all his life. But this didn't seem to dampen his affection for all of us whom he continued to support and influence as well for many years, as we inevitably took our places in the American experimental-music family.

To get back to the story, it seemed to me that with all the discussions about utopia, anarchy, etc., the interesting thing is that we (MEV) were clearly making a new kind of chance music—not made from known or invented systems, but based on the risk (in every sense) of bringing people together to make music anywhere without a score. This is something that Cage could not consider nor likely ever approve of. And in view of his voracious imagination and rigorous radicalism, it is curious to imagine that this one small step toward liberating the music from the composer and ultimately from itself, is one Cage never took. That is, for all his dedicated commitment to freedom, liberation of the spirit, mind, and body, he remained a modernist composer true to his time—fully horrified at the thought of taking one's own music and throwing it away. This may be in essence the most significant contribution made by the MEV group. It was our manifesto: music made with no composer, no conductor, no written signs, no music, no money, and no expectations. And for this we have to thank John Cage; it would have been impossible without him. It's very much like what Maryanne Amacher says: it was the next step, the next evolutionary notch. Spontaneous music is now being practiced all over the world and very much alive—thanks to Cage.

My professional baptism occurred on December 31, 1969, in Palermo, where as part of *Winter Music,* performed by Rzewski, Cardew, Teitelbaum, and myself, we were instructed to open all the doors and windows of the Teatro Biondo at a given time. The glacial music along with the added noises from the street caused a near riot in the theater. In 1984 I invited John to collaborate as one of the ten soloists in my *Maritime Rites* project. I asked him to record five monosyllabic words of his choice ("Ice, Do, Food, Crew, Ape") for me. "Is that all?" he asked, ingenuously. I paired those beautifully soft-spoken words—in hocketed loops—with one of the most powerful foghorns ever built, installed on the *Nantucket Lightship II.* On two occasions—one a seventy-fifth birthday party and twenty-four-hour concert broadcast live by the Studio Akustischer Kunst of the Westdeutcher Rundfunk—I played roles in his delightful *Hörspiel, An Alphabet,* and once he honored me with the part of Satie. In the late eighties, as he was preparing his *Europeras* in Frankfurt, he had heard that I had made a mix of some seventy operas all playing at once and wanted to hear it. He listened and loved it—he thought he might like to include that in the foyer of the theater since he didn't think he had time to do a similar one. Of course he found the time, as he always did, but his invitation remains a precious memory.

One more thing: Cornelius Cardew. Cornelius was one of my early mentors. He came to Rome in 1964 on a study grant with Petrassi at the Accademia Santa Cecilia. Cornelius too was a revolutionary and very magnetic person. He revered Cage and as you know performed his piano music a lot. In a genuine search for a coherent belief, Cornelius passed from Buddhism to Marxism, Maoism, and finally to Hoxa-ism. In this latter period he wrote inflammatory manifestos denouncing all forms of bourgeois behavior, and personally attacking his former mentors, Stockhausen and Cage. I happened to be on hand with Cornelius—performing with Steve Reich in Pamplona—when Cage read Cardew's denunciation of him. Cage did not take it lightly, nonetheless he always reminded me how much he admired my solo piano work: *For Cornelius,* pacifically linking himself to all the wayward sons and daughters.

MARYANNE AMACHER: I would like to continue some comments made by Jim and Christian. Rather than start with music's historical tradition, let's imagine more radically. Imagine a "time before music"—a world without music, so different from the world we are in, where we have so much recorded music and every possible form of so many sounds. Imagine ancient beings listening long before music appeared on the earth. No one knows exactly what they were listening to—some say that is how all the legends and myths got started—that they were listening to their "own voices." These were virtual sounds, existing in their minds only. They had no music, and the young nerve cells were restless—so they began producing sonorities and rhythms inside their minds to satisfy them. Mind became an instrument they played, creating the colors and rhythms of voices and stories. For there was nothing outside to match neural rhythms and movements, no corresponding shapes to complement their patterns of "aliveness" (as music provides). And the young receptors needed partners complementing their existence.

Was this perhaps the origin of our first music? Did the sonic traces of music exist first in the mind, responding to an essential biological coding? Consider the sonorities John Cage created, illuminating a "life" of the mind—before grammar, before musical conditioning—in *Empty Words* and *I–VI*. Letting the sonorities of his voice project the numinous radiance of his mind, he elicits fluent geographies of consciousness: liberating the mind from the automatic responses of musical conditioning, intelligence awakes to unrecognized and new perceptual modes.

The beautiful writings of the great nineteenth-century scientist/thinker, Hermann Helmholtz, articulate the urgency of bringing the "listening mind" into the picture. I am reminded here of a passage from *On the Sensations of Tone:* "There arises in our mind a feeling that the work of art which we are contemplating is the product of a design which far exceeds anything we can conceive at the moment, and which hence partakes of the character of the illimitable. . . . The contemplation of a real work of art awakens our confidence in the originally healthy nature of the human mind, when uncribbed, unharassed, unobscured, and unfalsified."[3] Helmholtz's detailed and penetrating investigations were the first in a young tradition of music science to explore human auditory responses to sound and music, to appreciate the sensitivity of the "listening mind's" range, and the variations of its operation. His monumental research was the very beginning, the foundation for a new understanding that advanced to new levels with Cage's cognitive methods and explorations.

3. *On the Sensations of Tone,* trans. Alexander J. Ellis (New York: Dover 1954), 367.

In a wonderful essay, "On Thinking about Thinking," Lewis Thomas proposes that "[m]usic is the effort we make to explain to ourselves how our brains work."[4] I returned recently to Thomas's inspiring essays, because of my desire to understand how neurobiology informs in some very basic ways the music I create. These short essays are beautifully concrete; Thomas's insights into some of the more profound features of musical response are exhilarating. For example, he recommends that instead of using thought to explain the nature of music, we begin with music to see what it can tell us about the *sensation* of thinking: "We listen to Bach transfixed because this is listening to a human mind. The *Art of the Fugue* is not a special pattern of thinking, it is not thinking about any particular thing . . . it is about thinking. . . . [A]s an experiment, to hear the whole mind working, all at once, put on the *St. Matthew Passion* and turn the volume up all the way. That is the sound of the whole central nervous system, all at once."[5]

Thomas considers music to be among the most profound problems for human biology. In "Things Unflattened by Science," he includes music in his list of top-priority puzzles, things that puzzle him more than anything else. Urging biomedical researchers to pursue critical questions about the experience of music, he proposes an imaginary situation in which he is allowed to ask neurobiologists three or four questions. One of the scenarios he describes was completely startling to me.[6]

In the early 1980s, the German government set a large advisory committee to work out the next scientific mission of the Max Planck Institute. After a long time, the committee recommended that the new mission be dedicated to the problem of music—"What music is, why it is indispensable for human existence, what music really means—hard questions like that." The government turned down the idea. Thomas says that the U.S. will have grown up when we assemble a similar committee for the same purpose and begin developing a National Institute of Music, such as other national research organizations.

In 1977, I put similar questions to Marvin Minsky. He later wrote a paper, and I wrote detailed "treatments" for a fictional screenplay, set some years in the future, addressing a number of these questions: Why do we seem to need music? Why do people like music? Why do people enjoy experiencing the same rhythms, melodic patterns over and over again, day after day, even year after year? Why is so much taken for granted about music, while at the same time there is so little under-

4. *The Medusa and the Snail: More Notes of a Biology Watcher* (Toronto: Bantam, 1980), 127.

5. Ibid., 128.

6. *Late Night Thoughts on Listening to Mahler's Ninth Symphony* (Toronto: Bantam, 1984), 79.

standing of its operations? (As Wittgenstein suggests, "Animals come when their names are called. Just like human beings.")[7] Why is music profound?

"Other People Think" was written by John Cage in 1927.[8] He was fifteen years old. We all know the incredible scope of his influence on twentieth-century art. But I think he will come to influence the science of mind as well. I imagine that his procedures, multidirectional methods, and radical questionings will one day be examined very carefully, and that they will become part of cognitive science in the twenty-first century.

About seventy-five years after Helmholtz published *On the Sensations of Tone,* Cage took a critical step: he investigated cognitive approaches to music. His unique, multifaceted ways of thinking opened radical questions that were the beginning of a totally new "musical mind." I believe that Wittgenstein's remark is important here: "What a Copernicus or a Darwin really achieved was not the discovery of a true theory but of a fertile new point of view."[9] This applies equally to Cage and the potential evolution of musical thought. Cage created a point of view that did not exist before him. There were no recognized cognitive procedures for advancing thought and imagination out of the more mechanical conditioned responses. There existed minds driven by stereotypical musical responses.

Cage understood many of the problems that had built up over time, that accompany the habitual practice of music: namely, that it becomes difficult to "hear" new thoughts. Only by the creation of new methods of listening and studying can we transform these automatic thought processes. What Cage understood was that the main activity of most composers is not that profoundly creative, after all. He realized this long before our current digital technologies, which make it very clear, since we now have software even more adept at carrying out many familiar "compositional" procedures. Most "composing" had not meant isolating acoustic features, beginning with the physical spectrum itself, discovering its energies, and shaping it accordingly (as did Varèse). The unsettling truth was that most approaches to creating music began with *existent figures*—melodies snatched from the great fragments of musical memory.

In truth, composing usually amounted to a rearranging and modifying of these patterns, that is, other men's tunes, giving them personal-

7. *Culture and Value* (Chicago: University of Chicago Press, 1984), 67.

8. *John Cage: An Anthology,* ed. Richard Kostelanetz (New York: Da Capo Press, 1970), 45–49.

9. *Culture and Value,* 18.

ized sequences in time. Throughout the ages, new musical compositions were made by rearranging and individualizing such figurative patterns and giving them personalized time frameworks. ("Silicon composers" are now achieving this faster and often better.) More dramatically, Cage understood that music had come to mean "nod and tap" recognition of secure tunes, melodies, and shapes, prepared *ages ago*. What developed from this approach was a music sustaining itself through memory patterns—figurative fragments snatched out of the air and rearranged in time. He decided new, more fertile approaches were needed. It was time to open minds. Now composers would have to listen in ways they had never listened before. They would have to hear, think, and explore the "unformulated." And with prevision, he foresaw our time now.

It's 1937. How do minds approach the creation of music?

Visualize the time. John Cage was twenty-five years old when he delivered the lecture "The Future of Music: Credo" in Seattle. And consider his birth year, 1912. Women were still wearing long skirts, and musical activity was dominated (perhaps more than today) by unquestioned and habitual patterns. Simulate the time, and imagine his presence in it. In the halls of conservatories, musicians are practicing eight to ten hours a day, filling the building with every kind of possible melodic pattern; composers scribbling "notes without ears." (Yes, today this still goes on and on, owing to that unfortunate aspect of music that is mechanical, "without mind," grounded in habit.)

Imagine Cage in this environment, questioning how minds approach the creation of music; initiating totally new models of cognition into the "hitherto unheard or even unimagined" (Cage's expression for the future sonic worlds he anticipated).

What antennae did Cage use? He looks into the musical environment around him and understands percussion music to be a contemporary transition from keyboard-influenced music to the "all-sound music of the future." How will these sounds become available? How did he arrive at this observation? Why is he thinking about such future developments at all? Cage announces in "The Future of Music: Credo": "I believe the use of noise to make music will continue and increase until we reach a music produced through the aid of electrical instruments which will make available for musical purposes any and all sounds that can be heard. . . . [I]t is now possible for composers to make music directly, without the assistance of intermediary performers." Sweeping across the field of thought, how does his mind know what it knows?

He looked outside his own musical activities, discovering the first traces of these developments, in film studios and acoustic laboratories. Totally alive to his time, he recognizes the very beginnings of a sonic expansion to be achieved with electronic technologies. Interpreting, synthesizing this information, his imagination distinguishes how the course of music will benefit. He is alert to trends in other disciplines—engineering, physics, and acoustic research. He is informed about the library of "sound effects" recorded on film that every film studio had at the time; especially film phonographs which made it possible "to control the amplitude and frequency of sounds and give them rhythms within or beyond the reach of anyone's imagination."[10]

He imagines the sound of things unheard, and considers them to be future musical instruments. Today, we take for granted this world of all possible sounds, available to us through synthesizers, computers, recorders, microphones, and various means of sound modification. Cage did not only foresee the availability of the "total field of sound," including noise, he also imagined the precise modification of the harmonics, frequency, and intensity of this sonic spectrum years before it became a reality.

It's the turn of a new century. Why choose music to cultivate mind?

In a few years, neuroscience may provide some important clues. Composers today live at a moment of extraordinary transition. Discoveries, especially in the fields of biotechnology, neuroscience, and molecular engineering, as well as ubiquitous digital, converging media, and VR (virtual reality) platforms and the all-encompassing habitation of the Internet, will profoundly affect the multisensorial arts. Already a number of such innovations have appeared. There are parallels today that correspond to 1937. In the immediate future, breakthroughs in emergent technologies will act as catalysts for unprecedented changes in the creation and reproduction of musical experiences, as the advent of new technologies did in the second half of the twentieth century, radically advancing the development of musical thought in the next twenty years.

Visualize John Cage, twenty-five years old today. Imagine how he would approach the emergent evolution in knowledge and technologies. Simulate his far-reaching, telescopic mind, look forward in time, as he did in 1937, to the next half century. Model his approach; recognize the first traces of future developments.

For example, today's CD has a memory of 640 million bytes. The predictions are that this will increase to 10 billion bytes in five years, and in ten years to 100 billion bytes and beyond. Recent research includes optical discs the size of a quarter, capable of storing eight days or more of music; memory sticks the size of a piece of gum; ubiquitous sensory

10. "The Future of Music: Credo" (ca. 1938–40), in *Silence: Lectures and Writing* (Middletown, Conn.: Wesleyan University Press, 1961), 3–5.

particles the size of dust motes; and bio- and molecular engineering promise even greater capacity.

New visual and aural experiences are being explored as a result of recent advances in multisensorial and immersive technologies, some unlike any past experiences, particularly those being created for converging media platforms, such as 3-D sonic imaging and graphics, telepresence, and cyberspace.

Modeling Cage's telescopic perspective, we can ask: How will such developments affect our thinking about the content, duration, and presentation of experiences in the works that we create? How will we take imaginative account of these and other developing trends in planning new work for the future? I believe that it is especially urgent to give serious attention and recognition to groundbreaking innovations in the field of the "emerging arts."

Today media exist that begin to approach the range and subtlety of our perceptual modes. As immersive technologies expand and grow to mirror the sensitivity of our responsive energies, will the auditory arts delve consciously into these expansive sensory worlds? And in what ways? Or instead, will our sonic worlds be created with simpleminded "variation makers"—computer software that makes subtle or not so subtle variations and developments of preexistent musical materials?

In "The Future of Music: Credo," Cage described percussion music as a contemporary transition from keyboard-influenced music to the "all-sound music of the future." A similar transition is occurring now, as we move from concert, CD, and DVD temporally based music to media with infinitely greater memory. Instead of the availability of all sounds, it is the availability of vast memory that will make possible an unprecedented expansion of musical time and influence a new course of composition: the "all-time" music of the future.

The development of this expansive time spectrum in emergent technologies is for me today what an extended sonic spectrum that included noise was for Cage in 1937. As the possibilities of the "all-sound music of the future" were to Cage, the possibilities of "all-time music" are to me. In the twenty-first century, new time worlds will be explored just as composers in the twentieth century explored new sounds.

Music will be filled with extraordinary surprises. These will be achieved through a new mastery of time, which composers will gradually acquire. To paraphrase Cage, the present methods of writing will be inadequate for the composer who will be faced with the entire field of time. I believe that there will be magnificent changes in how we create musical forms over time. Completely new worlds of musical experience will be produced in the next fifteen years.

What becomes exciting to think about in creating this music is that it will require the creation of completely new ways of thinking about duration and structure developing over time. Composers will "sculpt new time" in totally new ways. Long-standing time conventions that have applied to the creation of musical experiences will no longer apply. We may choose to keep them, but there will be an infinite range of temporal choices: a complete "spectrum of time dimension" in the reproduction of music. For example, there will be the possibility of creating multisensorial or entirely musical worlds to be experienced over twenty-four hours, or over much longer or shorter periods of time. In theory, years, months, weeks, days, minutes, seconds will be possible. As Cage said in his "Credo": "The principle of form will be our only constant connection with the past."[11]

But more significant and ultimately more intriguing than the extension of the macro-time dimension will be the advent of something unprecedented in musical experience. It will no longer be necessary to produce music as uninterrupted sound, to have it continue nonstop, as in the past, or as on current CD and DVD formats. This will be the most unique feature of the new musical worlds produced with advanced memory technologies. Expansive memory will allow composers to create sonic worlds that may last many hours yet include long periods of silence. For example, music might sound for ten minutes, followed by a long span of silence, say an hour or two, and then maybe three minutes of sound. In any given twenty-four hours, for example, there can appear many wonderful musical surprises. Music will now take on a totally new dimension, similar to our experiences of time with its events in life.

I think of this unprecedented feature as a magnificent temporal-magnification of "musical form," as though using a macro- or telephoto lens to expand the silence and differentiation of phrase structures, enhancing their scale and presence over time. The challenge of composing its dimensions is very exciting. It will involve learning a number of new composing skills.

Advanced memory will inspire new ways of presenting music. Imagination is no longer limited solely to pieces, or continuous sonic installations, and nineteenth-century concert halls. Even now, I compose "Sound Characters" that interact with each other in different ways, depending on the architectural staging of my installations. One of the most vivid things I learned from Cage is how much everything we do is taken for granted and that we have to turn it around, discover other views. I

11. Ibid., 5.

remember shortly after having read *Silence,* I was preparing to present one of my first works, but I did not like the hall where the concerts were being given. I thought, "Why do you have to produce your work in this concert hall? Go out and find a beautiful space, a wonderful architecture." Right now we have no buildings dedicated solely to sonic experiences, other than frontal concert stages built for presenting nineteenth-century music. This has been a serious problem, even in the last half of the twentieth century, alive with electronic media, multi-loudspeakers, and interactive media.

Rather than being staged frontally, as in traditional concerts with the audience seated, immersive aural architectures are often best experienced interactively, as the audience explores the sonic world by listening at different locations in the space. There is a critical need for buildings that are dedicated completely to these new musical and sonic worlds, just as galleries are to the visual arts. And I believe in the immediate future we will be able to provide the kind of enriched public experiences of these new musical environments that can only result from architectural staging, and that are absolutely impossible to experience in one's home, even with multichannel systems.

All possible sounds and their modifications are available with current technologies. However, there remains one area of sound that has not been fully explored, though I anticipate it soon will be: specifically, the tones and patterns our ears produce in response to music, which is unfortunately referred to as "psychoacoustics." Produced interaurally, these virtual sounds and melodic patterns originate in our ears and neuroanatomy. In fact, recent scientific experiments at Johns Hopkins have shown that our ears continue to emit sound for a few seconds after death, establishing that our ears not only receive and absorb sound, but also emit sound (referred to by researchers as "otoacoustic emissions"). Such response tones exist in all music, but they are usually registered subliminally, often masked by complex timbres. They are a natural and very real physical feature of auditory perception, similar to the fusing of two images resulting in a third three-dimensional image in binocular perception, and they play a crucial role in the experience of music. I like to think of our ears acting as neurophonic instruments, sounding their own tones and melodic shapes. I expect in the future more composers will want to release this music produced by the listener, to bring it out of subliminal existence and consciously make it an important sonic dimension.

Jim talked about Cage introducing at a historical moment a real focus on the experiential. This focus is also very much part of our time. No longer limited to writing notes on paper, with current sound technologies composers may access real-time auditory experiences. In the process of composing, they can investigate in depth the aural worlds they create; they can examine different ways of hearing, whether sound is very far away, very close up, vibrating an elbow, appearing on top of their head, or "inside" their head and streaming out of their ears into space in front of their eyes.

Amazingly varied, abundant possibilities exist for creating interactive worlds in art and popular entertainment. (How different from today's CDs played over and over again.) Instead of preparing scores that only musicians play, composers will prepare new kinds of "scores" for listeners to explore at home. We have seen how the emphasis shifted with Cage from the composer to the musicians who perform the score. Here it will shift from the composer to anyone who might have the "score" in their living room. With recent developments, we may delve into even more intense possibilities: entering the interior of the music in startling new ways, perceptually. Composers will soon learn how to develop the "perceptual geographies" that will become the maps for vivid, personalized experiences in the sonic worlds of these "home scores."

A widespread conception about music is that it has to be for millions of people, whether in the form of pop music or art music. Beethoven in every bar, Bach in every bookstore. In the coming decade of customization, the expectation that music be created for millions only, will no longer exist. Of course, it will still be an option, but composers will also be able to tailor sonic experiences, individualizing them for specific rooms, architectures, and listeners. I think there are many exciting possibilities to think about—and to think about them as Cage would have. Imaginative narratives and experientially adventurous, compelling scenarios can be created in stunning, transformative worlds.

The experiential designs of real-time "first-person" sensory interactivity in converging new media are powerful because they individualize changing perceptual viewpoints, expanding visual, auditory, tactile, and motion-based experiences. Even more specific customization will be possible through materials science, neuroscience, and genetics, in health, in medicine—all these will have a relation to music as well. Perhaps we will soon tailor our sonic worlds for each individual's uniquely personalized bio-neuro profile, because it is clear that in the next fifteen years the foundations for a real knowledge of neurobiology will be achieved. Quite possibly, composers, besides learning harmony, will learn more about synaptic modulations. Recently I read an interview with Nicholas Negroponte (author of *On Being Digital*); he discusses ways in which biotechnology will become increasingly important for computer science in the twenty-first century. Current articles describe research advances in quantum computing and detailed computing systems based on biological memory (DNA) instead of silicon that eventually may become very interesting for composers. Perhaps one day, composers will make scores that will include bioenhancements for hearing, ornamenting our auditory system.

In 1980, during the New Music America Festival in Minneapolis–St. Paul, I created *Living Sound, Patent Pending (Traveling Musicians Being Prepared),* the first large-scale multichannel installation in my "MUSIC FOR SOUND–JOINED ROOMS" series for the Walker Arts Center. The music and visual sets were staged architecturally throughout the nearly empty Victorian house of the conductor Dennis Russell Davies and filmmaker Molly Davies. The house, on a hill in St. Paul with its panoramic view of Minneapolis, was lit by tall quartz spots, as if a movie set. The time: midnight. The visual elements gave clues to a story discovered in the different rooms, and in the outside garden. Davies's music room, where two grand pianos had stood, was now an "emergent music laboratory" where twenty-one petri dishes with "something" growing in them (the musicians and instruments of the future) were placed beside metal instrument cases marked "Fragile: Traveling Musicians Being Prepared" and "The Molecular Orchestra." TV story boards referred to "symbiotic aids" (biochemical companions tailored to enhance neurophonic recognition) and "making new scores." DNA photos and biochemical diagrams were placed on music stands. Meanwhile, the entire house was full of sound, circulating throughout the rooms, out the doors and windows, down the hill, past sedate Victorian mansions. For me, what was most interesting about this work was that I did not know that the law to patent life forms was about to be passed. I was thrilled to discover that this law (the Diamond V. Chakrabarty decision) followed a few days later. As the possibilities of biocomputers and emerging media approach, perhaps this work was not as much fantasy as it may have seemed at the time.

For music students, I hope that Cage's influence gets deeper and deeper, that right now we've only touched the tip of the iceberg and that one day we'll have minds for music. Imagine, there are six listening posts where people are currently studying sound on the sun in a project called "The Gong." In the last few decades, interferometry techniques have revealed defined patterns of acoustic oscillations corresponding to a series of harmonics produced as sound waves reflect off the thermal boundaries surrounding the sun's core. Separated from us by 93 million miles of vacuum, the sun is in effect a big silent gong. In its interior, middle C (which on our earth has a wavelength of roughly four feet in air at room temperature) has a length of about one half mile. Imagine the sound.

NINE

James Pritchett (chair), James Tenney,
Andrew Culver, and Frances White

Cage and the Computer

A Panel Discussion

It took six weeks to teach the computer how to toss three coins six times. Somewhat worried, I tossed the coins manually to discover from the *I Ching* how *I Ching* felt about being programmed. It was delighted.

—John Cage, "Diary: How to Improve the World (You Will Only Make Matters Worse) Continued 1969 (Part V)"

JAMES PRITCHETT: Let me welcome everybody to this session, which deals with Cage and the computer. We have three panelists.

James Tenney is a pioneer of computer music, of the application of algorithms to composition with computers. He was there before the beginnings—in the 1960s at Bell Labs, contributing to the development of the first computer music languages. I thought the first such language was called Music 4, but he informs me that he had worked with Music 3. That's like reading galleys from the Gutenberg Bible.

Andrew Culver collaborated with John Cage on computer-related projects. I think of him as John's "human-user interface for the computer." He filled this important role for many years, making Cage's ideas happen on the computer.

Frances White writes music using the computer largely for the synthesis of sound. She worked with John on his *Essay* pieces.

JAMES TENNEY: Cage's relationship with the computer was rather tenuous in the beginning. Before Andrew Culver began working with him he was interested in it, but aside from his connection with Lejaren Hiller and the development of *HPSCHD,* I don't know of any direct involvement that he'd had.

Long ago I was active at Bell Labs in the very early development of computer sound generation. Beginning in 1961, I was employed there for two and a half years. This was a period in my work when I not only was involved with this medium but also followed with great interest what Cage was doing. These two things were not separate; both were central to my concerns as a composer at the time. In thinking about what I might say here, I realized that this coincidence—my being caught up in the early development of the medium and my interest in Cage—made his ideas a very important early influence on the development of computer music simply because certain things I wanted to do were greatly stimulated or inspired by his ideas, and I had been brought to Bell Labs to help them develop the medium.

This was a fantastic situation, the start of what we all now take for granted as digital sound recording and processing. But what my colleagues at Bell Labs were doing then was generating digital sound completely from scratch, not working from recorded sounds. Basically this involved the same technology that we use with compact discs. Bell brought me in fresh out of graduate school from the University of Illinois with a mandate to work with the medium and, by trying to use it, propose developments of it. I was in the incredibly privileged situation of being asked to give input. What Bell didn't realize but gradually became aware of was how subversive my activities there were bound to be, due to the fact that my aesthetic philosophy was very close to Cage's thinking, whereas that was not the case with the people at Bell Labs. They didn't have the faintest notion of what he was up to.

To be more specific, when I got there even the sound-generating process itself was limited to oscillators and the equivalent of mixers. How about that! You could make a series of these and produce what Max Mathews called an instrument, which was in effect a series of blocks of computer code that you strung together. My first proposal to them, because of what I needed for the first piece, *Noise Study,* was, "You need a random noise generator in this"; they didn't have one. So, although they were primarily engaged in developing the tools that were designed already, they also started to expand in an unexpected direction.

Soon after this there were other things I felt I needed, for example, filters that would control timbre. These would produce sounds from a conceptual model based not on the sounds of traditional musical instruments but on sounds of the world outside, which are very complex and rich and full of noise. I didn't want to imitate them but to create a world of sounds that might approximate the variability that we hear when we listen to environmental sounds. The so-called instrument had to be very complicated, and a number of what were called unit generators had to be added to the set of possibilities.

Soon I was saying to myself, "We have an interesting situation here." The user would compose a piece, presumably in the conventional way or in whatever way, coming up with a series of numbers that became input specifications for the instrument. According to the numbers you gave, this series went into the computer, and sounds were generated that had their characteristics determined by these numbers. I thought, "Now what would happen if one could write another program that would generate numbers that went into the input to control sounds?" In other words, I became interested in what in other quarters and later would be called algorithmic composition, which is to say, working from a computer program to generate not just the sounds but the controls on the characteristics of the sounds. I proposed this to Max Mathews. It took him a few hours to set up a programming situation in which, if the user wanted to learn a little programming, he or she could write such a program, which would determine the nature of a particular piece. When I began to use this, I was immediately working with random number generation in a kind of process that I ended up calling a stochastic process, adapting the term from Xenakis's writings, but redefining it in a way that seemed more suitable to my own musical ideas and that is also applicable to a good deal of Cage's work.

I define a stochastic process as a constrained random process. The constraints are very important, although one condition that has to be included is the completely unconstrained random process; that's the default condition of constraints, namely, no constraints at all. But of course I don't think there's a piece by Cage that doesn't involve some kind of constraint. Every choice that he made precompositionally entailed one or more constraints on the interpretation of the *I Ching* results.

Near the end of my work at Bell I did two pieces, *Ergodos 1* and *Ergodos 2,* which represented for me not just the culmination of the experiments that I'd done in developing the range of timbres I wanted but also a manifestation of a compositional approach that I felt, that I still feel, brought me closest to Cage's aesthetic. Since then, I've gone in other directions, but then I was consciously trying very hard to come to terms with the implications of Cage's aesthetic. These two pieces represent that, and they are both dedicated to him. I was not surprised when, fifteen or twenty years later, I heard that he was using the computer for his own process.

There is a kind of mystique about the *I Ching* that may or may not be true: that you have to be right there to handle the coins or whatever to make it meaningful. I never took that seriously enough to see it as creating a problem in my use of the computer for generating random sequences, and it seemed to be a confirmation of my attitude when Cage started to do the same.

ANDREW CULVER: What's up on the screen is a table of the computer programs (table 9.1) between 1984 and 1995 that John and I used and others used for him. In the battle with technology, I've had to leave out the credits for who wrote the programs. Only two names should appear, mine is one and the other is Jim Rosenberg's. He wrote the two programs Mesolist and Mesomake, which were quite powerful utilities for generating the two kinds of mesostics that John was making.

In considering what I might say today, a number of recollections and thoughts came to mind. The first thing I want to tell you about is a blue proofreader's pencil. For a while John was never far from it. He may have gotten it from Paul Sadowsky, the autographer who, even when I started with John in 1981 on *30 Pieces for 5 Orchestras,* was producing copy for Peters, the publisher. Anyhow, John had this blue pencil. One day I opened my copy of Kernighan and Ritchie's *C Programming Language,* which is the bible for C programmers, and I saw that on the sly somebody had been underlining numerous words, several on each line, with the blue pencil. They were just words like "hard disk"; they were even more general words. It was as though someone—I assume John—had detected some special meaning in the words he underlined, words like "system," "language," "structure," "constant," "general purpose," "low-level." This underlining went from the beginning of the introduction all the way through the first page. I thought, "This is amazing, he's actually studying on his own." The underlining went on to page 2 and then it stopped abruptly, in mid-sentence. There was a time when John had expressed the hope that he would lay things aside and tackle the computer, and I think that this was the beginning and the end of that effort. I thought maybe he'd come in and say, "Let's talk about this C programming language," or at least, "Let's talk about these words of Kernighan and Ritchie's," but it never happened. He never brought it up, and neither did I.

Here I want to throw together the word "computer" with a few things that John did, the first of which is of course music. Recall that I was with him full-time from December 1983 through 1988, then on and off always in contact, still working but often at home, from 1988 until he died. My observations will center on the changes that the computer made in our various activities.

Major change brought about by the computer vis-à-vis Cage's music can be summed up in the word "notation." John was intensely interested

TABLE 9.1 Computer Programs Used by Cage

Name	Description	Year	Type	By	Language
Babbrook	Generated record player and sound parts for *Truckera*	87	process	Culver	C
Chairbar	Generated chair positions for *Essay* installation in Barcelona	91	process	Culver	C
Europera	End-user, integrated program for *Europeras 3 & 4* and *Europera 5:* setups, lights plots, gels list, light cues, and parts generation for photo flashes, phonographs, and *Truckera*	93	database	Culver	PAL, C
Flatcues	Generated the time plan for flat movements in *Europeras 1 & 2*	87	process	Culver	C, ZIM
IC	Generic command-line *I Ching* number generator with options: sort, nonrepetition, bias, immobile bias	84–91	utility	Culver	C
Imagecue	Generated image selections for the Frankfurt flats of *Europeras 1 & 2*	86	process	Culver	C, ZIM
Lghtcues	Light event generation for *Europeras 1 & 2* (Frankfurt version)	86	process	Culver	C, ZIM
Lieop	Light event generation for *Europeras 1 & 2* (Zurich version)	91	process	Culver	C
Liess	Light event generation for *Essay*	90	process	Culver	C
Lilcu	Light cue compilation for lieop or liess output	90–91	utility	Culver	C
Mattress	Generated chair and artwork positions for the changing installation at the Mattress Factory	91	process	Culver	C
Meso	Combines all mesostic routines in one program (incomplete)	89	process	Culver	C
Mesolist	Finds all the words in a source text that match all the letters in a string	85, 89	process	Rosenberg	C
Mesomake	Takes a source text and a source string and produces a "writing through" mesostic	84	process	Rosenberg	C
Mesorule	Proofs a mesostic poem for conformity with the 50% rule	88	utility	Culver	C
Mlcount	Counts the number of words for each mesoletter found by mesolist	85	utility	Culver	C
Mlfind	Finds one word for each mesoletter in a mesolist list	85	utility	Culver	C
Mlfmt	Formats a text for mesolist processing	85	utility	Culver	C

TABLE 9.1 *(continued)*

Name	Description	Year	Type	By	Language
Muoyce	Generated performance times for *Muoyce*	91	process	Culver	C
Musicfor	Generates time brackets, pitches, dynamics, specials for the *Music for*... series	88	process	Culver	C
Piaggs	Lists all three, four and five note piano aggregates	84, 89	utility	Culver	C
Rengamix	Chance mixes a group of mesostics with identical strings	85	process	Culver	C
Rover	End-user program for *Rolywholyover: A Circus;* integrates the design of the chance operations with every process necessary to run the main circus	93–95	database	Culver	Object PAL, C
TB	Generic time bracket generation (numbered pieces style)	90–91	process	Culver	C
TIC	Time values version of IC	84–91	utility	Culver	C
Yroverx	Generates pencil and stone selections for *Ryoanji* drawings	87	process	Culver	C

in notation. He made the anthology called *Notations;* his early autography has been exhibited in museums and published in books of graphic art. Right from the beginning (August 1981), when I arranged to help him with *30 Pieces for 5 Orchestras,* I came in, and on the round table in the loft was this extraordinary collection of tables and charts with the chance operations that came out of Bell Labs. And way over here, lost among everything, was the manuscript. The first thing he did was to give me a pencil and ask me to write notes on the manuscript. I couldn't believe it. I thought that manuscripts were revered things (perhaps I was suffering from a musicological imperative or something). What he did was keep the chance operations going. He diligently marked off whenever we used a number, and after that anytime we worked together John stayed at the chance-operation end of the process. He pushed the notation in the process my way. I have mentioned Paul Sadowsky's place in the final step, and now in the intermediate step there was I. Not to say that John never put his hand on notation anymore, or on a manuscript, but when we worked side by side he generally left it up to me. He was distancing himself from notation, letting go of it. Or he had already let go of it. The computer brought this development to greater extremes.

There were notations like the *Europeras* databases, for instance—such things as were given to the lighting crew or the stage director: dances, charts, drawings, costumes. Cage's interest in how these things looked was about what you'd expect, though many times he had nothing to say about how they were designed. Frequently their layouts stemmed from the constraints of our printer. The size of the fonts, for example, was based simply on how much data had to fit across the page. As to all the notation that carries instructions to the performers, its designs were left completely to others; it was a kind of indeterminacy. I'm not referring to the early pieces for which John made scores giving the player the kinds of choices and freedoms that came to be known as indeterminate scores. I mean that the process of making the notation had become indeterminate from his point of view, that he had stepped back from the process and was willing to let it go wherever it would. The computer and my involvement along with that of others, including Paul, were the agents of that happening.

In the years before Cage had a computer and the operators to work it, he was making large mesostics, the earlier of his writings through *Finnegans Wake.* Making these was terribly laborious and demanded an incredible discipline. And all of a sudden comes the computer, and Jim Rosenberg writes the program that does all the searching automatically, so the devotional aspect of composing a mesostic is usurped by the machine.

This had several side effects, the most immediate of which was that he sought outlets that required that kind of devotion in other places. It was auspicious that around that time Kathan Brown and Crown Point Press provided the opportunity for John to make visual artwork on a regular basis. His need to undertake difficult tasks was addressed by his making drawings where one of fifteen stones was placed by chance operations on a brass plate to be etched or on a piece of paper; then one of seventeen pencils was chosen by chance and a drawing was made around the stone. Sometimes the process went on as often as—was it a power of fifteen?[1] And several hundred placements of a stone—was it two to the fifteenth? In place of making mesostics, John had a new outlet for his desire to have a laborious task at hand.

I think there was another side effect, which affected performance, computer performance. You know John's famous aphorism about composing a piece of music having nothing to do with performing a piece of music, which has nothing to do with listening to a piece of music. Well, with the computer and the removal of the devotional aspect of making the mesostic, you now have a situation where making the mesostic has nothing to do with producing the mesostic, which has nothing to do with performing the mesostic. The producing, the middle stage, was

1. It was 15^2, 225, the most often one of the fifteen stones was outlined on one drawing—A.C.

taken over by the machine. John would thereafter be involved in the early stages, composing the selection of texts, the mesostic string; this is a compositional process. Then the performance of these processes would be given over to the machine in the end; this can be seen as a type of performance. He was removed one step from the composition of the material by its production by the machine and was now free to step in as a noncomposing individual, to become a performer at the final stage. Concurrent with this was the removal of other performance outlets. Piano and percussion were now behind him because of his arthritis. And, significantly or coincidentally, after a few years of composing using a computer, he stopped touring with Merce Cunningham and David Tudor, so he no longer had the third main component of his performance outlet. With percussion performance, piano performance, and the use of electronics relegated to the past, all he had left was text reading.

In the theater John had few chances to take charge of the light system, until the computer allowed him to work with this medium. With the Cunningham Dance Company—his main theatrical outlet until *Europeras*—he was only rarely and with little success given general control over lighting. The dancers complained that they couldn't see what they were doing. Only in the late 1980s comes the computer facility as well as the invitation to make the *Europeras* and, later, the *Essay* as installation. Cage now had machinery and lightboards that were computerized; he had the opportunity to do something brand new. He was very excited about being able to do his own lighting. He spoke of it as the principal experimental aspect of making the *Europeras* and as theatrically the most radical result of the whole process. He wanted to treat light as he'd been suggesting people consider sounds, that is, as individual points each the center of its own universe, the multiplicity of the interpenetration being without regard for what the viewer experiences. In lighting the phrase generally used was "without regard for illumination."

You may have noticed the words "utility," "process," "database" in my table (table 9.1). These name the three main ways to categorize the software that was generated over the years. Utilities are such programs as IC or TIC or the various mesostic formatting programs that facilitate some sort of task, whether it's searching for a mesostic word or tossing coins. Next are the processors. These are programs that call the utilities internally, so they're the next level of a Russian egg. They include lists of procedures and parameters and algorithms. The procedures are put into effect, and the program acts on the procedures according to the results of the chance operations and according to the parameters and lists of parameters. The program that made all the time brackets for all the "number pieces" is one of these; the other significant one is Musicfor, significant because it's the process program that embodies, more than any other, the entire compositional process.[2] It goes 99 percent of the way. It left one thing for John to do. Much as I tried to suggest that we automate that too, he wouldn't let me.

Beyond utilities and processors, the third kind of program involves the databases. The database programs contain within themselves process programs, which in this context are called "utilities." The significance here is that with the databases you not only can generate results, you can gather results—observe them in different ways and output them in different ways. If you look at these three in comparison with all types of computer programs that are possible, you will see where John's interests lay. The database is really the most complete and accurate analog to his use and interest in the computer.

FRANCES WHITE: In preparing for this session, I found myself thinking a lot about computers in general and about John Cage and computers specifically. I feel that the relations of musicians to computers are frequently problematic. (I know they have been for me.) I don't like to make a distinction for computer music, and anyhow, it seems to grow increasingly less valid. Years ago you had to go to specialized centers and work on very specialized equipment to make sound with computers, but now they are almost ubiquitous, and it's a much less specialized field. You see composers who never think of themselves as computer musicians now write tape pieces and work with computer sound generation. The historical distinction is fading, and I think that's a good thing.

One of the big difficulties for me personally in dealing with computers is that I think the essence of music is ultimately something very mysterious. Somehow with computers some of the mystery seems to be lacking. Certainly what I don't know about computers would fill hundreds of books, though I am interested in the essence of what computers are. Part of the problem involves a composer's or performer's relationship to a computer as opposed to a traditional acoustic instrument. Both are artifacts made by human beings, but for me computers are more than just an instrument and also somehow less than that. To some degree they do incorporate human ideas about human thought, and here my remarks should return to John Cage. Cage once said that he thought it might be very interesting if you had a computer that acted more like nature than like human beings. I interpret this statement as getting at something like what I am talking about, the whole aspect of mystery.

My dealings with Cage and the computer occurred when I was doing

2. See Culver's comments below regarding the "special column" in the Musicfor outputs.

the technical work on the *Essay* pieces. I saw his interaction with technology only in a very limited way; he didn't work on the system every day. I always picked up from him a certain shyness around the technology. The equipment was intimidating; it was not user-friendly. He was eager for us to tell him what we were doing with the signal processing and such. He wanted to know what was behind the speech synthesis work we were doing. He never seemed to have an interest in a hands-on approach to the equipment. I observed a sort of reserve from him about technology. We think of him as focusing on the future of music, and yet he didn't get involved in the technology directly and personally.

AUDIENCE QUESTION FOR TENNEY: What were you doing before going to Bell Labs and how did you get your job there?

TENNEY: I attended the University of Illinois because I had read a tiny little notice in the *New York Times* saying that for the first time anyplace, certainly for the first time in North America, a course in electronic music was going to be given at that university toward the end of 1958. (There was a primitive electronic studio at Columbia University, but it was not accessible to students. Only Otto Luening and some invited guests could use it; it was not part of the teaching program.) I had been casting about for a place to do graduate work. Here was a course that was to be given by Lejaren Hiller, the guy who with a collaborator (Leonard Isaacson) did the famous or infamous *Illiac Suite,* which resulted from the first significant use of the computer in a quasi-compositional process. They weren't really trying to create original music, but rather to simulate existing styles. I went to Illinois and took Hiller's course. He also gave a course in musical acoustics and information theory, which was fabulous. At the same time, I had the fantastic good luck of getting to know and work with Harry Partch.

The university had a very primitive studio—nothing but a few tape machines and Lafayette oscillators that you had to set by hand. You'd record a note, then take the tape and splice it to the next. This was before Moog and Buchla came up with their synthesizers, which made it possible to program, in analog fashion, a whole sequence of sounds, so the task was horribly tedious and cumbersome. I had been turned on by Varèse's vision of electronic music in the future. When I saw this studio, I said, this is not the future, this is terrible!

So in desperation I got the idea of using concrete sounds or, in this case, Elvis Presley. In one week of twenty-three-hour days in the studio I made the piece called *Blue Suede.* It was done in spite of the medium (the medium being electronic music), not because of it. Before I had finished, Hiller mentioned an article by Max Mathews in the *Bell System Technical Journal* that described a new computer sound generation process. After the difficulty I had had, reading this article about the new process made me think that that was the medium for me, that would work. There was something about it I liked. I'm not a knob turner; I'm not particularly comfortable with equipment. So I went back to New York during the Christmas break and made an appointment to see some of the people at Bell Labs. I wanted to learn if outsiders could make use of the equipment. I had an interesting conversation with Mathews, John Pierce, and another person at Bell Labs. After going back to Illinois, I got a letter from Pierce saying, "We enjoyed talking with you, and we want you to know that you are welcome to come and use our system." I responded by saying "Thank you, it's a fantastic opportunity, and if I am nearby next year I will take you up on that. I don't know where I'll be because I have to find a job." They sent me back a letter offering me a job.

Just incredible. I wanted to move back to the New York area if possible, so this was an enormous opportunity. It put me in contact with the new technology and also with the whole artistic climate in New York in the sixties, which was pretty amazing. Of course, John Cage was central to that as far as I was concerned.

AUDIENCE QUESTION: How did Hiller meet Cage?

TENNEY: I believe they met when Cage came out to Illinois with the Cunningham dance troupe for a performance. By this time I think he was beginning to open up to new technological possibilities, and Hiller got to him at just the right moment.

PRITCHETT: I know that it was in 1953 at the University of Illinois that Cage put on one of the first concerts of electronic music in the country. Tape pieces by Boulez and Cage were played, including the ones that were part of the project called Music for Magnetic Tape that resulted in *Williams Mix.* So I think Cage may have had a long-standing relationship with the University of Illinois. Did you learn about him when you were there?

TENNEY: No, I had met Cage in 1954 when I was a student at Juilliard. My roommate was Stan Brakhage, the filmmaker; I had done the music for his first film. His third or fourth film, called *In Between,* used some of Cage's *Sonatas and Interludes* as soundtrack, and he wanted to get Cage's permission—he had put the music on the film without actually getting permission. So he called Cage and made an appointment to meet with him, and I tagged along. We met at a little bar down in the Village, and Cage bought us a beer. This was in 1954, and I'll never forget what Cage said: "You know, I'm into something else now. I am no longer interested in the *Sonatas and Interludes* or any of my music from that period. You can do what you want with it." It was like he was washing his hands of all that earlier music. He had no proprietary feelings about it. (Incidentally, a little clip from *In Between* was shown in the MOCA exhibit *Rolywholyover.* When you hear *Sonatas and Interludes* there, it's from Stan's film.)

AUDIENCE QUESTION FOR ANDREW CULVER: When you talked about the Musicfor program, you said that there was only one thing left for Cage to do, and I didn't hear you say what it was.

CULVER: The program outputs something called the "special column." Either it is empty or it has an asterisk. If it has an asterisk, it was up to John to devise something for the player to do that was special, unusual, depending on the instrument. For a string instrument, he might come up with little glissandi, for instance.

PRITCHETT: Since Cage wasn't much of a hands-on technologist, to what degree was he insulated from the changes that technology could have made in his composing?

CULVER: I think John liked to be the first person in on a new technology rather than the second or later. Perhaps this was a heritage from his father, the inventor. I'll tell you two anecdotes. One day he introduced me to someone he wanted me to know; he said. "This is Andrew Culver, he understands Buckminster Fuller." I said, "John, I never understood Buckminster Fuller." I found out that what John meant was that I could read texts in "Fullerese" and he couldn't. He'd trip over the first word, couldn't get past it. He just didn't want to go with it.

TENNEY: But he said many times that he lost interest in things once he understood them.

CULVER: Well, in this case, he never even got started. The other anecdote concerns his father. I gave John this little stopwatch, which I had bought at Radio Shack. I told him I thought it was the ultimate musician's stopwatch. He took me up on it, but he used it more for cooking, of course.

I showed him how it worked: "Look, John, it has this amazing little thing on the back which can hold it in place in three different ways: it's a clip, so you can clip it to your pocket or your music stand; it's got a magnet on it, so you can stick it on your refrigerator or something else; and it's got this little bar that you can flip down and then you can put it on a table." John is sitting there, looking at this thing, investigating all three ways, and now he wanted to get the clip flat again. He's holding onto it with his fingers—you remember the big post-arthritic fingers—and trying to push this little thing in there and get his fingers out before it closes on them. I say, "Oh here, John, just turn it upside down and let gravity do it," and he answers, "That's something my father would have said!" I took that to mean that he wasn't interested in gravity, never got into it, because his father had talked about gravity.

This may be exactly what we mean when we say he wasn't interested in technology. He saw something that was already there, and he wasn't going to explore it. It was something human beings had made, and so he didn't want to devote himself to its exploration.

TENNEY: Doesn't this connect also to what he used to say about 100 percent unemployment? He wanted the computer and you to do the work, which left him free to find other challenges. That's exactly what his economic arguments meant when they talked about what automation is going to do for us.

WHITE: Certainly I have always felt that I was working against the technology to some extent, and I too feel a desire to get closer to natural sounds. For me and for every composer that I have talked to who has worked with computer music, a strange thing occurs that affects the way you think about writing for acoustic instruments as well. I have gotten used to the idea of making sounds by hand, and with it comes a personal involvement with the sounds; I have tried to bring that to my writing for instruments. I can't even imagine what it was for Cage not to be involved on that level, not to have had hands-on experience. I do know that the whole *Essay* project would not have happened the way it did if before proposing the piece he had sat down at a computer and experimented with the speech synthesis programs and such. I really don't think the project would have taken the path it did. So I definitely think that the fact he didn't work with it affected the piece.

AUDIENCE QUESTION FOR ANDREW CULVER: Concerning the computer version of the *I Ching* coin oracle, how did it compare with the original? How does it differ from just generating random numbers? Also, was there any special care given to your brand of number generator, and did Cage care about that?

CULVER: There was a great deal of care on my part, but John couldn't have cared less, didn't want to know about it really. There was a pseudorandom number generator down at the bottom of it that has been through several generations. I ran across something in a magazine—*chi*-square tests on random number generators and such. The one that's in there now is a deck-shuffling scheme. The dirty little random number generator down at the bottom is used to stack a bunch of decks, which are shuffled. The cards are read to a point, and if a certain event occurs, that whole shuffle is thrown out and done again. All this is used to produce a zero or a one, a head or a tail. From then on it's strictly the *I Ching*. So three times you get a head or a tail, add it up to get a broken or solid line, or a changing broken or changing solid line. That's done six times. You get a hexagram, you look at it. If there's a changing hexagram, that's what you find.

AUDIENCE COMMENT: So those numbers aren't random in the same sense . . .

CULVER: . . . as the random number generator underneath it all? Right.

TENNEY: Just a different distribution of random numbers. They are pseudo-random. You can regenerate the same sequence if you want.

CULVER: There is one more difference. With the *I Ching* not only do you produce a string of numbers, but more often than not, because there is a changing line involved, you generate one more number hanging off one of those numbers. Let's say ten numbers come up. That's not ten numbers out of the random number generator. It might really be six numbers of which the first, third, fourth, and second are changing. You have a changing hexagram hanging on to it.

AUDIENCE COMMENT: When you flip coins there very often tend to be streaks, but depending on your random number generator, you may have more variety and a greater tendency toward streaks. Some may have different flavors of number generators.

CULVER: There are definitely different flavors to the different uses of this whole package of algorithms. One time you ask for a number from 1 to 33, and you ask for it again immediately and the second group is different from the first. Whether that can be traced back to the random number generator or not I don't know. I hope it can't be because that's why I went to all the trouble to find a good one.

AUDIENCE QUESTION: Did it have a noise source in it?

CULVER: No. Way down at the bottom is a random function.

AUDIENCE QUESTION: Are you against using random numbers per se?

CULVER: I think it is like standing on a bridge and facing in one direction or the other. If you are concerned about the randomness of your music, say, the way the music sounds, you are standing on the bridge, with the generator behind you, looking over at the other side of the river, which is where the results are. But John was doing the opposite. He had his back to the results and was looking at what was coming out of the *I Ching*. Does that make any sense? I think that the reason he didn't like the term "randomness" or "stochastic" was because he felt it described the results rather than indicating what he was up to when he was doing it. He liked to use chance operations because it emphasized that *he* was asking questions.

AUDIENCE COMMENT: I thought that what was crucial were the uneven probabilities.

CULVER: He was excited about that. He'd sometimes jump up and down, saying "Oh look at all those!"

AUDIENCE QUESTION: Why did he like unequal probabilities more than equal probabilities?

CULVER: You know he also invented this little thing called "bias." Anyone who has used IC knows that it has a bias flag. *A* minus *B* after all your other input produces a biased output. What does the bias do? We talked about the random number generator becoming the *I Ching*. The output of that is numbers 1 to 64. Then there is another layer where you relate the numbers to the number range of the questioner; it might be 33 to 62. It's different from 1 to 64. The way we did it was to use the "mail slot" concept: we had sixty-four slots and we needed thirty-two slots, so we took the first two and put them into slot one. Then 3 and 4 go into slot two. But if you want a bias, then the program will ask for a number from 1 to 64 and make dividing points by chance. It will ask itself to make a chance redistribution of the sixty-four slots.

PRITCHETT: Which was a process that he had developed early on. *Music for Piano* of 1952 uses just such a process, in which the notes are supposed to be muted or plucked or normally struck, and the way you decide, which is to divide the sixty-four into three, would be first to toss two numbers with that being the division point. So if the numbers are 2 and 6, there are two very rare possibilities, and then anything from 6 to 64 up. The points are randomly chosen. Then perhaps another number will determine how often the distribution is to be used; for a while you'd have a certain flavor of bias for so many notes and then go on to the next.

For me this raises the issue of the degree to which the computer made a difference, if any at all, in John's work. I remember seeing manuscript pages of long division that Cage was forced to do to get those fractions of seconds. I mean, we might have had a panel of "Cage and the Calculator." I was trying to express the same idea by talking about technology changing what we do. What is involved seems to be largely reimplementing existing processes. The computer influenced him by relieving him of having to think about the earlier implementations anymore.

CULVER: Which gave him time to think about something else, not necessarily something he'd planned but by necessity something else. One day he told me, "I have never wasted my time."

AUDIENCE QUESTION: Did Cage ever mention or discuss the main difference between the IC computer program and flipping a coin, which was the pseudo aspect of it? Did he ever want the program to be able to repeat stuff?

CULVER: No, he never asked for stuff to be repeatable. Well, actually what happened was that as we moved from the 8086 to the 286 and the

486 computer. I discovered I was getting the same "seed" over and over again because it was running so much faster and not enough time had elapsed. And that was the day I looked down at a page of ones and twos and saw to my horror that starting with the fifty-eighth item it was repeating what had started with the first one.

AUDIENCE COMMENT: In one part of *Empty Words* there occurs a repetition of a large text segment, which resulted from a computer error that Cage decided not to correct. Maybe this happened more than once.

ANOTHER COMMENT FROM AUDIENCE: I am interested in asking the panel generally about how, if at all, the computer inspired any new technique or new method.

WHITE: I feel strongly that the way he used the computer was to implement more easily what he was already doing. I don't believe that it *changed* what he was doing.

CULVER: But the example of *Essay* itself says exactly the opposite. For instance, *Essay* is the only sound installation that I know of that ever toured galleries and was installed for months on end as a sound installation of John's. And this came about because somebody had told him that there was a computer program capable of stretching or compressing his voice without changing the pitch; that's when he called up Charles Dodge to see if it was true. And Charles said, "Yes, we can do it." Cage wasn't intending to make an installation; it could never have come about without the technology.

WHITE: That's right. But it does seem to me that this is primarily the trajectory of an individual piece. True, he could not have predicted this trajectory, but as for his work in general I don't think of *Essay* as having changed it.

PRITCHETT: As the flip side of this I would ask, How many of his number pieces are there that differ from one another but for which the technique is conceptually, essentially, the same? Or take Musicfor, which is one program that still could be generating pieces.

TENNEY: And when you increase quantity beyond a certain number of orders of magnitude, you get a different quality. For example, would Cage have lived long enough to have realized *Europeras* if he'd had to do it the old way? I don't think so. The technology made possible some large-scale projects that he otherwise would never have thought of embarking on.

PRITCHETT: Such as "writings through" that became more and more elaborate.

TENNEY: A relevant personal experience may explain my position. I remember flying over Arizona and seeing all the land forms and realizing that, if I were down there on the ground, I wouldn't be able to see these incredible land forms. And I thought, "That's what working with a computer is like!" It gives you the possibility of distance. You can all at once take in this large thing that you couldn't take in without the technology. Instead, you'd be involved in details.

AUDIENCE COMMENT: But the advantages his chance operations actually gained from technology are hard to specify.

PRITCHETT: Maybe that's why he left that one thing to be done by hand. I say this partially in humor, but it may be true. It is true when you think about a program's being a composition that has all these various realizations. You could do something like the trombone piece; just say, "Do something special." In fact, I myself did something of this sort with some pieces that were never intended for such treatment. In doing research on some pieces from the 1950s, I tried to reconstruct what the systems were and thereby discovered that Cage was perhaps the first algorithmic composer. He was so systematic that you could look at his leftover papers and reconstruct how a piece was made. And to make sure that I had reconstructed it correctly, I would go ahead and do the piece; this was very educational. I strongly recommend doing this sort of thing. To learn what it's like to compose such a piece, just sit down and start working it through. You'll find out how laborious and tedious it is. And I had a calculator, too. Even in a finished piece there is always a level at which decisions still have to be made. John always left decisions, questions to answer, and judgment calls like the special codes.

AUDIENCE QUESTION: You said that at some point Cage had stopped being devoted to throwing coins and was focusing on other aspects. What were these aspects?

CULVER: Well, it depends on the period, but the example I gave was the automation of mesostic-making. Concurrent with that seemed to be the arrival of the laborious drawings. Cage quite simply went from the laboriousness of making mesostics to the laboriousness of making his drawings. A laborious process was chosen on purpose, I am sure; from the start he could have made it easier.

AUDIENCE COMMENT: But he kept on making mesostics. It became easier for him to do more.

CULVER: Yes, but since the difficulty was removed from mesostic-making, he found it elsewhere.

AUDIENCE QUESTION: Did he perhaps put some of that extra energy into the performance of the mesostics?

CULVER: I'm not sure about that. I think the need to perform was lifelong, and it ended up in the mesostics because, as I've said, his hands and the rest of his body made piano and percussion performance impossible. Then the need to do *Europeras* ruled out electronics, that is to say, touring with Merce and David. So by process of elimination he ended up with mesostics, readings as performance.

PRITCHETT: Let me ask James Tenney: Having written algorithmically oriented pieces, would you say that your act of composing ended when the program was designed and ready to roll or, after the piece was finished, would you have to make changes with it or reserve the right to change what it would be?

TENNEY: Generally, the decisions about instruments and other decisions that have to be made are compositional decisions. Nobody can just push a button and turn out a piece. However, someone could make similar decisions; they are not impossible for me to imagine. I'm wondering if I should put them in my will.

CULVER: A composition doesn't change. Take *0'00"*. Anybody can do anything with it; the piece won't change if I do something with it different than anybody else. The score is still the same.

TENNEY: I would like to speak to this issue. Until recently I don't believe I have ever used the same computer program for more than two pieces, even though I wrote a program that could generate a whole series of pieces. Finally, in the last year or so, I have gotten past this point, maybe emboldened by Cage's example. I am now working on what I call a family of pieces all generated by the same basic algorithm but with different kinds of input specifications that not only are determined by a particular instrumentation but also have to do with the shape of the piece, how it evolves in time.

I am beginning to have new feelings about the work. Even though at one time I imagined generating a series of pieces by the same algorithm, my ideas about what I want have changed so rapidly that I've had to write a new program. In addition, I sometimes (in fact, quite often) compose in other ways even within the field of algorithms. My desire changes so fast; it doesn't last long. In this recent series I felt I was able to distinguish each member of the family; each had its own personality.

I have developed a certain feeling about John's two series, the *Music for* and the number pieces. What he was really making was a very generous gesture to the world at large. All kinds of people wanted him to write pieces for them, and nobody could dream up new ideas that fast. I think he said to himself, "Well, they want some music from me, and so I'll give it to them."

PRITCHETT: I remember going up to John's one day and—Andrew, you were there, talking to John about all the things he had to do before he went somewhere. You were laughing about it. Among the items on his list was, you know, write that orchestra piece. And indeed it got done!

CULVER: Yes, he called Mimi Johnson that day to ask if the tickets were ready and such. He said to her, "Oh, by the way, I wrote that orchestra piece. It took twenty minutes." And she said, "Oh my god, don't tell them about it. I haven't even answered their request. You don't have a contract or anything."

PRITCHETT: To be fair, that's one of the pieces in which everybody plays in unison, so there really weren't that many notes to be generated. It's a beautiful story, in any event. It seems that by having the whole orchestra play in unison Cage was trying to make a qualitative difference in the sound that would come from this mysterious place. I recall being very excited by that. It was a beautiful sound. The last time I spoke to Cage he told me about this microtonal music he was working on, trying to find a way to make the freedom that happened in the time domain in those pieces happen with pitch and timbre, in all domains. These are things that no computer is going to redo. These are the sorts of things that went with him.

AUDIENCE COMMENT: In 1982 Cage was asked if he still enjoyed composing music, and he said no. Then, asked why he was still composing, he said, "People keep asking me for new pieces. I never want to say no." As you all have suggested, the computer actually helped him to say yes as best he could.

CULVER: "Just say no," we should have said to him.

WHITE: I know he changed his answer to that question periodically. Mostly he answered yes, but just at some moments he felt no.

PRITCHETT: He said it in the sixties as well. It's one of those statements that should be taken with heavy grains of salt.

AUDIENCE COMMENT: He gave a reason for it. He said, "I have said everything I have to say in music, and I would now rather do different things," which is why he began to do more word pieces, radio pieces, installations, printmaking, and such. He had many outlets rather than being just a composer.

CULVER: Before we close, something I ought to tell you is how John decided to buy a computer and how I got involved in helping him learn to operate it. For years he had been thinking about working with a computer, but he kept saying no, no, no. Then, when he was in Banff in November 1983, he met a man who had been teaching photography. This was Hubert Hohn. In his spare time Hugh had begun poking around on Apple II computers and discovered that every Apple II has its own thumbprint. He managed to write a program that, before it did anything else, could print out the initial conditions of all the memory bits, whether they were zeros or ones. He then printed them all out and stuck the printouts on the wall. You could look at them; you could put the Apple II below it and say here's this computer's thumb print. And you'd look around the room and see that every computer had its own thumb print. He took that to Apple and the engineers couldn't believe it. Anyhow Hugh was telling all this to John, who gets excited and enthusiastic. He found enjoyment in it. He came right back from the trip and called me up. He said, "Now I think I should get a computer, but I don't want to operate it myself," and so he asked me to do it. He lined himself up with both the promise of great enjoyment and the security of escaping the bother of having much to do with it. So I came in, and we went shopping and bought a computer.

TEN

Jackson Mac Low

Cage's Writings up to the Late 1980s

I myself feel more committed the more diverse and multiplied my interests and actions become.

Somewhere in Virginia, I lost my hat.

And so we hesitate before crossing the great waters.

—John Cage, "Lecture on Commitment," *A Year from Monday*

To give a complete account of John Cage as a writer one would have to consider his work as a composer, thinker, mycologist, and unorthodox Buddhist as well as his other activities, and to show the relation between these activities and his writings. The following survey, however, does not deal with all his writings and touches only peripherally and generally upon his work in music and the visual arts or upon his other interests. Instead, I discuss a limited number of his writings, certain poems in particular, describing each as completely as possible. I also examine his principal motivations for writing as he did.

"Cage's Writings up to the Late 1980s" is a thoroughly revised and expanded version of an essay entitled "Something about the Writings of John Cage," the first version of which appeared in the catalog *Music Sound Language Theater: Etchings from Crown Point Press* (Crown Point, 1980). Its first revised version appeared in *Writings about John Cage*, ed. Richard Kostelanetz (Ann Arbor: University of Michigan, 1993). The last of these earlier versions was revised and expanded, after Cage died, for presentation at the Cage conference, concert series, and exhibit "Days of Silence" (Warsaw, October 1993). That version was further revised and expanded for the conference "Here Comes Everybody: The Music, Poetry, and Art of John Cage" (Oakland, November 1995) and again revised, with the addition of several examples, at the end of November 1995. During the final stages of the most recent revision, Anne Tardos gave me invaluable editorial help and suggestions for improving the text.

What Cage said in a 1979 interview can provide a theoretical groundwork for the descriptions and interpretations of particular works:

> [V]alue judgment . . . [i]s a decision to eliminate from experience certain things. [Dr. D. T.] Suzuki said Zen wants us to diminish that kind of activity of the ego and to increase the activity that accepts the rest of creation. And rather than taking the path that is prescribed in the formal practice of Zen Buddhism itself, namely sitting cross-legged and breathing and such things, I decided that my proper discipline was the one to which I was already committed, namely the making of music. And that I would do it with a means that was as strict as sitting cross-legged, namely the use of chance operations, and the shifting of my responsibility from that of making choices to that of asking questions.[1]

Cage often called the use of chance operations and the composition of works indeterminate as to performance "skillful means" (Sanskrit: *upaya*, a Buddhist term for means employed by Bodhisattvas to help all sentient beings attain enlightenment). I think he viewed the experiences of composing, performing, and hearing such works as being equally conducive to the arousal of *prajña*—intuitive wisdom/energy, the essence/seed of the enlightened state—by allowing the experience of sounds as perceived in themselves, "in their suchness," rather than as means of communication, expression, or emotional arousal or as subordinate elements in a structure.

These considerations are as relevant to his writing as to his music—especially to the poems he wrote from 1967 to 1992, most of which are alogical and "asyntactical" collage word-strings of language elements: letters (which Cage seemed not to distinguish from phonemes), syllables, words, phrases, and/or sentences. By "asyntactical" (Cage often used the term "nonsyntactical"), I mean that these strings are ones "departing from conventional [normative] syntax"—freed from "the arrangement of an army," which Norman O. Brown told him was the original meaning of "syntax," derived from the Greek word σύνταξις. Such "asyntacticality" rendered (or was meant to render) the component linguistic units, like the sounds in the music he wrote after 1950, perceivable in themselves, as are objects of perception when one regards them with "bare attention" during *vipaśyanā* (contemplation leading to insight), the basic form of Buddhist meditation.

There is some question, of course, as to whether any arrangement of language elements, no matter how different from normative syntax,

1. Interview with Cage conducted by Bill Womack at the Los Angeles County Museum of Art, March 27, 1979, *Zero* 3 (1979): 70.

doesn't in itself constitute a new, non-normative syntax. (For this reason I never use Cage's term "nonsyntactical.") Some theorists would say that Cage and others who eschew normative syntax are "evading the army" by producing their own *new* syntaxes, over which the "generals" have no sway (or, at least, less than they usually do). Nevertheless, such non-normative syntaxes may well conduce to the reader's or listener's giving words, phrases, phonemes, and other linguistic elements something approaching "bare attention." To utilize a term introduced by Russian Formalist critics, notably Viktor Shklovskii, non-normative syntaxes "defamiliarize" their linguistic elements, thereby bringing them into the foreground of the reader's awareness. "The habitual is 'made strange'; it is presented as if it were seen for the first time."[2] The transition from this awareness of familiar linguistic elements as "strange" to giving them "bare attention" is not of course inevitable, but it is certainly possible and probably does take place for a certain number of readers and listeners from time to time.

From 1961 to 1986, Wesleyan University Press published five substantial volumes of Cage's writings: *Silence* (1961), *A Year from Monday* (1967), *M: Writings '67–'72* (1973), *Empty Words: Writings '73–'78* (1979), and *X: Writings '79–'82* (1983, 1986). Moreover, the University of Tulsa Press published his first *Writing through Finnegans Wake* as a special supplement to the *James Joyce Quarterly* (vol. 15) and as number 16 in its Monograph Series (1978), and Cage himself, as a member of the now defunct publishing co-op Printed Editions, published in 1978 a deluxe edition of his first two writings through *Finnegans Wake*.[3] In addition, Station Hill Press published his *Themes & Variations* (1982). While most of what Cage wrote before the late 1980s is included in the Wesleyan collections, many of his writings have also appeared in magazines, anthologies, record brochures, and exhibition catalogs, and as forewords to other people's books. Several of his verbal works are available on LP records, audiotapes, and compact discs.

Cage wrote verbal works from time to time throughout his life, although the earliest work in the Wesleyan volumes, "The Future of Mu-

2. Victor Ehrlich, *Russian Formalism: History-Doctrine*, 3d ed. (New Haven, Conn.: Yale University Press, 1981), 76. See also 177 and other pages indexed under "Disautomatization vs. automatism (of perception)." Formalism was a school of literary scholarship and criticism that originated in 1915–16, flourished in the early 1920s, and was suppressed by the Stalin regime around 1930. It was informally allied with the Cubo-Futurist poets, notably Velimir (orig., Viktor Vladimirovich) Khlebnikov (1885–1922), Alexei Yeliseyevich Khruchenykh (1886–1970), and Vladimir Vladimirovich Mayakovsky (1894–1930).

3. He wrote five of them, the last two of which, "Writing for the Fourth Time through Finnegans Wake" and "Muoyce (Writing for the Fifth Time through Finnegans Wake)," appear in *X: Writings '79–'82* (Middletown, Conn.: Wesleyan University Press, 1983), 1–49 and 173–87, respectively.

sic: Credo," dates from 1938–40.[4] While his principal subject was music, of course, especially modern experimental music, he discussed other music of the past, present, and future as well. And in addition to writing extensively on his own music, he often commented on that of other composers, including Earle Brown, Henry Cowell, Morton Feldman, Charles Ives, Erik Satie, Arnold Schoenberg, Karlheinz Stockhausen, James Tenney, Edgard Varèse, Christian Wolff, and myself. He dealt, too, with visual artists such as Marcel Duchamp, Morris Graves, Jasper Johns, Joan Miró, Nam June Paik, Robert Rauschenberg, and Mark Tobey; the social and religious thinkers Norman O. Brown, Buckminster Fuller, Marshall McLuhan, D. T. Suzuki, and Henry David Thoreau; and dance and dancers, in particular Merce Cunningham and his choreography. He also wrote on "something," "nothing," and mushrooms.[5]

Much of his writing consists of elegantly composed expository prose and skillfully told stories, most of them drawn from his friends' lives or his own. However, the discussion that follows is limited to the writings he composed by *I Ching* chance operations, by use of materials originally composed to generate realizations of indeterminate musical works, by "writing through" certain texts to produce "mesostics," and by related methods. These fall ostensibly into two categories: lectures and poetry, much of it "asyntactical," but as we shall see, the categories are really "not-two."[6]

The *I Ching,* or *Book of Changes,* is a "wisdom book" and one of the basic Chinese classics. It is consulted by means of certain chance-operational methods—involving yarrow stalks or coins—in which the probabilities of particular answers occurring are not equal. Cage not only derived from it basic attitudes toward the world and toward questions and answers but also—around 1950—adapted the coin method of consulting it to musical composition, and somewhat later, to writing lectures, poems, and the like. By "chance operations," he meant preeminently ones involving unequal probabilities like those he considered to be embedded in the somewhat ritualistic methods through which the *I Ching* is consulted.[7]

4. In *Silence: Lectures and Writings* (Middletown, Conn.: Wesleyan University Press, 1961), 3–6.

5. "Lecture on Something," in *Silence,* 128–45; "Lecture on Nothing," ibid., 108–15; "Mushroom Book," in *M: Writings '67–'72* (Middletown, Conn.: Wesleyan University Press, 1973), 117–83.

6. A Zen Buddhist term often alluded to by D. T. Suzuki and other writers on Zen, "not-two" implies that polarized aspects of reality, e.g., matter and mind, are neither/both the same nor/and different.

7. See *The I Ching, or Book of Changes,* the German translation by Richard Wilhelm rendered into English by Cary F. Baynes, foreword by C. G. Jung, Bollingen Series 19 (New York: Bollingen Foundation and Pantheon Books, 1950). A composer-friend who understands the mathe-

In the 1950s and 1960s Cage composed several works for speakers, most of which he called "lectures." An early example is "45′ for a Speaker." Here he adapted the numerical rhythmic structure of his *34′46.776″ for Two Pianists,* in which the structural units of each piano part become different in duration through use of a factor obtained by chance operations.[8] When he applied the chance factor to the numerical rhythmic structure of the speech, he obtained 39′16.95″, which proved to be too short a time for him to perform the speech. After experiments he found that forty-five minutes for the whole, two seconds for each line, was the shortest practical duration: "Not all the text can be read comfortably even at this speed," he writes, "but one can still try." Material from previously written lectures along with new material, make up this work, and by chance operations he obtained answers to six questions that determined all the characteristics of its spoken contents and silences.

When the poet, potter, and educational author M. C. Richards asked him "why [he] didn't one day give a conventional informative lecture," which she called "the most shocking thing [he] could do," Cage replied, "I don't give these lectures to surprise people, but out of a need for poetry." Then he added: "[P]oetry is not prose simply because poetry is in one way or another formalized. It is not poetry by reason of its content or ambiguity but by reason of its allowing musical elements (time, sound) to be introduced into the world of words."[9]

In writing "Where Are We Going? and What Are We Doing?" for delivery by four readers at the Pratt Institute, Brooklyn, in January 1961, Cage used the materials for his *Cartridge Music* to compose four texts that are to be heard simultaneously.[10] They are divided into lines, twenty-

---

matics of probability better than I do has informed me that Cage was mistaken: that the probability that any particular hexagram, or place on one of Cage's charts, would be arrived at by the coin-oracle method, is equal to the probability that any other would. I have not yet been able to investigate this matter further.

8. "45′ for a Speaker" can be found in *Silence,* 146–92. *34′46.776″ for Two Pianists,* a piece for prepared pianos, was commissioned by the Donaueschinger Musiktage in 1954; it's also known as *34′46.776″ for a Pianist.*

9. *Silence,* x. See also M. C. [Mary Caroline] Richards, *Centering: In Poetry, Pottery, and the Person* (Middletown, Conn.: Wesleyan University Press, 1964); *The Crossing Point: Selected Talks and Writings* (Middletown, Conn.: Wesleyan University Press, 1973); and most recently, *Imagine Inventing Yellow: New and Selected Poems of M. C. Richards* (Barrytown, N.Y.: Station Hill Press, 1991).

10. "Where Are We Going? and What Are We Doing?" in *Silence,* 194–259). *Cartridge Music* was composed in 1960. "(A cartridge is an ordinary phonograph pick-up in which customarily a playing needle is inserted.) This is a composition indeterminate of its performance, and the performance is of actions which are often indeterminate of themselves. Material is supplied, much of it on transparent plastics, which enables a performer to determine a program of actions (causing amplification and modification of small sounds by insertion, use, and removal of various objects from a cartridge and production of auxiliary electronic sounds)" (from Cage's note, in the catalog of his works compiled by Robert Dunn [New York: Henmar Press/C. F. Peters Corp., 1962], 34).

five of which may be read in one, one and a quarter, or one and a half minutes, so that the printed relationship between the four texts is only one of many possibilities. Empty lines indicate silences. Despite these pauses, which come at different places in each of the parts, much of the lecture (I was there) was unintelligible because of the simultaneity. Two sentences in one of the texts tell us more about Cage's conceptions of poetry (they are broken as indicated, but so printed that lines of the other three texts, as well as spaces, separate their segments):

> We who speak English were so
> certain of our language and that
> we could use it to communicate
> that we have nearly destroyed its potential for poetry. The
> thing in it that's going to save
> the situation is the high percentage
> of consonants and the natural way
> in which they produce discontinuity.[11]

These "lectures"—in which discontinuity in the form of silences longer than punctuational pauses and abrupt shifts in subject matter, tempo of delivery, and other aspects have been brought about mainly by use of chance operations and materials for realizing musical compositions indeterminate as to performance—are really Cage's earliest published poems.

In 1967 he began composing two types of works that are avowedly poems: (1) "asyntactical" sequences of letters, syllables, words, phrases, and/or sentences drawn from the *Journal* of the American philosopher and naturalist Henry David Thoreau and arranged by *I Ching* chance operations; (2) poems in which the capitalized letters of a name run down the center of each strophe, for which Cage adopted the term "mesostics."[12]

Many of the latter, for example, "36 Mesostics Re and Not Re Marcel Duchamp" are haiku-like poems that are normatively syntactical, if often elliptically so, but most of them are "asyntactical," or fragmentarily normative, compilations of phrases, words, and/or word fragments. A large group, "62 Mesostics re Merce Cunningham," which are both visual poems and performance texts and comprise over seven hundred type faces and sizes, was drawn from Merce Cunningham's *Changes: Notes on Choreography* and other works on dance. A later "mesostic poem," "Writing through the Cantos," comprises linguistic strings drawn from Ezra Pound's magnum opus. However, by far the largest number of mes-

11. *Silence*, 224.

12. The *Journal of Henry David Thoreau*, edited by B. Torrey and F. H. Allen (New York: Dover, 1962).

ostics were drawn from James Joyce's *Finnegans Wake*. I discuss each of these works below.[13]

Cage's first "asyntactical" poems are the texts of *Song Books (Solos for Voice 3–92)*, which he began in 1967. I quote the first three and last three strophes of the irresistibly beautiful "No. 30," which appears in *M* as "Song."[14]

Wasps are building
summer squashes
saw a fish hawk
when I hear this.

Both bushes and trees are thinly leaved
few ripe ones on sandy banks
rose right up high in the air
like trick of some pleasant daemon to entertain me
and birds are heard singing from fog.

Burst like a stream
making a world
how large do you think it is, and how far? To my surprise, one
answered three rods.

* * * * * * * * * * * * * * * * * * * *

The field plantain, the narrow cotton grass
tobacco pipes still pushing up dry leaves
like the wild cat of the woods
pine wood.

I am surprised to find these roots with white grubs.

One or two flashes of lightning, but soon over
ridge of meadow west of here
naked eye.

Each solo in the *Song Books* is either "(1) song; (2) song using electronics; (3) theatre; [or] (4) theatre using electronics" and "is relevant or irrelevant to the subject, 'We connect Satie with Thoreau.'"[15] Each

13. "36 Mesostics Re and Not Re Marcel Duchamp" and "62 Mesostics re Merce Cunningham," in *M*, 26–34, 4–211, passim; Cunningham's *Changes: Notes on Choreography* (New York: Something Else Press, [1965?]) and other works on dance; "Writing through the Cantos," *Unmuzzled Ox* 23 (1984): 5–13; *X*, 109–15; James Joyce's *Finnegans Wake* (New York: Viking Press, 1939).

14. *Song Books (Solos for Voice 3–92)* (New York: Henmar Press / C. F. Peters Corp., 1970); *M*, 86–91.

15. *Empty Words: Writings '73–'78* (Middletown, Conn.: Wesleyan University Press, 1979), 11.

exemplifies one of the twenty-five possible combinations or single instances of five linguistic units: letters (presumably any of the phonemes—or any *English* phonemes—each letter may stand for), syllables, words, phrases, and sentences, all drawn by *I Ching* chance operations from Thoreau's *Journal.*

His first extensive "asyntactical" text, "Mureau" (1970), includes all the possibilities and was written "by subjecting all the remarks of . . . Thoreau about music, silence, and sounds he heard that are indexed in the Dover edition of the *Journal* to a series of *I Ching* chance operations. The personal pronoun was varied according to such operations and the typing [in a number of different typefaces that often begin or end within a word] was likewise determined. Mureau is the first syllable of the word music followed by the second of the name Thoreau."[16]

"Mureau" differs significantly from the texts in the *Song Books* in that it is a poem to be read, aloud or silently, rather than a text to be, in some sense, sung. Hearing Cage read it aloud on the very fine sixty-five-minute S Press tape offers one of his "asyntactical" poetry's most accessible delights.[17] As he reads in his calm, precise voice, the sequence of language elements and silences glides through the listener's mind as "naturally"—reader, choose your own adverb—as the constantly changing configurations of the water in a stream flow between its banks. It is curious how this continuum of discontinuities seems always to be speaking directly to us. Even the separated and recombined letters function as speech—enigmatic interjections in this stream of language and silence about silence and sound.

Subsequently (ca. 1973–75), Cage subjected the whole *Journal,* including eventually Thoreau's sketches, to *I Ching* chance operations to produce the long four-part poem "Empty Words." In this work a transition takes place, as Cage says, "from language to music." All four parts include silences; however, part 1 includes no sentences, but mixes phrases, words, syllables, and letters; part 2 mixes the last three; part 3, the last two; and part 4 includes only letters and silences. The language elements throughout were not only drawn from the *Journal* by *I Ching* chance operations but also placed on the page by them. Cage also used such operations to answer the question, "Of the four columns on two facing pages which two have text?" and to select and place the Thoreau drawings, which had been photographed by Babette Mangolte.[18]

16. *M,* ix.

17. S Press Tonband/Tape No. 14 (Hattingen, [West] Germany: Edition S Press, 1972).

18. *Empty Words,* 65, 33.

Here are the first "strophes" (i.e., series of lines before empty lines) of the four parts of "Empty Words":

I: notAt evening1
right can see
suited to the morning hour

II: s or past another
thise and on ghth wouldhad
andibullfrogswasina - perhapes blackbus
each f nsglike globe?

III: theAf perchgreathind and ten

IV: ie tha h bath
i c r t
o no[19]

Cage often performed one or more parts of "Empty Words" sitting quietly at a small lamplit table with text, stopwatch, and microphone, emanating an aura of quiet even when he spoke. Mangolte's photographs of Thoreau's sketches were often projected beside him.

Thoreau's writings, not only his *Journal* but also *Walden* and the essay "Civil Disobedience," were the sources of the collage performance text "Lecture on the Weather," composed by means of *I Ching* chance operations. The work fulfilled a 1975 commission from Richard Coulter of the Canadian Broadcasting Company for "a piece of music to celebrate the American Bicentennial." Cage had returned to Thoreau after looking in vain for "an anthology of American aspirational thought," in searching for which he "began to realize that what is called balance between the branches of our government is not balance at all: all the branches of our government are occupied by lawyers."[20] Cage's preface to this work is his strongest and most direct political statement before the late poems dealing with anarchism (or "anarchy"). This affirmation is reinforced by his "stating his preference that [the twelve speaker-vocalists and/or speaker-instrumentalists] be American men who had become Canadian citizens," presumably to avoid being forced to fight the Vietnamese.[21] He writes that although chance operations may seem

> counter to the spirit of Thoreau, [who] speaks against blind obedience to a blundering oracle, [they] are not mysterious sources of "the right an-

19. Ibid., 12, 34, 52, 66.
20. "Preface to 'Lecture on the Weather,'" in *Empty Words*, 3–4.
21. Ibid., 1.

swers" [but] a means of locating a single one among a multiplicity of answers, and . . . of freeing the ego from its taste and memory, its concern for profit and power, of silencing the ego so that the rest of the world has a chance to enter into the ego's own experience whether that be outside or inside. . . .

We would do well [he concludes] to give up the notion that we alone can keep the world in line, that only we can solve its problems. . . .

Our political structures no longer fit the circumstances of our lives. . . . I dedicate this work to the U.S.A. that it may become just another part of the world, no more, no less.[22]

Norman O. Brown suggested to Cage the term "mesostics" to distinguish such poems from acrostics, in which a person's names or other "index words" run down one or the other side, rather than the middle of the verses. Cage's earliest mesostics were poems written for friends on various occasions, somewhat akin to Mallarmé's "Vers de circonstance."[23] His "first mesostic was written as prose to celebrate [the poet and dance critic] Edwin Denby's birthday":

Present

rEmembering a Day i visited you—seems noW
as I write that the weather theN was warm—i
recall nothing we saiD, nothing wE did; eveN so
(perhaps Because of that) that visit staYs.[24]

"The following ones, each letter of the name being on its own line, were written as poetry. [As Cage used it, the word "poetry" seems usually to have denoted verse.] A given letter capitalized does not occur between it and the preceding capitalized letter [Cage's first Mesostic Rule, see below]." His earliest extensive group, "36 Mesostics Re and Not Re Duchamp," is normatively syntactical, with either "Marcel" or "Duchamp" running down the middle of each verse, as in the first one:

a utility aMong
swAllows
is theiR
musiC.
thEy produce it mid-air
to avoid coLliding.[25]

22. Preface, ibid., 5.

23. *Oeuvres complétes* (Paris: Gallimard, 1945), 81–186.

24. *M*, 94.

25. Ibid., 26.

It was only when Cage began "62 Mesostics re Merce Cunningham" that he began to write "asyntactical" mesostics, employing *I Ching* chance operations and "writing-through" methods, or as I prefer to term them when I use such methods, "reading-through text-selection procedures." In these procedures, the writer searches through source texts to find, successively, words and/or other linguistic units that have specific characteristics—or uses a computer program to conduct the searches. In writing the Cunningham series, Cage

> used over seven hundred different type faces and sizes available in Letraset and, of course, subjected them to *I Ching* chance operations. No line has more than one word or syllable. Both syllables and words were obtained from Merce Cunningham's *Changes: Notes on Choreography* and from thirty-two other books most used by Cunningham in relation to his work. The words were subjected to a process which brought about in some cases syllable exchange between two or more of them. This process produced words not to be found in any dictionary but reminiscent of words to be found everywhere in James Joyce's *Finnegans Wake*.[26]

These poems thus intrinsically anticipated the long series of mesostics constituting Cage's writings through *Finnegans Wake*.

The "62 Mesostics re Merce Cunningham" not only constitute dazzling visual poems that "resemble waterfalls or ideograms", but have been performed by Cage and others, notably the late Egyptian-born vocalist Demetrios Stratos, who recorded them in 1974.[27]

Of the five writings through *Finnegans Wake*, all except the last follow Cage's principal Mesostic Rule: "[T]he first letter of a word or name is on the first line and following it on the first line the second letter of the word or name is *not* to be found. (The second letter is on the second line)." At Brown's suggestion, Cage omitted punctuation marks from the first "Writing through Finnegans Wake," but kept the omitted marks "not in the mesostics but on the pages where they originally appeared, the marks disposed in the space and those other than periods given an orientation by means of *I Ching* chance operations."[28] (These marks are omitted from the example below.) The beginning mesostics of the first "Writing through Finnegans Wake" must serve to exemplify the mesostics of all of them:

26. Ibid., x.

27. Ibid.; see *Gli anni di Demetrio: Nelle immagini di Giovannetti, Silvia Lelli, e Roberto Masoti* [photographs of Stratos and essays by the photographers, Daniel Charles, and others], ed. Gianni Sassi, Milano-poesia 1989 (Milan: Cooperativa Nuova Intrapresa / Ente Autonomo Milano Suono / Fondazione Mudima, 1989), 8.

28. *Empty Words*, 134, 135.

wroth with twone nathandJoe
A
Malt
jhEm
Shen

pftJschute
Of finnegan
that the humptYhillhead of humself
the knoCk out
in thE park[29]

"Writing for the Second Time through Finnegans Wake" differs from the first "Writing." As Cage explains, "I did not permit the reappearance of a syllable for a given letter of the name. I distinguished between the two J's and the two E's. The syllable 'just' could be used twice, once for the J of James and once for the J of Joyce, since it has neither A nor O after the J. But it could not be used again. To keep from repeating syllables, I kept a card index of the ones I had already used. . . . [T]his restriction made a text considerably shorter" than the first "writing-through."[30]

"Writing for the Third Time through Finnegans Wake" follows a rule suggested by the late Louis Mink, a professor of philosophy at Wesleyan University. Between any two letters of a name or other index word, it does not let *either* letter appear in any intervening word (hereafter referred to as "Mink's Rule.") When composing "Writing for the Fourth Time through Finnegans Wake," Cage followed both his Mesostic Rule and Mink's Rule; in addition, as he had when composing the second "writing-through," he kept a syllable index and did not permit the reappearance of any syllable for a given letter of the name "James Joyce."[31]

"Muoyce (Writing for the Fifth Time through Finnegans Wake)" is not a series of mesostics, but was composed by means of *I Ching* chance operations, jumping from chapter to chapter, and is made up of four sections, which comprise, respectively, eight "strophes," four, four, and one "strophe," all formatted as narrow, justified, unpunctuated paragraphs of very different lengths, which reflect, more or less, the proportions of the seventeen parts of *Finnegans Wake*. The "stanza" paragraphs are not

29. *Writings through Finnegans Wake* (Tulsa: University of Tulsa Press, 1978), unpag., first page of poem.

30. *Empty Words*, 135–36.

31. "Writing for the Fourth Time through Finnegans Wake," in *X*, 1–49. As far as I know, the third "writing-through" has never been published in a book. But I hope it has.

initially indented, though they end with indentations from the right, and none begins with a capital letter. "*Muoyce* [Music-Joyce] is with respect to *Finnegans Wake* what *Mureau* [Music-Thoreau] was with respect to the *Journal* of Henry David Thoreau, though *Muoyce* . . . does not include sentences, just phrases, words, syllables, and letters. . . . [P]unctuation is entirely omitted and space between words is frequently with the aid of chance operations eliminated."[32]

An interesting variant of the writing-through method is found in "Writing through the Cantos [of Ezra Pound]."[33] In writing this poem, Cage followed Mink's Rule. He also observed the same restrictions on syllable repetition as he had when composing the third and fourth writings through *Finnegans Wake.* "Writing through the Cantos" was first published in issue 23 of Michael André's magazine *Unmuzzled Ox* as "Canto CXXIII." This issue was the first part of André's project "The Cantos (121–150) Ezra Pound," which appears in issues 23–25 and includes "fake Cantos" by many poets, including Cage and myself. These issues are in "tabloid" format, with pages measuring 11½ by 16¾ inches, and Cage's "Canto" extends over eight double-column pages and half of a final column. It comprises 344 mesostic strophes (28 on each page), having "Ezra" and "Pound" alternately down their centers, and a final line with "E" in the center.

In *X,* however, this poem does not consist of mesostic strophes but of flush-right lines, each made up of five or more words: in alternate lines the letters of "Ezra" and "Pound" are capitalized in the words selected through Mink's Rule and the syllable index. (In both this and the earlier format, a small number of other words that accord with Mink's Rule sometimes appear between successive name-letter words.)

Each mesostic strophe of the version published in *Unmuzzled Ox* has become a single line in the one published in *X;* also, the empty lines between the strophes in the first version have been eliminated. As a result, the poem occupies only seven much smaller pages (7 by 8¼ inches) in *X.* Below are the first two mesostic strophes of the *Unmuzzled Ox* version (in which a double space appeared between the first two words), followed by the first two lines of the *X* version:

and thEn
with bronZe lance heads
beaRing yet
Arms

32. Ibid., 173. It is not clear whether Cage considered *Muoyce* "prose" or "poetry."

33. *Unmuzzled Ox* 23 (1984): 5–13; *X,* 109–15.

sheeP slain
Of
plUto
stroNg
praiseD

and thEn with bronZe lance heads beaRing yet Arms
sheeP slain Of plUto stroNg praiseD[34]

As far as I know, this radical change of format between two publications of a text is unique in Cage's poetic oeuvre. Unfortunately, I had forgotten the earlier mesostic format by the time I saw the version in *X*, so it didn't occur to me to ask Cage about this change. I can only speculate about why he made it. While the second format preserves the mesostic generative structure, it does change the way the poem would be read aloud. I think that most people would read the earlier one, with its many short lines and line and strophe breaks, much more slowly and deliberately, and probably with more breath pauses and longer silences, than in reading the later one. Though the words and capitalized letters are the same in both formats, the *verse* is quite different. The more I read aloud sections of each one, the more I am convinced that they are two different, though verbally identical, poems.

It may be relevant that Cage seemed to be dissatisfied with "Writing through the Cantos," and that he more than once remarked, to my surprise, that he thought that my "Canto" was "better" than his. Mine was made by applying a "diastic," or "spelling-through" text-selection procedure, which in this case selected words and "ends" of words successively from the source. Each "end" was either the final letter of a word or a string running from any letter except the first to the last. These words and ends have the letters of Pound's name (capitalized) in places corresponding to those they occupy in Pound's two names (sometimes I was forced to go back into a previous word to achieve this correspondence). Unlike Cage's "Canto," mine was drawn from only the first thirty of Pound's *Cantos*. Later it became the first section of a ten-part work, as I expanded it by applying the procedure to the rest of the *Cantos*, into the book-length poem *Words nd Ends from Ez*.[35]

If Cage's assessment of his "Canto" was correct, the difference in our results may have been due to the fact that he was basically much less in sympathy with Pound—aesthetically as well as politically—than with Joyce, Thoreau, and the other authors from whose works he often drew.

34. *Unmuzzeled Ox* 23 (1984): 5; *X*, 109.

35. Jackson Mac Low, *Words nd Ends from Ez* (Bolinas, Calif.: Avenue B, 1989).

On the other hand, while disagreeing profoundly with Pound's political ideas as represented in the *Cantos* and elsewhere—my finally voicing my disagreements in fact ended our ten-year correspondence when he was held in St. Elizabeth's Federal Hospital for the Insane, in Washington, D.C.—I still felt sympathetic to him as a poet. His early work especially had been an inspiration to me, both in high school and later. Like others, notably Robert Duncan, Allen Ginsberg, and Charles Olson, I was able to value his poetry highly, while abhorring his fascism, and by reading and writing through the *Cantos* as I did, I may have all but purged the latter from the former—peeling from that great verbal collage most of the fascist montage with which Pound had burdened it. (Charles Bernstein makes this valuable distinction between collage and montage in his essay "Pound and the Poetry of Today," near the end of which he writes, "At an allegorical level, *Words nd Ends [from Ez]* exorcises the authoritarianism that underlies the *Cantos*").[36] That I was able to make this highly problematic and fiercely contested distinction between great poet and abysmal political thinker may indeed have helped to give my poem the qualities that led Cage to like it better than his.

The change of format from the first to the second publication of "Writing through the Cantos," then, may have been due in part to Cage's dissatisfaction with the poem. Though he did not want to disown the poem, he may not have wanted it to occupy a large number of pages in *X*. In addition, he may have needed to keep the length of the book within certain limits, which would have reinforced his choice of the reduced format.

The "writing-through" methods used in composing the first four writings through the *Wake* and "Writing through the Cantos" are not chance operations. For one thing, the inclusion or omission of "wing words" (single words or strings on either side of a "name-letter word") in mesostics (and the analogous non-name-letter words in the *X* version of "Writing through the Cantos") was a matter of *choice*, as long as the writer obeyed the Mesostic Rule, Mink's Rule, or the Syllable Rule. Cage's "tendency was toward more omission rather than less." More important, the name-letter words were already there in the source, waiting to be found, even though Cage could not predict them, and he strove for accuracy: "I read each passage at least three times and once or twice upside down." As he explained, "It is a discipline similar to that of counterpoint in music with a cantus firmus."[37]

In 1994, while discussing my acrostic and diastic reading-through text-selection procedures (developed respectively in 1960 and 1963),

36. *Yale Review* 75 (summer 1986): 640.

37. *Empty Words*, 135, 136; Charles Bernstein, *My Way* (Chicago: University of Chicago Press, 1999), 165.

my son, Mordecai-Mark Mac Low, who is an astrophysicist, remarked that though they are "nonintentional"—in that I cannot predict to any extent what will be brought into a text through using them—they are at the same time "deterministic." If followed out to the letter, they must find, and bring into the work being written, the same linguistic units in the source texts each time. However, human errors (and when these methods are automated, computer errors) provide an unlooked-for but inevitable element of chance. One can check the work—as Cage did—many times, but still errors will creep in, and one must eventually accept the ones that have not been found and corrected before a certain time. This acceptance is the last act in the making of the work; often (in my experience) it takes place only after the work's publication in a book.

Acceptance can only take place if the writer feels that the accidental departures from the deterministic writing-through procedure do not impair the overall aesthetic value of the work. This requires that the work as a whole be considered more important than the minute details of its structure and unerring accordance with its generative procedure. These acts of valuation would seem to be departures from the original project. For me, they are ineluctable.

How Cage might have dealt with such departures is something we can never know unless there is some record of his thoughts on this matter that is as yet unknown. However, what he said to Joan Retallack about accepting the results of errors in a computer program is relevant. He discovered, while writing the poem "Empty Words," that he was getting repetition:

> I knew that it was impossible with the process that I was using for a repetition to occur! So, I examined the chance operations I was using and discovered that the error lay in the chance operations themselves, hmmm? In other words, in the computer program that made them. So they were not chance operations "correctly," hmmm? They contained repetition, which is the great no-no with chance operations! *(laughter)* So what should I do? I was momentarily nonplussed . . . until I realized that at no point had I wanted . . . that to happen, hmmm? And that now, in discovering there was an error implanted, I realized that I had continually worked, not intentionally, but non-intentionally. I felt now that I had to accept the error in the chance operations as part of the "stance of acceptingness" that was at the basis of what I was doing. That *it* was at the basis, more than the specific chance operations [that had an error in them]. That allowed me to continue with ease, rather than guilt.[38]

38. *Musicage: Cage Muses on Words, Art, Music,* ed. Joan Retallack (Hanover, N.H.: Wesleyan University Press, University Press of New England, 1995), 140. Cage and Retallack carried on an intermittent series of conversations from September 6, 1990, through July 30, 1992, thirteen days before his death on August 12.

Cage made clear to Retallack that though the result of the error "can be seen as very beautiful," it only altered his frame of mind about repetition "temporarily": "It was like a disease." But more important, I think, if he had not accepted it in this case, he "would have had to redo everything." It seems to me that after a work is published in a book, one is confronted with a similar situation when finding a substantial error in the work itself, that is, not a printer's error, even if it is "one's own" and not an error in a generative computer program.

What writing-through (or reading-through) methods have in common with chance operations is that both involve a large degree of nonintentionality, "diminish[ing] the value-judg[ing] activity of the ego and . . . increas[ing] the activity that accepts the rest of creation," as Cage put it.[39] Note that he speaks of *diminishing* the ego's value-judging activity, not doing away with it entirely. What he meant by "the ego" would make the latter impossible.

I think that Cage assumed the Zen Buddhist psychology that considers all parts of the psyche, including the psychoanalytic "Unconscious," to be "parts" of the individual ego. (Those who write about Zen in English, such as Dr. D. T. Suzuki, use the term "unconscious" as a synonym for the "no-mind," which is not individual but universal.)[40] From this point of view, writers and other artists exercise value judgment when *any* components of their minds make choices, even in the course of "automatic writing," "action painting," or other activities supposedly proceeding in whole or part from the *psychoanalytic* Unconscious. Procedures operating from *any* level of the ego, in the Zen sense, I call "intentional"; "nonintentional" refers only to those procedures or components of procedures that do not do so. Thus that part of a mesostic writing-through method that consists in finding each successive name-letter word is nonintentional, since the poet does not consciously or "unconsciously" select the word, but as accurately as possible, *finds* it. Whereas the activity of selecting the wing words in mesostics and the analogous words between name-letter words in the later version of the *Cantos* poem—deciding which ones to bring into the poems and which to leave out (with the proviso that each "kept" word is contiguous to, or part of a string contiguous to, a name-letter word)—is intentional.[41] Thus, when making mesostic poems, Cage had to make valuations for

39. Womack interview, in *Zero* 3: 70.

40. D. T. Suzuki: *The Zen Doctrine of No-Mind* (London: Rider and Co., 1949), 60, 140–43; see also 56–63, 101, 115.

41. These are not Cage's terms or formulations but my own. The exception is "wing words," his term (or if someone else's originally, the term he adopted) for the words and strings to the right and left of name-letter words in mesostics.

every line. This shows us that, at least in producing these kinds of poems, he was intent upon diminishing, not eradicating, valuation.

As we have seen, Cage often described his way of working as asking questions and abiding by the answers given to the questions, usually by *I Ching* chance operations. However, it is clear that a certain degree of intentionality—perhaps a large one—is involved willy-nilly in the devising of procedures and in the choosing and framing of both the questions and the gamuts of possible answers, as well as in the selection of source texts. The point is not whether he ever entirely evaded his individual ego and its predilections, but that he diminished to some extent the value-judging activity of the ego that excludes possibilities, and that he thereby let in, to the same extent, "the rest of creation."

I cannot attempt in this short essay to describe all of Cage's writings from the 1950s to the late 1980s, or all the methods used in composing them. Instead I shall focus on two works of the early 1980s: "James Joyce, Marcel Duchamp, Erik Satie: An Alphabet" and *Themes & Variations*.[42]

The title of the former work alludes to the fact "that the artists whose work we live with constitute . . . an alphabet by means of which we spell our lives," but it is really "not an alphabet but a fantasy." The three artists of the title, now ghosts, made works that "in different ways have resisted the march of understanding and so are as fresh now as when they were first made." They made the two kinds of art that Cage liked best: "art that is incomprehensible (Joyce and Duchamp) and . . . art that is too nose on your face (Satie). Such artists remain forever useful . . . in each moment of our daily lives."[43]

Though Cage in his introduction first characterizes the "Alphabet" as a "lecture," it is actually a play, divided into thirty-seven scenes, involving, in addition to the three of the title, other "actors . . . mostly people with whose work [he had] become involved." It was produced as a *Hörspiel* at Westdeutscher Rundfunk (WDR, the West German Radio Network) in Cologne, and on stage at the end of WDR's second Acustica International sound art festival at the Equitable Branch of the Whitney Museum of American Art in New York, on April 29, 1990—a performance in which I took part.[44]

During the scenes, each ghost is either alone, "in which case he reads

42. "James Joyce, Marcel Duchamp, Erik Satie: An Alphabet," *X*, 53–101, and *Themes & Variations* (Barrytown, N.Y.: Station Hill Press, 1982).

43. These quotations concerning "An Alphabet" come from its introduction (*X*, 53–55).

44. The term *Hörspiel*, "radio play," has acquired an extended meaning, "sound-art work," mainly because of the so-called *Neue Hörspiel* developed and encouraged at Westdeutscher Rundfunk Köln by the producer and director Klaus Schöning.

from his own writings," or "together with another sentient being or beings, ghosts or living, or with a nonsentient being or beings." This schema yields twenty-six possibilities: "the three ghosts alone, each in combination with one to four different beings, the ghosts in pairs with one to three different beings, [and] all three with one or two." Cage "used the twenty-six letters of the alphabet and *[I Ching]* chance operations to locate facing pages of an unabridged dictionary upon which [he] found the nonsentient beings that are the stage properties of the various scenes." These scenes constitute a kind of narrative in "Minkian" mesostics on the names or initials of the three ghosts, among which are interspersed ten prose paragraphs, each drawn from the writings of one of the ghosts. The mesostic "narrative" gives the "stage directions," introductions of the actors (read in radio and stage productions by a narrator), and together with the prose paragraphs, the speeches of the ghosts and other personae.

Themes & Variations is "one text in an ongoing series; to find a way of writing which though coming from ideas is not about them; or is not about ideas but produces them." It is "a chance-determined renga-like [and 'asyntactical'] mix" drawn from "fifteen themes" and sixty "variations" constituting a "library of mesostics on one hundred and ten different subjects and fifteen different names."[45] The subjects are "one hundred and ten different ideas which [Cage] listed in the course of a cursory examination of [his] books" written before 1979. The first and last ideas on his list are "[n]onintention (the acceptance of silence) leading to nature; renunciation of control; let sounds be sounds" and "[g]oal is not to have a goal."

The names are those of fifteen men important to Cage in his life and work, ranging from Norman O. Brown and Marshall McLuhan to Arnold Schoenberg and Suzuki Daisetz (Dr. D. T. Suzuki). Each "theme" and each "variation" (there are four on each name) is a mesostic on one of the names, derived from three, four, or five mesostics of equal length written on the same name and on any of the hundred and ten ideas.

This complexly composed "asyntactical" text "was written to be spoken aloud. It consists of five sections, each to take twelve minutes. The fourth is the fastest and the last one is the slowest." The tempo of delivery is regulated by numbers in the right-hand margins denoting minutes and fractions of minutes up to 60.00, each carried out to as many as four decimal places (e.g., 0.244, 10.344, 33.4786, 41.5636), which indicate how long the reader should take to read the lines between

45. A renga is an extended Japanese poem traditionally written by a group of poets, successive lines being written by different poets. These and the following quotations concerning *Themes & Variations* come from its twelve-page introduction. (The book is unpaginated.)

them, and thus also how quickly or slowly. "The lines that are to be read in a single breath are printed singly or together as a stanza [strophe]. These divisions or liaisons were not chance-determined, but were arrived at by improvisational means." At the end of the introduction, Cage offers as an example "the first part of all five [source mesostics on] DAVID TUDOR DAVID . . . which were material for the renga but . . . not themselves the renga," followed by "the corresponding parts [i.e., the theme and variations, some truncated, derived from them] of the finished mixed nonsyntactical ['asyntactical'] text." The first part of the first Tudor source mesostic appears below:

we Don't know
whAt
we'll haVe
when we fInish
Doing
whaT we're doing
bUt
we know every Detail
Of
pRocess
we're involveD in
A way
to leaVe no traces
nothIng in between
herDed ox

The first page of the renga itself reads as follows:

it was a Juncture
to go thAt way or this

Most
no longEr
doeSn't

it is Just
hOw

of the manY benefits
Coming to us

nErvous system

Notice that in the renga, the beginnings and ends of mesostics do not coincide with those of the renga's strophes.

What these two remarkable texts, "James Joyce, Marcel Duchamp, Erik Satie: An Alphabet" and *Themes & Variations,* have in common—despite the fact that one is, for the most part, normatively syntactical and even narrative, and the other "asyntactical" (except for its source mesostics) and very much fragmented—is their "speakability." Compared to performers of such typographically and performatively difficult poems as "Mureau" and "Empty Words," not to mention the Cunningham mesostics, the actors who perform the "Alphabet" and the soloist who speaks *Themes* aloud are given very clear and easily spoken word strings to enunciate.

Not that these texts are "easy" to perform! Making the transitions from character to character and projecting each persona believably is no trivial task for performers of the "Alphabet." And accurately delivering the exactly timed segments of *Themes,* while sensitively conveying the meanings of the words, demands plenty of practice despite such helpful directions as "slower" and "faster" at the beginning of each twelve-minute segment after the first. Nevertheless, Cage's relation to the readers, performers, and hearers of these works can credibly be characterized as "genial." As a Zen teacher might put it, they clearly evince the "grandmotherly kindness" that, often less apparently, underlay and motivated all of Cage's work as an artist.

In conclusion, I want to examine certain terms and ideas crucial not only to Cage's writings but to his work after 1950 in all the arts: "nonintentionality" (or "nonintention," as he often preferred to term it), "chance," and "indeterminacy." Intentions are states of mind that involve commitments to action. They cannot be conflated with desires and beliefs, even though they may be closely connected with them. When someone intends to do something, they plan to do an action or series of actions conceived of as being within their powers to do. Conversely, the elements of plans are intentions. It may seem paradoxical, then, that Cage, who was uniquely devoted to "nonintention," made, at certain levels of generality, very elaborate plans for each of his works. These plans usually were based on minute analyses of the possibilities offered by the materials works were conceived of as using or comprising, and not seldom by the specific persons who would realize the works in performances. Even "nonintention" itself, "opening to the world," and "diminishing the ego's [value-judging] activity" can be seen as intended goals aimed at by Cage's ways of making artworks ("Goal is not to have a goal"). Nonintentionality at certain levels was severely constrained by clear intentions at higher (more general) levels.

Similarly, what Cage meant by "chance" and "chance operations" was not by any means "just anything that came along." It was only when he had clearly delineated (probably in very general terms) what was to enter a work (and what was *not* to do so) that he employed chance operations, and those usually of a specific type: ones wherein (as he believed) the possibilities did not have equal chances of occurring. (It is irrelevant that he may have been wrong here: that the possibilities of particular outcomes may actually be equal when *I Ching* chance operations are used.) It was only at the levels on which there was a "multiplicity of [acceptable] answers" that he employed chance operations or analogous means. Chance was always constrained, to a greater or lesser extent, by his intentions. (This matter is highly complicated by the fact that it is impossible to determine exactly at what level(s) he began to ask the questions whose multiplicities of answers were acceptable.)

Even Cage's beliefs and desires were not irrelevant to his compositional intentions. This can most clearly be perceived in his "Lecture on the Weather" and in very late poems that I have not discussed, which by design are relevant to political ideas that he grouped under the term "anarchism." It was at the level where it was a matter of indifference *which* statements and ideas about anarchism (among those he found acceptable) emerged in the poetry that nonintentional means were used to select among them.

Cage's taste also operated in his compositional actions (musical, verbal, and visual) despite his diminishing its effects by using nonintentional and mixed procedures. (By "mixed procedures" I mean nonintentional actions completed by choice, as in the making of mesostics.) His choices of source texts, especially the works of Joyce and Thoreau, are significant illustrative cases. In contrast with practices such as mine in 1960 and after, when I often drew upon anything I happened to be reading, Cage always carefully selected his sources. It is notable that when he drew upon Pound's *Cantos,* a source that must have been much less congenial to him than others he worked with, he produced a poem that, as we have seen, did not finally satisfy him.

Careful analyses of his working methods in all the arts may eventually show at what points his taste was determinative before or during his use of nonintentional procedures. Nevertheless, his methods and his patient perseverance in carrying them through assured that his taste would be effectively reined in by those procedures.

Finally, "indeterminacy": compositions "indeterminate as to performance," or even as to proximate score, are never completely indeterminate, but have a "constrained indeterminateness."[46] They do not allow

46. I have borrowed this phrase from Stephen K. White's discussion of Jürgen Habermas's principles of justice in *The Recent Work of Jürgen Habermas: Reason, Justice, and Modernity* (Cambridge: Cambridge University Press, 1988), 74.

"just anything" to happen in a performance or to be placed in a proximate score, but only those actions and notations that are prescribed by the general account or plan given by the composer as being within the work's gamut of possibilities. When Cage's prescriptions were violated by performers or audiences, as happened more times than one cares to recall, he often became quite upset. He frequently ascribed such violations to lack of goodwill or to "silliness."

These concluding paragraphs are not meant in any way to depreciate the importance of Cage's decision to use chance operations and other nonintentional procedures. I think he clearly realized the extent to which his taste and beliefs and even his desires were determinative at crucial points. (Certainly a person who uttered the words "beautiful" and "beautifully" as often as Cage did understood the extent to which valuation is inescapable.)[47] He knew very well that if he did anything at all, it would be done by or through his ego. His development of methods that at least diminished the ego's dominance did indeed conduce to "letting in the rest of creation" and to certain hearers', viewers', and performers' giving "bare attention" to the audible, visible, and intelligible elements his works comprise.

What is most remarkable is that his works and the ways in which he produced them helped him to *change* his own ego: often he came to see as beautiful what he had not seen in that way previously. He mentions this more than once during his conversations with Joan Retallack, notably in an October 1991 conversation:

> [When you work with chance operations,] you can then number [the possibilities] and ask which one you're to use. Get the answer, again, through chance operations, so that if you work with chance operations, you're basically shifting—from the responsibility to choose, you're basically shifting to the responsibility to ask. *(pause)* People frequently ask me if I'm faithful to the answers, or if I change them because I want to. I don't change them because I want to. When I find myself at that point, in the position of someone who *would* change something—at that point I don't change it. I change myself. It's for that reason that I have said that instead of self-expression, I'm involved in self-alteration.[48]

It is now well known that Cage's works and ways of working have, even when misunderstood, influenced artists in all media. I think he felt badly about some unintended side effects of his work and of his explanations of his methods and reasons for using them. I'm sure, how-

47. See *Musicage*, passim.

48. Ibid, 139.

ever, that at times he appreciated the positive results of some "fruitful misunderstandings."

Eventually he looked with equanimity upon some unintended consequences of his influence that seemed to him less fruitful or even deplorable. For instance, he remarked to me that he forgave the putative founder of an art movement who, along with some (but by no means all) of its adherents, had been, in his estimation, negatively influenced by misunderstandings of his practice—"now that the poor man [was] dead."

It was at least as true of Cage, who never boasted of it, as of Whitman, who did, that he "contained multitudes." Unlike Whitman, however, he endeavored to be consistent rather than contradicting himself, and to provide a rationale and a theorized transition for each of the many changes that over time inevitably occurred in his ways of working and in his works.

For many years to come, John Cage and his works, despite innumerable misunderstandings of them and reactions against them, will continue to help artists in every field to find their own ways to make new, enlivening kinds of art and to bring about the interpenetration of art and life.

ELEVEN

Constance Lewallen

Cage and the Structure of Chance

Remarkably, John Cage was regarded by many as the enfant terrible of the avant-garde right up to his death in 1992 at the age of seventy-nine. This view was especially unjustified since, no matter how disconcerted audiences may have been by his unconventional lecture-demonstrations or musical works arrived at by chance operations, he never set out to shock; rather, he spent the last fifty years of his life approaching calmness.

Cage's most innovative and provocative musical concept was that music cannot be separated from all other sounds. In other words, he agreed with Thoreau, whose influence on him was long-standing and profound, in believing that music is a continuous presence in the environment, that only listening is intermittent. Extending this idea to visual art, Cage said, "art is everywhere; it's only seeing which stops now and then."[1]

From 1978 until his death in 1992, Cage devoted a good deal of time to the creation of visual artworks, especially in the medium

1. "John Cage: An Interview by Robin White," *View* 1, no. 1 (April 1978): 6.

of intaglio printing. Since Cage, of course, was known as a composer and thinker, not as a visual artist, Kathan Brown took a leap of faith in inviting him to make prints at her etching studio Crown Point Press in 1978. But Brown's faith was grounded in her knowledge both of Cage's considerable influence on many visual artists, including Jasper Johns and Robert Rauschenberg, and of his receptivity to the ideas generated by artists from Marcel Duchamp to Mark Tobey. (It should be noted here that as a very young man Cage was equally attracted by music and painting, only giving up the latter at the insistence of his teacher Arnold Schoenberg.) Cage had also participated in the activities of Fluxus, a disparate group of unconventional, international artists, poets, composers, and performers who shared a desire to widen the boundaries of art. Several future Fluxus members (George Brecht, Al Hansen, Dick Higgins, Toshi Ichiyanagi, and Allan Kaprow) had been Cage's students at the New School in New York, where Cage taught a dialectical class in the composition of experimental music in the late 1950s.

Cage accepted Brown's invitation, later confessing that he had resolved not to refuse such intriguing offers, since, after once having declined an invitation to trek in the Himalayas, he did not get a second chance. He returned to Crown Point Press nearly every year until his death, and from 1988 he also tried his hand at watercolor painting and paper making.

Not surprisingly, Cage's first project in etching, *Score without Parts (40 Drawings by Thoreau): Twelve Haiku,* was based on the score of one of his musical compositions (plate 1). In *Score without Parts,* he replaced conventional music notes with graphic notations in the form of photographic reproductions of sketches from Thoreau's journal, showing leaves, insects, and other observations from nature. In these and all his subsequent prints and watercolors, as in his musical compositions, Cage arrived at decisions by chance operations derived from the *I Ching.* Traditionally one receives answers from the *I Ching* by tossing coins to obtain combinations that refer to one of the sixty-four possible symbols or hexagrams the oracle contains. In 1969 Cage began using a computer program simulation of the *I Ching,* which facilitated the procedure of translating the hexagrams into their numerical equivalents. He was less interested in the *I Ching* as a book of wisdom than as a mechanism of chance operation that produces random numbers from 1 to 64.

Cage's complete fidelity to chance operations is both the most widely known and the most misunderstood aspect of his methods—misunderstood because it is often mistakenly believed that Cage used chance to avoid making choices. But, as he said, "[M]y choices consist in choosing what questions to ask." (From the time he first used the *I Ching* in the

1950s, the creation of his works in all media began by way of questions rather than answers.)[2] In starting a project, Cage set certain parameters. These might be the size and type of the paper, the palette from which the colors would be derived, and so on. The technical and procedural decisions were then made with the aid of the computer charts, and the images that resulted were a record of the answers given by chance operations. Cage used chance as a discipline (in the sense of "giving yourself rather than expecting things to give themselves to you") to circumvent personal taste and memory so that he would be more open to outside experiences. As he so modestly put it to me once when I asked him why he used chance in creating his prints, "It enables me to draw a line without embarrassment."[3]

Several of Cage's prints and watercolor paintings relate directly to the fifteenth-century Zen-style garden Ryoan-ji in Kyoto, Japan. His engagement with Zen Buddhism began in the late 1940s, included his attendance at Daisetz Suzuki's lectures at Columbia University, and remained central to his endeavors from that time on. The ultimate development of the dry landscape garden as abstract representation of nature, Ryoan-ji is a 360-yard rectangular plane of gravel raked, to resemble water, with fifteen rough stones placed upon it. The garden inspired Cage's 1985 series of thirteen drypoint prints titled *Ryoku,* a conflation of Ryoan-ji and haiku.[4] (Drypoint is a form of intaglio printing in which the artist makes a line by scratching into a copper plate with a needle. As the artist incises the line into the copper, a burr is raised on either side. The line and the burrs hold the ink during printing, producing a soft, variable line.)

Cage began each of his print projects with an intricate "score" based on the *I Ching,* using the same methodology he would in composing music. Just as in musical composition the score guides the musicians, tells them what notes to play, and when, how loud, and how long to play them, the score for a Cage etching project similarly provided the guidelines for the printers.

Cage used fifteen stones (to correspond to the fifteen rocks in Ryoan-ji) and seventy-five small copper plates, five for each stone. The printers cut the plates, in the shape of triangles and tetrahedrons, from discarded end pieces of copper. Cage determined where the cuts would be made by chance operations. Next Cage arranged the plates into fifteen sets (five plates, numbered 1 to 5, for each of the fifteen stones). Addition-

2. Ibid., 5; see also Joan Retallack, "Poetics of a Complex Realism," in *John Cage: Composed in America,* ed. Marjorie Perloff and Charles Junkerman (Chicago: University of Chicago Press, 1994), 268.

3. David Revill, *The Roaring Silence: John Cage, a Life* (New York: Arcade, 1992), 117; Cage in conversation with the author, January 1991.

4. Printed by Marcia Bartholme with the assistance of Peter Pettengill, Crown Point Press.

ally, each plate was assigned a number from 1 to 15 to denote the stone that was traced on it. For each of the thirteen planned prints, the plates to be used, fifteen in all, were drawn from the entire pool of seventy-five, so that a particular tracing might appear more than once in the same image. Some of the plates were used more times than others, and two were never printed at all.

Cage had gathered the stones from all over the world and had used several in an earlier print project. For *Ryoku* he determined by chance that each stone would be traced five times using the drypoint technique, that there would be a single tracing of a stone on a piece of copper, and that the stone had to fit entirely on each plate. After the plates were cut, Cage paired the plates with stones as he wished—as long as the stone fit entirely onto the plate. Each stone had a front side and back and was always drawn in the same orientation.

Before printing, Cage outlined the plates with graphite on transparent sheets of paper in the order in which they were to be printed. Each sheet in the map set corresponded to a run through the etching press. The outlined shapes bear a large number in the middle with superscript number and another encircled number to the right. The large number from 1 to 15 refers to which stone in the set of fifteen was used; the superscript number from 1 to 5 refers to which plate of that stone; the encircled number from 1 to 10 identifies the color.

Cage confined the placement of the plates during printing to an imaginary rectangle (proportioned like Ryoan-ji) situated in the lower half of the sheet of paper. Cage determined by chance operations that the image would be placed inside an imaginary rectangle 5¾ by 18 inches situated 3⅜ inches from the bottom and sides of the paper and that the rectangle would sit on the lower half of a 24-by-18-inch sheet of handmade Farnsworth paper. Although each tracing had to fall within the rectangle, the end or edges of the plates could fall outside its borders. This explains the impressions one can see extending above the imaginary horizon line. The printers positioned all the plates within the grid to see which ones would extend beyond the edges of the paper. Since Cage did not want this extension to occur, he instructed the printers to cut these according to chance operations but within sets of marks which were about the width of the 3⅜-inch margin area.

Cage again consulted the *I Ching* to determine how to combine seventeen (for the seventeen syllables in a haiku) earth and mineral pigments that made ten colors—yellows, greens, browns, and violets—and to select which of those colors he would use for each stone. The pigments were mixed to make ten colors (the number was chance-determined). Each color is the combination of two pigments; one color, cobalt green deep, came up mixed with itself, so it was the only pure pigment used.

Not all the colors appear on all the prints. Because some of the earth colors are gritty, they left small scratches on the copper plate as the printers wiped it. These scratches held some ink and, when printed, created a light tone on the print over the whole plate area. This is especially true of the cobalt green and some of the browns.

On the second day of working, Cage was still trying to resolve the final composition. He considered doing combinations of images printed one on top of the other and asked the printers to print a combination of *Ryoku No. 1* and *Ryoku No. 2*—a total of thirty impressions. When he compared the proof to *No. 2* printed alone (with fifteen impressions), he felt that individual sets of fifteen tracings were more "lyrical," the tracings more apparent, and the repetition of tracings, when it occurred, was "very pleasing and easier to notice" than in the combination working proof. So he decided to continue with single sets of fifteen rock tracings and a total of thirteen prints as he had originally determined. This is only one of many examples of how Cage remained flexible rather than shackled by his self-devised systems.

The thirteen *Ryoku* drypoints are abstract works that combine embossed straight lines and sharp angles of the plates with fine, delicate, sometimes tentative, irregular earth-colored lines. The earth colors, the organic forms and their placement below an imaginary horizon line, the plate impressions that extend into the space above the invisible horizon line like craggy mountain peaks—all suggest but do not represent landscape. As Cage said repeatedly, he wished his art to be in the *spirit* of nature. Each of the thirteen prints has a different but always nonhierarchical arrangement of elements. For instance, in some of the prints the forms are more clustered, in others they are more evenly spread across the page; in all, the drawn lines and plate marks link together and overlap harmoniously in what are among Cage's most elegant and delicate works.

Cage subsequently used Ryoan-ji as a musical compositional device, and in 1988 and 1990 he continued his involvement with the Japanese garden at the Mountain Lake Workshop of the Virginia Tech Foundation in Blacksburg, Virginia, where he accepted the invitation of the director, Ray Kass, to make watercolors. Cage again used stones as templates, this time painting around them with feathers and then with brushes dipped in watercolor paint. He had always resisted using a brush before, believing the results would be too reflective of his personal touch. When asked if he was now allowing gesture into his work, he said he was, with the following caveat: "On the other hand, this is a very circumscribed gesture, because it has the support of the stone."[5]

5. Interview by Vincent Katz, *Printcollectors Newsletter* 20 (January/February 1990): 109.

When he returned to Crown Point Press in 1989, Cage built on his experience with watercolor painting and employed brushes to paint around stones, creating his two largest (54 by 41 inches) and most colorful prints, *75 Stones* and *The Missing Stone*.[6] Two plates of slightly different dimensions were printed at once to create these large works, which therefore contain diptych plate marks; in *The Missing Stone* the larger panel is on bottom and the smaller on top; this is reversed for *75 Stones.*

As in the *Ryoku* series, Cage used fifteen stones in the creation of these two prints. To correspond with the larger format, however, he used several much larger stones he had brought from Telluride, Colorado, along with the smaller stones used in the *Ryoku* series. The stones were always placed on the plate in the same orientation, which makes their repetition easy to recognize.

As at the Mountain Lake Workshop, Cage derived the color palette of transparent and opaque greens, browns, oranges, grays, and blues from the colors in the stones themselves, not, as he had always done in the past, from chance operations. He cited Ludwig Wittgenstein's "Remarks on Colour" as having suggested to him the idea of communicating color through matching. Cage painted with brushes directly onto the metal plates and used the etching techniques of sugarlift, aquatint, and spit bite. In sugarlift, the artist blocks out a gestural mark on the plate with a sugar and water solution. When an aquatint is laid in the area, it yields an even, hard-edged tone (fig. 11.1). In spit bite, the artist paints with acid directly on the plate and the resulting swaths of color are modulated and soft-edged.

In *75 Stones,* Cage layered five different arrangements of fifteen stone tracings (plate 2). In comparison, *The Missing Stone,* which contains a single layer of fourteen tracings, is spare and contains few overlapping contours (fig. 11.2). Whereas in the *Ryoku* drypoints the drawing is linear and fine, in the two etchings the tracing simulates a brush stroke, which at times is thick and gestural. Before printing, the printers "smoked" the paper. Cage and the Crown Point Press printers had developed the technique of smoking in 1985 for the purpose of creating atmospheric effects. The printers ignited a wad of newspapers and suffocated the flames with the dampened printing paper, which then bore the traces of the smoke. When this technique is used, no two prints within an edition are identical as each has its unique pattern of smoke residue.

Both *75 Stones* and *The Missing Stone* are characterized by colorful, broad, irregularly shaped silhouettes, at times overlapping, dancing across the lightly smoked page. In *75 Stones,* Cage decided beforehand to

6. Printed by Pamla Paulson with the assistance of Lawrence Hamlin and Renée Bott, Crown Point Press.

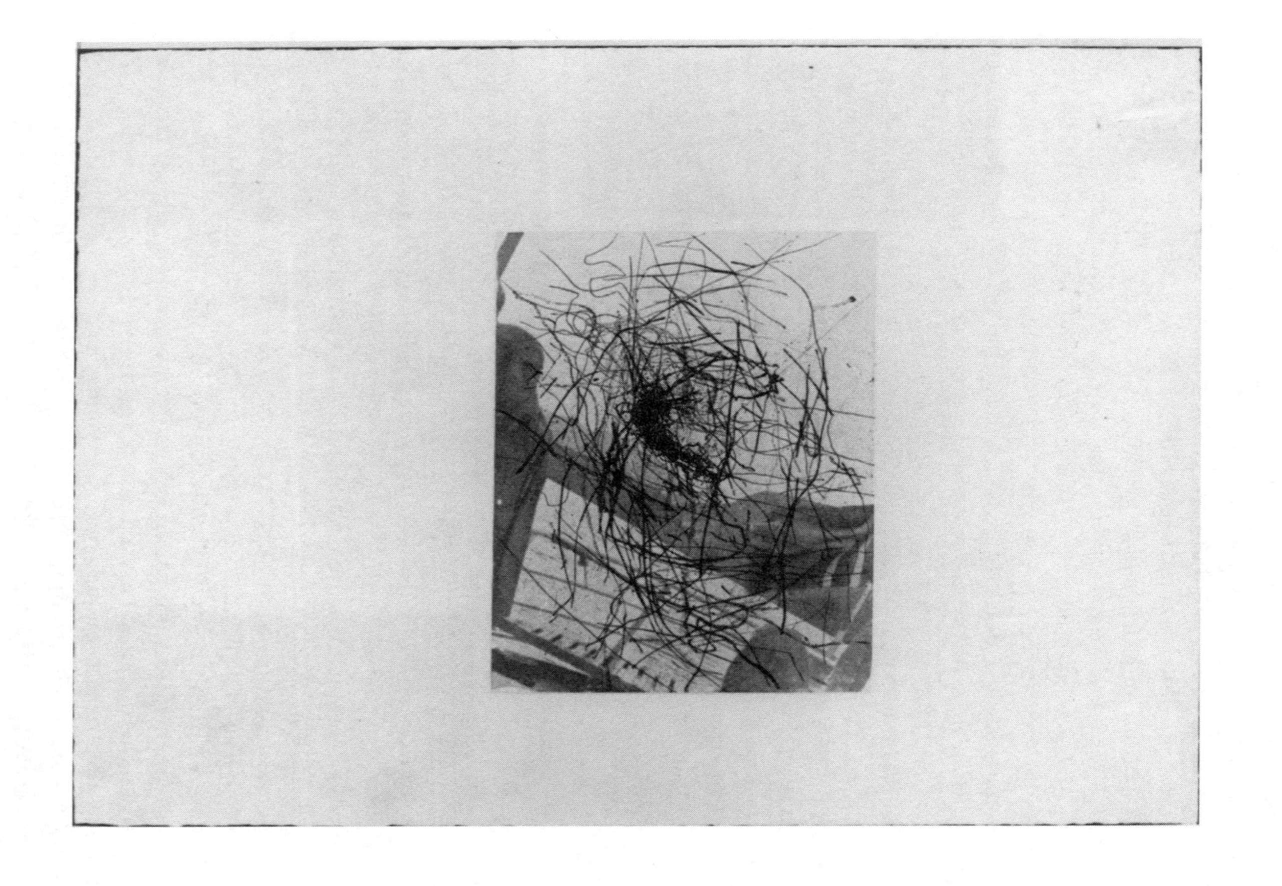

FIGURE 11.1
Seven Day Diary (Not Knowing), 1978, Day 6 from a portfolio of seven hard- and soft-ground etchings with drypoint, sugarlift aquatint, and photoetching, 12 × 17 in., Edition 25. Published by Crown Point Press, printed by Stephen Thomas.

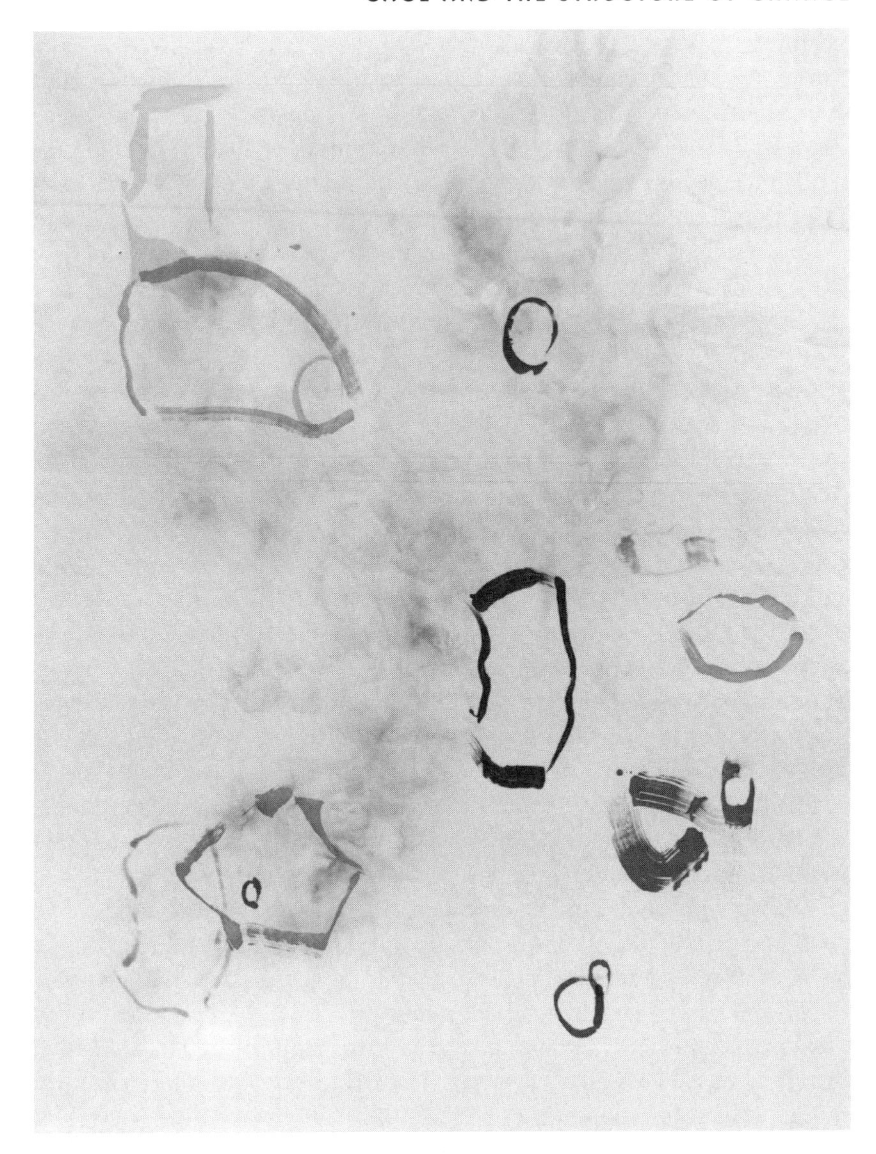

FIGURE 11.2
The Missing Stone, 1989, color spit bite and sugarlift aquatints on smoked paper, 54 × 41 in., Edition 25. Published by Crown Point Press, printed by Pamela Paulson.

repeat the process of placing and tracing fifteen stones until he achieved a satisfying density of forms, which occurred after five rounds. In this instance Cage allowed himself to make a subjective judgment during the process. He said that all his life he had eschewed gesture and aesthetic decision-making, but as time went on he found he could change ideas he thought were fixed. He liked to quote Margaret Mead, who said, "Since we live longer, we can change what we do. We can stop whatever it was we promised we'd always do and do something else."[7] For *The Missing Stone,* Cage limited himself to one set of tracings. He had intended to use fifteen stones as always but discovered after proofing the print that he had inadvertently omitted one. Since he liked the spare, elegant etching as it was, he decided not to add the missing stone. He took pleasure in the relationship between this "mistake" and the fact that the garden of Ryoan-ji is designed so that one can never see more than fourteen rocks from any single vantage point.

New River Rocks and Smoke, Cage's last painting, was made during his third visit to Mountain Lake Workshop. During this session he decided to use the smoking technique in combination with watercolor for the first time. Before Cage set to work, assistants smoked the paper in successive six- to eight-foot sections. Cage used large stones that had been collected from the New River in Virginia. The flattest surface of each stone was designated as the bottom, and their vertical orientation was fixed. Cage used brushes two- to eight-inches wide selected by chance from a group of twelve. The thirty-two-foot-long horizontal scroll combines fifteen watercolor brush tracings around large rocks situated along the lower portion of the paper, as if in a riverbed, with smoke stains above.[8] The yellowish smoky areas in *New River Rocks and Smoke* act as ethereal counterpoints to the more deliberate, though hardly emphatic, calligraphic brush strokes below. The combination of elements—fire and water—is underscored by the visual suggestion of flow.

With his predominantly modest works on paper, Cage managed to challenge just about all of Western culture's received ideas about what art is. If, from the Renaissance on, art has been regarded as a means of communication, Cage instead defined art as self-alteration, a means to "sober the mind."[9] If art has served to give form to the chaos of life's experiences, he created an art that as nearly as possible combines with, rather than gives shape to, life. If art has been regarded as a giver of truth through the "self-expressed individuality of the artist,"[10] Cage saw

7. "How to Improve the World (You Will Only Make Matters Worse) Continued 1969 (Part V)," in *M: Writings '67–'72* (Middletown, Conn.: Wesleyan University Press, 1969), 69.

8. Just before creating *New River Rocks and Smoke,* Cage made another scroll painting almost identical in size, *New River Rocks and Washes,* in which he did not smoke the paper. Instead, after tracing around the rocks, he painted transparent watercolor washes over the entire surface with large, custom-made brushes. *New River Rocks and Smoke* has the same constellation of rocks and colors, although the colors are considerably lightened to correspond to the smoke.

9. "45′ for a Speaker," in *Silence: Lectures and Writings* (Middletown, Conn.: Wesleyan University Press, 1961), 158.

10. Calvin Tomkins, *The Bride and the Bachelors* (New York: Viking Compass Books, 1966), 69.

it rather as an exploration of how nature itself functions as a means to open the mind and spirit to the beauty of life with a minimum of artistic expression or interpretation. Finally, if art has traditionally expressed meaning through symbol or metaphor, he preferred that viewers provide their own meaning according to their individual personality and experience. ("I don't want to spend my life being pushed around by a bunch of artists," he said once, explaining his objection to expressionist art.)[11]

Given that nonintentionality was Cage's guiding principle, it may come as a surprise that there is a consistency throughout all his visual work. This can be attributed in part to the types of basic elements and procedures Cage established as he began a work. Though he varied the forms, the colors, and the techniques from project to project, Cage's open-ended strategies resulted in the sense of a moment snatched from the constant flux of nature, as if whatever is occurring on the page is continuing outside its physical borders. This is particularly true of *New River Rocks and Smoke* because of its exaggerated horizontality. Most of the time the overall look of a Cage work is light and gentle—one could say dramatically understated—but even when exuberant, it is never strident. If a stylistic development can be discerned, it is that there was a loosening that culminated in the radiant lyricism of Cage's last works. That there is an overriding harmony in everything he created accords with Cage's belief in the essential, if unknowable, order in nature, as revealed by his chance operations.

11. Richard Kostelanetz, *Conversing with Cage* (New York: Limelight, 1988), 177.

TWELVE

Ray Kass

Diary: Cage's Mountain Lake Workshop, April 8–15, 1990

If there were a theory of colour harmony, perhaps it would begin by dividing the colours into groups and forbidding certain mixtures or combinations and allowing others. And, as in harmony, its rules would be given no justification.

—Ludwig Wittgenstein, "Remarks on Colour," I-74

In conjunction with John Cage's first visit to Mountain Lake in 1983, an exhibition of his musical scores and other works on paper was held at the Student Union Gallery at nearby Virginia Tech, which introduced his work as a visual artist to many people who knew him only as a composer. Since 1978, the development of his visual work had been enhanced by Crown Point Press, where he had frequently investigated printmaking techniques, especially etching, in the open and exploratory spirit that characterized his composing and writing. His later printmaking series had evolved to some extent toward the execution of unique or individualized impressions, with attention to specific processes and random effects that surpassed the typical printmaking goal of creating multiple images in an edition.

In the graphic works of the 1983 exhibition, Cage had employed random gestures through chance operations to achieve abstract patterns in which fifteen small stones had been used as stencils to create circular linear contours. These configurations represented the automatic reflexes or spontaneous gestures that revealed the softness or hardness of the actual pencils, intuiting the Zen sensibility of Chinese or Japanese "zenga" paintings of solitary and spontaneous calligraphs that reflected both inner and outer nature.

Such a strategy could be applied to the watercolor medium and its brushes. Cage admired the collection of smooth stones from the remote site of Ripplemead on the New River in southwest Virginia, and after consideration, he agreed to make three experimental pieces using New River stones. These were painted in my studio in 1983 to demonstrate how such a workshop might proceed. The result was John Cage's 1988 Mountain Lake Workshop, in which fifty-two paintings of four series entitled *New River Watercolors* were executed (see plate 3).

In the spring of 1990, Cage conducted his second workshop. The paintings from 1990 represent his further investigation of the watercolor medium and of the relationships between his printmaking activity and his experience with painting. His most recent etchings from Crown Point Press had utilized the "rock" imagery printed on papers that had previously been impressed with the amorphous burn patterns of fire and smoke. These indeterminate naturalistic effects were analogous to a watercolor wash contrasted with wet brushwork for the stones: a provocative Heraclitean image of fire and water.

We consulted with Crown Point about their procedure for smoking paper: newsprint had been placed over the dampened paper and ignited. Then a wool blanket was thrown over the flame and the entire ensemble quickly run through the press, leaving the gray essence of the smoke impressed on the paper, along with a few ghostly traces of newsprint. We wanted to achieve "smoke" impressions without the use of a press, which would limit the paper sizes for the paintings. A simpler method utilized a large piece of dampened blotter paper (6 by 8 feet) laid flat on concrete; on it we ignited pieces of newspaper sprinkled with mineral spirits. We quickly covered the flames with dampened watercolor paper, overlaid with a 4-by-8-foot panel of quarter-inch masonite. Larger papers were hosed with water, damp-dried, and smoked by this method. They were then rewashed to remove carbon particles.

To eliminate the local, sooty effect of the newsprint, we burned straw. If spread tangled on wet blotter paper, burned straw created a greater range of color from the smoke, and the shafts often left silhouettes imprinted on the paper. We associated these delicate shapes with the fragments of newsprint transferred in the etchings, and called this process "straw writing" on smoke. We settled on straw for smoking all of the paper for the workshop. Twenty-eight sheets were smoked during three separate sessions in the weeks before the workshop began.

Upon his arrival, Cage met many of the twenty volunteer assistants and was shown the layout of all painting materials, grouped and numbered for convenient access for chance operations. On the floor at the rear of the studio lay thirteen different papers, including six types of rag on rolls, a diverse group of mold-made hot- and cold-press single sheets, and three types of Japanese mulberry (or "rice") papers. Tables held boxes of fifty-seven different watercolor pigments and dozens of cups, pans, and other containers in which to mix paint. Two plastic buckets contained forty of the rigid glide-feathers he had used in three of the four series of paintings made during the 1988 workshop.

Eighty brushes of different types and sizes were organized in groups from small to large. Eight of these were oversized wash brushes made by combining either 5- or 7-inch Hake brushes in customized armatures. These had been constructed with "handle frames," which allowed as many as twelve large brushes (each between 10¼ and 84 inches long) to be assembled as one brush. All of the wide brushes were designed so that Cage could walk upright while holding the brush to paint. The most extraordinary was the "body frame" constructed for the 84-inch brush, used by gripping two laminated wooden handles fastened at midpoint to the weight-balanced space frame. The painter "stepped into" the center of the frame to lift the brush and then could adjust the rear handle weights to modify the pressure with which the tilted brush was applied to the paper. This elegant brush evoked images of early pioneering days of aviation. Wooden troughs of various lengths were built to contain the paint mixtures for specific brushes. The brushes and their pine troughs recalled ancient tools, or perhaps modern sculpture.

Finally, 129 of the 1,312 New River stones used in the 1988 workshop were combined with 33 additional rocks from the Ripplemead site to comprise a group of 162. We also assembled an additional group of 59 stones, somewhat flat and angular, gathered from Sinking Creek at nearby Eggleston Springs. Each group of stones was divided by size categories of small, medium, and large.

Monday, April 9, 1990

On Monday morning at 8:00 A.M., the work began. The week had been scheduled so that five assistants, Peter Lau (an architecture graduate student and the workshop coordinator), and myself would assist Cage as the work proceeded. One of the assistants, Dan Yates, a literature student, was asked to be a scribe to record each day's activities.[1]

One of Cage's most important new decisions at the 1990 workshop

1. Dan Yates's diary of the workshop is the basis of the following exchanges with John Cage. In some cases, I amended or paraphrased and/or clarified his entries through further discussion with Cage.

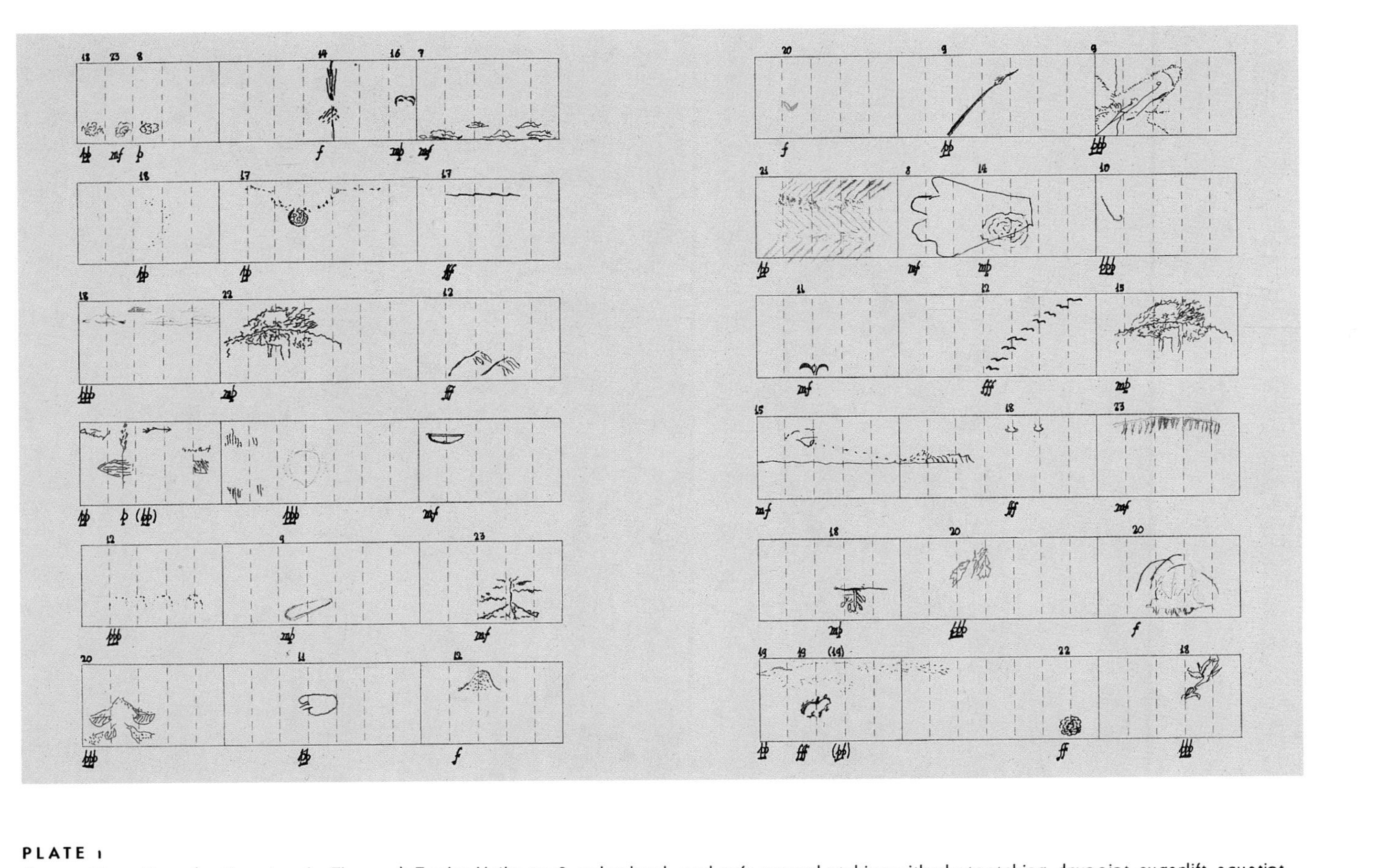

PLATE 1
Score without Parts (40 Drawings by Thoreau): Twelve Haiku, 1978, color hard- and soft-ground etching with photoetching, drypoint, sugarlift, aquatint and engraving, 22 x 30 in., Edition 25. Published by Crown Point Press, printed by Pamela Paulson.

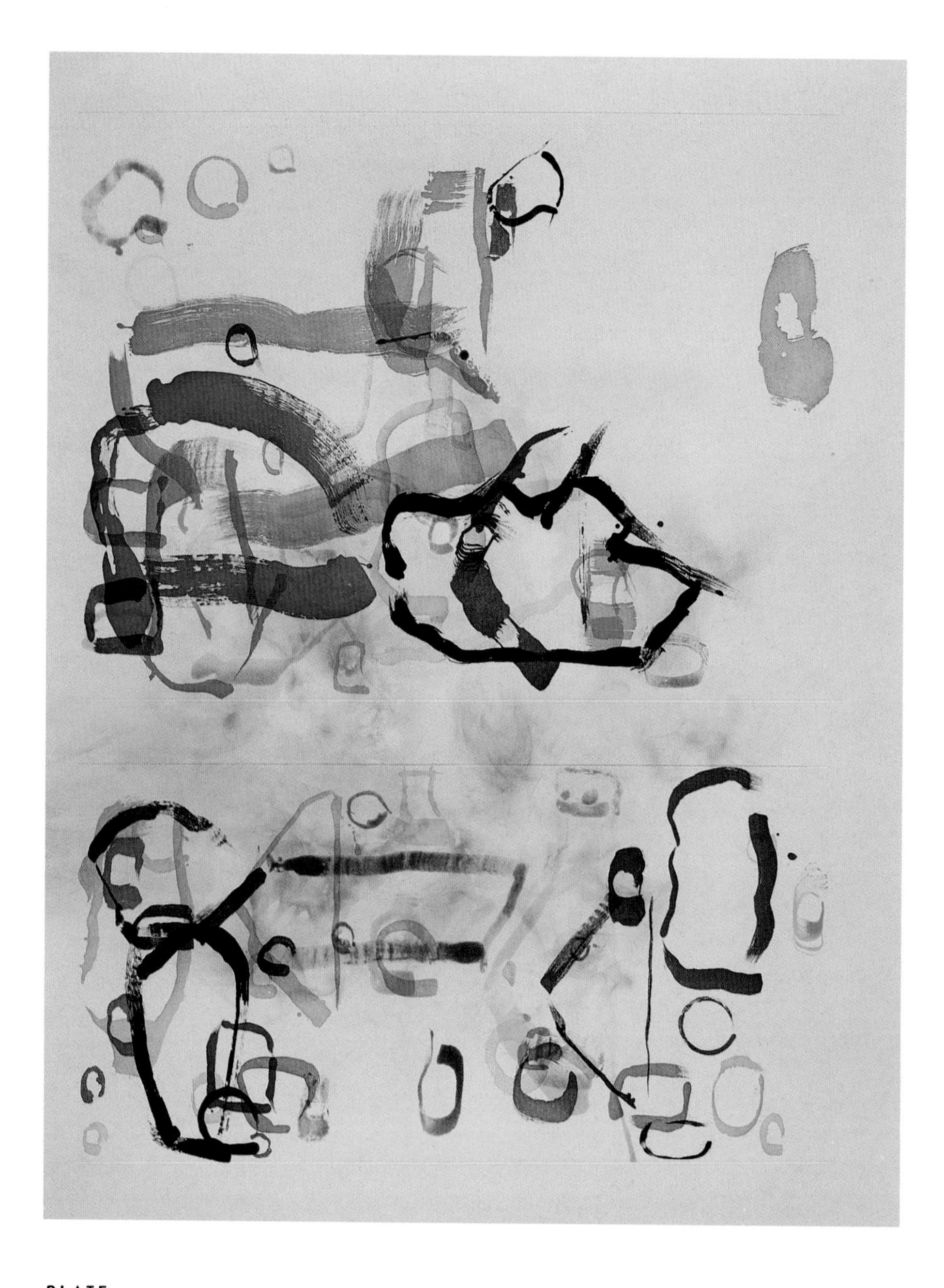

PLATE 2

75 Stones, color spit bite and sugarlift aquatints on smoked paper, 54 x 41 in., Edition 25. Published by Crown Point Press, printed by Pamela Paulson.

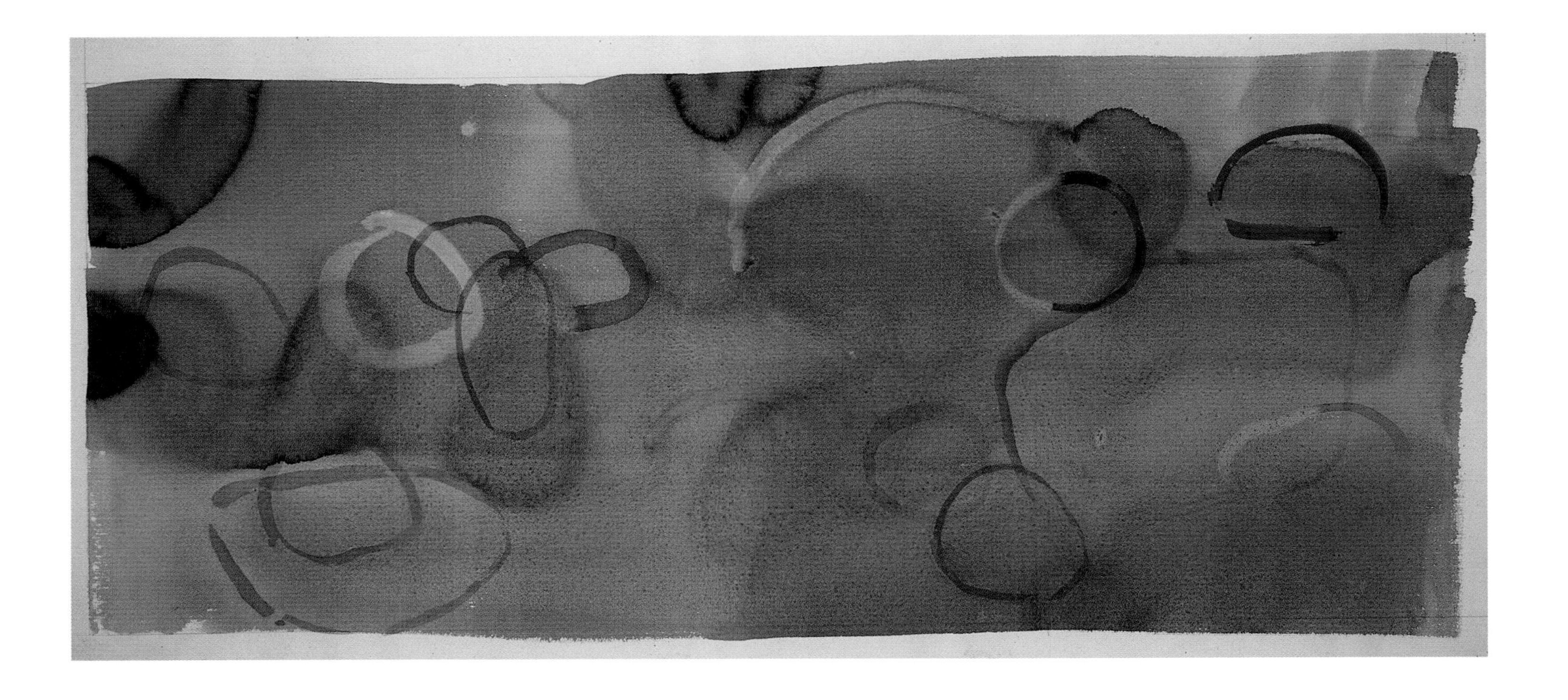

PLATE 3
New River Rocks, 1983, 24 x 52.25 in. Private collection. Photograph by Virginia Tech Media Services, courtesy of the Mountain Lake Workshop.

PLATE 4

Untitled No. 9 and *Untitled No. 12,* from Series IV, 4/13"90, each 52.5 x 15 in. Private collection, New York. Photograph by Virginia Tech Media Services, courtesy of the Mountain Lake Workshop.

was to create divisions in the plane of each painting, which suggested that he might attempt to relate the new paintings to the general characteristics of modern musical composition. He began by working on the eight largest sheets, both smoked and white examples, and decided that their longest dimensions would be the vertical heights of these paintings. The *I Ching* would be asked to determine as many as six internal vertical divisions, or "panels," along the horizontal width of each painting. The number 6 was based on the six size-categories of the two groups of stones. He considered that each panel would contain the image of a single stone (fig. 12.1).

The *I Ching* determined that the forty-eight-inch widths of the first paintings would be divided into five panels (out of a possible six), commencing from left to right, and according to the process of elimination. The first division referred to the printed page 640 of random numbers from 1 to 48, from which the next available number, 20, was assigned as the width of the first panel. The next was determined by the correspondence of 28 (the remaining number of inches of the paper's width) with page I-28 of random numbers, from which the number 15 was assigned as the second panel's width. The remaining thirteen inches of the paper's width, handled in the same way, established a third ten-inch panel. The final three inches of the original forty-eight would contain a further one-inch division, leaving only two inches of width for the fifth and final panel. The dimensions of the remaining paintings were established in the same way.

His method by which to determine the vertical placement of the stones on the panels, including provision for the possibility that the images of the stones would be "invisible," was a variant on the theme of continuity and division. For vertical placement, he "chose" to align the "base" positions of all of the configurations of the stones on a parallel border four inches from the bottom of the painting. The horizontal adjustment of the stone within each panel would be limited by a further vertical division based on each panel's width as determined by chance operations. He added one inch to the width of each panel, and consulted the corresponding page number (equal to width in inches plus one inch), to select the horizontal parameters of the stone's appearance in that panel. Each stone entered the panel from the right moving left, until its right edge met the termination point established by the *I Ching* (also measured from right to left). By this method, it was possible that the numbers selected to determine the extent of the stone's appearance could be "one inch" greater than the actual width of the panel, thereby "pushing" the stone beyond the predetermined field of vision.

The *I Ching* determined that as many as four washes could be used

FIGURE 12.1
John Cage painting at the Mountain Lake Workshop, 1988. Photograph by Rick Griffiths, Virginia Tech Media Services, courtesy of the Mountain Lake Workshop.

in each panel of each painting, and Cage determined that the heights and widths of the washes would be the same as that of the panels. The wash colors would be decided by "choice," that is, by mixing paints that represented our interpretations of the natural colors of the stones.

At first Cage thought that the pigments mixed to configure the rocks should be determined by each rock's intrinsic coloring: this was suggested to him by Ludwig Wittgenstein's text, "Remarks on Colour," which led Cage to muse that "when we say blue, we don't know what that is." He changed his mind, however, when he eliminated, according to his view of their functions, the "colors" white, black, and gray for use for stones: "White shows what a color is . . . [and] allows for the presence of all colors. Black is their absence." At last, chance operations selected the colors for the stones; each color would consist of two hues mixed together in varying proportions graduated by measurements of 10 percent.

The five rocks selected for the first paintings were examined for the positions they should take on the paper. At first Cage wanted to use chance operations to decide their orientations. But when he realized that some stones might be perceived as having several sides (between three and six), and that uncommonly round stones might be thought to have "no" sides at all, he concluded that the flattest surface should be the bottom, and that an assistant should select their vertical orientations by writing their numbers on masking tape applied to the stones to be read in the "up" position.

He elected to work with brushes rather than with feathers (as he most often did during the 1988 workshop), and a group of sixty-five small to medium brushes were selected and numbered. The *I Ching* was asked to make the final selection of brushes, the mixes of colors, and number of washes specific to each panel of the first painting. After these final considerations, we decided together that two versions of the first two paintings should be executed simultaneously. Thus Cage repeated the same configurations and procedures on both presmoked and white sheets of the same sized paper.

After the two versions of the first paintings were completed, a program was organized for the next set of paintings. These were to be done on two 25-by-72-inch papers, one smoked and one white. Cage decided that the two narrower versions should be divided into three or fewer panels, rather than five, but otherwise the procedure was identical to that for the first paintings. Chance operations determined that these paintings would have only two panels, and that the image of the rock would appear, in each case, as a limited fragment hugging the left side of the panel.

Our critical impressions of the four paintings of Series I determined the direction of the rest of the workshop, and led to later modifications. The Series I paintings lacked unity. The *I Ching* had determined that a middle panel ten inches wide would be the only division not to receive a wash color, which visually divided each painting in half. To reestablish unity, we applied a final gray wash or neutral tint over each. The *I Ching*'s selection of the rock contour for the first painting had been rendered "invisible"; the panel, however, was well defined by its four vertical washes, which suggested the various hues of the rock, as if the absent stone had left its color behind. In fact, the nearly complete image of a rock contour appeared in only one panel, and the other rock images were represented only by unrecognizably fragmented strokes of paint.

During the course of the painting, Cage had "chosen" to modify the procedure for locating the stones in the two narrowest panels (of one and two inches, respectively). Thereafter he arbitrarily changed the one-inch scale of graduation for panels narrower than two inches to divisions by four, six, eight, or more and asked the *I Ching* to determine minute parts of the lateral placement of a stone. Apparently he was somewhat uncomfortable with these paintings: the dramatic "striped" effect of the panel washes seemed incompatible with the poetic spirit of the "invisible" rock. Moreover, the washes combined to obscure the smoke effect and to fracture the illusion of depth.

Next he began a new series, painted on two additional sheets of the larger 48-by-72-inch smoked paper. No washes would be used. Rock placements and imagery would be determined by the system of area divisions as previously described, but the panels themselves would now be "invisible," that is, undefined by the vertical stripes of washes.

The *I Ching* determined that these paintings would contain three and six panels, respectively. Each displayed the entire painted contour of a stone and also fragmentary outlines. The effect of the smoke seemed to expand to hold the weightless perimeters of the rocks in an ambiguous space. These were the first two paintings of Series II; it was late afternoon and we decided to continue the work the next day.

Tuesday, April 10

Cage continued the Series II paintings without the use of washes, and began with the four remaining large sheets of presmoked paper. We would need to smoke an additional roll of number 844 Bee paper, which would be cut into fourteen 48-by-72-inch sheets. Two narrower sheets, 25 by 35 inches (which would be used later in the workshop) came from the end rolls.

Our scribe, Dan Yates, had begun to include workshop commentary in his daily record of the activities:

> [Tuesday A.M.] Conditions have changed. Mr. Cage likes the two paintings without the washes that he did last on Monday. He wasn't happy with the effect that the washes had on the panels. This is what brought about the notion of change. Change the rules. . . . There was talk of ghost images. We spent the first part of the morning smoking paper and preparing the sheets for the next four paintings.
>
> [Tuesday P.M.] This afternoon a series of fourteen additional paintings were completed, similar in concept to the four completed this morning. Eight are 8 × 72 inches, and the other two are 25 × 72 inches. These last two pieces accentuated the vertical greatly, and by chance there appeared only one stone in each. Mr. Cage likes this configuration and has said that he would like to do a series like that.

Wednesday, April 11

Dan Yates's commentary continues:

> [Wednesday A.M.] A [variant] on the Golden Rectangle was considered for the next series of paintings. [Mr. Cage and Ray] stood over a piece of smoked Whatman paper, 27 × 42 inches (England, 1949). Mr. Cage said that the ". . . idea is to use fifteen rocks in a horizontal band across the 42-inch length of the paper. Maybe only the small and medium sized rocks should be used?" Rather than decide to limit the sizes of the rocks, he suggested that [we restrict] the categories of rocks to be subjected to chance. All six categories are eligible for use.

For the Series III paintings, the *I Ching* selected fifteen rocks from the six categories, to be used in all nineteen works, which further utilized two different types of paper. The first seven were painted on 1949 Whatman (hot-press, 210 lb., 27½ by 42¼ inches); the next twelve used recent Waterford (cold-press, 260 lb., 26 by 40 inches). As in Series I and II, Cage decided the positions of the rocks, two inches from the bottom edge of the paper. This change nevertheless preserved the use of invisible divisions across the paper, but eliminated the correlations between the positions of the fifteen stones and the (possible) fifteen panels that might occur in each painting. The positions of all the stones that might appear in a single painting were established simply by referring to the computer pages corresponding to the entire width of the paper "plus 1" (random numbers 1–42 for Whatman; 1–40 for Waterford). Chance determined the number of panels—from one to fifteen—in each painting. The stones would enter and traverse the paper from right to left as before, and would be "right justified" as they were in relation to former panel divisions. Wherever a division vertically crossed a stone placed on the paper, only that aspect of the stone as it appeared on the right side would be rendered. On the left side the stone would be "invisible." In this way, the panels continued to function as barrier zones. Yates explains:

> [Wednesday A.M.] This [procedure] allows for rocks to overlap one another. This is exciting. Ray asked, "What do you think of this color?" Mr. Cage answered, "I like it. The trouble is that I like all of them."
>
> When it was possible for overlapping images of stones to smear the paint, we placed several small pieces of wood, ½ inch thick, at strategic contact points to elevate a new stone above the previously painted stone's configuration.

Five paintings on Whatman paper had been completed in the morning session. Viewing these paintings inspired a discussion of their similarities to traditional Zen painting, which seemed, to us at least, so remarkable for their lack of stylistic development. Dissatisfied with his own brushwork, which seemed to him insufficient to convey the character of the brush, Cage decided to practice with the feathers before painting again.

The irregularities of the feather strokes were very different from brushwork, which allowed him to concentrate more objectively on effect. Soon he asked, "These are better, don't you think? And I learned to do it from a feather!" He returned to the brush and began the next painting of Series III.

He now applied each brush and color to a practice sheet before using it on the painting. I suggested that he begin each practice stroke with a paint-saturated brush, continuing the stroke until the brush was dry. He was particularly interested in the paler effects of the dry brush, and asked for colors to be mixed in progressively lighter hues and values. He most preferred the brushstrokes that appeared to emerge from the smoke-colored paper rather than "float" on its surface.

Three of the least satisfactory paintings from the morning session were treated with all-over washes. He agreed to my suggestion that I now use my own judgment to mix warm or cool washes to complement the colors in each painting; in this way, smoke effects and brushwork might be better unified. We widened an adjustable wash-brush to cover the paper with a single pass and, standing over the paper, he delivered the wash. We concurred that a wash softened the stronger colors of some of the rock contours. Cage asked, "Do you still feel the smoke?" The smoke was not as strong as before, but it was still present. The wash helped to unify the painting. Two more were treated in a similar manner. He then resolved to continue to work with even lighter colors to unify the paintings by preventing one color from dominating another.

Thursday, April 12

The eighth painting of Series III was on cold-press Waterford paper the same size as Whatman, but slightly heavier and more softly textured. This paper was also used in the 1988 workshop; the smoking process made it less "wavy" than the Whatman.

We reviewed the larger paintings done on Tuesday. Of particular interest were the last two, which were narrow because they were made from the end rolls of the sheets for Series II. They measured 72 by 25 and 72 by 35 inches, respectively, and each contained the image of a single stone.

They inspired Cage to begin a similar series. The *I Ching* selected a roll of Arches cold-press paper, 52½ inches wide by 10 yards long. By chance operations, each sheet was made 15 inches wide, whereas Cage himself decided that the entire roll would be cut into pieces of that size and smoked.

As Dan Yates describes, Cage used increasingly lighter colors for the paintings of Series III:

> [Thursday A.M.] Mr. Cage said, "Two years ago I couldn't see anything. Then when I saw [those paintings] in the traveling exhibit, I thought they looked better every time. At first I didn't care for [the nearly invisible strokes] at all, but I like them quite a bit now. Yes. We're trying to go very light. The whole situation seems to me to suggest that."

> [Thursday P.M.] Mr. Cage thinks that painting twelve [of Series III] achieves a consistency of light color nearly aligned with the atmosphere of the smoke, and remarked, "Yes, it's working, but we could go further." We increased the number of brushes to include additional very small ones, because he liked their effects. In the fifteenth painting the strokes had virtually disappeared.
>
> Mr. Cage said, "It's almost like Morty," and asked whether we had heard the music of Morton Feldman. "Nobody plays his music as softly as he meant it to be played. He collected rugs, and used the patterns, the repetitions, in his music. If he were making these [paintings], he would make five or six of each."

> J.C.: "Do you see it? " (meaning the stroke around the stone).
>
> R.K.: "Oh, let me see. It's this right here, right?"
>
> J.C.: "Yes, it goes around."
>
> R.K.: "Yes, it's quite visible."

J.C. (laughing): "Oh, it's a little gaudy, don't you think?"

The next to the last painting of Series IV has only one panel division, which virtually encompasses the width of the paper.

J.C.: "In this one, Ray, the colors should be especially light. I'll tell you why. In this one there are only small rocks, they're all small rocks, and I'll be painting around all of them."

R.K.: "Very light, especially light . . ."

J.C.: "Yes."

R.K.: "Lighter than anything so far. Lighter than the colors that we're not sure we can see . . ."

J.C.: "Lighter than most everything."

Friday, April 13

Cage wanted to work on the twenty narrow sheets of paper cut and smoked the previous day, as Yates describes.

> [Friday A.M.] Mr. Cage contends that "There are ways to approach the smoke, either through color [hue] or through intensity [value]. For these next [paintings] I am thinking of the rock as a person, a small person in a gigantic world." Ray has suggested that to create a more subtle relationship between the smoke and paint hues, they might mix the color chosen by the *I Ching* with a 20 percent component of its complimentary color. This would soften the intensity of the hue. On the other hand, Mr. Cage suggested that they might mix the hues with an "earth color," such as sepia, raw umber, neutral tint or charcoal gray. Each way to gray the color was tested, and Mr. Cage's idea prevailed. Sepia was selected by chance operations from among the brown or gray pigments on hand. After sampling the effect of the sepia on a few test colors, he decided that Ray should add a small amount of black to the colors. They [experimented] with the darker values, and Mr. Cage accepted the increased value and stronger hue, and decided that they would approach the paintings [of Series IV] in this direction. [He then] changed his mind concerning the mixing of the paint, and decided to ask the *I Ching* to choose the color and also select from among all of the earth colors [including] sepia. The mix of the two was still fixed, however, with 80 percent color, and (approximately) 20 percent earth tone, and a small amount of black to darken the value. Ray suggested including black in the group of earth tones in addition to its use in every mixture. [This would] create the possibility that some of the prepared colors would be very dark or black. Mr. Cage agreed.

> In seeing the stones as people, perhaps Mr. Cage's idea for using vivid dark colors [serves] to describe the nature of our individual existence in the shared moment, [and that] in attempting to see ourselves as a part of the nature of all things, we must first acknowledge our own contrasting value, or difference, and that our movement toward harmony with the rest of nature takes place "alone" for each of us.
>
> In this new series [IV] some of the other rules have also changed. The rock will be positioned along the bottom of the 15-inch width of the painting by using chance operations to determine an additional orienting feature. After the horizontal placement is fixed by referring to the I-15 page of random numbers, the *I Ching* is asked on which side of the line of demarcation the rock should be placed (i.e., by citing the I-2 computer page, a "1" puts it on the left side of the line, and a "2" puts it on the right).

Cage decided that all the bases of the stones would be placed four inches from the bottoms of the paintings. He commented, "Well, we're ready for anything." The twenty paintings of Series IV were completed by 10:00 A.M. (see plate 4).

Immediately after completing Series IV, the workshop set out in a new direction. He had decided to use the big brushes on a very large painting. We examined a roll (102 inches wide) of heavy rag paper and used half of its 20-yard length. From this, a 30-foot length was stapled to the floor. Yates continues:

> [Friday A.M.] Mr. Cage remarked, "I think for the long skinny one, I'd like to do a parade by chance, a parade of stones . . ." To establish the horizontal positions of the rocks, he graduated each foot of the paper lengthwise into sixths, or 168 total divisions. In keeping with the subject of the Ryoan-ji garden, which had earlier inspired his series of etchings and drawings called Where R = Ryoanji (some of which had been exhibited at Virginia Tech in 1983), Cage decided that the painting would include fifteen rocks, all large, and they would be centered on their respective horizontal positions in a row which he arbitrarily place 1 foot from the bottom of the paper. The colors were a mixture (80 percent/20 percent), determined by chance. These were chosen from the list of all colors and a selected group of neutral colors (larger than the previously-mentioned group of earth tones), the latter of which included white, flesh tint and raw sienna. He painted with brushes selected by chance from a group of twelve large brushes ranging from 2 to 8 inches in width. The entire length of the painting was to be washed in an admixture of all of the leftover colors from the workshop.

[Friday P.M.] Finally we all gathered attentively around a wet drop of paint beside the last rock image to be painted, and waited for it to dry before applying the washes. Peter has prepared the 84-inch wide brush with the help of Mike Sonnichsen, who fabricated most of its armature.

M.S.: "The paper is 8½ feet wide, and the brush is 7 feet wide. Do you want to start at the top [of the paper] or in the center?"

J.C.: "More or less centered."

M.S.: "And so you'll let it go up and down as you want?"

J.C.: "I'll let it go up and down as it happens."

The brush was carefully "loaded" with paint. Pete and Ray lifted it over Mr. Cage's head and into waist-high position, and he was guided to his starting point at the long end of the paper. The wash went just over the tops of the rocks. Mr. Cage seemed somewhat pleased by the effect, and repeated the application three times, commencing each new wash about 3 feet farther down the length of the paper.

We decided that the remaining lower portion of the paper, containing the rock images, should also be "washed." This was done with a 28-inch-wide brush, which covered the margin. Cage seemed less happy with this last wash, but when the completed painting was trimmed for viewing, he seemed more pleased. The washes had absorbed the colors of the

FIGURE 12.2
New River Rocks and Washes, 1990, 101 × 354 in. the Menil Collection, Houston Texas. Photograph by Virginia Tech Media Services, courtesy of the Mountain Lake Workshop.

rocks without obscuring them too much. We titled this piece *New River Rocks and Washes,* and noted its resemblance to a huge scroll (fig. 12.2). I suggested that he might be able to apply smoke to a similar huge piece of paper.

> [Friday P.M.] Mr. Cage would like to paint another version of the giant "scroll" painting, this time using smoke instead of washes. It doesn't seem possible [to smoke such a huge paper]! Charles Layman and Joe Kelley, the volunteers who had most often led the "smoking brigade," wanted to try. Another assistant, Bob Camicia, proposed that it be smoked in successive 6- to 8-foot sections. Then we rehearsed it.
>
> We threw the paper onto the fire, worked intensely, and spoke very little. By the time Mr. Cage saw it, we had reached a crucial moment. Then the wind picked up, and ripped the wet paper so badly that it

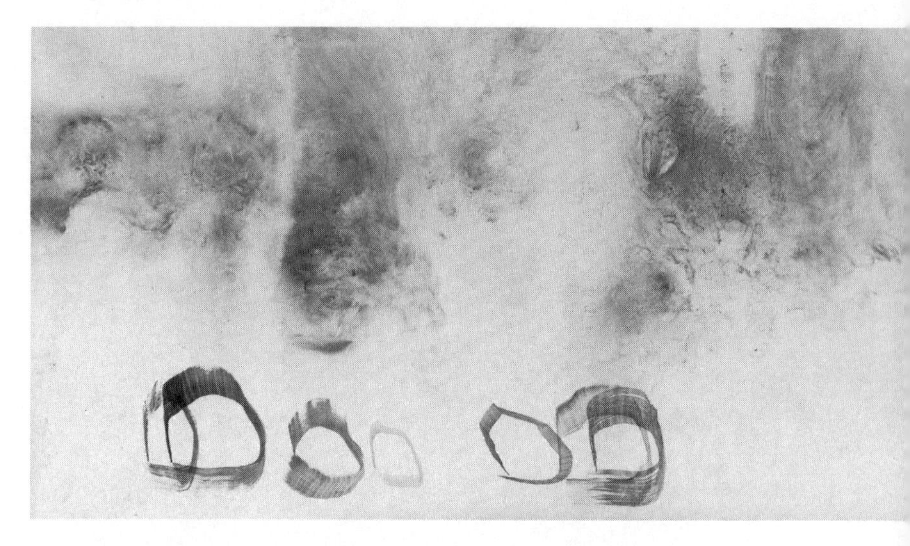

couldn't be salvaged. Smiling, Mr. Cage said, "[This is] like an Irish tragedy." One of the assistants, Bruce McClure, asked Mr. Cage how he began to use smoke in his work. He said, "It came from trying to understand a work that I love by Mark Tobey, and how he achieved the effect that's in it. Maybe it's a monoprint. There is almost nothing in it . . . reddish gray. I wanted to achieve a sense of opposites—fire and water. [At Crown Point] I did the first pieces with a hot iron tea kettle." Then Ray proposed that we try again with a new paper. Everyone rushed into action, and this time we succeeded. The paper was placed on the studio floor, and we all sat quietly with Mr. Cage and listened to the sound of the paper as it stretched and dried. I've never heard anything like it.

Sunday, April 15

Cage painted the last scroll by repeating the same painting operations with the identical rocks used for *New River Rocks and Washes,* but he asked for much lighter versions of the colors so that they would correspond with the smoke. The rock images against the background were extraordinary. He admired all the rips on the edges of this scroll, so we delayed the trimming of the completed work. This one was titled *New River Rocks and Smoke* (fig. 12.3). The completion of this painting concluded the workshop.

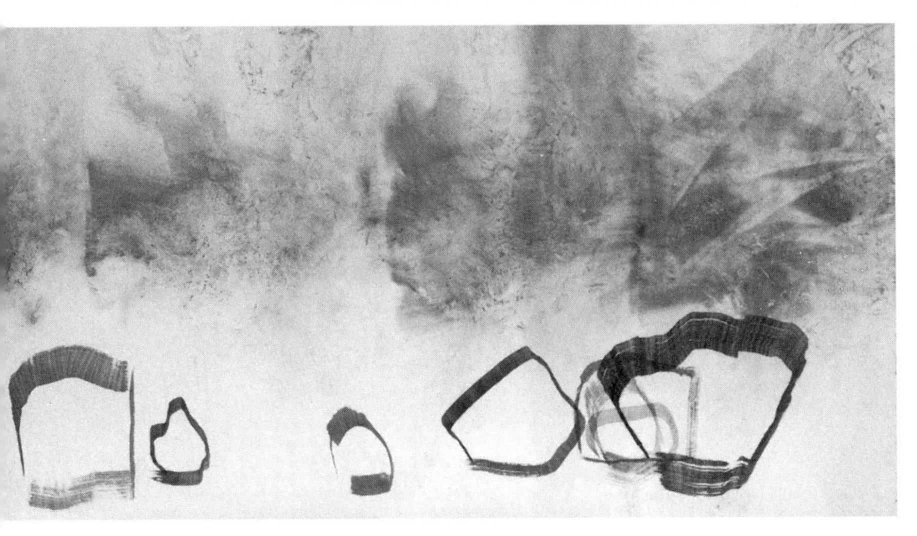

FIGURE 12.3
New River Rocks and Smoke, 1990, 102 × 384 in. The Menil Collection, Houston, Texas. Photograph by Virginia Tech Media Services, courtesy of the Mountain Lake Workshop.

THIRTEEN

Henning Lohner

The Making of Cage's *One*^{11}

One^{11} is a film without subject.

—John Cage

This essay documents some moments in the making of the film *One*^{11}. Of course this work of art, which John Cage and I created, speaks for itself. Any information I can now retrieve about the process of its making is limited by the mechanical means and coincidental nature through which the evidence was recorded.[1] It is my view that the greater part of the compositional process falls within the realm of the irreconstructible: the myth and immediate reality of feeling floating around, people interacting while *something* is happening. This process is within, and pertains only to, the individuals who are *in actu esse* and are therefore outside the observation of others and even outside their own observation. As Cage frequently said, "My memory of what happened is not what happened."

Cage resisted the idea of making this film for at least two years; the whole thing did not get off the ground until, as a result of my persistence, he gave me an opportunity

1. Throughout the period I was with Cage, I informally recorded our conversations from time to time. I also collected our correspondence and other documents, which now reside in my personal archive. Presently, there exist plans to make these materials available through the John Cage Trust.

to explain my idea. Years went by before he expressed any of his own ideas in this matter. During that time I was deeply insecure, anxious about the world and myself, impatient yet constantly drifting, vague, and evasive. Yet Cage must have sensed in me something that he recognized as sincere and to which he took a liking. Today I can say that Cage's particular confidence in a part of me I had no clue existed paved the way for the completion of his last full-feature work, the work I consider to be his credo: *One*[11].

When I asked Richard Serra about Cage, he said:

> As a moral, ethical, courageous person—although you don't think of Cage as being heroic in the John Wayne sense—Cage probably fulfilled for a lot of artists what we lack, because American artists, in particular, and German artists among others tend to have a heavy-handed *angst,* a defensive orientation in relation to the world. Cage seemed free of that. He seemed enlightened in a way that you hope that people as they get older become enlightened. He was one of the few people I've met in my lifetime who I thought had an awareness of a bigger construct. (Among the others were Huxley, Margaret Mead, and Bucky Fuller.) Cage had that same overview of a universal situation, particularly the language of sound. And I think that anyone who seems to have a language to explain the potential for opening up any other language is undeniably a teacher. In my opinion, Cage was a teacher without trying to be.

May 10, 1982, Frankfurt

John Cage was sitting at a café table after a concert of his *Etudes Australes* at the TAT in Frankfurt, Germany. For the first time, I saw John Cage "live" in front of me. I got myself together and went over to him, thanked him for the concert, and asked him whether he would teach me composition. As I would find out later, his response was typical: "I don't 'teach,' but we can have a talk."

April 2, 1985, Cologne

John Cage had just finished a reading of his mesostics in St. Georg, a Romanesque church in Cologne. I asked him for an autograph. He said, "What would you like me to write?" I said, "The first thing that comes to your mind." On the cover of the program booklet he wrote, "a cloud."

December 18, 1987, Frankfurt

JOHN CAGE: The advantage of the use of chance operations in filmmaking is that you can then use all the material which you make, rather than being confronted with the conventional problem, which is that you have to edit. You remove the editing in the sense of making judgments because with the chance operations you don't make judgments! *(laughs)* That way you don't waste any film, you can use it all.

HENNING LOHNER: What are your plans and visions in film so far?

JOHN CAGE: Well, there's a five-minute one we made on 35 mm, I think, and in color. It was a game of chess, not a game, but it was the playing of chess, myself together with the widow of Marcel Duchamp. You don't see her face or mine, and very rarely do you even see our hands; you just see the board. The camera is up above and all the parameters of changing the camera, focuses, and so forth, were controlled by chance. It was taken, if I remember, in ten-second strips, and they were put together with chance operations—very beautiful.

HENNING LOHNER: So if you wanted to make a "larger" project . . .

JOHN CAGE: Then I'd think on from that point.

HENNING LOHNER: What would you think of?

JOHN CAGE: I'm not thinking in terms of preparation. *(laughs)*

HENNING LOHNER: But this would be an extension, I imagine, of your having gone into opera (for the first time) and into the visual field.

JOHN CAGE: No, it would be an extension to film! Of the possibility of setting material into flux.

December 19, 1988, New York

To whom it may concern:

In the course of an interview in Frankfurt with Henning Lohner, I developed the idea in which I am interested to make a 90-minute film, a composed film by means of chance operations applied to all the variables; I now give him exclusively the right to do whatever is necessary to bring this project to realization. He likes it; so do I. I think (he is a composer also interested in film and film-experienced) we could make something interesting.

John Cage, New York, Dec. 19, 1988

June 27, 1989, Mainz-Lerchenberg

The administration and broadcasting center of the ZDF, the Second National Broadcasting Channel of German public television, is located on a hill in the midst of vast farmlands on the left bank of the Rhine. From the top stories of the building, you can see for hundreds of miles into the distance. My friend Harro Eisele, an editorial producer there, listened to my proposal: I wanted to make and finance a film about "nothing," a film that had no apparent content and that nobody knew anything about, and the one person who did (Cage) wasn't going to say anything about it except that magic word "chance." Harro introduced me to Maria Kasten, the editorial producer of music programs for "3sat," which is a cultural satellite for German, Austrian, and Swiss public TV. Meeting her, I realized that, years before, we had studied musicology together in Frankfurt. From here on, it took two years of typically difficult in-house negotiations before we were able to secure a studio and the first funds toward producing the film. During this time my brother and I had tried in vain to obtain funds or grants from film institutes or film commissions so that television actually became, as a last resort, the home of the film.

December 23, 1989, New York

JOHN CAGE: What I propose to do is leave the TV studio empty, but keep the light present that is ordinarily in a TV studio—at the ceiling, but also have lights available on the floor and in other parts. Therefore the film will actually be about the effects of light on an empty room—but no room is actually empty, and light will actually render—show—what there is in it. Also, the light is in interaction. And it is of course very productive of shadows. All of that space and light will be directed by means of chance operations, in terms of direction of numbers of lights as well as the changes of light.

We haven't come up to Buckminster Fuller yet, so the room will look like a box instead of a sphere. There's a beautiful Buckminster Fuller dome in Montreal—the one that burned, but the structure is still extant, and it is absolutely beautiful. In our film there is nothing inside the picture, except the shadows. But of course, there are things: in every empty thing there are things. The place is full of lights! On the ceiling, now on the floor, and in between, so that the lights themselves will make the shadows, or also the corners of the room, etc. It's very curious!

The room will not be a constructed room; it will be an empty room. I don't want anything made [specifically for this film]. It should be the studio room as is available without being artificialized as they do in TV. This studio could be any size with any number of lights and lighting available; however, I will need to know the exact size of the studio we are to work with as well as the exact number of lights available, so as to set up the composition. Also, there's a good possibility of changing the nature of the walls of the room from what they are to some other material, so as to accommodate the reflecting or absorbing qualities of different lights.

Of course, there should be a variety of different camera angles and also a parallelity of cameras, bearing in mind that the editing will be sequential as well as superimpositional. I'd be glad to make music to it, though in many cases the film will look very well without sound, but since it will be a long film (ninety minutes), it should have some kind of sound in some instances and that will be very interesting. Likewise, one will move from color to black and white. The music would be music for acoustic instruments, since my ear is in that field at the moment. It would be in the same vein as *Four,* my latest piece for the Arditti String Quartet. The sound of the film would furthermore be a composition of the actual sounds made during the shooting of the film, including any verbal or other utterances that are made by the people involved in the shooting.

Because the making of the film is all written out beforehand in the composition, there will not be the conventional form of shooting and editing in which you make your judgments, and so forth. It will simply be the continuation of the work, and the material that is taken won't be wasted, but will all be used. Mostly, with photography and film, people waste material, but I don't approve of that!

I think in the course of doing the work, the effect of the chance operations will be to make a kind of scenario of its own. And the scenario, instead of being known in advance, will develop organically out of the work. Almost no one, to my knowledge, has become interested in light in itself. Paying attention to light is generally paying attention to how light affects something else, but this film will be light in itself. It is very easy to describe, and I think it will be a pleasure to see.

July 28, 1990, Darmstadt

Cage had received a check that he wanted to cash. The German bank we went to was different from most others I had seen in that it had a big black leather sofa in the middle of the room. He and I sat down in it, and we asked our turn to be called while dozens of people all around us were waiting in lines.

A question entered my mind that I had always wanted to ask Cage: "How do you stay so well-balanced, cheerful, and friendly towards everyone?" Earlier in the day I had witnessed a horde people wanting all sorts of things from him, strangers with requests: a shopping excursion, a walk in the woods, mushrooms, a lecture, signing a hundred records for a poor publisher before two conflicting luncheons (neither of which he managed to attend because someone was busy asking him about the meaning of the universe). And so I was thinking: "How do you do it?"

I imagined an answer of great depth and intensity, a statement alluding to Buddhist philosophy or some insight only a wise old man could have, someone with the natural talent of equilibrium, a spirit beyond the constraints of emotional imbalance. His answer: "Well, I've been practicing all my life."

July 31, 1990, Berlin

HENNING LOHNER: We spoke about the unknown objects in different locations. Let's say when you come to Berlin there are certain buildings that I would assume that you know of, that you've seen before in pictures or that you've seen before when you were here, and when we discussed taking a trip around the city, you said it would have to be by chance to a place that we might know of.

JOHN CAGE: I prefer to go to a place, yes, that was anyplace rather than a well-known tourist place.

HENNING LOHNER: Why is that?

JOHN CAGE: Oh, I've spent my life on the side of the underdog. So, I'm more interested really in uninteresting things than in especially special places.

HENNING LOHNER: When do you think uninteresting things become interesting?

JOHN CAGE: When and if you pay attention to them.

HENNING LOHNER: So that's on the side of the viewer or the listener.

JOHN CAGE: I think so.

HENNING LOHNER: And what is your function as a creator or a composer, is it to make people listen?

JOHN CAGE: No, I don't want to make anyone do anything. I make music so that people can, if they wish, hear it, and I write books and so forth. The various things I do are available, but I don't want to force them upon anyone.

HENNING LOHNER: You've always said that there's a difference between the composition and the listener who finishes the composition. Where does that start?

JOHN CAGE: This starts with the listener.

HENNING LOHNER: And are you responsible for anything? As a composer?

JOHN CAGE: I try to do my best work.

HENNING LOHNER: How do chance operations fit into this idea?

JOHN CAGE: It's to keep me from doing always the same thing. That is, to save falling into my own habits, my likes and my dislikes. Chance operations are a little bit like sitting cross-legged. They keep you from doing only what you like.

HENNING LOHNER: But you've said many times that there are profound chance operations and less profound.

JOHN CAGE: It's not the chance operations that are profound or less profound, it's the questions that are asked. If the questions are not good, the chance operations are not good either.

HENNING LOHNER: Can you give an example?

JOHN CAGE: Yes. I have never liked—I'm now speaking of former times—now I like harmony, but formerly I thought I didn't. And what I thought I didn't like about it was the fact that it has always four voices: soprano, alto, tenor, and bass. So I thought if we leave one of those out, or two or three of them out, that that would be a way of refreshing harmony, and when I did that I got an interesting result from an interesting piece, and I got an uninteresting result from an uninteresting piece. So it was not a profound question. If the questions had been profound, the result of the use of chance operations would have been to make uninteresting pieces interesting and of course interesting pieces interesting, too.

HENNING LOHNER: What did you do then to change that?

JOHN CAGE: I separated the voices, the bass from the tenor and from the alto and the soprano, and I counted the number of notes in each line, and I found where the active points were by chance operations, and then I would have a sound start from the beginning and go to the first active point, and then a silence would begin and go to the next active point. The result was a series of sounds that had four voices, but which had single notes preceded and found by silence. The result was you had an image of centers of activity moving in all directions. And that's a powerful image which is, so to speak, the Buddhistic notion of creation. This actually refers to a piece called *Quartets.*

HENNING LOHNER: When you find out that a certain question is not as profound as you thought it might be, who asks the new questions? Do you?

JOHN CAGE: Of course.

HENNING LOHNER: So, in the beginning it's you who asks the questions and then . . .

JOHN CAGE: I continue to ask them. And I keep going until I find a radical question.

HENNING LOHNER: Is your idea or your vision of what musical anarchy is related to this radical question?

JOHN CAGE: I guess it must be related because they're ideas that came into my head, but I don't know what the relation is.

HENNING LOHNER: The reason I'm asking is that when I hear the word "anarchy" I think of something being ungoverned. Isn't that true?

JOHN CAGE: True. Yes.

HENNING LOHNER: When you compose a piece which goes in this direction, aren't you still provoking an ungoverned situation or making an ungoverned situation, and isn't that a contradiction? Do you know what I'm trying to say?

JOHN CAGE: I don't know, Henning. When I'm making an ungoverned situation, I don't do any thinking like that. So I don't know what I'm doing. I literally don't know. As I said in Darmstadt, I don't have any ideas, I don't have any tastes, I don't have any feelings, I'm just doing my work, so to speak, stupidly. And it turns out to be beautiful. It's very hard to explain. I don't know how else to explain it.

HENNING LOHNER: What is tradition to you?

JOHN CAGE: When you say the word, I think of society rather than an individual, and I think of the past and the acceptance of the past.

HENNING LOHNER: Can you define past in respect to future, let's say?

JOHN CAGE: Well, it's things which took place.

HENNING LOHNER: And how do you become aware of them?

JOHN CAGE: I guess we're being told that they've happened. I don't cultivate my memory. So I have to be told. The reason I don't cultivate my memory is [that] Marcel Duchamp, who I admire so much, stated, as an ideal, attaining the impossibility of transferring from one like-image to another, the memory imprint. So, you see, if we can't remember one Coca-Cola bottle and we see the second one, then we can look at the second one as though we were seeing something new. And that helps very much in this day and age. It helps you to remain a tourist in a state of great duplication. And it's true because each Coca-Cola bottle is at a different point in space and a different point in time. The result is light falls on it in special ways. So no two Coca-Cola bottles look the same.

HENNING LOHNER: Now with digital tape and computers you can reproduce something exactly as it was before.

JOHN CAGE: I guess so.

HENNING LOHNER: And yet it's . . .

JOHN CAGE: It's different.

HENNING LOHNER: So are we actually getting back, closer to nature?

JOHN CAGE: Maybe.

HENNING LOHNER: You haven't thought about that yet?

JOHN CAGE: Well, I've thought that the proper future of technology would be to disappear, without really disappearing, to give us the impression that we were without technology. I've noticed that technology, when it improves, gets smaller. And carrying that through logically, it would be at its highest point when it disappeared entirely. Don't you think? *(laughing)*

HENNING LOHNER: But if technology can go to nowhere, where do you think that human beings and living beings are going?

JOHN CAGE: Well, our present technology, according to [Marshall] McLuhan, is the extension of the central nervous system, so we're in a situation of a greater number of ideas and interconnection of ideas. McLuhan says our proper work now is simply rubbing ideas against ideas.

HENNING LOHNER: Do you have any idea where this is going to lead?

JOHN CAGE: That's the future! We have yet to see what's going to happen. That's why I'm trying to remain, if I can, alive. So that I find out what's going to happen to us. I'm not sure that I'll succeed, but I'll try. I hope that we get to a point where everybody has what he needs to live as he wishes. I find very stupid and painful the division of the world into those who have what they need and those who don't.

HENNING LOHNER: How do you think it can change?

JOHN CAGE: So that everyone has what he needs to live as he wishes. The last time when I came back from a trip from London, as I was approaching the door to the house where I live, there was a young man in the middle of the day lying on the street as though he were on a cross, crucified. And he was bleeding somewhere. No one paying any attention. We, in New York, we see day after day sights that . . . it's a wonder we can experience them with the maintenance of conscience.

HENNING LOHNER: Did you help this man? Or what did you do?

JOHN CAGE: I didn't do anything. Nor did the other people.

HENNING LOHNER: And why?

JOHN CAGE: Well, he was asleep, for one thing. It didn't occur to me to wake him up. He was, so to speak, at home in his homelessness. He hadn't put out a sign saying, "Do not disturb," but he might have. He was acting as though he were at home.

HENNING LOHNER: You feel in all of this that each individual is still his own individual self?

JOHN CAGE: What else! I was at one time homeless.

HENNING LOHNER: When was that?

JOHN CAGE: When I was very young, I was homeless in New York, and before I got to New York, sometimes when I left it. I didn't have any money and I didn't have any place to live and I would lie down on the street to sleep.

HENNING LOHNER: Was that during the Depression?

JOHN CAGE: Yes.

HENNING LOHNER: You mentioned recently that that's when your interest in mushrooms came about, isn't that right?

JOHN CAGE: Yes, not on the East coast, but on the West.

HENNING LOHNER: That was out of necessity—that there was nothing to eat?

JOHN CAGE: I didn't have anything to eat, and I knew, as you say, from "tradition" that mushrooms were edible and that some of them are deadly. So I picked one of the mushrooms and went in the public library and satisfied myself that it was not deadly, that it was edible. And I ate it and nothing else for a week. And after a week, I was living in Carmel; I was invited to lunch. I had met someone, and I was invited to lunch and it was down at the other end of town. And I set out for the lunch, but found I didn't have the strength to get there. Mushrooms don't give you much strength.

HENNING LOHNER: What happened then?

JOHN CAGE: I decided that I had to have some food. So I got a job of washing dishes in the Bluebird Tearoom, and they gave me—at that time I was young and I wasn't macrobiotic—they gave me steak. Three times a day. And I had to wash all the dishes and wash the floor and so forth, but I had some strength to do all those things.

HENNING LOHNER: And so you became a mushroom expert, didn't you?

JOHN CAGE: But much later.

HENNING LOHNER: So that interest in mushrooms certainly persisted.

JOHN CAGE: I'm still a kind of a—I'm what you would call an amateur mushroom hunter, and so far I haven't killed myself or killed any other person. *(laughs)*

HENNING LOHNER: Like us the other day.

JOHN CAGE: We had mushrooms together, didn't we?

HENNING LOHNER: Yes.

JOHN CAGE: And no one got sick.

HENNING LOHNER: No, we survived.

JOHN CAGE: But there was no pain or anything?

HENNING LOHNER: Neither. We were quite happy the next day.

JOHN CAGE: So, we didn't really "survive," we just had a good dinner!

HENNING LOHNER: Oh yes! Many people think that because of the views you have on general issues in the world, that your music has a political connotation. Is that true?

JOHN CAGE: Well, I think of myself in terms of politics as being apolitical or anarchistic.

HENNING LOHNER: And music has nothing to do with politics?

JOHN CAGE: Well, it can serve as an example of society, yes. You can make a social situation that is an image of government as an orchestral work with a conductor is, or you can give an example of an orchestral work without a conductor as an anarchistic situation. I think painting is not as social as music. Music, when it's played by a number of people, can follow a model of society or be a model for society. I often think of it that way. That's why I speak of anarchy so much.

HENNING LOHNER: Do you feel that you have been influenced by certain people in your work?

JOHN CAGE: I think everyone influences me. If I were at any moment asked to write down who influences me, I would write as many names as I could on a piece of paper in front of me. And then if I didn't have any more time and looked at the list later, my first thought would be, "Oh, I failed to mention so and so."

HENNING LOHNER: When you write music, do you have any preferred sounds? Anything that you personally like—I mean, outside of composition—just sounds that you like.

JOHN CAGE: I try not to think that way.

HENNING LOHNER: But you find yourself thinking that way sometimes?

JOHN CAGE: No. I just make the habit of not thinking that way.

HENNING LOHNER: What is music?

JOHN CAGE: *(sighs)* It's one of the arts. It's a way of paying attention, and I think attention is paid to sounds.

HENNING LOHNER: And what is art?

JOHN CAGE: The same thing. But if you're referring to visual art, then I would say it's paying attention to looking or seeing.

HENNING LOHNER: And what is love?

JOHN CAGE: We don't know. We think it's loving someone, but we suspect that it may be loving ourselves. We just don't know.

October 18, 1990, New York

JOHN CAGE: I believe that the purpose of music is to sober and quiet the mind, thus making it susceptible to divine influences. The responsibility of the artist is to imitate nature in its manner of operation. Our view of what that manner of operation is changes with our scientific awareness. Our scientific awareness in recent years includes chaos. We call it the butterfly effect or ecology. There is nothing that is free of the network of cause and effect. Everything causes everything else; everything else results from everything else.

I'm not sure that I remember correctly, but today knowing that you were going to ask me questions about chaos, I took down a book of Kwang-tse which has a passage in it about Hyung Mung, which is a name for chaos, and he was one of the winds. He was wandering about slapping his buttocks and hopping like a bird. Someone else asked him what he was doing, and he said he was enjoying himself.

And then the other person said that everything in the world was in a mess, you know, and he wanted to correct things and make everything better, and Hyung Mung didn't say anything. He just went on hopping and slapping his buttocks. But the third time—as in such stories—he answered and said, "Oh, you just want to improve matters, and you end by simply making them worse." That's where I got the title for my diary, "How to improve the world, you will only make matters worse." And it was Hyung Mung's "chaos" idea that we should let things be as they are, and it's our desire to improve them that ruins everything.

Each day provides an example of chaos. Either in the form of telephone calls or in the mail coming. *(laughing)* We never know what's going to happen. The kind of trouble that people have with the weather, we now have with every aspect of our lives. *(laughing)* I think the thing that I like about the butterfly is that it's like a grain of sand or that little bit of dust. It doesn't seem important. And yet for a scientist to say that it is important and that it's part of the network of cause and effect is pleasing. In other words, it takes our minds away from a hierarchical attitude towards nature which would, for instance, prefer a mountain to a bit of dust.

What I like in music, as you know, is silence, which is to say, all of the sounds that take place when we ourselves don't make them, so that experience through our hearing is constantly changing. Sometimes it has sounds that many people don't like or that they think interrupt whatever else is going on. But I've changed my mind to the fact that I enjoy all the things that I hear, whether they act as a truck does when it passes down the street blocking something or not. Everything as a result is interesting. And we're living now more and more not only in a world full of noise, but in one full of all kinds of things that we can perceive through our senses and also a world of more people than ever before.

It was in the late 1940s that I heard for the first time the expression "population explosion" and at that time the number of people living on the planet was higher than the number of people who had lived before, all added up together, and since that time it has doubled. And our education, our schools, our laws, and everything have to do with a world of not such great population, but just a few philanthropic rich people and everybody else more or less well-to-do. But now we have the homeless. We have in fact everybody. And a lot of the people we don't take care of. Well, I don't want to give a talk, but I think we tend to worry about some people and forget others.

I started out in my music trying to give noise as much value as so-called musical sound. And I think that we should do that socially, giving just as much regard to the poor as to the rich. In other words, make our lives so that the poorest elements or the worst elements in it would receive some kind of honor.

My use of chance operations brings me into friendship with chaos. The first piece of that kind was the *Music of Changes.* And the title of the piece comes from the "book of changes": the *I Ching,* which is the oldest book on the planet. It comes from China. It deals with the number 64 and its mechanism is used as an oracle. It uses binary mathematics, and it turns out that our DNA and RNA do the same thing, so that when our parents conceive us, they do so by means of a chance operation: in other words, we are born as a result of chaos.

That's why two parents reproducing more than once don't produce the same child; even when they produce two at the same time *(laughing),* they're frequently very different. They are so amusing, those twins. They are like puns brought to life. There's one in particular—she and her sister both live in Paris; they look absolutely the same. So if you're with either one, you think you're with the other or vice versa. The same is true with Philip Corner, who has a twin very much the same as he is, though I think he has got a bit fat and the other may not have. *(laughing)*

What has interested me very much in both sound and sight, graphic arts and music and so forth is to experience each sound and/or each thing we see as itself rather than as representative of something else. So that when we look even as we do at things that we think are identical, if we actually look at them, we see that they are not. The reason that they are not is that each thing is itself at its own center and that center is a center with respect to everything else. So a light for instance falls on each Coca-Cola bottle differently so that if you looked at each Coca-Cola bottle with light in mind, you'll see that they're entirely different. That idea of being at one's own center is a Buddhist idea. It goes that every time a baby is born, its cry means, "I'm the world-honored one. I am at the center of the universe." And creation is seen as an interpenetration of centers. Whereas our Western idea has been often that the center doesn't exist in anything, but often [in] some world of ideas that no one has access to. *(laughs)* When you have an idea off in the distance where nobody has access to it, then you have the possibility of a separation between God and man, for instance, and tragedy like Prometheus or any tragic figure such as Hamlet and so forth.

But if you have chaos and if you enjoy it rather than not, then you have Hyung Mung hopping around like an idiot slapping his buttocks and enjoying himself. *(laughs)* There's no possibility of tragedy in such a world of multiplicity of centers. There is good in the sense of comedy. Joyce preferred comedy to tragedy. I find him more or less essential to the twentieth century and "Here Comes Everybody" is the overpopulation that we're living in. And one of the meanings of "Anna Livia Plurabelle"—Alp—is in German, "nightmare"; isn't that the word for nightmare? If we take a tragic point of view, which Joyce didn't, then we could laugh it off, for instance, by saying: "Well, it's just a nightmare." *(laughs)*

It's true, the first things you have to get free of, if you take the attitude of a sober and quiet mind, are your feelings and your ideas. When you see how many things there are and you make more connections between things, I think that is the result of the acceptance of all the things. If you stick to your feelings and your ideas, you may be impoverished then and have just the same ideas you've always had plus 2 + 2 = 4 and that will be the end of it. But if you let chaos come in, you have no idea how far you will go. My motive is to have a sober and quiet mind and thus become susceptible to divine influences, which is another way of saying: and thus enjoy what happens.

HENNING LOHNER: What is a divine influence?

JOHN CAGE: Everything that happens.

HENNING LOHNER: So it's chaos?

JOHN CAGE: Of course!

July 4, 1991, Fernsehstudios München

Cage was in Munich on the occasion of a retrospective of his artwork, prints, monotypes, watercolors, drawings. My brother, Peter, had joined the film as producer, and we took Cage over to the film studio that had been designated for us. Cage said it would work out fine, which meant that the studio met the demands of the composition he had in mind, and he felt capable of tailoring the composition to meet the "demands" of the studio (see figs. 13.1–13.3).

July 30, 1991, New York

Frank Zappa was another great American composer with a big heart. I remember him dearly and miss him. So does Van Carlson, the wonderful photographer I met through Frank in 1989. Van hadn't met Cage yet. When Cage asked Van where he thought we should begin discussions

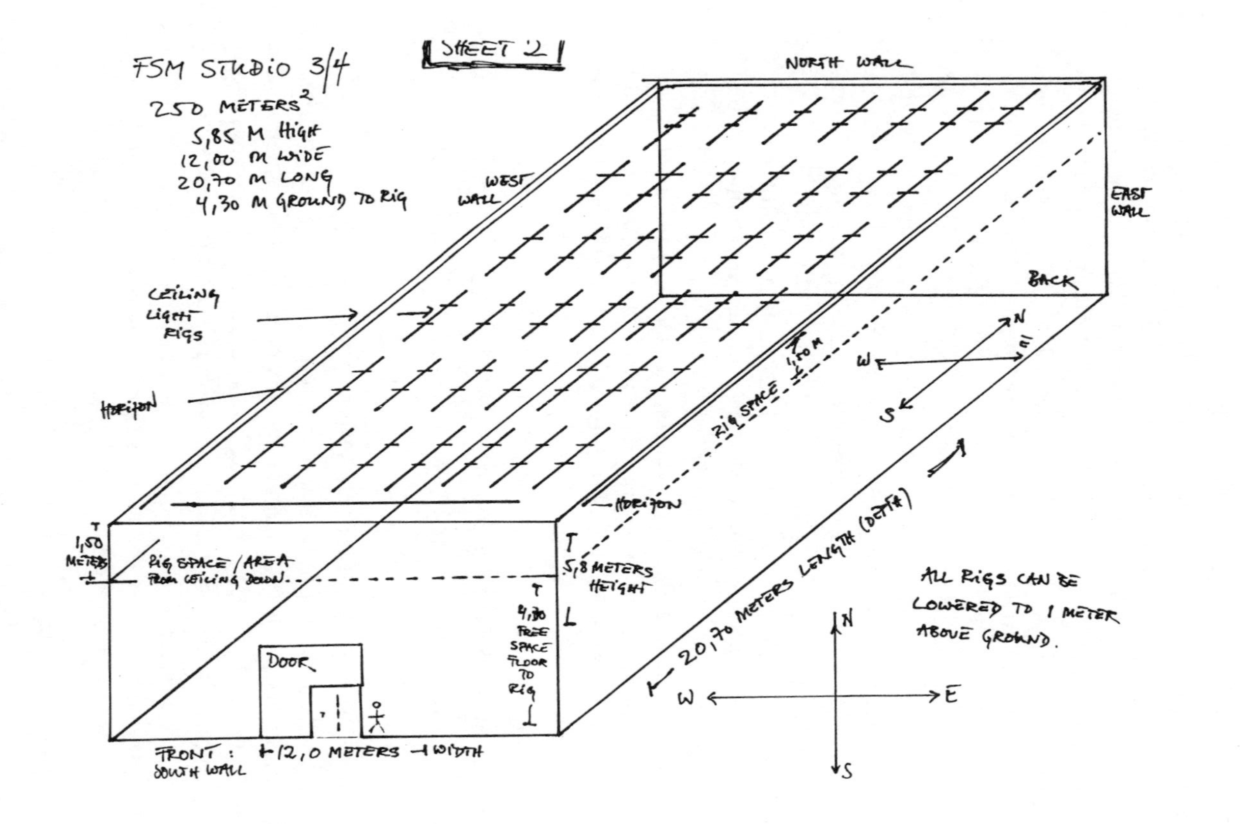

FIGURE 13.1
Studio dimensions for *One"*, sheet 2. © John Cage and Henning Lohner.

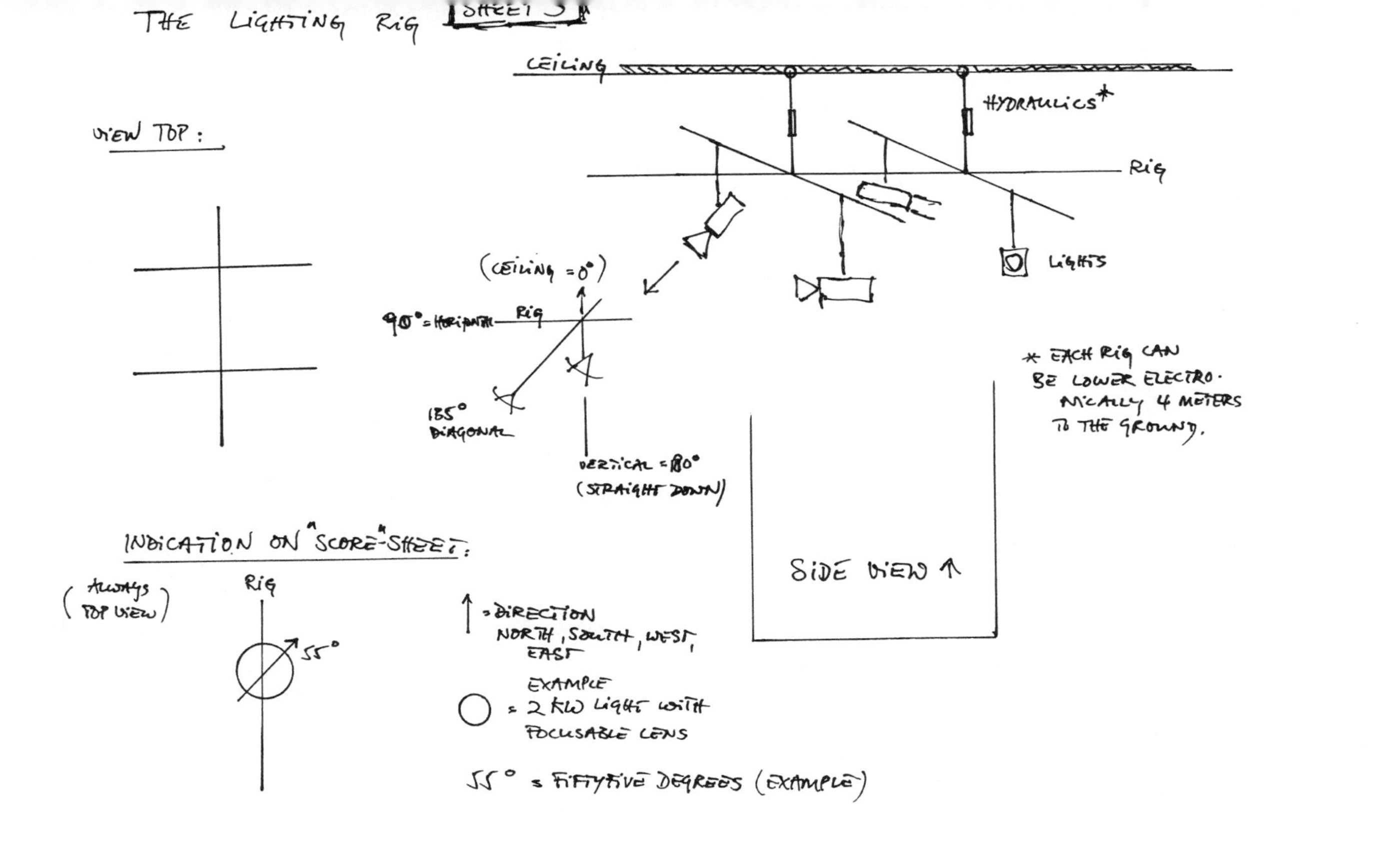

FIGURE 13.2
Lighting rig setup for *One*", sheet 3. © John Cage and Henning Lohner.

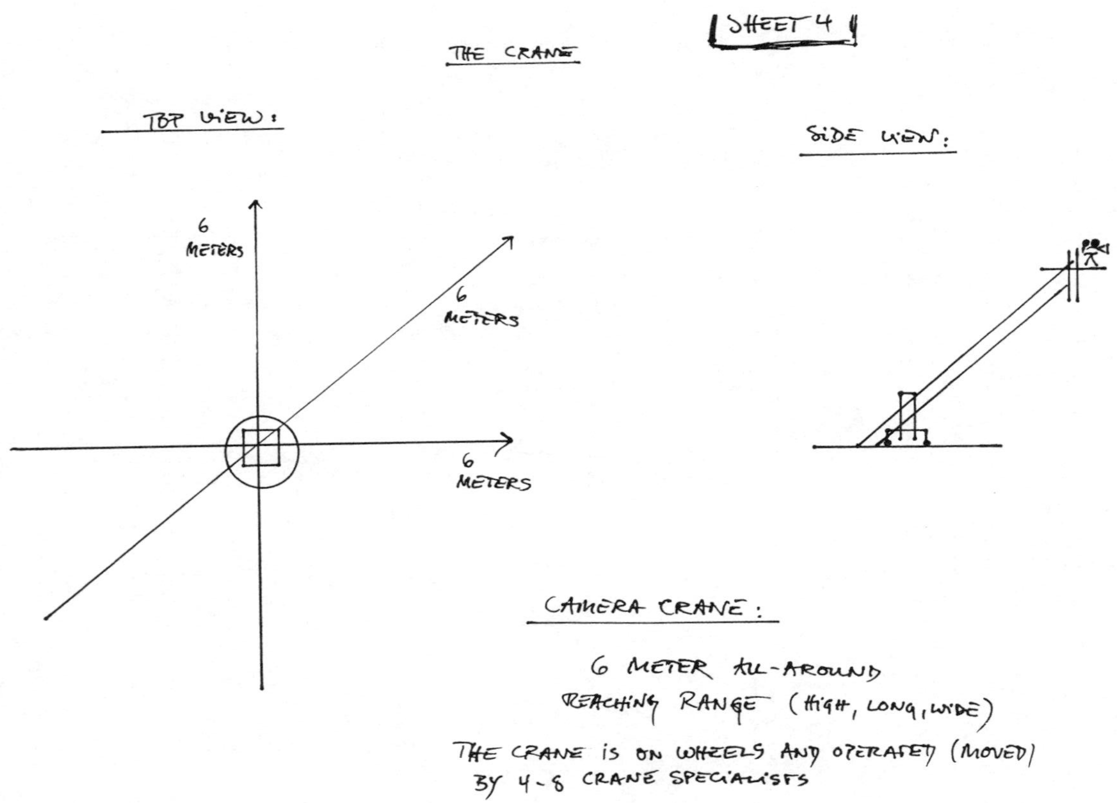

SHEET 4

THE CRANE

TOP VIEW:

6 METERS

6 METERS

6 METERS

SIDE VIEW:

CAMERA CRANE:

6 METER ALL-AROUND
REACHING RANGE (HIGH, LONG, WIDE)

THE CRANE IS ON WHEELS AND OPERATED (MOVED)
BY 4-8 CRANE SPECIALISTS

FIGURE 13.3
Camera crane setup for *One*", sheet 4. © John Cage and Henning Lohner.

about the film images, Van replied: "I am interested in anything that fits in a frame." Cage laughed.

In order for the TV studio to become an empty stage, it would be draped on all sides by one continuous huge screen called a "horizon." The lights would perform their movements in this space, and the performer would also be there, performing on his instrument, the camera. Before writing the screenplay-score of *One*[11], Cage wanted to be familiar with all the variables of what the camera was capable of doing, the modes of operation it had to offer. His process of discovering this film instrument was similar to the way he would have approached a musical instrument he wasn't familiar with.

February 25, 1992, New York

Cage, Van, and I sat eagerly in front of the computer monitor that Andrew Culver, Cage's assistant and computer programmer, had set up in a corner of Cage's loft. He pressed a button and within the wink of an eye the first scene of the film appeared on screen, in graphic form (see fig. 13.4), depicting the placement and rotation of the lights.

Each light was now in a position to perform its "duty as an instrumentalist" and to play "light" notes or tones. Figure 13.4 illustrates the movement of five fictitious lights (A, B, C, D, E) over a time change defined by five value increments, in this case all beginning with value zero. The curve drawn for each light movement indicates a so-called ADSR (attack-decay-sustain-release). This is the type of movement that, in musical terms, describes a moving "light field" similar to the "sound field" an orchestra produces (and in our film the amount of light used is comparable to the size of an orchestra).

Each ADSR movement of a light is like a musical note: there are the attack and delay phases by which the initiated light wave reaches its dynamic peak, and then there are the sustain and release phases, where the light wave is held, and finally recedes back to zero value. In the score these values would be written out numerically. All in all, in ninety minutes of film there were going to be about twenty-four thousand of these light changes, divided into seventeen scenes, equaling approximately twelve hundred cues, with an average of twenty light changes per cue.

April 9, 1992, New York

> [From] John Cage and Andrew Culver [to] Van Carlson, Peter and Henning Lohner
>
> *One*[11] Takes:
>
> Instructions for each take are given in drawing and table form. The table shows the time bracket for each take—a time within which a take

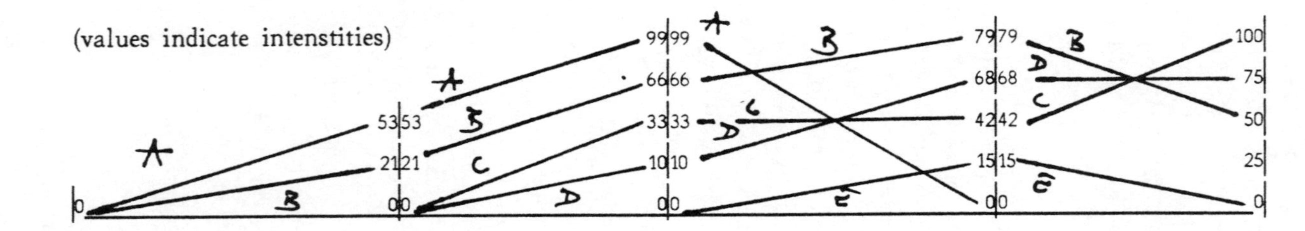

FIGURE 13.4
Plot sequence from the shooting manual for *One*", item 10. © John Cage and Henning Lohner.

must begin together with a time bracket in which the take must end. In most cases, successive takes overlap (by 10, 15 or 20 seconds) (fig. 13.5). Some takes, however, have fixed beginnings and endings (these are very short), and the different scenes abut at fixed times. The lens for each take is also given in the table.

Finally, the table gives the use of a crane or not (on "foot"), and the "from" and "to" grid positions. If no "to" position is given the take is without movement. Crane "from" positions are that of the base of the machine. The crane "to" position may be used to indicate the direction that the crane arm takes. Further details of crane direction, rotation, movement, etc., will be determined on the spot by chance operations with respect to practicality. On the drawing, "foot" "from" positions are circles, those for the crane are squares. The dotted line shows the trajectory to the "to" position (figs. 13.6 and 13.7).

[From] John Cage and Andrew Culver [to] Van Carlson, Peter and Henning Lohner

One^{11} Lights:

The lighting setup is described in twenty-four drawings, at least one for each of the seventeen scenes (either *Deckenlicht* or *Bodenlicht*), some of the scenes having both (2, 5, 6, 10, 11, 13, 16). Each drawing has a table in the upper right corner, giving, for each circuit, the numerical value of the horizontal rotation, the distance above the floor on the scrim of the lamp's hot-spot, and the gel (Rosco #114 or Lee #228), if any. The rest of the drawing is self-explanatory. Not indicated [are] the shape, edge and size characteristics of the light beams. These will be determined on the spot using chance operations with respect to practicality.

The light cues are given in a separate 138-page document (fig. 13.8). Each of the seventeen scenes begin[s] again at cue 0, a special cue with no duration that describes the intensities of all lights at the beginning of the scene. Cues from 1 on up have a duration and a "Perftime" which is the accumulated time of all durations up until that cue. Circuit and intensity numbers are joined by either a "<" (crescendo—intensity increasing during the cue) or a ">" (intensity decreasing). After every twenty cues a "State Current" is given, which is the actual intensity of all circuits at that point; this is given as a means of proofing the entry of intensities. During shooting, the lighting operator will have to be able to stop and start the cues in sync with the time-code used for filming.

One[11]

4

Take	Begin time bracket	End time bracket	Lens	Foot/Crane	From	To
6	0:36:30<->0:37:15	0:37:00<->0:37:45	85mm	Foot	G 1	O 2
7	0:37:25<->0:38:25	0:38:05<->0:39:05	50mm	Foot	B 5	H 3

SCENE 8

Take	Begin time bracket	End time bracket	Lens	Foot/Crane	From	To
1	0:39:05<->0:40:05	0:39:45<->0:40:45	32mm	Crane	K 1	D 8
2	0:40:25<->0:41:25	0:41:05<->0:42:05	50mm	Crane	N 3	C 1
3	0:42:05	0:42:20	100mm	Foot	A 8	
4	0:42:20<->0:43:05	0:42:50<->0:43:35	20mm	Crane	N 5	J 4

SCENE 9

Take	Begin time bracket	End time bracket	Lens	Foot/Crane	From	To
1	0:43:35<->0:44:05	0:43:55<->0:44:25	85mm	Foot	B 9	B 7
2	0:44:05<->0:45:05	0:44:45<->0:45:45	50mm	Foot	F 3	I 5
3	0:45:25<->0:46:25	0:46:05<->0:47:05	20mm	Foot	J10	E 9
4	0:46:45<->0:47:45	0:47:25<->0:48:25	40mm	Foot	C 6	A 7
5	0:48:15<->0:48:45	0:48:35<->0:49:05	85mm	Foot	J 9	H 3
6	0:48:50<->0:49:35	0:49:20<->0:50:05	100mm	Foot	F 7	G 2

SCENE 10

Take	Begin time bracket	End time bracket	Lens	Foot/Crane	From	To
1	0:50:05<->0:50:35	0:50:25<->0:50:55	85mm	Foot	O 7	J 7
2	0:50:55	0:51:45	24mm	Foot	N 9	
3	0:51:45<->0:52:30	0:52:15<->0:53:00	40mm	Foot	L 5	M 1
4	0:52:50<->0:53:20	0:53:10<->0:53:40	85mm	Foot	C 8	I 5
5	0:53:25<->0:54:10	0:53:55<->0:54:40	40mm	Foot	J 4	I 7

SCENE 11

FIGURE 13.5
Time bracket list for *One*[11], marked by Van Carlson during shooting. © John Cage and Henning Lohner.

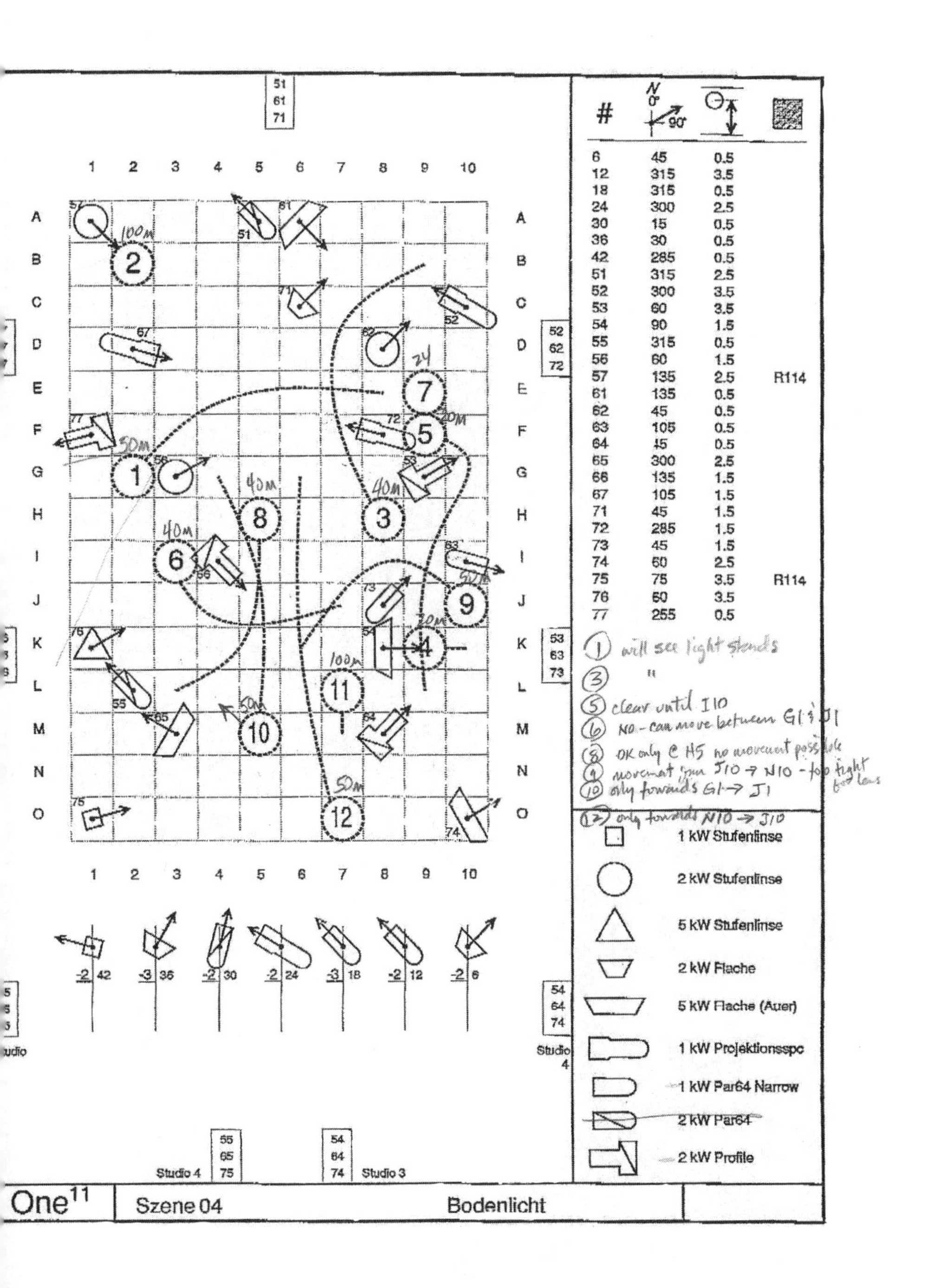

GURE 13.6
mera graph for *One*^{11}, marked by Van Carlson during shooting. © John Cage and Henning Lohner.

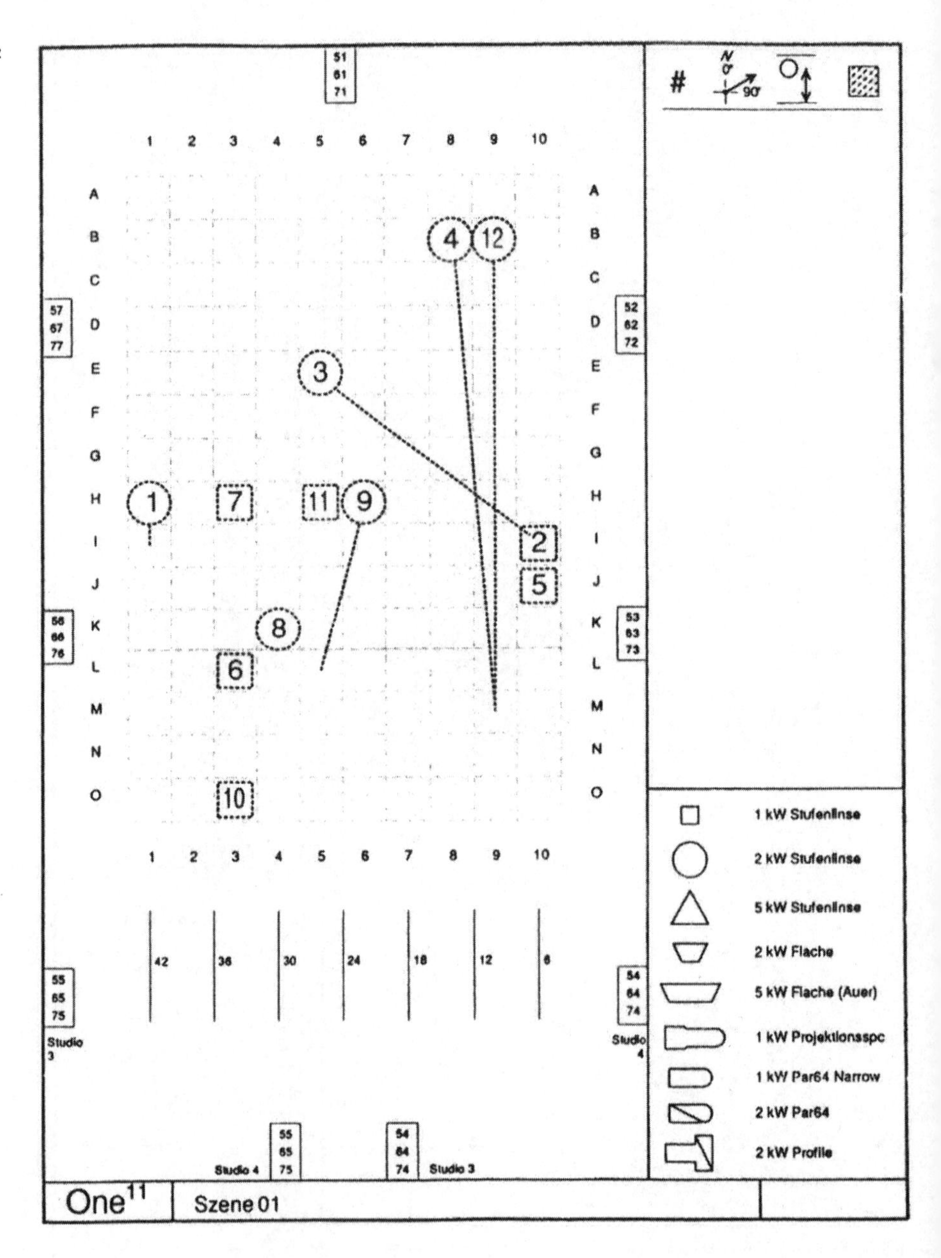

FIGURE 13.7
Scene grids for *One*^{11}. © John Cage and Henning Lohner.

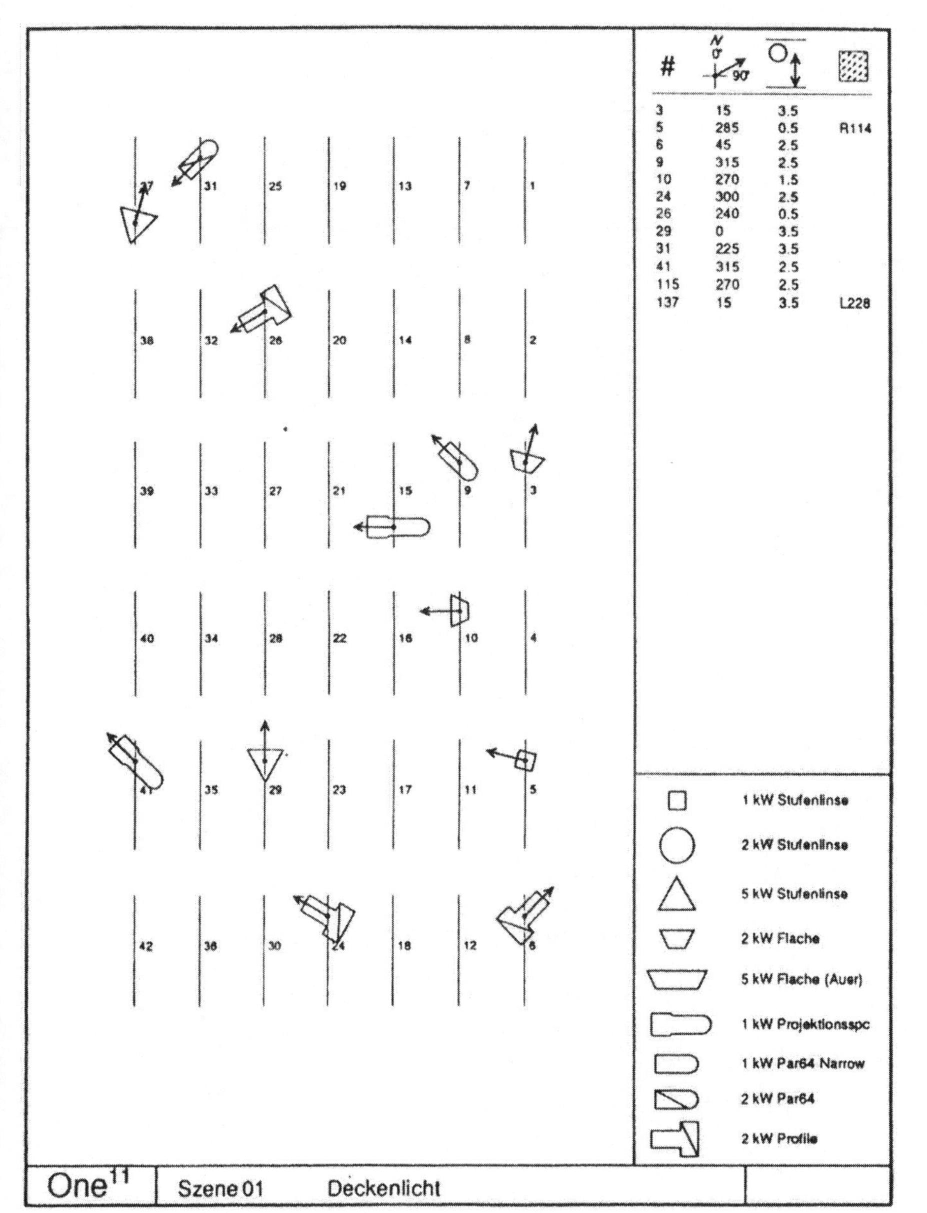

#
N
0°
90°
3 15 3.5
5 285 0.5 R114
6 45 2.5
9 315 2.5
10 270 1.5
24 300 2.5
26 240 0.5
29 0 3.5
31 225 3.5
41 315 2.5
115 270 2.5
137 15 3.5 L228
1 kW Stufenlinse
2 kW Stufenlinse
5 kW Stufenlinse
2 kW Flache
5 kW Flache (Auer)
1 kW Projektionsspc
1 kW Par64 Narrow
2 kW Par64
2 kW Profile
One11
Szene 01
Deckenlicht

One11 | Scene 01 | 1

CUE: 0 | PERFTIME: 00:00:00 | DURATION: 00:00:00

3<035 5<035 6<035 9<035 10<063 24<064 26<035 29<074
31<091 41<099 115<091 137<035

CUE: 1 | PERFTIME: 00:00:00 | DURATION: 00:00:11

3<042 5<052 6<041 9<057 10>060 24>060 [illegible]76 29>066
31>071 41>082 115>081 137<057

CUE: 2 | PERFTIME: 00:00:11 | DURATION: 00:00:09

3<047 5<066 6<046 9<076 10>058 24>057 26>072 29>059
31>054 41>068 115>072 137<075

CUE: 3 | PERFTIME: 00:00:20 | DURATION: 00:00:09

3<053 [illegible]31 6<[illegible]51 9>072 10>055 24>054 26>[illegible]
31>037 [illegible] 11[illegible]63 137<093

CUE: 4 | [illegible]FTIME: 00[illegible] | [illegible]ION: 00:00:01

3:053 5>078 [illegible] 068 29:052
31>035 41[illegible]

CUE: 5 | PERF[illegible] | DURATION: 00:00:11

3<060 5>042 6<058 [illegible] 24>050 26>063 29>043
31<044 41>035 115>051 137>0[illegible]

CUE: 6 | PERFTIME: 00:00:41 | DURATION: 00:00:02

3<061 [illegible]>035 6<[illegible]59 9>066 10:052 24:050 26>062 29>042
31<045 41<037 115[illegible]049 137>076

CUE: 7 | PERFTIME: 00:00:43 | DURATION: 00:00:06

3<065 5<042 6<064 9>063 10>050 24>048 26>059 29>036
31<050 41<044 115>043 137>069

CUE: 8 | [illegible]FTIME: 00:0[illegible] | DURATION: 00:00:01

3:065 [illegible] 9:06[illegible] [illegible]0 24:048 26:059 29>035
31:050 4[illegible] 137>[illegible]

FIGURE 13.8
Lighting cues for *One*[11]. © John Cage and Henning Lohner.

Scene 2 Page 2

```
    5<037    10>063    17<053    18:020    21>033    26:046    74<033    75<081

CUE:     12              PERFTIME:   00:13:46             DURATION:   00:00:01

    5<040    10>061    17>045    18:020    21>031    26:046    74<034    75<084

CUE:     13              PERFTIME:   00:13:47             DURATION:   00:00:03

    5<052    10>055    17>020    18<022    21>023    26>044    74<037    75>076

CUE:     14              PERFTIME:   00:13:50             DURATION:   00:00:01

    5<056    10>053    18:022    21>020    26:044    74<038    75>074

CUE:     15              PERFTIME:   00:13:51             DURATION:   00:00:14

    5>044    10>020    18<032    21<045    26>032    74<052    75>035

CUE:     16              PERFTIME:   00:14:05             DURATION:   00:00:02

    5>043    18<033    21<048    26>031    53<022    74<054    75>029

CUE:     17              PERFTIME:   00:14:07             DURATION:   00:00:01

    5>042    18:033    21<049    26:031    53<023    74>053    75>026

CUE:     18              PERFTIME:   00:14:08             DURATION:   00:00:02

    5>040    18<035    21<053    26>029    53<026    62<023    74>050    75>020

CUE:     19              PERFTIME:   00:14:10             DURATION:   00:00:08

    5>032    18<043    21<069    26>021    53<038    62<037    74>038

State Current:
     5:032    10:020    17:020    18:043    19:020    21:069    24:020    26:021
    29:020    32:020    34:020    53:038    55:020    61:020    62:037    73:020
    74:038    75:020

CUE:     20              PERFTIME:   00:14:18             DURATION:   00:00:01

    5>031    18:043    21<071    26>020    53<039    62<038    74>037

CUE:     21              PERFTIME:   00:14:19             DURATION:   00:00:03

    5>028    18>041    21<077    29<026    53<045    62<043    74>032

CUE:     22              PERFTIME:   00:14:22             DURATION:   00:00:07

    5>021    18>035    21>067    29<042    53>041    62<056    74>020
```

April 14, 1992, Munich

[To] John Cage and Andrew Culver

Greetings from Germany,

We have arrived safely thanking always the wings that lift. After closely studying the camera positions, I have some notes on what the camera will and won't see through the lens.

Scene 1	take 4: a crane shot with the 100 mm lens could be shaky
Scene 1	take 12: a crane shot with the 85 mm lens could be shaky
Scene 2	take 3: 32 mm lens field of view may see lights at O-1 & K-4
Scene 3	take 1: 100 mm lens and crane move = vibrations
Scene 4	take 1: camera position & lens will see light stands
Scene 4	take 3: camera position & lens will see light stands
Scene 4	take 5: camera OK until I-10 position then light stands
Scene 4	take 6: camera can only move between G-1 & J-1 in that position
Scene 4	take 8: camera OK only at H-5, no other movement possible
Scene 4	take 9: camera moves possible only from J-10 to N-10
Scene 4	take 10: camera moves only towards G-1 to J-1
Scene 4	take 12: camera moves only towards N-10 to J-10
Scene 6	take 3: movement only A-4 to A-6 or D-1 to G-1
Scene 7	take 3: 100 mm lens on foot will be shaky
Scene 9	take 3: movement to E-9 may be too far
Scene 9	take 5: 85 mm lens on foot may be shaky
Scene 9	take 6; 100 mm lens on foot may be shaky
Scene 10	take 1: no movement—only L-10 possible
Scene 10	take 3: may see light stands at L-1 to N-2
Scene 10	take 4: camera moves only from A-10 to C-10 or A-8 to A-9
Scene 11	take 4: camera moves only from K-10 to O-10 or A-6 to A-10 or O-1 to K-1
Scene 11	take 5: camera moves only from O-10 to I-10
Scene 11	take 6: camera moves only from O-1 to K-1
Scene 12	take 1: 100 mm lens on foot shakes a lot
Scene 12	take 2: distance to cover in time allowed is very great
Scene 13	take 1; 100 mm lens and distance covered may be a problem
Scene 14	take 1: distance in time allowed is tight
Scene 14	take 4: 20 mm lens may see top of lighting grid at J-6
Scene 15	take 3: end point at N-5 may be too far & light stand appears
Scene 16	take 1: 100 mm lens traveling from F-2 to O-2 may be too far

Now is it clear? Perhaps I am jet-lagged and need to adjust to this Bavarian atmosphere. All I can say is it's not the takes that take time, but the time between the takes that takes time.
Van Carlson
München Kammeraman

April 22, 1992, Fernsehstudios München

First day of shooting: In order to complete the full ninety minutes of film within the seven given days, we had calculated that we could spend no more than fifteen minutes per take, regardless of the difficulty of any particular take. In completing each shot on schedule, we had to accommodate a variety of decisions and operations.

Changes in lighting. Changes in lighting were made scene by scene. Since there were seventeen scenes total, most days we set up one lighting rig in the morning and a second in the afternoon; on some days three lighting rig changes were necessary. The schedule was divided up so that on those days when we were shooting three scenes, comparatively fewer changes would be shot. As it turned out, a certain number of lights needed adjusting with every take: spurious reflections (the angle by which light falls between cyc-screen and camera) were the greatest problem, but also spurious shadows (where one light produces a shadow because another light has interrupted it).

Camera setup, positioning, and motion. There were three different possibilities for setting up the camera: (1) "flying" the camera on the crane, (2) using a hand-held camera, and (3) keeping the camera stationary on a tripod. This decision had to be coordinated with what the camera could actually see, that is, the lens choice and focal range, along with the "in" or "out" of focus options included in the compositional scheme. There were instances where the choice of lens would expose too much or too little of the area needed for the shot, and we would have to make ad hoc changes. Frequently Cage would consult his briefcase filled with chance operations, but not always: sometimes sheer practicality made the selection evident (or "commonsensical").

Film stock controls and magazine changes. We'd change the magazine with every eleven minutes of shot film. After each take and with each change of lens, the machine would also be checked, since there was the danger of the camera jamming or dust getting into it, thereby ruining the image. We actually had problems here during shooting only once or twice, so we were lucky.

Ad hoc decisions by John Cage. Early on during shooting, Cage decided to give Van's motion with the camera more "freedom" in order to follow the light motion more closely. Such decisions were often made during the rehearsal for each take. Also, decisions on the exact range and height of the crane were left until the crane had been moved into its base position for any given take.

Coordination of video playback and rehearsal of all motions. Once all the individual "characters" of the play were in place, the time code clock for the particular take was started. It was slated to the camera, then spread across several monitors for everyone else to see, not just in the studio, but up in the two control rooms located under the ceiling for video playback and lighting cues. In addition, I would launch a simultaneous reverse countdown so that lighting and camera motion were in sync, and call the magic word: "Action."

Troubleshooting. Peter Lohner balanced the shooting inside the studio with the demands of the "outside world." He kept everything on schedule, solving any and all problems, usually before they could occur, from securing all the lights before the morning shooting to making sure that the film negatives were delivered and developed properly in the evening.

In effect, all of these processes leading to that long-anticipated moment "action" had to happen simultaneously. The lighting cues were programmed and triggered in a separate studio control room located in a corner under the ceiling of the studio, and while we were recording one take, the lighting cues for the next takes would be programmed. The video playback room (both the time code reference monitor track and the monitor of what we had just shot) was located in another part of the building, above the actual studio, and "wired" down to the stage monitors; their coordination was done by intercom.

April 24, 1992, Fernsehstudios München

Cage came to the shooting stage and said: "I dreamt color." He had left the day before worried about the film becoming too dark, literally, that it had not enough light in it. We had found that the movements of the camera sometimes did not correspond well enough to the area in which the lights were moving. Although Cage later discarded the idea of color, the problem of "lightness" was solved by Van's suggestion that we do one rehearsal for each take and pay attention to the movements, and then move the camera towards the light action.

April 26, 1992, Fernsehstudios München

CAGE: Van, it's very nice to have some of those greasy, those difficult-to-see lights.

VAN: Over here?

CAGE: These are very beautiful over on this side.

VAN: Yeah, we were going to start here and just swing this way.

CAGE: Good!

April 26, 1992, Fernsehstudios München

Van and I discuss the video-replay of a shot in which documentary cameraman Henry von Barnekow's shadow coincidentally wound up in the filmed picture: Cage likes it and wants to keep it in the film. (Henry was shooting video for a documentary about the making of *One*[11].)

April 27, 1992

HENNING LOHNER: Can you describe the compositional process to achieve such a film? In general steps?

JOHN CAGE: Well, I've worked with Andrew Culver for several years—I think it's around ten years now—and the first work we did together was the *Europeras 1 & 2,* and since then we've had installations of a work called *Essay,* which is writing mesostics through the "Essay on Civil Disobedience" by Henry David Thoreau. It was conceived as a present to give to Satie in another work called *The First Meeting of the Satie Society.* So, in all those cases, Andrew Culver has made different lighting installations, that is to say, a multiplicity of lights facing in different directions. In the case of the *Europeras,* it was in the Opera at Frankfurt before it burned. And in the case of the *Essay,* it was in a darkened room, and we gave the light its own life. That is to say, it didn't light the action or the scene or the decors, it simply existed as light independent of what it lit, which is the way the sun exists during the day, wherever it shines: it doesn't know what it's doing. And frequently the most "important" things, like presidents and kings and so forth are in the dark. *(laughs)* OK?

HENNING LOHNER: Can you describe the surroundings we are currently working in?

JOHN CAGE: This is, so to speak, an empty room in which the light is not in relation to anything but itself. And it reminds me of what Immanuel Kant in his *Critique*—I think in his *Critique of Pure Reason*—said about music and about laughter: that without meaning anything both music and laughter—and I think we can now add light, too—give pleasure without having any meaning whatsoever.

And it's true: there are changes, changes that take place with sounds and the changes that take place in the sound of laughter and the changes that take place in intensity and differences between light and dark; noticing such things, one is free of the problems of politics and economics, I think. Even, perhaps, free of oneself.

HENNING LOHNER: Other, perhaps, than my asking you to do it, is there any reason that you would like to make a film?

JOHN CAGE: Well, I'm getting rather old, so if I have the opportunity to do something, then I jump at it, instead of hesitating, because there isn't much time left! *(laughs)*

HENNING LOHNER: Can you describe the process of chance operations as it relates to this project? In other words, we have spontaneously been deciding certain things . . . can you explain?

JOHN CAGE: Well, the program specifies the number of lights to be used in a particular scene and for this composition we have, if I recall correctly, we have seventeen scenes. It's about the number of chapters in *Finnegans Wake* or *Ulysses*. When you have a large work, it's better to divide into parts like of that number rather than, say, three, because three parts would produce very long sections. In this case, dividing ninety minutes into seventeen sections, we have the experience of both what seems to be long and what seems to be short. And we're carried through the ninety minutes with differences of light, differences of numbers of lights. I look forward to the pleasure of seeing a film that isn't—doesn't have a plot, doesn't have characters, which has, so to speak, nothing. And that gives us, I think, in this day of violence and overpopulation, war, and economic collapse, I think it gives us something to enjoy. *(smiles)*

HENNING LOHNER: The computer program is based on the *I Ching?* Is that correct?

JOHN CAGE: No. It's not based on the *I Ching;* it uses the *I Ching* in order to make choices or [to show] how to make selections, if you wish, among the plurality of possibilities.

HENNING LOHNER: Now, I noticed you have in your briefcase pages with long lists of numbers; you use them to help us make decisions when we have a problem. Can you explain those numbers to us?

JOHN CAGE: Oh, I carry around *I Ching* numbers with respect to a large number of numbers—particularly those below 64, from 2 to 64, and only a few above 64. The higher numbers are for special circumstances, but the lower numbers are frequently useful. Particularly in this situation, the number 2 has been extraordinarily useful. So it's a page full of numbers between 1 and 2. They're either 1s or 2s. If we want to know whether a light should be focused or not focused, we use the sheet for 2. If we want to know whether there is the possibility of one thing or the other, then we use 2. We use 5 on other occasions, I imagine, where there's a sweep of possibilities. So that it goes from 1 to 2 to 3 to 4 to 5. *(makes gesture with arm)*

PETER LOHNER: So, Van, tell us whether you think the director is giving you enough creative freedom or not?

VAN CARLSON: Oh, well, that's a thing: there's too much freedom!

JOHN CAGE: Too much freedom?

VAN CARLSON: Yes.

JOHN CAGE: Well, when you want some—some constraint? We know where we can get it! *(laughs)*

VAN CARLSON: Yes, I think we've done a good job. We're done with the choices. *(Cage laughs)*

JOHN CAGE: Yes, if you want more constraints, you simply ask for it.

VAN CARLSON: Yes, good.

JOHN CAGE: I think one of the problems in making this film was that the constraints we gave originally about your position and so forth were difficult, some of them, to handle, or didn't result in much visuality because we didn't know what the specific directions of the lights would be when we did the chance operations. So I think you who are so experienced with the camera and know what the camera can do with respect to the light, you, I think, can use freedom or constraint more efficiently on the spot, so to speak.

VAN CARLSON: Yes, I think we've gotten to that. And, really, the whole piece is a performance for the camera.

JOHN CAGE: Right.

VAN CARLSON: Within the . . .

JOHN CAGE: Within the lighting situation.

VAN CARLSON: Which is maybe like a dream come true!

JOHN CAGE: I think light gives me the pleasure that sound gives!

VAN CARLSON: Well, and always, of course, I think because of your references to Joyce about the ineluctable modality.

JOHN CAGE: What! Now, isn't that marvelous! I was trying to think of what those words are! I don't have my copy of *Ulysses* with me, but "the ineluctable modality of . . ."

VAN CARLSON: "The ineluctable modality of the visible."

JOHN CAGE: ". . . of the visible." Isn't that marvelous! And then in the next paragraph: ". . . of the audible." And that's how we live together, I would say, in society: We live with light and we live with sound. We live with what we see and we live with what we hear.

VAN CARLSON: Good.

HENNING LOHNER: All right, you can . . .

JOHN CAGE: . . . I can be quiet now? *(all laugh)*

(Cage gets off the crane and walks back toward his table at the studio entrance.)

June 12, 1992, New York

One[11] and *103*

One[11] is a film without subject. There is light but no persons, no things, no ideas about repetition and variation. It is meaningless activity which is nonetheless communicative, like light itself, escaping our attention as communication because it has no content. Light is, as McLuhan said, pure information, without any content to restrict its transforming and informing power. Chance operations were used with respect to the shots, black and white, taken in the FSM television studio in Munich by Van Carlson, Los Angeles cameraman. The producer and director was Henning Lohner. The executive producer was Peter Lohner. The light environment was designed and programmed by John Cage and Andrew Culver, as was the editing of the film, done in video format at Laser Edit East in NYC, with the help of Gary Sharfin and Bernadine Colish. This edit was then transferred to the original 35 mm film negative at ARRI, Munich.

103 is an orchestral work. Like the film, it is ninety minutes long. It is divided into seventeen parts. The lengths of the seventeen parts are the same for all the strings and the percussion. The woodwinds and the brass follow another plan. The shots of the cameraman still another. Following chance operations, the number of wind instruments changes for each of the seventeen parts. Thus the density of *103* varies from the solo trombone of Section Eleven, the trumpet and horn duo of Section Ten, the woodwind trio of Section Six, to the tutti of Section Five and the near tuttis of Sections One, Eight, Thirteen, Fourteen, and Sixteen.

—John Cage[2]

September 19, 1992, Cologne

The film and music were premiered in Cologne on September 19, 1992, with the Radio and Symphony Orchestra of the WDR. I remember going on stage after the concert with Van, Peter, and Andrew, to take our bow for Cage, and as I looked out to the fifteen hundred spectators I somehow located my mentor, Gerhard Richter, raising his thumb up in the air.

I found out that night that Cage had dedicated the music to Wolfgang Becker-Carsten and me. I met Dr. Becker in 1990 on a wonderful sunny afternoon in Zurich. I had come there to see Cage's exhibit at the Kunsthaus; a great show of his artwork, smoke paintings, etchings, etc. Cage was there, too, and after we had our usual game of chess (a ritualistic occasion by which Cage would make me the present of a book for every

2. Preface to the screenplay/lighting score from *One[11]*.

time that he lost), he hooked me up with Dr. Becker, who is a unique figure in contemporary European music. Through his enthusiasm and his position at the WDR radio in Cologne he has been able to sponsor and commission countless pieces of contemporary music. Dr. Becker made the music of *103*, as well as its use with *One*[11], possible.

Sometime during the process of making the film, Cage's ideas about sound for it changed. He completed the score to *103* early in 1991, and he called me in Germany specifically to tell me the good news. *103* was meant to go with *One*[11], and vice versa. So, whereas both *One*[11] and *103* can anytime be performed separately, they were not to be premiered separately; in terms of their composition, they are closely related. I consider them to be twins.

[From] Heinz-Klaus Metzger:

There is no precedence in film history to *One*[11], not even a single piece of work referentially precursory; the avant-gardists of "abstract film" referred at least to platonic ideas or products of human imagination such as geometrical figures or figurations. *One*[11] introduces *ex abrupto* a new era. At a time when television has fully substituted reality with its mere likeness so that any former hope of a better world has been transmutated into the wish for better TV programming, *One*[11] surfaces as the first film that applies without compromise an achievement of civilization, that, although it is thousands of years old, has very rarely been realized, which is the biblical Second Commandment:

> Thou shalt not make unto thee any graven image, or any likeness of any thing that is in heaven above, or that is in the earth beneath, or that is in the water under the earth. (2 Moses [Exodus] 20, verse 4)

For *One*[11] the camera recorded nothing but light impressions unto themselves, emitted by lamps that do not illuminate anything, but simply expose the film material. . . . It may surprise that this work of art required a whole team to produce it, . . . while it functions under the title-numeral *One*. What "counts" with [Cage's] number pieces is the personnel necessary for the performance: here, one projectionist suffices.

For many years Cage's compositions had necessitated the revolutionary postulate of the fall of the art empire *(Kunstprivileg)*, thereby admitting ordinary and everyday noise into them, so as to soften the borders between art and its surrounding reality, and this was furthered even more by incorporating the enemy art industry into the compositions, such as converting radios and record-players into musical instruments. However, Cage's late works—like *Etudes Australes* for piano, the *Freeman Etudes* for violin, or all the "number pieces"—announce in blinding purity and solemnity their critical difference from the real world and the ideas that rule it, both literally and figuratively. Given the rigor with which Cage declined that like-image of, to, or from the real world, the completely singular quality of *One*^{11} very possibly make it Cage's most radical work of all, a play of light that neither belongs to nor has any tradition in any aesthetic discipline, the least of which in film art: *One*^{11} cannot be integrated, it is outside of everything else, and very possibly Cage's most founded archimedic center of enlightenment.[3]

October 10, 1992, Wiesbaden

In order to make the broadcast copies of the film, the 35-mm positive was transferred to Betacam-Sp videotape, where the standard contrast ratio of 0 to 100 is further narrowed by about 30 percent because of the nature of electromagnetic waves: whether you overexpose or underexpose the video, you run the risk of frequencies "crossing out" which in turn can lead to the broadcast signal's "caving in." Also, the resolution of television is less than a third of a 35-mm film.

Cage asked that the 35-mm theatrical copies not be cleaned of the dust that naturally collects on them the more often they get shown; this idea he took from a film Nam June Paik once made, where the film changes through every theatrical performance. The video copy, however, will never collect dust. So the television version of the film has its own "look" to it.

Initially, I had proposed a length of ninety minutes for *One*^{11} because that is the average length of a feature film, and we had set out to make a feature film. Having done so, the logical consequence was for us to show it in its entirety. However, it is not necessary for the audience to watch it all at once; rather, they can take it any way they like. Cage mentioned that he could conceive of the film being viewed for only moment just as well as in an infinitely repeated "loop"—for even the shortest moment would suffice, if that's what one chose to pay attention to. Also, the film can be shown anywhere, not just in a movie house, and the audience can do whatever they like while viewing it.

I saw those fading images, dying out, white and black light born again, coming in and out, that flickering craziness we call *One*^{11} on my television screen—this was television alive (figs. 13.9 and 13.10)! And I knew from "documentation" that we achieved something unprecedented in television. After the broadcast, response from public television officials was unanimous. One of the directors of broadcasting came up to me: "Great film—just don't do it again."

3. This text, which I have translated, appears in the program booklet for the premiere of *103* and *One*^{11}: *John Cage: 103 für Orchestra und One*^{11}, *ein Film ohne Thema* (Cologne: Westdeutscher Rundfunk, 1992), 15–16.

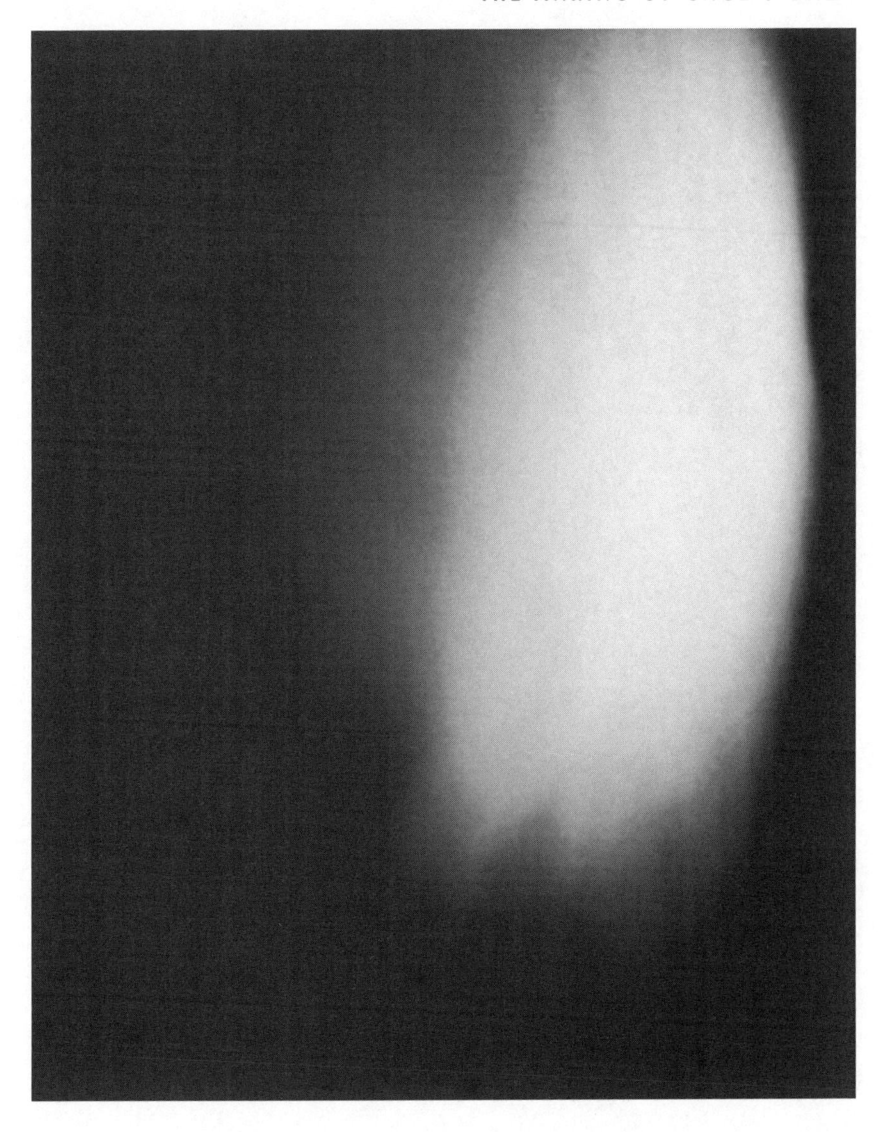

FIGURE 13.9
Frame from *One*''. Photograph by Henning Lohner.

Cage asked that there be no "end" credits, since he didn't like the notion of something being at the "end" as opposed to anywhere. Since we didn't want to leave the credits out altogether and because for a variety of reasons film credits are mandatory, we decided to put them all before the actual film started. It was Peter's idea to use the film leftovers from the editing room's garbage can as visual background to the credits. Cage liked it; we did it.

FIGURE 13.10
Frame from *One*". Photograph by Henning Lohner.

However, Cage did have a personal suggestion for a title to "end" the film. One afternoon during the editing in New York, we were sitting around his writing table, and he told us this story: Many years ago, much before the war, when he was traveling like a hobo through Europe, he came to an Italian mountain village. On a poster he saw the announcement that a movie would be screened in the marketplace in a few days' time. Back then, there were not many cinemas, and it was common that on a given day in a week a truck would come to town with a projector and screen, and the townspeople could gather to see a film. Cage returned to the town the evening of the screening and took his place in a café; sure enough, there a huge white screen had been set up in the square. Waiting for the film to start, Cage took in the atmosphere of sounds and images around him, the chatting of the people, the clacking of plates, the sounds of the wind and weather. Lost in his observations and his imagination, Cage suddenly realized that it had become fairly late and the film had not even begun showing yet. He went to the owner of the café and asked what was happening. The café owner answered that the film couldn't be shown this evening because the film hadn't arrived in town.

So, fifty years later, when Cage had completed his own black-and-white film, he thought it would be pleasant to announce "The End" in fancy script, just as the black-and-white films of his youth used to do. In a way, this was a sentimental joke, an elegant little twist, typical of Cage's gentle and eloquent humor. It was a way of saying, You don't have to take all this too seriously.

And I find this interesting when we consider *One*^{11} as Cage's artistic credo. I remember at the world premiere in Cologne, the organizers tried stopping the film before it could end with "The End," which seemed to them "silly," an obvious error of production. However, they didn't know where the end was before the end title came up, so they couldn't stop the film in time for "The End" not to occur.

To date *One*^{11} has had nearly a hundred public performances in ten countries. It's been broadcast in Germany, Switzerland, and Austria and was part of *Rolywholyover*—a circus exhibit curated by Julie Lazar in 1994–95 that traveled the United States and Japan. There have been a total of five performances with live orchestra: the Cologne premiere, in Prague, at Chatelet for the Festival d'Automne in Paris, at the Venice Biennale, and at the Spoleto festival in Charleston, South Carolina.

One^{11} was Cage's last completed work of a larger scale. As for myself, I am grateful that his final work would turn out to be my first.

CONTRIBUTORS

Maryanne Amacher, a composer and installation artist, is a pioneer in the exploration of forms of sounds in space. Since 1973, Amacher's work has been mounted in museums, galleries, and concerts in Europe, Asia, and the United States. In 1975, she was invited by John Cage to compose the storm environment for his *Lecture on the Weather,* and in 1978, to compose *Close Up,* the sonic environment that accompanied his ten-hour solo voice composition *Empty Words.* They presented the latter work together in performances in Canada, Germany, and the United States (1976–84).

David W. Bernstein is an associate professor of music at Mills College. He has published articles on Schoenberg's tonal theories, the history of music theory, John Cage, and the avant-garde. He edited, with Christopher Hatch, the collection *Music Theory and the Exploration of the Past* (University of Chicago Press, 1993). In 1995, Bernstein organized the conference/festival "Here Comes Everybody: The Music, Poetry, and Art of John Cage."

Deborah Campana serves as conservatory librarian at the Oberlin College Conservatory Library. Prior to this, she was a librarian at the Northwestern University Music Library, where she oversaw work on the John Cage Archive and, in 1992, coordinated the weeklong festival "John Cage NOW." Since her dissertation, "Form and Structure in the Music of John Cage," her research has focused on Cage's life and work, on which she has written many articles and given lectures. She was a performing member of the Chicago ensemble Kapture and a founding member of New Music Chicago.

Austin Clarkson is professor emeritus at York University. His critical editions of the music of Stefan Wolpe appear under the imprint of Peer Classical (New York and Hamburg), and he is editor of *On the Music of Stefan Wolpe: Essays and Recollections* (forthcoming). Clarkson coauthored *Reginald Godden Plays* with the Canadian pianist, who shared Cage's enthusiasm for mushrooms and who developed the fungus spore imprint as an art form.

Andrew Culver, a composer whose interests include the musical application of R. Buckminster Fuller's tensegrity principle, worked closely with John Cage from 1981 to 1992. He developed computer programs for Cage's music and poetry and directed his theatrical and installation pieces. Culver also designed the software for Cage's *Rolywholyover: A Circus* (1993). With Frank Scheffer, he made a group of four award-winning films entitled *From Zero,* based on materials from Cage's life. Culver is the composer of *Ocean 1-95,* the orchestral component of *Ocean,* conceived by John Cage and Merce Cunningham, with choreography by Cunningham, electronic music by David Tudor, and design and lighting by Marsha Skinner.

Alvin Curran, the Darius Milhaud Professor of Music at Mills College, began his career with the renowned group Musica Elettronica Viva (MEV), which he founded with Frederic Rzewski and Richard Teitelbaum. Since 1965, his music—embracing the sounds of the world—has been featured in major new music venues and festivals. He collaborated on several occasions with John Cage.

John Holzaepfel received a Ph.D. in musicology from the City University of New York, where he wrote his dissertation, "David Tudor and the Performance of American Experimental Music, 1950–1959." He is currently preparing a biography of David Tudor.

Allan Kaprow, professor emeritus of visual arts at the University of California at San Diego, is among the most influential figures in contemporary American art. Famous for creating the "Happenings" of the 1950s, Kaprow is also widely known as an author, having published a series of essays and other writings, from his first major work "The Legacy of Jackson Pollock" (1958) to "The Meaning of Life" (1990).

Ray Kass is the founder and director of the Mountain Lake Workshop, an art project that draws on the practices of resource use of the New River Valley and the Appalachian region. In 1983, 1988, 1989, and 1990, Kass welcomed John Cage to this workshop to experiment with watercolors. Kass, a painter and professor of studio art at Virginia Polytechnic Institute and State University, Blacksburg, Virginia, has written *Morris Graves: Vision of the Inner Eye* (1983) and *John Cage: New River Watercolors* (1988).

Jonathan D. Katz is chair of the Department of Gay/Lesbian/Bisexual Studies at City College of San Francisco and the first tenured faculty in Gay and Lesbian Studies in the United States. He has published widely on queer contributions to American art and culture, especially of the cold war era. He recently coauthored a book with Moira Roth entitled *Difference/Indifference: Musings on Postmodernism, Marcel Duchamp, and John Cage,* and has written extensively on Andy Warhol, Jasper Johns, and Robert Rauschenberg as well. A long-time political activist, he founded the Harvey Milk Institute and the Queer Caucus of the College Art Association, the professional body of artists and art historians.

Constance Lewallen is senior curator at the University of California Art Museum, Berkeley. She received her education at Mount Holyoke College, Columbia University, and California State University, San Diego. As well as teaching at the San Francisco Art Institute, the University of California, Santa Barbara, and other California colleges and universities, she has lectured and written widely on contemporary art and served as associate director at Crown Point Press, San Francisco.

Henning Lohner began working as musical advisor as well as apprentice director for Louis Malle (1989-90, on the film *May Fools*) and has since focused both on sound and visual media. His films include *Peefeeyatko* (1991, in collaboration with Frank Zappa), *One¹¹* and 103 (1992, by John Cage), *The Revenge of the Dead Indians* (1993), and *In a Metal Mood* (1996, starring Pat Boone). Lohner's audiovisual installation *raw material: vols. 1–11* (1995, on tour in Europe) has been followed by scores for *The Polar Bear* (1998, by Til Schweiger), *The Great Bagarozy* (1999, by Bernd Eichinger), and the restored silent classic *Orlac's Hands* (1925/2000, directed by Robert Wiene). He is currently living and working in Los Angeles as member of the Media Ventures group of composers.

Jackson Mac Low is a poet, composer, and writer of performance pieces, essays, plays, and radio works. He has read, performed, and lectured throughout North America, Europe, and New Zealand and has taught at universities and writing schools in the United States and Europe. Of his twenty-seven books, the most recent are *42 Merzgedichte in Memoriam Kurt Schwitters* (1994), *Barnesbook* (1996), and *20 Forties* (1999). The compact disc *Open Secrets* (1993) features ten of his musical and verbal performance works, realized by Anne Tardos, seven instrumentalists, and the composer.

Gordon Mumma is professor emeritus of music at the University of California, Santa Cruz. He worked as composer and performer with the Merce Cunningham Dance Company; he was a cofounder of the ONCE Festivals of Contemporary Music in Ann Arbor, Michigan, and a member of the Sonic Arts Union. Mumma's compositions and recordings include *Music for the Venezia Space Theater* (1963), *Megaton for William Burroughs* (1964), *Hornpipe* (1967), *Some Voltage Drop* (1974), and *Than Particle* (1985).

James Pritchett is a writer and pianist specializing in contemporary music. His publications include *The Music of John Cage* (Cambridge University Press, 1993) and a series of essays to accompany recordings of Cage's music released by Mode Records. Pritchett has performed works by Cage and Frances White. His recording of White's *Still Life with Piano* (written for him) appears on the *Cultures Electroniques 5* disc put out by Le Chant du Monde.

James Tenney's teachers and mentors have included Carl Ruggles, Edgard Varèse, Harry Partch, and John Cage. He is a performer as well as a composer and was a pioneer in the field of electronic and computer music. He has written works for a variety of media, both instrumental and electronic, many of them using alternative tuning systems. He is the author of books and articles on musical acoustics, computer music, and musical form and perception, and is now on the composition faculty of the California Institute of the Arts.

Paul van Emmerik received his Ph.D. in 1996 at the University of Amsterdam, where he studied musicology, library science, and American studies. He is a faculty member at Utrecht University, where he currently teaches music history, with an emphasis on twentieth-century art music.

Frances White is a composer working primarily in computer music. Her teachers were Lawrence Moss, Charles Dodge, and Paul Lansky. In

1985, White assisted John Cage in the technical realization of his *Essay* pieces for computer-generated tape. Her music has been performed in the United States and in Europe and appears on several compact discs. In 1993 she composed *Winter Aconites* for six instruments and tape, commissioned by the ASCAP Foundation in memory of John Cage.

Christian Wolff holds a professorship in classics and music at Dartmouth College. In the early 1950s he was an associate of John Cage, Morton Feldman, Earle Brown, and other members of the New York school. Wolff later studied classics at Harvard University, where he also taught until 1970. The American Academy of Letters has honored him with an award, and among his many compositions are works commissioned by West German Radio, the Wesleyan Singers, and pianist Ursula Oppens. In 1996, he received the John Cage Award for Music, and in 1999, became a member of the Akademie der Künste in Berlin.

INDEX

Locators in boldface refer to figures and musical examples.